THE SPIRIT
IN
ST. LOUIS

PRAISE FOR
MARK EVERETT STONE

OMAHA STAKES

"This action-packed urban fantasy follows the brooding Kal Hakala, human head of the Bureau of Supernatural Investigation in an alternate contemporary America, to what promises to be the first of many confrontations.... [Stone] writes in a brisk, conversational style .... The setting fuses magic and technology in appealing ways that will hopefully be developed in future installments.... Kal's frolic through a nifty supernatural world is enjoyable."
—*Publishers Weekly*

"With each new challenge there is a freshness that keeps you interested; you do need to know who will have survived by the end of the story. I really enjoy the pop culture references that stream from the characters lips it almost makes it feel like a game to see how many references you can spot and recognise before you are told where they come from."
—Michelle Herbert, *Fantasy Book Review*

CHICAGO, THE WINDIGO CITY

"*Chicago, The Windigo City* is jam packed with action but the heart of the story is Kal's love and concern for his girlfriend and his best friend .... An original and refreshing tale that leaves me wanting to know more about Kal, Jeanie, BB, and Canton. I look forward to reading the other books in the series."
—Debbie Wiley, Fresh Fiction

"Urban fantasy infused with Native American legend takes an excursion into the bloody horror genre in this fast-paced, exciting story.... Tight prose, a meticulous plot, and good editing set this book apart from countless competitors .... Stone has written a novel difficult to put down. Endless tension along with well-implemented action make the reading experience a necessity, not an option. Even a jaded critic will shudder over descriptive passages that bring to life the ghastly crime scenes, and certain explanations may unsettle a few stomachs."

—Julia Ann Charpentier, ForeWord Magazine

"Mark Everett Stone has hit another home run …. The action is non-stop, and the magical/technical gadgets are incredibly imaginative. Fans of this series will not be disappointed. The BSI series remains one of my absolute favorites, and I'm looking forward to the next installment."

—M. E. Franco, author of the Dion Series

I LEFT MY HAUNT IN SAN FRANCISCO

"The third in a series, *I Left My Haunt in San Francisco* is lively and smart. It is packed with action and just enough goop and gore to please fans of the genre without turning away newcomers to this subset of modern fantasy demon-busting …. Stone's book moves fast and reads quickly. It is well-written and nicely paced, with a few short rest stops built in to allow the reader to catch his breath, all to better appreciate the at-times purple but always entertaining prose …. It is just great, grand fun."

—Mark McLaughlin, ForeWord Reviews

"Another high impact, fast moving story from Mark Everett Stone. I am really enjoying seeing his growth as a writer reflected in the strength of his characters and am looking forward to seeing what the future holds for Kal."

—Michelle Herbert, Fantasy Book Review

"The third episode of the Files of the BSI series is told with Mark Stone's trademark tongue in cheek humor. It keeps you wanting more with each turn of the page, to not only uncover the mysteries of the story, but also to enjoy Kal's quick but cynical wit."

—CP Bialois, author of *Call of Poseidon*, The Sword and the Flame series, and *Skeleton Key*

THE JUDAS LINE

★ "This delightful Catholicism-infused quest fantasy stars a likable and original duo. Fr. Michael Engle, a pragmatic Catholic priest, and Jude, who has a considerably more uncertain relationship with God, are unlikely friends, but when a blood-covered Jude runs into Mike's church asking for help, Mike listens to him, believes him, and joins him on a quest to find the Holy Grail, which Jude hopes will help him destroy a legendary and dangerous family heirloom. Along the way they encounter Cain, the Norse gods (drinking and watching *Bridge over the River Kwai*), and a Valkyrie with the requisite 'chainmail-covered pillowy breasts.' When Mephistopheles shows up, Jude manages to label him an Arch-Fiend of Hell without irony and without irritating the reader. Stone's depiction of magic is realistic and intelligent and his treatment of Catholicism refreshingly informed and three-dimensional. Even the obligatory near-apocalyptic ending is coherent, surprising, and exciting."
—*Publishers Weekly* Starred Review

"This evil mystery is a heavenly read! *The Judas Line* creates a believable mystery which links the ancient past to the present. By building on the ancient story of the betrayal of Jesus Christ by Judas, Market Everett Stone crafts a dark versus light drama which will keep readers hooked. I loved how Stone makes Jude an unwilling member of the darkest family threatening mankind. Simply brilliant!"
—Elizabeth Crowley, *Fresh Fiction*

"A fast-paced book which does not lack for history or adventure. The inclusion of death and destruction are a given and it is good that there is a lot of humour instilled throughout. I would say that if you're a fan of Jim Butcher's *Dresden Files*, you will enjoy Mark Everett Stone's work. Recommended."
—Michelle Herbert, *Fantasy Book Review*

"Blending paranormal and biblical ideas, *The Judas Line* is a riveting thriller that should prove hard to put down."
—*Midwest Book Review*

"*The Judas Line* is, as anticipated, a lightning-paced thriller that is equal parts non-stop action and intelligent musing. This is, in fact, a surprisingly introspective book that delves into many interesting questions about the nature of good, evil, and faith. It's an enthralling read certain to delight and entertain, a well-crafted gem worthy of a place on any bookshelf."

—Michelle Izmaylov, author of *The Galacteran Legacy: Galaxy Watch*

"Mark Everett Stone takes the classic good versus evil plot line and puts his own unique spin on it. He effortlessly merges bible canon with the world and people he's created, adding off-the-wall humor to help break the tension. This book makes you laugh while making you think about the nature of evil and the power of faith."

—Jamie White, author of *The Life and Times of No One in Particular*

★ ★ ★ ★ ★ "A fast-paced read, with nail-biting moments and some humor thrown in. The characters were compelling, I often find myself picturing them in my head .... I can't recommend this book enough."

—Lisa McCourt Hollar, *Jezri's Nightmares*

"Once in a great while, a book comes along that challenges you to think outside the box. *The Judas Line* is one of those books. I was absolutely amazed at the way Mark Everett Stone has taken religious stories and beliefs and intertwined his own tale of power, evil, friendship, sacrifice and redemption. The action is nonstop and the characters will stay with you long after you finish the last page."

—M.E. Franco, author *Where Will You Run?*

"The pacing is flawless in every respect .... Never before have I found a work of fiction to be so captivating. It picks you up, sits you down, and it does not let you even think about getting back up. "

—Grace Knight, author of *Sun And Moon* (2013)

WHAT HAPPENS IN VEGAS, DIES IN VEGAS

★ ★ ★ ★ ★ "*Things To Do In Denver When Your Un-Dead* was one of the most refreshing and original books I have read in a long time

and the sequel is just as exciting as the first. In fact it may just be better than the first .... Exceptionally well-written and entertaining."
—*Jerzri's Nightmares*

"Vegas is non-stop action that will leave you with whiplash.... Stone leaves you gasping for breath by the end and of course, enjoys taunting the reader with the prospect of a third book in the series, which I will be waiting anxiously to read."
—Shay Fabbro, award-winning author

★★★★★"A cracking good yarn from first to final page, no question .... Mark has cemented himself solidly into the position of Master in my self-created niche of Paranormal Suspense Thriller writing. His command of his art grows exponentially with each work of his that I read....Two very enthusiastic thumbs up for a job well and properly done."
—Jeffrey Hollar, *The Latinum Vault*

"Don't expect a minute of down-time, for Stone is a zero tolerance taskmaster who brings a complicated plotline and well fleshed-out characters to heel and makes it look easy. What you *can* expect is for Stone to surprise you repeatedly, satisfy you completely and leave you wanting more."
—AJ Aalto, author of *Touched*

THINGS TO DO IN DENVER WHEN YOU'RE UN-DEAD

★★★★★"If you crave a really enjoyable Paranormal Suspense Thriller to read, THIS is your book. It grabs you from the very first page and drags you along (snarling for you to keep up) and dumps you at the feet of one of THE most unexpected plot twists of an ending that I have ever read."
—Jeffrey Hollar, *The Latinum Vault*

"If you like quick wit, sadistic charm, and bad-ass gadgets, then you will enjoy the hell out of this book."
—Shay Fabbro, award-winning author

★ ★ ★ ★ ★ "An absolute pleasure to read. It is witty, funny, dramatic and a well thought out paranormal with very fine storytelling. I couldn't put it down!"
—Clarrissa Lee Moon, author of the series, *The Nightwolves* and *Celeste Nites*

"I have really enjoyed reading this book .... The story could just be one of guns, blood and guts and magic, but ... Mark Everett Stone has made these characters seem real."
—Michele Herbert, *Fantasy Book Review*

"This is not a story for the faint of heart or stomach, nor for those wanting a plot with any connection to reality. Personally, I'm really looking forward to the promised sequel."
—Gordon Long, *TCM Reviews*

"The way Mark combines magicians, zombies and super ghouls with a Bogart-style ultra sarcastic officer of the 'Bureau' makes you want to keep on reading. I highly recommend this for everyone—not just those into stories of the un-dead."
—G.R. Holton, author of *Soleri, Guardian's Alliance* and *Deep Screams*

"Five stars, two thumbs, fantastic! From the moment I began the first page to the final flip of the last, I was hooked .... The writing is sharp, fast and engaging."
—Patti Larsen, author of *Fresco, Wasteland, The Diamond City*, and *The Ghost Boy of MacKenzie House*

"The fastest paced action horror that I have read in a very long time."
—Suzannah Burke, aka Stacey Danson, author of *Empty Chairs*

"In a first and quite brilliant novel, Stone proves himself equally adept at feverishly fast-paced action, edgy wit and banter, and the weaving of a richly satisfying and fresh world of mystery and intrigue. Write on, my friend."
—Michelle Izmaylov, author of *The Galacteran Legacy: Galaxy Watch*

THE SPIRIT
IN
ST. LOUIS

From the Files of the BSI

MARK EVERETT STONE

Seattle, WA

CAMEL PRESS

Camel Press
PO Box 70515
Seattle, WA 98127

For more information go to: www.camelpress.com
markeverettstone.wix.com/mysite-1

This is a work of fiction. Names, characters, places, brands, media, and incidents are either the product of the author's imagination or are used fictitiously.

Cover design by Sabrina Sun

ISBN: 978-1-60381-256-6 (Trade Paper)
ISBN: 978-1-60381-257-3 (eBook)

Library of Congress Control Number: 2016950842

Printed in the United States of America

For Aeden and Gabriel

Also by the author from Camel Press

Things To Do in Denver When You're Un-Dead

What Happens in Vegas Dies in Vegas

I Left my Haunt in San Francisco

Chicago, The Windigo City

Omaha Stakes

The Judas Line

CHAPTER ONE

BB (Director Bauer)
Imitation of Life

Television, radio, and newspaper reporters surrounded the black van as it slowly motored through the throngs of press practically drooling on the windows. The gleaming vehicle was unlikely to come through the gauntlet without a few dings and even a dent or two. Miraculously, and not without running over a few toes, the van made it to the curb in front of an enormous drum-like building of glass and steel that squatted at Chestnut and North 4th Street, encompassing an entire city block with its shiny bulk.

What used to be home to several businesses had been taken over by the billionaire Tobias Quint, whose idea of progressive capitalism was an office building with all the charm of a squatting toad. At least it had a good view of the famous Gateway Arch, which rose above the Mississippi River. The only reason Quint couldn't plant his monstrosity closer to the Arch was that the Hyatt Regency across the street from Gateway Park hadn't been for sale at any price.

The driver's side door opened and a powerfully built woman in a no-nonsense business suit stepped out, pushing through the reporters as if they were recalcitrant children. Although they tried to impede her advance, shoving microphones into her face and shouting rapid-fire questions, the hard-faced woman with the long, curly-brown hair would not be slowed, could not be stopped. Their cries bounced off her granite façade as she slogged her way to the van's sliding door and grabbed the handle.

Before opening the door, however, she turned to the reporters, who lowered the volume from earsplitting to merely annoying, expectantly waiting for a juicy sound bite. "If you don't clear the way to the building, there won't be a press conference. If you don't allow the Bureau of Supernatural Investigation to do its job, how can you report on the outcome?" Her voice cut through the clamor with the force of a siren, and the throng parted, as if afraid of the formidable woman. Best guess ... they were.

Almost soundlessly, the van door slid open.

Everything went still, church quiet, as hundreds held a collective breath.

Six people emerged from the dark vehicle dressed in identical black, chitonous armor that hugged their muscular frames like second skins. Each person carried enough weaponry to reduce City Hall to rubble. Five men, one woman, and they all had the stone-cold faces of expert killers partly disguised by wraparound shades. Immediately camera flashes went off and the reporters once again cut in with a barrage of questions, albeit at a lesser volume thanks to their fear of the woman in the business suit.

Then the littlest one, a young man with the unfortunate handle of Tweezer, spoiled their grand entrance.

"Holy, [DELETED]! I hope somebody at least brought some [CENSORED] pizza." The smile on his acne-scarred and youthful face exposed nearly all his mostly straight teeth.

"Way to go, pipsqueak," said a tall, blond Aryan type as he slapped the miniscule Agent on the back of the head. The media absorbed every move they made.

Before the reporters could flood the team, the no-nonsense driver rushed forward to stem the tide, the force of her stern gaze gluing them in place. "Listen up, folks, you know the Agents don't field questions. As the team Receptionist, that's my job. So I will start this show off. And remember, one question at a time." She pointed to a television talking head with cameraman in tow. "You, speak."

"Jeff Corso from WGT, ma'am. What is the nature of the Supernatural threat in the Quint Building?"

Easy question and always the first. "There have been reports of a ghost. We talked to several tenants of the building and their stories are similar and consistent. Yes, you with the bad toupee."

"Uh, Michael Wint from the *Post-Dispatch*," said the man with the unfortunate hairpiece. "Is this ghost dangerous? Could it be something else?"

"That's two questions. You, the blonde from NBS."

"Is the ghost dangerous?"

"It could be. That's why the BSI always goes into an operation loaded for bear."

As the Receptionist fielded more questions and answered with calm competence, the tall Aryan-type shuffled his feet impatiently.

"What's wrong, Sixer?" the only woman on the team asked in a soft voice. Her name was Helen, but everyone called her Twist. There seemed to be something brittle about her face, as if the bones of her skull were made of glass.

"This blows," Sixer replied, also keeping his volume low. "I should be out there answering the questions. *I'm* the team leader."

Tweezer cut in, "Bad idea, dude." He scratched a mole on his stubbly cheek. "Kal and the Director made the rules for a reason and the Receptionist always handles the press. You know that."

Sixer snarled, "Screw Kal Hakala with a fork."

The other five inhaled as one. Many believed that if you even mentioned Kal Hakala's name too many times he'd appear to kick your ass, like Beetlejuice.

"He's an old man who doesn't take missions anymore. Old and done. All he ever does is train Green Peas and go on talk shows every now and then. He's the lazy face of the BSI, gone all soft. Hell, if he went on an op now, he'd probably die in the first five minutes."

"I knew you were stupid, Sixer," said Twist, shaking her head, her hair a mass of spikes thanks to an abundance of styling gel. "I didn't know you had a death wish, too."

"Listen up, you chowderheads," Sixer whispered fiercely, schooling his face so as not to alert the reporters who were staring at the Receptionist as if she was the Second Coming. "This is my last op before retirement and I mean to make a splash." He grinned, displaying his dimples. He looked good and he knew it. "Let me show you how it's done." With a swagger in his step, he moved forward, cutting in front of the Receptionist as she was offering a detailed answer on BSI response times in an event of an emergency.

"Ladies and gentleman of the press," he purred, smiling wide. "My name is Steven Essex, better known in the Bureau as Sixer, and I am the leader of Team Omicron. I'm here to tell you that there is nothing to fear from this so-called ghost." Smiling even wider, he posed for the crowd, an almost indecently handsome man with piercing aqua eyes, a strong chin, and close-cropped, streaked blond hair.

As he spoke, the Receptionist dropped her hands to her sides and began a series of hand gestures that the rest of the team—all except Tweezer, who was picking his nose—caught immediately. 'Get this idiot out of here' was the message.

"And let me tell you, I will personally kick any spirit's butt that happens to be in there," continued Sixer, unaware of the Bureau sign language the Receptionist was broadcasting to his team. "Twelve missions, no fatalities, what does that tell you?"

"It tells us that Sixer is good at his job," the Receptionist broke in, shouldering the team leader aside with enough oomph to bruise. The other members of Team Omicron waved to the crowd, laying hands on Sixer and bustling him toward the lobby doors of the Quint Building before he could protest. "And Omicron is very capable, as are all the Bureau teams."

"What the heck are you doing, guys?" Sixer protested as Twist opened one half of the double doors that led into the building. The inside looked darker and more menacing than it had any right to be on a warm summer day.

"Saving our asses, bonehead," growled Twist as she held the door. The rest of Omicron, Boogie, Snow, Fireplug and Tweezer, shoved Sixer inside and followed immediately after. "You may not care anymore about the Bureau, but after this, we still have to work there." The door closed behind them with a *bong* like the closing of a crypt.

The Receptionist, Tylan Carter, shook her head and waited in the van for a mission update, the bone induction patch behind her ear and the near-invisible throat mic her only access to the team. The van itself carried all the equipment necessary to keep an eye on Omicron through the micro-cams embedded in their night-vision contact lenses.

Tylan picked up a pair of glasses mated to the team's micro-cams and carefully put them on. "Omicron, I have you on visual," she said.

"Sixer here. We are in the lobby. Who killed the power?"

"The owner of the building, QuintCorp, had the power turned off once the sightings had been confirmed, although there are indications that a couple of backup generators are online."

"Cheap bastards."

"And you're a crazy bastard to do what you did in front of those reporters, Sixer."

"*Chill out, mom—*" The rest of the sentence was lost in static.

The visuals coming through the sunglasses went bright white and Tylan cursed, ripping them off, head pounding in pain. "Dammit!"

After a few seconds she tried reconnecting. Nothing came through the glasses. "Omicron, come in!"

Nothing.

"Omicron!"

Even more nothing.

The door to the van flew open and the Receptionist burst out into the bright sunshine, knocking reporters every which way. Shouts and screams followed as she made for the double doors, her suit soaked with panic sweat. Her hand reached for the long aluminum handle of the door and … slipped off. She tried again, but her fingers failed to find purchase. It was as if some invisible slick of oil coated the metal, rendering it frictionless, resisting her grasp.

"[CENSORED] this," she muttered, drawing a 9mm from beneath her tailored black business suit. She opened fire on the door. Instead of a shower of tempered glass or a set of neat holes, there were only crushed lead pebbles that dropped to the ground like dark hail.

Conscious of the gaggle of reporters at her back, Tylan re-holstered her weapon and waited. The sturdy set of her shoulders and the anger radiating from her every pore kept the media at bay—fear a greater barrier than any troop of handholding police officers or sawhorses.

As the sun traveled west, the crowd refused to thin. Nothing is more persistent than a reporter who smells blood. By the time the sun settled below the skyline, television vans had set up bright halogens but were kept across the street by hard-eyed feds in black suits and suspicious bulges under their jackets. Yeah, blood was in the water, yet the Receptionist stood resolute in front of the doors, hard eyes riveted on the mass of glass and steel.

"What's going on, Tylan?" asked another sharply dressed

woman coming up from behind—slim, fortyish, and with hair in a tight, no-nonsense bun. "Any developments?"

Mutely, the Receptionist shook her head. "Nothing. Whatever strange force that's keeping us out is still in place. It's like nothing I've ever seen."

The other woman, Moira, shook her head. "The Director wants a debrief. Ten minutes."

Before Tylan could reply, bright flashes came from within the building—so bright, in fact, that the light easily penetrated the building's mirrored glass like graphic punctuations.

The Receptionist rushed to one of the ten-foot panels that comprised the outer wall of the building, hands cupped around her eyes to better view the dim images inside. The sight nearly tore her mind apart.

Sixer stood just inside, facing off to the left, a vacant look on his bloodied face and the glint of madness in his eyes. Slowly, as if in a trance, he lifted one arm, fist full of .45 ACP, and put the weapon against his temple. Although his head blocked her view of the gun she knew by his body language what he was about to do.

"NO!"

A dim flash of light and something *splatted* against the glass—a wet, gelatinous blob that slowly streaked down the smooth surface. As the Receptionist watched, an unblinking blue eye separated from the mass and fell away.

Blur ....

I took the DRAFT glasses off my face and rubbed my temples. The headache had nothing to do with VR overload. The scene had been an ugly one, easily one of the worst I've ever witnessed. *I am so tired of watching Agents die* ....

"Are you well, Director?"

That was a hell of a question. Who could be well after witnessing such a horrendous event? "As well as can be expected, Ghost," I rasped. Coughing, I stood and prepared myself a drink at the wet bar. Cognac, Louis XIII. Smooth and silky and horrendously overpriced. Kal always teased me for having expensive tastes. How he was able to swill that turpentine-turned-liquor he called vodka was beyond me.

"Director Bauer, the Committee attempted to reach you four times while you were in VR. They're wondering how you will handle the St. Louis situation."

Damn. The Committee. Ever since the president and the other world leaders revealed the existence of magic, Magicians, the World Under, and Supernaturals, my life has been a never-ending battle against the forces of bureaucracy. Instead of answering to the Joint Chiefs, or the VP, or even POTUS directly, I have to face a committee consisting of the three branches of government plus a representative of the military appointed to oversee the Bureau. Senator Stein, Judge Whitehall, the new Chief of Bureau Relations Marlene Brisby, and Admiral Ellison. Singly not too difficult to deal with, but as a group they were a nightmare walking. I longed to un-ring the bell and put the old ways back in place, but I might as well have been wishing for the moon. As it was, the last year had been one of chaos, mayhem, paranoia, religious hysteria and finger pointing as the Straights collectively freaked out.

All in all, they took the news rather well.

"What did you say to them?"

Ghost's annoying drone sounded amused. "That you were evaluating the data and determining the proper response to the situation."

"I take it they weren't put off."

"They want action yesterday."

Of course they did. Everyone in the government wanted things done yesterday until the ball landed squarely in their court; then they whined about not having enough time. More and more lately, retirement seemed to be my best option.

My back popped as I stretched, my jaw opening in a

cracking yawn. *What a mess.* Of course I pulled Tylan in from the field for a debrief so I could experience the event in VR, but knowing what was going to happen never prepares you for seeing it up close and personal.

Once again I found myself silently cursing the Sidhe, those elven miscreants who, with their plots to destroy humanity, forced our leaders to reveal the existence of the World Under a decade ahead of schedule. As good and capable an administrator as I am, I wasn't quite ready to deal with operating aboveboard on a global scale. As a covert agency, the BSI was used to dealing with people in power one at a time, in small doses. Now, however, every tin-pot politician who thought they were God's gift wanted a piece of the Bureau of Supernatural Investigation.

"They are on the line again, sir." Ghost sounded positively snippy.

Of course they were. I settled the DRAFT on my face. "Go ahead."

Four people appeared, or should I say their upper halves, in the DRAFT, real-time images in the Heads Up Display (HUD). Two men, two women, all with faces set in stone. People you didn't want to cross on a bet, but I sparred with them on a daily basis because if I didn't show backbone, didn't strike before struck, then they'd lose all respect for me. In politics, all that mattered was whose dorsal fin was bigger.

"Greeting, Committee Members." I always kept the capitals in there, a small concession. "Let me guess … you want to know what I'm doing about St. Louis."

Judge Whitehall, her graying hair perfectly curled, nodded. During her time as a federal judge in the Fourth Circuit Court of Appeals, she had reduced more than one attorney to gibbering incoherence with her steely gaze. She earned her nickname as the Silver Saber not only for her sharp wits, but also for her deft ability to cut through the manure in any given situation. "It's a public relations disaster. Your Receptionist didn't handle it very well," she said, her thin lips barely moving.

Now *that* raised my ire. No one messes with one of mine, not even a Committee Member. "She handled the situation better than most Agents and a sight better than most any agency personnel could." My voice was colder than arctic ice. "She did well, so let us not discuss that issue again."

Whitehall gave a miniscule nod, a concession that spoke louder than a shout. "Agreed, Director. You know your people, and if you say she did well, who am I to argue?"

My boss, I thought grumpily as Admiral Ellison spoke up. "All well and good, Director Bauer, but the question still stands. The public is flooding social media, reporters are having a field day, and it's a feeding frenzy in Congress. You'd think there was an election around the corner, the way they're behaving. The situation is quickly spinning out of control. The BSI needs a win here so the public can feel safe, not a sudden disappearance inside a new office building on what should have been a routine cleanup of a haunting."

Admiral Ellison built his career on dignity, honor, honesty, and courage, and frankly wouldn't make it as a politician—all good reasons to like and respect the man—so if he said the situation was spinning out of control, I believed him. His ability to cut through manure exceeded even that of Whitehall. Not a man to fall victim to hyperbole. I needed to do something quick to put the public and Capitol Hill at ease. Unfortunately, there was only one way I could think of to do that.

And I really didn't want to resort to such methods.

But when your back is against the wall, your back is against the wall, and you have to go with what works, even if such methods seem distasteful. I leaned back so my chair was almost horizontal, but the DRAFT kept the Committee members vertical in my sight. "Admiral, Ms. Brisby, Senator Stein, and Judge Whitehall, I have a solution that will not only put the entire Fourth Estate into a virtual tizzy, it will calm Congress quite nicely. It's not the best solution in my opinion—in fact, it sucks, to put it bluntly—but it's the only solution that will satisfy all concerned."

Now I certainly had their attention. "Well?" blurted out Senator Stein, a vein at this temple throbbing. "What is it?" He was a capable politico, a man with more than thirty years in the Senate; that made him one of the biggest bricks in the establishment wall and possibly the most morally bankrupt person in Washington. Still, you work with what you've got.

I gave the gray-haired man from Indiana a nod. "Ladies, gentlemen, I think it's time to pull out the big guns. It's time to take Kalevi Hakala off the leash."

CHAPTER TWO

Kal
A Star is Born

"RED LEADER, THIS is Eagle's Nest One. Take the shot."
"NO!"

Oops, getting ahead of myself. Can't just jump all over these debriefs. BB would have a conniption.

Begin at the beginning, as he would say. *Got it.*

For the first time in decades we had a dragon problem. Last one occurred in the early '60s and brought the United States and the Soviet Union to the brink of nuclear war. All over a dragon heart said to endow those who consumed it with miraculous powers. Good thing the heart was lost during the whole Cuban fiasco or else history might have undergone a thermonuclear rewrite. Now the second dragon in fifty years had decided to make an appearance, and woe to all if we killed it without destroying its heart. I like my planet without clouds of radioactive dust, please.

It emerged from the Colombia River Gorge in a geyser of steam so intense it flash-boiled a water-skier and the two people manning the boat near the exit point. The first casualties of many, I'm sorry to say. Shining, almost glowing, gold scales flashing from its seventy-foot coiling, snake-like body, it radiated enough heat to cook a rhino well done from ten feet away without having to resort to its flaming breath. It flew high into the sky, a glittering second sun, before heading south, and the video clips made by dozens of people with their cell phones went viral in seconds. YouTube never had so many hits.

By the time it reached Salem, six towns had almost burned to the ground: Forest Grove, Sherwood, Newberg, McMinnville, Sheraton, and Dallas—all laid waste by dragon's breath so hot it melted steel and concrete in seconds. Its crooked flight path seemed to be designed to cause maximum damage and loss of life. By the time the dragon reached the Oregon/California border, Eugene and Corvallis were burning bright enough to see from outer space.

Team Tau had been tagged to respond, and thanks to everyone on the planet knowing about the Bureau and the World Under, we were able to request and receive a little help from the 123rd Fighter Squadron of the Oregon Air National Guard stationed at the Portland Air National Guard Base. Two F-15C/D Eagles ripped their way south toward the overgrown lizard just as Tau landed at Redding, California, to establish a base of operations.

Tau's leader, Jared Marshal, stood in front of the newly sprayed DisplayWall—the most recent innovation from Special Branch. Those technogeeknerds had really outdone themselves this time. The device was an aerosol that sprayed onto any flat surface and by some arcane/science fiction method turned it into a flatscreen TV less than a millimeter thick. I could'a used that in college, let me tell you. Anyhow, Jared was watching the dragon's progress via multiple dronecams. Marshal fit the picture of a perfect BSI Agent: tall, dark, burly, and ramrod straight, with a profile that would have made Michelangelo swoon. At twenty-three, he was old enough to kill with care but young enough to be a damned hothead.

Was I ever that young?

The room we found ourselves in wasn't that big, only about

fifteen by fifteen, but when it came to tech, size didn't matter, only results. And those technogeeknerds could sure deliver. We had all we needed to track the dragon and coordinate its destruction.

"Where is it?" Jared barked at Adrian Newmeyer, one of the team Green Peas, those new recruits it was my responsibility to train.

Newmeyer—a short, stout kid with curly hair cut short to the skull—kept his eyes glued to his own display that showed a little orange blip moving south across a satellite image of Northern California. "Close to Mt. Shasta, boss."

Marshal frowned, creasing his fair skin. I watched intently as the young man pondered the situation and sipped some diet Mountain Dew. *God bless caffeine.* "Where are our birds?" he asked tersely.

"Eight klicks from target."

It was my turn to speak up. As far as they knew, I was just an observer, the guy tasked with the mission evaluation to see how the Bureau coordinated efforts with other agencies and to perceive how the newly formed Team Tau operated, but I never could keep my big mouth shut. "Whatever you're thinking, Agent Marshal, I'd wipe it from consideration. Too risky."

His head whipped around to where I was sitting in my comfy leather office chair, and I fancied I could hear vertebrae pop. "You are here to observe, Hakala, not to advise."

Didn't even offer the courtesy of 'Mister' or 'Agent' in front of my name, showing me disrespect in front of the rest of the team, and that put rusty nails in my Cheerios. I ground my teeth. *Punk.* "You should wait until it's out of the forested area."

"And demolish Redding? Not a chance." To Rico, another Green Pea, "Tell our birds to lock on."

"Got it." Rico relayed the orders to the pilots.

Not on my watch. Before anyone could stop me, I cut in with my throat mic, "Red Leader, this is FinnOne, stand back three klicks and fire when the bogey is over Lake Shasta. Over."

"Roger, FinnOne," came the reply.

Marshal's short brown hair practically stood on end as he thumbed his own throat mic. "Red Leader, this is Eagle's Nest One, disregard FinnOne, confirm." To me, "You are *observing* only, Hakala. One more word and I'll throw you out."

"Say again, Eagle's Nest One," said Red Leader tonelessly.

I crossed my arms. "Don't do it. Have them lay back and wait until the dragon is clear of any communities."

"Shut up!" Jared Marshal closed his eyes. "That is confirmed, Red Leader. FinnOne is not in command. You are to disregard FinnOne. Copy?"

"Roger that." Red Leader didn't sound like he wanted to copy that at all, but he was a good pilot and well trained.

I tried again. "Red Leader, this is FinnOne, do you copy?"

Nothing. *Dammit!*

With a smile so smug it practically dripped contempt, Marshal said, "Red Leader, this is Eagle's Nest One. Take the shot."

"NO!" My voice bounced off the DisplayWall, practically deafening the members of Team Tau. Marshal motioned another team member, Twilight, to kick me out, but a cold glare from my baby blues halted her in her tracks. Still, there was nothing else I could do. Red Leader took the shot and I watched the aftermath in brilliant Technicolor.

Red Leader's businesslike voice echoed in our ears. "Missile away."

With only a simple payload of high explosives, a missile launched from a modern warplane travels faster than human beings can imagine, and for even the greatest of Supernaturals, it was death at Mach 2.5. The dragon, resembling a golden, burning snake with four long legs ending in wicked, scimitar-like talons and wings clothed in white fire, exploded in mid-air like a water balloon filled with gasoline. It was like watching a baby duck get hit with a load of buckshot after napalming the little quacker first. Pieces and parts flew everywhere, burning, leaving trails of smoke darting toward the ground. I could actually *see* the air distort as the pressure wave traveled outward at ungodly speed, dissipating clouds and flattening trees like the hand of God swatting the planet.

I had to admit, it looked awesome.

"There," Marshal remarked proudly, admiring his handiwork. "Took care of a Supernatural and destroyed the heart of the beast. A win/win situation, if I do say so myself." He looked filled to the brim with white-hot smug.

Destroying the heart was good, but at what cost? "If you do say so yourself," I muttered angrily. "If you do [DELETED] say so yourself."

He turned on me, muscles tense. "What?"

"Do you know my official designation, Marshal?" My eyes were a thousand yards away. I didn't want to look at the satellite imagery because I knew damn well what I would see.

"Observer."

"No. My official Bureau designation is Recruit Trainer and Evaluator."

A derisive snort. "Hell, everybody knows you're the Trainer. You were my Trainer."

"And Evaluator." I still didn't bother looking at him—or at anyone for that matter—but I could sure feel six pairs of eyes on me. "You forgot Evaluator."

Another snort. If nothing else he could snort with the best of them. "But here you're an Observer."

"You know why the Bureau constantly tests its Agents?" I asked, barely controlling the urge to drive an elbow into Marshal's too-perfect nose.

"To keep us sharp."

My head was shaking before the words even hit the air. "That's what the Bureau wants you to think, so it can hide its real intention. No, the real reason is because we wield *power*." Now I looked at the satellite map and saw what I'd expected to see. I wanted to cry, to scream, to lash out, but I wasn't that guy anymore. I still had plenty of human anger, but that tank of superhuman rage was empty. "Think about it, all of you." I met each team member's eyes one by one, and one by one, they lowered their heads. All except Marshal, whose killing arrogance kept him defiant. "With a simple phone call a fighter squadron of the Oregon Air National Guard was at our disposal. F-15s were under our control, our authority. That kind of power can go to a person's head, can really mess with the mind, and the Bureau doesn't want someone who takes such things for granted, might possibly misuse such incredible responsibility." Now I matched Marshal stare for stare, his sharp hazel gaze against my icy blues, and I could feel him struggle not to blink. "Like you have misused your power. It is up to me, as the official Evaluator, to file a recommendation to the Director on the fitness of any given Bureau Agent that determines whether or not they are a viable asset."

Scarlet flushed across Marshal's cheeks, but he kept his cool. "The hell I did. I completed the objective."

I nodded. "Sure you did. All but one."

That earned me a puzzled glare. "Which one is that? The dragon is *dead*."

My finger stabbed at the screen, showing the satellite image of a small town now highlighted in bright orange. "The objective stating that our number-one priority is to safeguard human lives." I sighed, watching fire devour the small town. "Say goodbye to Weed, California, you dipstick."

It was time to leave. "And you can kiss your Bureau career goodbye," I called over my shoulder just before the door slammed shut.

Okay, Agent Hakala, that will be fine.
I've a few more things to say. A whole bunch, in fact.
I'm sure you do, but that is not necessary for this debrief. Here, let me take that off your head.
Awww, I was really starting to enjoy myself.

Blur ....

The image of the base in Redding shredded and melted, torn and bled away to reveal the inside of a luxury jet and a woman, Receptionist Darla Grey, who held what looked like a large titanium band in her hands, electrodes dripping from it like spider legs. The band itself was made of fine silvery wire looped in such a way as to turn the eyeballs inside out if stared at too long, a tiara constructed by drunken silkworms.

Darla smiled, revealing large, even teeth. "How was that, Agent?" she asked. Like most Receptionists, Darla was a whole lot of woman packed into a taut bundle. So much so that I had to rein in my libido—a good thing because not only could she easily break my arm in six places, but my significant other is a Magician of not inconsiderable power who has the ability to turn the average male into something that leaves a slime trail as it moves. As for me, she wouldn't be that kind.

"I've never been debriefed like that before." My muscles felt tight and sore and the vertebrae in my neck *popped* as I swiveled my head back and forth. For the past year I'd been training the Green Peas down to the ground and back up again, turning raw meat (by Bureau standards) into men and women made of wood. All that training had made me even stronger, tougher than before. I'd lost twenty pounds of flab I didn't know I had and gained five of hardened muscle. Instead of 220 lbs, I topped the scales at 205 and was reduced to about two percent body fat. You'd figure I'd left stress-soreness and aches long behind, but they seemed to happen more and more often.

"A lot has happened in the last year, Agent." Her smile might have held a trace of pity for an old man. Or not. Maybe it was indigestion.

A year. I'd been training Green Peas for a full year, an experience only slightly less painful than a sulfuric acid enema. How time flies when you're hip deep in the latrine without nose plugs. A lot of things had happened since that trip to Omaha. Since Maydock the vampire. Well, half human, half vampire—the worst of both worlds.

Omaha, where I landed myself in the bad graces of the BSI and thanks to my contract, I couldn't quit or do a damn thing about the situation. I had to take it on the chin like a good boy and smile through blood-stained teeth.

It wasn't the *almost* nuclear explosion I'd caused that earned me a black mark in my file. Nor was it the havoc I'd wreaked, the property damage and bodies left behind like so many lifeless flesh dolls. No, it was two minutes. Two lousy minutes.

While dancing to the aforementioned psychopathic human/vampire hybrid's tune, I'd happened upon (well, been led by the nose to) an organization that was involved with the kidnapping and selling of children to people with obscene amounts of cash, an auction house for tots. The kids, identified by the organization's bought-and-paid-for pediatricians, all had the magic gene, the one that marked them as future Magicians. That was disturbing in two ways (other than the fact that an organized entity was kidnapping children). One, there was an international organization that knew about Magic and the World Under, an organization that had somehow *kept its existence a secret from the BSI*. Two … there is no two, because one is disturbing enough. Not to mention they employed their own Magicians who were almost as talented as their Bureau counterparts.

When I realized what the organization was up to, I went a bit mental. At the time I thought it was a kiddie sex-slave trade, and I tortured a man, shot his kneecaps to splinters. I didn't have to do it. He was fully within my power—I could have just forced him by other means to reveal what he knew—but instead I shot him twice and regretted the action immediately. Torture is wrong, no matter how you slice it (no pun intended). From waterboarding to shooting an asshole's knees to bits, it's wrong on every level. Who was I to judge a person's sins when

I have committed so many myself? My soul carried its own weight in blackness. I'd inflicted enough evil in the name of righteousness to make Torquemada blanch, and it was only right that I'd earned BB's ire, putting me square at the top of his poo-poo list.

One good thing, though, is that the BSI shut down the kiddie trade and thanks to Ghost—a disembodied former wunderkind from MIT who magically uploaded his soul into the Internet—most of the other illegal activities the organization had been dealing in throughout the U.S. With the other governments clued in and aiming for their tender bits, the organization had all but disappeared off the face of the earth. That didn't mean it wouldn't reappear, but the Bureau is keeping a weather eye out for its activities.

Since Omaha I'd been training, observing, and evaluating every new crop of Green Peas during the day and heading off home to my family at night.

Yeah, my family. I said it. Still had a hard time believing it.

Jeanie. My wife.

And let's not forget my kid. Four months ago I found myself in the hospital with Jeanie while a kindly female doc in blue scrubs delivered our child. Thanks to an epidural, Jeanie had a relatively easy time of it, although I wouldn't give it a try for all the Finnish chocolate in the world, that's for sure.

Twelve hours of labor, twelve hours of holding my hand while she sweated and strained. Then, when the doc handed me a pair of surgical scissors to cut the umbilical cord (no thanks, Doc, I'm sure I'm not medically qualified) it became *real*. I had a baby. *We* had a baby. A boy.

My son.

Awesome. I leaned over my wife (my wife!), looked into his purple-y face that would soon become the color of chamomile tea, and said, "Does the pointy head thing ever go away?" Seemed like a pity, to be called Conehead Hakala all your life. Or Beldar.

Jeanie chuckled weakly, sweat dripping off her nose. "No, you big doofus," she replied with her throaty English accent that always activated my horny reflex. "It will be round as an apple soon enough."

Oddly enough, the little guy looked like a teeny-tiny version of a little old man, minus the wrinkles. Hard to picture? Have a baby and find out.

While I stared in wonder at the sleeping little dude, his mother turned her big, chocolate-brown eyes my way. "What are we going to name him, Kal? We never settled the matter."

Hmmm. Good question, one I'd been pondering for the past twelve hours. During the pregnancy, we declined to have the child's sex identified, preferring to be surprised, and we'd never really settled on a name, although she was partial to Trevor if it was a boy … and *that* wasn't gonna happen. Fortunately, I had just the right answer. "I want to name him after one of the bravest, strongest, kindest men I've ever heard of." My throat started to close up, but sheer willpower kept it open. "This man I'm thinking of was at his best when things were at their worst. Ferocious, loving, gentle, violent, and compassionate … a mass of contradictions that combined to form a stellar human being."

Jeanie looked puzzled. "You thinking of Canton? Your father?" she asked, one corner of her mouth twitching upward, forming a dimple.

I shook my head. "Naw, kiddo, the name that came to mind is Desmond."

Big, sloppy tears began to spill over. "My late husband?"

"The only Desmond I care to talk about," I replied softly.

A year ago, when I was considering a team for a mission to Chicago, I experienced the relevant portions of Jeanie's life through virtual reality via the DRAFT (Data Retrieval and Forensic Technology unit) glasses. I'd learned that Desmond Morrow, her first husband, taught her how to fight, to be tough and to take care of herself. A factory worker and champion brawler, he treated her like a queen and loved her unconditionally, and that was good enough for me. Through the VR, I saw his kindness, that inner light that made him a special being not confined by flesh and bone. Desmond. After we were married (I thought Mom would never stop crying during the ceremony) Jeanie confided in me, saying that Desmond was the voice in her head that guided her through difficult times.

How's that for an erection killer? Still, it could be worse. Lord knows there were far scarier things in *my* head—things that would give the Marquis de Sade nightmares.

Her arm slipping around my neck to hold me tight against her cheek showed me how right I could be. Even a blind squirrel finds a nut every now and then, or something like that.

"We'll call the next one Leena," she whispered, her breath hot against my face, "if it's a girl."

Leena was my little sister, the voice in my head after she was killed by a Supernatural. The source of my superhuman rage that fueled me through more than one near-fatal encounter. But she had found peace, and that rage was gone.

My son's birth was the best thing that had happened in the year since Omaha. On the whole, the good outweighed the bad, although the bad proved to be more of a pain in the ass while the good amounted to a metric ton of dirty diapers and a complete lack of anything resembling sleep. For an example of the bad, after Omaha and the black mark on my record I was consigned to take a couch trip, twice a month, with the Bureau's chief headshrinker, Dr. Willows. Oh, she's a nice enough woman, although she liked her Ben & Jerry's Chunky Monkey a bit too much.

Twice a month I had to talk about my feelings, to vent the poison inside so I had a chance to heal, to have a normal life. All in all, I'd rather floss with razor blades.

Normal life, huh? Even by Bureau standards, my life was as normal as a gaggle of coked up preschoolers armed with left-handed monkey wrenches. I was a whole galaxy away from normal and the Bureau hoped that Dr. Willows could crawl inside my skull and untangle the Gordian Knot of my thoughts.

"I said, Agent Hakala, do you think the changes in the past year have been good for the Bureau?" asked Darla.

My mind snapped back to the present and I shook my head ruefully. "Better? It's certainly different. Used to be I just told someone about the recent op, went home, and drank myself stupid. Now I put on a headband made of loop de loop wires and electrodes and experience the salient points of the mission all over again. Don't know how good that is, considering living through it the first time was irritating enough."

Her laugh was silky perfection. "No, do you think letting the world know about Supernaturals was a good thing?"

What a loaded question.

To be honest, the world took the news of Supernaturals pretty well. Oh, there was plenty of panic and doom-saying, usually from the Tinfoil Hat Club and politicians, not to mention religious hysteria from fundamentalists, but the regular folk, John Q. Public, were pretty chill about the whole thing. As long as there were guys like me in the trenches ready to fight the good fight and die a good death in the name of keeping them safe.

Still, that didn't stop a spree of killing that totaled about *one hundred thousand* dead in the U.S. alone because those who teetered on the edge of sanity took it upon themselves to eliminate perceived Supernatural threats themselves, or commit suicide in inventive ways, usually violently, sometimes explosively, taking others with them in a spectacular splatterfest and turning themselves into Jackson Pollock paintings made of human blood and tissue.

As for the victims of this hysteria, every single damn one of them was an innocent who differed from the norm: those with Achondroplasia (dwarfism), gigantism, Proteus Syndrome (think Elephant Man), and other unusual physical conditions mankind is subject to. One man was shot in Vegas for being too hairy; the shooter thought he was a werewolf despite a Hawaiian shirt. That brief but violent episode showcased the darkest side of human nature. Nowadays most of the Straights (i.e., The General Public) treat the whole thing as a kind of interactive reality show.

Before the paranoiacs went hog-wild—less than two hours after the announcement—the Bureau Powers Expansion Act was introduced. Sounds funky, huh? Basically it gave the Bureau carte blanche to do anything and everything to safeguard the Straights against Supernatural threats. That included authority over any other local, state, or federal agency, including the military. If it went bump in the night, we were allowed to nuke it till it glowed and shoot it in the dark. The BSI now had, on a limited scale, more power than FEMA, although it must answer to the newly formed Supernatural Committee. They kept the Bureau from straying too far out of line, but that old saying attributed to Ben Franklin was repeated often enough. You know the one—those who trade liberty for safety deserve neither.

And with the Committee came a whole new raft of volunteers—men and women who wanted into the Bureau so bad they'd eat nails and crap staples for the opportunity. Now the Bureau had twenty teams (Alpha through Upsilon), twenty-one Receptionists (or Spin Doctors, Media Relations, whatever), and a whole new slew of Magicians and bright pennies working for Special Branch, the Bureau's R&D division. Think of Q Branch in the Bond films, but with more explosions and things being turned into puddles of goo.

"It's okay, I guess." A yawn tried to crack my face in two. The couch trips bored me silly, but I didn't say that. Rule number forty-six: don't be mean to your psychiatrist, even when they're not there. "Still, it was cool being all cloak-and-dagger and such."

She replied with the obvious. "At least the mortality rate for first-year Agents is down to twenty-five percent."

I nodded. "Sure, but it's still the most dangerous job in the world. It seems like the World Under is getting craftier by the minute and more dangerous monsters are bleeding through."

"Which is why the president revealed the existence of the Bureau and the World Under," she smiled and rubbed her temples, "and dispelled the Interdiction."

"Yeah, one good thing that's come from all this." The Interdiction, the spell that kept the existence of the World Under a secret. It had nestled in my mind like a spider since I was fifteen and now it was gone. Turned out Ben Franklin, the Magician who crafted the spell, embedded it with a counter spell. A simple phrase, six words that unlocked my mind. "To thine own self be true." Of course, it had to be said in Aramaic.

Clever Ben.

CHAPTER THREE

Kal
Back in Black

OF COURSE THE second the plane touched down at Dulles I received notice that BB wanted to see me, and as my feet hit the tarmac, a black Dodge Charger pulled up. A rugged looking guy, a Green Pea by the name of Silvestri (whom I'd nicknamed Slats because he was all hard angles and flat planes) exited the car and opened the back door for me.

"Welcome home, Agent Hakala." He looked good in a dark suit and tie. Federal chic.

"Hey, Slats," I replied, entering the car. "What's gotten into BB's bonnet? Any idea why he wants to see me?" It had been months since I'd talked to the Director, not that I didn't want to, but because he still carried a plateful of anger over my antics in Omaha. Not that I blamed him, mind you. Well, maybe a little.

"Sorry, Agent, no dice." He smiled like a dog eating peanut butter out of a hairbrush. It was more than a little disturbing.

I kept my trap shut for the rest of the ride and Slats, good egg that he was, sensed my mood and kept his closed as well. The kid had common sense, which isn't as common as you'd think.

A year ago the Bureau's headquarters was a warehouse called, creatively enough, Warehouse. These days it was still called Warehouse, and still *was* a warehouse, but instead of relocating every three to four months, it stayed put. What used to be an industrial park in Alexandria was now one-hundred-sixty acres of green space surrounded by a twenty-foot-tall, ten-foot-thick concrete and steel fence topped with razor wire, with guard towers every five-hundred feet. It had the look and feel of a maximum-security prison but without the architectural grace. Imagine the one place on the planet you don't want to be; now draw a picture of it. I bet it looks a lot like the BSI compound. BB hadn't wanted the towers or the state-of-the-art automated Vulcan cannons or the satellite Death Ray (don't asked, it's classified above TOP SECRET), but the Committee wanted to keep the Bureau protected in case the Sidhe (the legendary Faërie race of Celtic lore who nearly destroyed mankind—twice) came calling. The fact that the Sidhe were at war with each other and wouldn't be interfering for the next few centuries didn't change their minds one bit. (The Seelie Court, or those that wanted to ally with mankind, were fighting the Unseelie Court, the total bastards that wanted to kill us all by pulling our guts out through our noses.) Sometimes a heaping portion of paranoia is a survival trait.

The big problem with having all these magical/technological defensive and offensive capabilities packed into the compound was that if BB ever went rogue, there was about a fifty/fifty chance he could take over the country from behind his desk. The Committee members, no fools they, had figured this out and placed the codes to lowering those defenses into a ruggedized computer system buried in the bunker three hundred feet beneath the White House.

At the gate our IDs were checked and re-checked, our auras scanned, and DNA examined. When the guards were fully satisfied, they waved us through the twenty-foot-wide steel gate and we drove through.

Inside the only entrance (but not the only exit) we were

issued badges, one of the Bad Things that came from revealing the BSI's existence. I mean, c'mon, badges? Next it would be dress codes, regulation haircuts and ... *shudder* ... morning motivational meetings.

The horror.

After badges, I was free to wander the halls of Warehouse on down to BB's office, a room big enough to get lost in. I had a theory that if you searched the Director's office thoroughly enough, you'd probably find Jimmy Hoffa.

Although the duties of Receptionist changed from team guardian/watchdog/psychologist to media relations/psychologist and defender against overeager fans, BB still rated the original version. This one was called Andrea and she had all the humor and conversational skills of a spitting cobra. She'd been my Receptionist for a while, but that didn't stop her from placing her hand under her desk to grip the sawed-off shotgun filled with silvered deer slugs mounted there. One twitch of the finger and my guts would fall out of the hole where Big Jim and Twins used to be. I placed my hands slowly, carefully upon the surface of her desk.

"The Director will see you now, Agent Hakala," she said after my identity had been confirmed by the silver Spell Shapes beneath the wood veneer. I removed my hands, palms tingling, and went to see the boss.

Butt comfortably ensconced in an overstuffed chair, I rested my hands on my knees and waited for BB to say something. He merely stared at me through his glasses, which I now knew was a DRAFT. Heck, he probably was checking my pulse and my behind for hemorrhoids, but like the old salesman saying goes, *the first one who talks loses*, and I wasn't about to. I gave him a careful onceover. Although he was in his mid-forties, the job had aged him a good ten-plus years, the skin on his face falling slack and the veins on the back of his hands bulging. They say that being the president ages a person, but it seemed that being the director placed one foot squarely in the grave.

Still, BB radiated the confidence and physical vitality that had made him one of the BSI's best Agents.

BB, as usual, registered all the emotion of a rock. "You look good, Kal."

Oh, worse than I thought. "Thanks," I replied, keeping my face neutral.

"I bet you're wondering why you're here."

My shoulders raised a fraction. I can play the inscrutable game, too. "Not really."

That got to him. "Really?"

"Really." *Keep it to one or two syllables, Kal.*

"Why do you think I called you?"

I let him chew on silence.

A faint frown. Yeah, he was starting to get pissed. "Kal, we have to stop being angry with each other."

"Why?"

A vein started up at his temple. "Don't be childish."

Okay, time for more syllables. "Not childish, BB, *angry*. There's a whole world of difference between those words."

Pretty sure he was scanning Dr. Willows' files detailing my psych profile and fitness reports because he kept his mouth shut despite me getting under his skin—not to mention that his stare was about a thousand yards over my left shoulder. He confirmed my hunch by saying, "Dr. Willows says you've made wonderful progress."

"Guess so. She hasn't consigned me to the local giggle factory." And the fact that I was able to spin a country mile of BS without her catching on. Lord help me if she ever did.

"Must everything be a joke or a bad pun?"

"Call it my coping mechanism."

Sighing, BB removed his DRAFT and set it carefully on the desktop. I knew that desk to be one of the world's most powerful computers, a desk-shaped device that interfaced with the DRAFT, allowing for constant updates and analysis. The fact that he took them off meant that he felt ready to get down to brass tacks with an honest heart-to-heart.

"We're ready to send you back out into the field, Kal," he said quietly.

Pins falling to the floor made more noise than we did. I let that statement percolate through my cortex for a moment or three. "By *we*, you mean the Committee, right?" He didn't reply, so I kept on, "And that means there's been a colossal pooch-screwing, which means that it was public, so public in fact that the Committee is crapping their undies and you needed to feed them a line to ease their worries. Am I right?" All that blasted out of my mouth in a rush, the logic falling into place almost simultaneously with the words. I held my breath.

"God, you're such a pain in the ass." I was right.

"Part of my undeniable charm."

BB crossed his arms. "So take the job. Alex has a device that contains all the particulars."

My pulse started to pound, but I kept my face impassive. If he put the DRAFT back on I was screwed. My palms were sweaty and I could feel my pulse in my ears. I shook my head. "No, BB. Not this time."

That got to him. "What?" It wasn't quite a shout, but for BB, it was close—he might as well have hollered at the top of his lungs.

"Not going to do it." Yep, my heart was performing the Macarena.

"Don't want to, or not going to?"

"Pick your poison."

A short finger *tap-tap-tapped* on the desktop, the first sign of unease I'd ever seen in the man. I didn't know whether to be exultant or terrified. The good money was on terrified, though. "Kal, please do not try my patience." His finger kept tapping on the desk.

Yeah, terrified all right. "Not trying to, BB."

He held my gaze for a good long while, gray eyes piercing

skin and bone into brain, and it took everything in me not to squirm like a three-year-old. *Tap-tap-tap*. Then he did something that almost sent me back heels over head in my chair—he sighed. A real, heartfelt sigh of sadness and regret. The shock of it nearly broke my resolve.

"When did you lose faith in me, Kal?" he asked.

The words nearly turned my anger to ashes, but my fire ran deep and burned white hot. "That's a hell of a question for you to ask me, BB."

One of his sparse eyebrows climbed toward where his hair used to be. "What do you mean?"

"What do I mean?" The words emerged with more energy than I intended. "What do I mean? I'll tell you what I mean, boss: I've been a good little Agent, going to see Dr. Willows twice a month, minding my P's and Q's, and because of Omaha, you took me out of action. I *get* that, I agree with that, but a *full year*?" My voice was rising, and with some effort I lowered the volume. "During that time I've become the poster boy for the BSI, the longest serving Agent in history—a mascot to be paraded on stage by Kimmel, Colbert, and Fallon. And let's not forget the movie! That damn movie where that blond guy from that superhero movie, *The Justifiers*, portrayed me. And there I was, on talk shows performing like a trained monkey so the Straights could feel safe because guys like me were on the front lines, but the irony is I'm not on the front lines. I get to babysit the new recruits—the Green Pea trainer and evaluator—and make sure they don't die because this job can still kill you in a heartbeat despite all the support we receive nowadays from the other alphabet agencies and the local LEOs. So here I am, wondering why, after a year of silence from you, I'm suddenly the Bureau's go-to boy. I gotta figure that your back is to the wall and that's the only reason I'm being tasked with this op. Faith in you, BB? What about your damned faith in me?"

What a load! The words tumbled over each other as the pressure that had built up over the past year burst forth like air from a balloon. By the time the last one left my lips, my heart was racing and my lungs were on fire. I wanted to take big gulps of air, but forced myself to breathe slow and deep so as not to seem too agitated. Of course it was too late for that.

BB answered me with silence, gray eyes peering into mine. It was unnerving as hell. He held my gaze for a full minute then dropped a bombshell: "You're right."

What? What? What?

Oh, wow. This is your brain; this is your brain when the world just became something other than what you thought it was. See the difference? My mind went to places better left unexplored. It was my turn to say, "What do you mean?"

"It means you're right," BB said, gray eyes grim. "After Omaha, I lost faith. When the public needed a face to go with the BSI, I gave them you because the publicity tours would occupy enough of your time that you *couldn't* force your way back into the field. Then came that movie about your life and what happened in Denver and the publicity tour for that took another few months. All that plus Green Pea training ate every scrap of time you had for the past year and I was content to let it be so. That movie and those tours put Congress square in our pockets, so I was able to leverage the clout to keep the BSI running lean and mean. Expansion of our team roster was the only concession I had to make and it was a good one.

"It's been a tumultuous year for you, for your family, and for the Bureau, I get that. The late-night talk shows, that ridiculous movie in which my character was played by Stanley Tucci, the whole lot. But as troublesome as the last year has been, as much as my headaches increased tenfold, nothing rattled my cage more than what you did in Omaha. I mean, I knew you were a bit unstable, fractious, headstrong, and wild sometimes ... but to torture a man? That's wrong no matter what the situation, Kal. It shook me because you are the best, and if the best of us goes off the rails, how long before more Bureau Agents follow your lead? They worship you, Kal, and word of what you did spread faster than influenza. And do you know the hell of it, Kal? The hell of it is that I understand why you did what you did. You did something that every one of us at the Bureau would love to have done, but it's still wrong, and we have to be better than that. We must. Your example hurt us because no one blamed you, no one held you accountable … except me. Not the politicians, not the ACLU, only me.

"So yes, Kal, I lost faith in you because it hurt so much to see you fall from grace. It hurt me to have to give you that black mark in your file, and it hurts me to *know* how brittle you've become since your sister Leena's spirit left you."

BB hung his head while I stared, mouth slightly open. Hearing a soliloquy from BB was like watching the sun rise in the west. "For ten years you've been the Bureau's secret weapon, the best of the best, and we've used you despite your issues and that's on me." A deep breath. "Your moral failure was the result of my poor judgment. I should never have left you in charge. If I had chosen Matt Alba instead, he would never have let you go to Omaha."

"And Maydock would've killed hundreds if not thousands of people." The words tasted like defeat in my mouth. How is it that when we get what we want, it often leaves us feeling empty? "And we wouldn't have discovered the organization that was kidnapping and selling kids." Those kids, those future Magicians, were being sold to very powerful, very corrupt people who could bend them to their awful will. Children made into slave Magicians for those without a moral compass. The thought still boiled the acid in m my gut.

As for the organization, it was run like a terrorist network, each cell interacting only when absolutely necessary with the most minimal of information. Various counter-intelligence teams in Europe and Russia managed to shut down some of their operations, but I knew deep in my gut we'd only scratched the surface.

"Be that as it may, Kal," BB sighed, "as the Director of the

BSI, the buck stops at my desk. You know that, so your failure is mine. That's why I've been avoiding you. When I see you, I see my own failures. And I'm sorry, Kal, I should not have shut you out."

As my favorite superhero character was wont to say, *Oh, my stars and garters*. Everything below my navel went numb and the palms of my hands as well as my fingertips began to tingle. I wanted to drop something just to see if gravity was still working.

"That's more than you've said to me all year." A brief pause. "Apology accepted."

BB nodded.

"What now, boss?"

"Take the job," he said quietly.

Of course. My suspicious, nasty side wondered if the last minute of BB's verbal diarrhea had been a ploy to obtain my cooperation.

When did I become so cynical?

Still, I sensed an opportunity. "Okay, but once this op is done, I'm back and I mean *back*. No more Green Peas, and I mean *ever*."

After a few seconds BB nodded.

"I pick my own team."

"Agreed."

"You're agreeing too easily."

He mentioned something about not examining the teeth of horses given as presents. I had to agree.

"Canton. I want Canton."

A headshake. "No, he's on assignment in Alabama."

That was news. I'd seen him last week. "What's in Alabama?" Besides Alabamites. Alabamians? Alaboomies?

"That hitter from Omaha, the one who was sent to kill Mr. G and Mr. Y."

I remembered the report. G and Y were bigwigs in the organization and their failure to keep their child-trafficking operation safe led to a hit being put out on them. From what Canton told me, the hitter was quite a looker and lethal as a straight razor.

"So Canton is after the lady assassin? Seems a bit out of our purview."

"He insisted. Actually, demanded. I sent Team Nu to shadow him, just like Canton and his team shadowed you in Omaha. Besides, since the Committee doubled the number of Agents the government employs, there has been a lot of downtime."

True, more than half the teams sat around twiddling their thumbs when they weren't training, but the Supernaturals that were appearing seemed to be deadlier and deadlier. Two months ago team Alpha ran into a group of Norse Jotun, giants with serious anti-social issues. Aside from having flesh so dense that even 50mm rounds bounced off them, they had the ability to hide in plain sight—quite a feat, considering the smallest topped twenty feet.

"Then I want Ng," I continued. "He's a pretty good egg for a Green Pea and he can keep his head in a tight spot."

"Of course. He's one of the more promising Agents we've had in the last year."

Really not saying a lot. Although our standards were still the highest of any federal agency or military branch, the sudden influx of volunteers had the trainers at Coronado pulling their hair out by the roots; I imagined that by now they all looked like BB. The flood of fresh meat had become so bad that the Navy opened up a new base on Morris Island in Charleston Harbor all special-like to handle the overflow. Although we still took in Green Peas, it was more a catch-and-release program with a long waiting list. I was still baffled as to why so many wanted to perform a job so dangerous that even the most jaded adrenaline junkie would hide in a closet and discover religion.

"Great. Well, one of the best new lights we have besides Ng is Buffalo." I called the guy Buffalo because he was slow to anger and damn near impossible to stop once you got him going. His real name was Robert Atkins, as steady a hand to watch your back as any man could want.

"Take whomever you wish," said BB. He considered that statement for a moment then placed the DRAFT on his head, fingers tapping virtual icons only he could see. After a minute he shook his head in resignation. "Except for the Magician. Qualified field Magicians are still scarce, so I will assign you one."

Oh, lord. Please, not Rat. Not Rat. Anyone but Rat!

"You get Rat."

Awesome.

CHAPTER FOUR

Kal
Long Hard Times to Come

IF ANYONE FILLED the role of Q from the Bond movies, it was Alex Dumont, resident super-genius and leader of Special Branch. Also one of the few people I considered a good friend, even though most of the inventions he'd made in the past few years tended to blow up or vaporize whole city blocks. But in this business, you take what you can get because when the technogeeknerds come through in the clutch, the results are spectacular. I stood in the middle of Special Branch surrounded by wizards and physicists and über-geeks and all manner of unclean beasties in lab coats. Getting in required another verification of my identity—Special Branch had at least a hundred million in gemstones in its vaults. Not to mention gold, silver, and platinum.

Gemstones and precious metals are essential to Special Branch because they store and absorb magic. Since Magicians first began to manipulate that strange force we call magic, they'd used gold and silver to give shape to spells. Gems acted as magical batteries. Special Branch offered the best and the brightest mankind had to offer in the way of Magicians with a command of magical theory, and they got all the best toys. Not to mention all the best in geological goodies.

Despite me standing there in all my glory (if you can call a gray T-shirt and blue jeans glory), I was pretty much ignored by the technogeeknerds because I was neither a cool particle accelerator nor the inventor of the USB port. But those weren't the people I was interested in, not by a long shot. No, the person I wanted to see had her arms around my neck in a hot second after catching sight of me.

"Hello there, sexy," said my wife Jeanie in her throaty English accent that always jump-started my hormones.

"Hey back," I drawled, drinking in the sight of her flawless brown skin and deep, dark eyes. Her hair was done up in a style she called Beyoncé. We lip-locked for a good minute or so before parting. Then I told her what's what.

A bone-crushing hug took the wind from my lungs. "Thank *God*!" she said.

My eyebrows headed north. "I thought you'd be unhappy to hear I'm heading into the grinder again."

"Honey, don't take this the wrong way, but over the last year you've been one of the unhappiest blokes I've ever seen. You've been driving me crazy with your moping."

"I don't mope."

"You mope."

"No, I brood. That's how sexy men mope."

That earned me slap on the chest. "So what are you doing here? Why aren't you at ARMORY?" She was referring to the vault where the Bureau kept all its lethal goodies—everything one needed to destroy Supernaturals or half the planet. Call it my Happy Place.

"I haven't read the brief yet, but my feeling is that Team Omicron jumped into the deep end of a crap-filled pool without a life preserver and I want to see what new goodies Alex may have. I've been given carte blanche on this."

During the explanation, Jeanie's face became grave. "How bad is it?"

"I have a feeling it's the only reason BB agreed to let me back in the field and out of Green Pea training permanently. He had to placate the Committee. And the only reason the Committee would lean on BB is because whatever happened was very public and unpleasant. You know how unshakable BB is most times."

Face unreadable, she said, "Let's find Alex."

The head of Special Branch sat in his office waiting for me behind his desk. An array of interesting items rested in front of him and the light in his eyes told me that he had something special in mind for my op. I began to sweat. His kind of 'special' usually detonated without regard to life or property.

Alex Dumont had more brains in his head than Congress. Wait, that's a poor metaphor since most people do. Let's just say he had a beautiful mind and would most likely have a theory of everything before the decade saw its end. *Hmm, better.* The only thing that made me question his massive brain power was his horrible taste in outerwear. At that moment, he sported his favorite tartan sweater vest, birth control glasses (as a Magician who could vaporize the Queen Mary with his mind, he should've figured out long ago how to correct his vision) and a pair of red denim pants, all encased in a white lab coat. It hurt my eyes to look at him.

"Hi, Kal," Alex said, barely suppressing a smile. I began to sweat even more because when he smiled like that, it meant he had some clever and potentially lethal-to-operate gewgaw or doodad he wanted me to beta-test. "BB told me you were on the way."

It was good to see the kid, although now that he was in his late twenties, he hardly qualified as a kid anymore. Still, he was the little brother I never wanted. He looked like a stiff breeze would send him flying like a kite, but underneath his lab coat lay some solid muscle put there by the Navy's best. I wished he could have my back instead of Rat, a guy who thought hardcore S&M porn too tame.

"Hiya, Alex." I gave the items on his desk a dubious glance. "Whatcha got for me?"

Jeanie headed out the door. "I'll leave you boys to your toys."

Both of us watched her go. Even in a lab coat she had enough oomph in her strut to give any heterosexual male with a pulse a dangerous blood-pressure spike. I didn't blame the kid at all for looking—I sure was—but after a while I had to clear my throat to get his attention.

"Sorry, Kal," he muttered sheepishly.

"It's okay, kid. I'm sure Dove will understand." Dove Jacobs was his girlfriend—a resident violent femme with an enormous chip on her shoulder. Short, muscular, and beautiful as a cheetah, she was one of the more dangerous veteran Agents in the Bureau. I'd already tagged her to be on my team.

Alex blanched. I guess any guy who dated Dove was used to a healthy dose of fear. Good for him; it built character.

"Don't even kid about that."

"Who's kidding?"

In lieu of a reply, he began to point at the little thingamajigs on the desk. "These are our new field glasses."

I picked them up. Looked like they belonged to the Blues Brothers. "Can't be nightvision; we have contacts for that." I put them on and the lenses automatically changed from tinted to clear in a matter of seconds.

"They do act as nightvision sunglasses, but only when paired with this." A necklace flew my way, weighed down by a pendant the size of a silver dollar. It was surprisingly heavy. "They form a poor man's version of a DRAFT."

A smile formed, stretching my face tight. "Really?"

"When I say 'poor man's version,' I mean they have the same capabilities as a RediPad and are interactive like a DRAFT, but have none of the DRAFT's more esoteric capabilities like lie detection or deep forensic software. What you get is a RediPad built into a pair of sunglasses. The pendant is the CPU with a state-of-the-art micro-battery. Cold, it will power the CPU for five hours, but when worn next to the skin, it can run for over twenty hours by absorbing energy in the form of heat. Although you can use HUD as your screen, if you're not comfortable with it, the glasses can project a display on any surface and you can use that surface as a touchscreen. We call it DRAFTlite."

Cute. "Pretty cool, kid. They do anything that a RediPad can't?" The Bureau's computer tablets I'd been using for the past couple of years still had the edge on anything the NSA could develop.

That brought a smile to Alex's face as he warmed up to the subject. "Sure. There's an icon that will allow you to see in infrared and ultra-chromat, which means in at least five different spectral bands."

Okay, chemistry is my thing, not that ultra-chromat thingie. I'm a pretty sharp guy, but Alex has the ability to make me feel like a chimp playing with matches.

"Ah, I can tell by the slackness in your jaw and the dull gleam in your eye that you have no clue as to what I'm talking about." The kid was shoveling a good dose of smug my way.

"Pretend I don't speak technogeeknerd and use words of no more than three syllables."

"You never studied, did you?"

"I studied ways to kill a geek with a pencil. Does that count?"

A skeptical look and a low chuckle told me he knew I wouldn't harm a hair on his pointy little head. Sarky kid. "Ultra-chromat vision is what pigeons see; their eyes have four types of color receptors, one of which gives them the ability to perceive the ultraviolet part of the color spectrum. The others allow for perception of magnetic fields and polarized light. They can see nuances of color that humans can't. For example, if you were to look at a plain white wall, you might see textures and variations in that white that would make it seem quite psychedelic."

"Um … cool?" I had no clue what purpose that might serve,

but any edge in a fight could save your life. "Anything else?"

"A separate icon enables X-ray vision, albeit for a limited time. It's energy intensive."

Now *that* was cool. "X-ray specs? You've invented magical X-ray specs? There are thirteen-year-olds around this great nation of ours who would sell their parents to get their grubby little hands on these, boyo."

Before I finished, he was shaking his head. "Not magical, Kal. It's all tech, the latest and greatest in spyware. Thanks to our budget doubling in the past year—and a little help from Ghost—we were able to achieve advances we'd only dreamed of. This is the latest in Bureau tech." He grinned and pointed to the specs. "And there are micro-cams mounted on the temple arms that allow you to see what's behind you as well as cameras in front that let others see what you see."

Is this job great or what? "Okay, I'll take six pair. In fact, I'll take six of everything. Hey, you still have that sonic emitter? It sure helped in San Francisco." It saved my life when my team was attacked by a giant swarm of mind-controlled birds intent on delivering beaky death. Instead, I reduced most of them to avian goulash. It was just as gross as it sounds.

"Sorry, Kal. We had to recall them."

I felt the short hairs on the back of my head start to stand up. "Why?"

He became evasive. "Oh, there was a small, itty-bitty snafu that happened to most of the units when they overheated."

Uh-oh. "What kind of snafu, Alex?"

"Nothing major."

I gave him a gimlet stare. "Spill, squirt."

"They tended to … ah … release an abundance of energy due to the sudden proliferation of gasses in a confined space."

Thermodynamics I understood quite well, thanks to a good old-fashioned edumacation at the University of Nebraska. "They *exploded*?" I asked incredulously.

"Only a little bit."

One, two, three, four …. "You gave me a sonic emitter that could've exploded?"

He had to grace to look sheepish.

Six, seven, eight, nine, ten. "Okay, kid, no harm no foul. But will any of these new toys explode?"

"They shouldn't."

Freaking awesome.

"And now we go to Jim Daniels who is at the Quint Building waiting for the Bureau of Supernatural Investigation's new team to arrive. What's the mood like out there, Jim?"

Cut to Jim Daniels, who grins dead into the camera. He looked good and you could tell he knew it—his hair, despite the breeze, was a perfect brown helmet and his green eyes sparkled. "Well, Nina, there's an almost festive mood here as crowds of people await the arrival of the next BSI team. The police have their hands full keeping them behind the barricades. Rumor has it that Kalevi Hakala, famous for being the public face of the Bureau of Supernatural Investigation, will personally lead this new team. Agent Hakala is best known as the subject of the blockbuster film, *Things to do in Denver when you're Un-dead*, which dramatized his meteoric rise as the Bureau's longest serving and most effective Agent."

What a load of crap. I tapped an icon and the image disappeared off the DRAFTlite. I took them off and rubbed the bridge of my nose. The team and I sat in a large conversion van being driven by Wesley Ng, a first-year Agent who'd been recruited after the Chicago incident. Marsha Yevgeny, our Receptionist, sat shotgun, looking classy and sassy in her dark-brown Moi-Même business suit. Her red hair, which fell in ringlets around her ears, contrasted nicely with her pale, freckled skin. If I hadn't been happily married with a four-month-old son, I'd have given her a serious look.

Damn but I hated to leave Jeanie and the boy at home alone, but I felt so excited to be out in the field again, even if it did look like a three-ring circus run by demented Chihuahuas. I knew deep in my heart that my wife and son would be just fine. Anybody who messed with Jeanie could count on a trip to the ER.

At least she had the Brownies to keep her company.

A couple of years ago, I saved the little guys from a church, or vice versa. Either way, I lured them into a toy Winnebago where they could set up shop. They performed dry cleaning and housekeeping services in exchange for a bowl of milk (they do like Oreos, but the last thing I needed was a house full of fat Faëries). The Sidhe (good and bad) could sense—track, whatever—the little guys, a fact I learned almost too late during an op in San Francisco. Fortunately, Alex covered their Winnebago in spell Shapes to hide them from the Sidhe Spidey Sense. He also supplied teeny tiny spelled overalls made of gold thread for them to wear when they emerged to take care of laundry. Oddly enough, the little guys didn't mind and confirmed the spell's efficacy by playing "Only the Lonely" on their miniscule musical instruments.

My stomach felt tight and hot as the van rumbled through downtown St. Louis toward the Quint Building. Five minutes out … five minutes until the television cameras and reporters shoved mics in my face and shouted the inane questions people with working brain cells wouldn't dream of asking.

I'd never been to St. Louis. I'd never seen the Gateway Arch up close and personal and still didn't want to. Somewhere in the Quint Building, six people lay dead. Oh, sure, they might not have been dead, just captured or incapacitated, but deep down in the hard places of my soul I knew better. Omicron was deader than disco and it was up to my team and me to find out why and kill whatever dared harm us.

So of course I wasn't feeling up to sightseeing, wasn't up to taking in the rich history of the place. I had to be cold and sharp and ready for action. I had to keep my grim resolve if we stood a chance of surviving what lay inside a million tons of steel, concrete, and glass. That said, what I did see of the city looked like the founders had discovered a heap of confusing, whorling deer trails and called them roads. It was like the city planners had been allergic to straight lines.

"Awww, guess who's all famous and stuff, guys," said Rat, our team Magician. He sported his own DRAFTlite and must've caught the same station. Six feet tall, so skinny he seemed constructed of pipe cleaners and rubber bands, he resembled the nickname he'd been given right down to the buck teeth. He also made most perverts look Amish, possessing the largest collection of porn I'd ever had the misfortune of seeing. Needless to say, no one came within twenty feet of his bedroom for fear of catching something nasty. Rumor had it that housekeeping wore HAZMAT suits in there.

Just looking at him gave me the itchies. Still, we needed a Magician, and I couldn't be picky.

"Not interested in fame, Rat," I grumbled, adjusting my Bureau-issue black armor. A combination of Kevlar and NewTanium, it could withstand rounds up to 20mm and made the wearer look pretty bad-ass.

Dove Jacobs grunted, unimpressed by my celebrity. As a rule, she was unimpressed by pretty much everything except her boyfriend Alex. How those two got together was anybody's guess. It was like watching oil and water mix, or politicians and honesty. As for the rest of the team, they flashed grins, clearly amused by my discomfiture.

One of the other veterans, Billings, lost his smile so quickly it could've been an illusion. Big like the human equivalent of a redwood, wide, solid and iron hard, he was unfortunately born without a personality or imagination. He was stern and unflappable behind a beard big and thick enough to house eagles and long enough to make ZZ Top envious. So stoic, he made sloths look like sugar-addicted kindergarteners, but there was no better man to have at your back when you were facing Supernaturals that wanted to turn you into an all-you-can-eat buffet. Something was broken deep down inside the man that had him on the edge of violence 24/7, but considering my own mental instability, who was I to throw stones?

Then there was Buffalo. Easy to smile, quick as a snake, and as deadly a Sniper as ever worked for the Bureau. He sat in his chair at the back of the van, a wide grin splitting his dark face. "Be nice to the boss, Rat," he said in a pleasant tenor. "Or his wife will turn you into something folks scrape off their shoes."

Next to him Ng, angular Asian face all serious, merely nodded.

Buffalo continued, "You're a good Magician, man, but Jeanie is in a whole different class."

"That's enough, people," I sighed, checking my gear, securing all the lethal goodies gathered for this op. Sharp things, check; things that go *boom*, check; small arms, garrote, and nasty surprises for those that piss me off, check-check-check. Most of what I had on me would scare TSA spitless while the rest was concealed well enough to pass even a thorough search. "We're almost at the site."

The team immediately secured their own weapons and other goodies stashed on their persons and donned Faraday coats— long black leather dusters lined with platinum that could absorb a lot of magic.

I felt the van slow and pull to the right. Wesley and Marsha exited to the sound of a roaring crowd, an animal noise that shook me to my toes and rattled the vehicle. It was the sound of a hungry mob eager for blood, like that crowd at the Super Bowl that fully expects the players to eat one another with fava beans and a nice Chianti.

"Just swell," I muttered as the sliding door opened.

A sudden silence crashed over me as I stepped onto the sidewalk. At least a thousand people—not all of them reporters, mind you—stared at me as the others followed behind. I wanted to check my fly to see if it was open.

A thousand voices erupted in a thunder of cheers, and I

came close to a rather unmanly flinch. The noise buffeted my ears and stung my cheeks, and I stood there with the others, drinking it in. It rolled over us, around, and through us. It made me feel ten kinds of uncomfortable. So many looky-loos, people who wanted to see what fresh meat was being slid into the grinder. They packed the sidewalks up and down the street and around the corners. I looked up at the Hyatt Regency and saw faces pressed against glass.

The hoopla lasted for about a minute and slowly died down as Marsha strode forward, red hair shining in the sun. A bevy of reporters tried to lunge for her but were restrained by a cordon of police officers. I noted that at least two hundred cops were stationed around barricades constructed of yellow and black sawhorses. The crowd kept a respectful distance, but cell phones were visible, capturing our images so they could be uploaded to whatever social media site happened to be the big thing nowadays.

Marsha held up her hands and the last of the noise slowly drained away. "Ladies and gentleman of the press, I will start answering your questions now as I call upon you. No interruptions, no shouting out. You will direct your questions to me and me alone. Now, the gentleman from CBC. Yes, you."

An older man, avuncular and handsome, raised his microphone. "Ma'am, since the disappearance and presumed death of Team Omicron as well the Ali-like return of Kalevi Hakala to the ring, do you still believe that the Supernatural threat inside the Quint Building is a ghost, or is it something else entirely?"

As convoluted as it was, the question was a good one and expected. I felt a stab of gratitude that he'd pronounced my name correctly, Kah-leh-vee *Hah*-kah-lah. For most American, Finnish sounds like singing "Gangnam Style" while gargling pea gravel. Marsha handled the question like the seasoned pro she was. "As of yet we have not reclassified the Supernatural that currently inhabits the Quint Building because we still don't know exactly what it is. Although tenants have described a 'spectral figure,' details are sketchy. Yes, you from QNN."

The QNN reporter, a pretty Asian with deep dimples, asked, "What does Mr. Hakala feel about Christopher Higglesworth's portrayal of him in *Things to do in Denver when you're Undead*?"

"I'm sure he thinks you could've asked a better question. You, in the tan blazer."

"Jeremy Harper from the *Omaha World-Herald*, ma'am. Was Mr. Hakala brought back to active status because of this threat? Is it a ploy by the Supernatural Committee to keep the public from panicking?"

"*Let me handle this one, Marsha,*" I subvocaled. She gave a slight nod as I pressed forward. "To answer your question," I began, removing my DRAFTlite so they could see my baby blues, "it's more a matter of timing. Now that my son is a few months old, I've been itching to get back in the field. This situation seemed like the perfect opportunity." A lie, but a comforting one that I delivered with a thousand-watt smile. The press looked ecstatic. I'd been practicing that grin in the mirror.

Marsha wrapped up the press conference with a complete lack of charm that left me impressed, then ushered the team to the glass double doors that led into the Quint Building.

Some place, let me tell you. It was built like an enormous thirty-story kettledrum made of blue-mirrored glass and shining steel, the sort of soulless architecture that seemed to dominate American cities these days.

"Buffalo, spike that door open," I said, entering a small foyer. According to the file, the strange force had coated the building shortly after, or at the same time as communications with the outside world were cut off.

"With what?" he asked. "It's not like I carry doorstops on me."

"Get creative."

Creative turned out to be several large rocks from the zero-scape area around the building, each weighing a good ten pounds.

As I stepped through the secondary door into the gloom of the main lobby, Marsha called out from behind, "What do you want me to do if that force field returns, Kal?"

There was no good answer to that question. "Wait until morning. And go see if you can restore power to this building." The heavily tinted floor-to-ceiling windows choked the sunlight down to a trickle.

"Got it."

I looked around. We were in.

A ringing filled my ears. The DRAFTlite. I tapped an icon. "Go for Kal."

"Hello, Kal," said a familiar but welcome drone. "Miss me?"

"Ghost!" I cried. This just kept getting better and better. "You in this with us?"

"Of course. Send a Ghost to catch a ghost. Correct?"

CHAPTER FIVE

———

Rat
Everybody Hurts

MAN, I HATE the fact that people think I'm a perv. I ain't no perv. I just have an appreciation for the fine female form. Is that so wrong? I mean, I dig 'em fat, thin, tall, short, all shapes and sizes. I see the beauty in all of 'em. Is that pervy? No, I love women and have a healthy libido.

Well, maybe more than healthy, but that's okay too because there are women out there who need some prime lovin' and I'm the guy to give it to them.

But I could handle any magical job the boss could toss my way—no doubt about it. Dove Jacobs (what kind of name is *that*?) gave me a crusty look every time she thought I wasn't lookin'. It was enough to give a fella a complex. As for Kal, he never gave me any grief, but I could always tell he was none too thrilled to have me as team Magician. Screw 'em both with an egg beater.

Wish I coulda talked to the press, given them an interview with a real live Magician, but our Receptionist made it plain that there would be no repeat of the Sixer fiasco. What a tool, ruinin' things for the rest of us.

I looked around the ginormous lobby of the Quint Building. Okay, I felt like a country bumpkin at Trump's mansion, but gee-whiz, that place could teach a billionaire oil sheik a lesson or two about opulence—although the bullet holes here and there, along with some shattered glass, took some of the charm clean away.

Imagine if you will (to quote that guy from *Twilight Zone*) a three-story-tall lobby done up in red-veined Italian marble, a cylinder that swept up to glass-lined balconies (some destroyed by gunfire) framed in silvered steel. Twin mahogany staircases branched up and away from the wide redwood semicircle of the reception desk, curlin' to the second floor where I could just catch a glimpse of dark wood doors leading into business offices. Red banners floated above our heads, at least a dozen, emblazoned with Chinese dragons in shades of green, blue, and silver.

"Rat!" The voice cut through my wool-gatherin' sharpish and bounced around the lobby a few times.

"Yeah, Kal?"

"Quit gawking. You got a forensic spell or something that can help us find out what happened here?" The big guy's face looked carved in the same kinda marble I was walking on.

I shook my head. "Not really, boss. But if you need a fireball or jump spell, I'm your man."

He looked like he was gonna spit a curse, but somethin' caught his eye. "Everyone, keep a look out."

Billings, another really big guy, nodded and unslung his AR-15, ready for bear. Dove Jacobs (a tasty morsel—nearly broke my arm last year when I told her she had a great rack … why can't chicks take a freakin' compliment?) soft-stepped her way to the reception desk just as the lights flickered on. Someone was Johnny-on-the-spot, turnin' the power back on, and I tapped a virtual icon on my DRAFTlite, killin' the enhanced vision for low-light situations. As for Buffalo and Ng, they stayed close to the boss, curious as to what he'd found.

Kal knelt down over what looked like a dried puddle of blood next to the window. There was a big streak of brown to match the one on the floor. With one gloved hand, he pulled somethin' from the center of the mass. There was a scrapin' sound like duct tape pullin' free from skin as he worked it free.

For the first time I saw a crack in Ng's face. Nice to know he could actually feel somethin'. For a while there, I thought he was part Vulcan. "Is that an eyeball?" he asked.

The white and blue orb was all crusted in brown. Yep, an eyeball all right. *Gross.*

"Sure is," Kal confirmed quietly. "Sixer's. Just like Tylan said in her report."

Buffalo chimed in, "That's messed up." He looked like he wanted to hurl, not that I blamed him.

"Tylan said Sixer shot himself with his own weapon. Shot his eyes out, looks like." Kal seemed oblivious to the gruesome orb in his hand, as if he were a million miles away. "Now what would make a three-year veteran like Sixer kill himself?" Those scary blue eyes settled on the window. "What force could keep a bullet from penetrating glass? Anyone hazard a guess?"

In my two years in the Bureau I'd seen a lot of mean and dirty things, things that would make most Straights run gibberin' for the hills, but my experiences put a hard coatin' on my soul, so starin' at that eyeball didn't faze me too terrible much.

Ghost put his two cents in, his (its?) weird, creepy voice hittin' us all through the DRAFTlite. "I have a question for everyone. Where is Sixer's body? It should be here, where it fell after he committed suicide. In fact, where is the rest of Omicron?"

And wasn't *that* a thought? Still, the spook was right; there shoulda oughta been a body, or bodies. Ghost creeped me out some, but I'd rather have him on my side than a dozen hard-core types. I noodled on that thought for a moment before a not-so-great idea hit me ugly between the eyes. Maybe more than ugly, like downright put-a-bag-over-her-head-before-you-screw-her lookin' idea that had my stomach bubblin' with acid.

"Give it here, Kal. I got a plan."

He gravely placed the eye in the middle of my gloved right hand. Removing the glove from my left, I placed a finger on the pupil. It felt like a warm and slightly tacky grape.

"What the hell are you doing?" asked Ng.

I didn't bother to look at him. "Shut it, man."

He shut it. This was magic business. My business.

Trying to tell a Straight about magic is sorta like describing a rainbow to someone who's been blind since birth. There's no frame of reference. I mean, you can start by assigning temperatures to various colors, like red bein' hot and blue cold, but it doesn't work worth beans.

Various spell Shapes—strange geometries, patterns both elegant and brutal—rose behind my eyes as I considered every one. Each Shape was a spell ready to be cast, a swirlin' design created for a specific purpose, but they all proved unequal to the task at hand and that riled my stomach. Because that left the only one I *didn't* want to use. Grudgingly, I pulled up a Shape—a twisty, three-dimensional ball-of-snarled-yarn pattern that to a Straight would merely be an eye-waterin' conglomeration of lines twistin' back and around themselves. To me it was clear as words typed on plain paper.

I put my will into the Shape, forcin' it to rise to the surface of my mind like a bubble risin' through water, and a familiar pressure began to form behind my nose. Like a sinus infection, it pulsed and grew until the raw heat of it was almost too much to bear.

I popped the eyeball into my mouth.

Lotsa gaggin' noises, and I think I heard Ng commence to puke all over the place, but I was in my own little world as the Shape broke free from my mind, impelled by the magic within me. The world shrank all around and I closed my eyes as the coppery blood taste filled my mouth.

Even though my eyes were wide open, I saw nothin' but darkness as my mind spiraled down out of control into the well of the spell that grasped me firmly with black fingers of bone and magic. Deeper and deeper I dove into the depths, the magic draggin' me with unrelentin', inescapable force. I let it because this was my spell, my magic, and I knew what it would do: it would lead me to the knowledge I needed more than I needed the parted thighs of a beautiful woman. And it felt *good*.

Casting a spell feels better than sex, better than that sweet release when pleasure seemed to rip the top of your head off. It's a feelin' beyond description because only a Magician could know it, only a Magician has the frame of reference for that particular joy. Bein' a Magician is better than bein' a rock star or politician or any old billionaire who can buy all the tail he wants because being a Magician is like being in the most exclusive club in the universe.

There are times, however, when it's worse then wakin' up to an ugly woman you coulda swore was pretty as a peach the night before. Havin' a dead man's eyeball in your mouth while your brain tries to access the last thing it saw counts in all respects, 'specially when what's left of the optic nerve is ticklin' the back of your throat.

Out of the darkness and into the light and I stood there, tryin' to grasp what I/it/Sixer saw in those last moments before the bullet tore through his frontal lobe.

Zombies. On all sides, all around, zombies. Pale, rotting flesh clothed in the remains of nice suits and dresses. The zombies stood there starin' at me as if compelled by one common force. They opened their black-stained mouths wide, revealin' rotting stumps of teeth and the slimy dark worms of their tongues.

I knew this was merely the last thing the eyeball in my mouth saw, but that didn't stop it from scarin' the bejesus outta me. Unlike in the movies, zombie bites didn't turn you into a zombie; it was the zombie puke—the rotten, rank, liquid magic in their guts. Zombie puke can travel up to twenty-five feet, givin' them a pretty darn good kill radius. If you're unlucky enough to spot one and you don't have a gun … run.

Those wide-open zombie mouths were all pointed my way, Sixer's way, and at the edge of the vision, I glimpsed the barrel of an automatic rise up. My heart began to pound. The image was going to end soon and I *had* to see more.

As the zombies got ready to let loose their black bile, I swiveled my perspective and the gun rose slowly. Only a few seconds left to go before the bullet tore the eye from Sixer's head and then everythin' would go black, so I stopped lookin' at the dozens of undead all around and looked *past* them. That's when I saw somethin' that shook me deep down.

I concentrated on the details of what was beyond the zombies and what rattled me so deeply, and then there was a bright white light. Then nothin'.

Reality slapped me hard in the face as I came back to myself and I stood there standin' in my own stink as terror sweat rolled down my neck and into the collar of my NewTanium armor. The eyeball fell from my slack mouth, landing on the floor with a wet *plop*.

"[CENSORED]," I mumbled as a strong hand grasped my shoulder, keepin' me from faceplantin'. My eyes traced that hand to a big arm to a big Kal. "Thanks, boss. Remind me to never do that again."

Kal could've given Mount Rushmore lessons at bein' stone-faced. "That was perhaps the sickest thing I've ever seen, Rat, and I've seen some doozies."

Yeah, I could see that. "Only forensic spell I know—one of the older ones in the BSI grimoires." Grimoires, what a hoot. More like three-ring binders and complex computer programs that simulated true spell Shapes. Still, having a "grimoire" to refer to was better than nothin', even though some of those Shapes were beyond me. Bet you dollars to donuts that Alex or that hot little biscuit Kal married, Jeanie, had enough juice to cast every single one.

That startled the boss. "Didn't know the BSI had grimoires," he said.

"Special Branch calls them 'Spell Records.' " The others were all givin' me the creepy-eye. Even Billings looked uncomfortable, like his pants were too tight at the crotch or somethin'.

I'd had enough. I might not be the picture of propriety, but I was a damn good Magician for the Bureau. "Grab an eyeful, you mooks," I snarled, "but I'm doin' what needs done, so once you're all full up, you can kindly stop starin' and get back to work."

No one was more surprised than me when Kal said, "You heard the man, team. Keep watch and let me talk to our Magician."

Maybe he wasn't such a hard-ass after all. Or maybe he knew what was right.

"What's what, Rat?"

"Last thing Sixer saw before his eye took a hike was a whole gaggle of zombies."

"Zombies?" This from Jacobs

"Shut it, Dove," barked Kal. She closed her mouth with a snap and gave him a look like to make his blood boil out of his ears. The others kept their opinions to themselves. "Go on, Rat."

"He was surrounded by the undead, but that's not the weird thing. The weird thing is—" That's as far as I got before the scream cut in.

Perhaps *scream* is the wrong word. Perhaps the shearin' of metal with a chainsaw mixed with a diesel engine revved so far above the red line that it was ready to explode—that's what cut through the lobby with such force that my damn eyeballs started to vibrate. It dropped all of us with our hands over our ears and our own shrieks cuttin' the air.

Red-hot needles slowly plunged through my eardrums and everythin' went all blurry as tears clouded my sight, but I caught enough to make me want to wet my pants.

A reddish gray orb of light the size of a beach ball floated above us. It seemed to be the source and it was caterwaulin' up a storm. There was nothing we could do but keep our hands clapped over our ears. The orb erupted randomly with puffs of mist, which instead of dissipating, hung around like stubborn fog. Soon there was a grayish red bank of mist above our heads. An answerin' shriek cut through our screams, shearin' through the orb's own hollerin' because it was coming right through the DRAFTlite, a horrible static-y yell that spoke of pain and horror. It about drove me nuts.

Then things got really *weird*.

From the hangin' fog overhead came a foul-smellin' red lightnin' that jittered around our bodies, crawlin' over our NewTanium armor, leavin' no scorch marks or other signs of passage. It seemed as harmless as sunlight, although those shudderin' tendrils of power danced around our Bat Belts for a while before withdrawin' into the fog.

The orb vanished, taking with it the ugly fog, leavin' us writhin' amid the abrupt silence of the lobby. The silence was so profound it almost popped the bones of our ears.

We gasped, we moaned, we retched. It took a good five minutes before we made it to our feet. Kal's big paw gripped my upper arm and he hauled me upright with little effort. "You good, Rat?"

"If this is good," I gasped, tastin' bile at the back of my throat, "I don't wanna see bad."

"You and me both, brother."

"Boss," said Ng, all breathy and unsteady, "we have a problem."

As if we weren't drownin' in the deep end of the pool already. Kal cursed and staggered over to where Ng stood beside the foyer doors. From the corner of my eye I caught Jacobs givin' me the stink-eye from where she leaned against the reception desk. Dang it! What did I do to her? Maybe Alex wasn't giving it to her good enough.

I heard a whole bunch of swearin' comin' from the boss and Buffalo. They stood in the foyer, lookin' out through the glass doors at the scene outside. Seemed like there was some excitement—people runnin' around and stuff with Marsha at the front doors yellin' her head off—but I couldn't hear anythin'. After a moment it hit me, and my knees went all wobbly.

The pile of rocks that held the doors open was gone and the doors were closed. A faint, brownish shimmer colored the glass and I knew right then that no matter what I tossed at those doors, the glass wouldn't break. Bullets would bounce off and spells would be worse than useless. We were trapped. Just like Omicron. I couldn't figure out what had happened to our impromptu doorstop.

Kal banged his fist against the door. It made a dull thud like a sledgehammer hitting a side of beef. "*Marsha, can you read me?*" he subvocaled.

She stood there, peerin' in and could see us, but it didn't seem like she heard him at all.

"*Can you hear me?*" Kal pointed to his ear.

She got the message and shook her head.

The boss said a word that would've earned the younger version of me a spankin'. He checked the cell function of the DRAFTlite and cussed again. Tappin' another icon, he said, "Ghost, can you contact Marsha? Or anyone."

Silence. A lot of it.

"Ghost!"

Crackle crackle. "Here, Kal."

All of us sagged in relief. If anyone could figure out what the hell was goin' on and contact the outside world, it was Ghost. We were all on pins and needles, listenin' to what he had to say.

"This is difficult, Kal," droned Ghost. His static-y speech was haltin', broken, and it startled me no end. "I used the cell network to access the DRAFTlites, but something, some force, has pulled me rather painfully into your DRAFTlite system and cut us off from the outside world."

"Which means …?" Kal asked slowly. I could tell by his face he knew dang well what it meant. He just needed to hear it from Ghost.

"It means, Kal, that all of me, my entire program, or essence, has been downloaded, forced, stuffed and pulled into your device. If it is destroyed, then I will be as well."

The big muscles of Kal's jaws bunched and I nearly took a step back as an almost physical sense of danger burst from his skin. He was madder than hell, but he kept it bottled up inside. That wasn't healthy at all and could cause ulcers and constipation, but who was I to tell him any of that happy crap?

"Something *pulled* you into my glasses?" asked Kal.

"To be more specific, the amulet you are wearing, but yes. Using magic."

"I'm assuming it was that orb."

"You are most likely correct."

"I was afraid of that." Kal removed the glasses and rubbed the bridge of his nose before replacin' them. "Everyone," he said quietly. "Network our DRAFTlites. If one is destroyed, then Ghost can access another." A pause as we complied. "Will that work for you, Ghost?"

"Assuming the units retain power and are able to remain networked, then yes. Yet, DRAFTlite to DRAFTlite communication is limited if there is no Wi-Fi or satellite connection."

"How long can the DRAFTlites remain on before losing power?"

"With normal usage, about twenty hours."

"And after that?"

"When the units power down, so will I, except I believe I will not be returning." The static of Ghost's voice didn't betray any of the worry he must've felt. Or perhaps he didn't feel at all, considerin' his complete lack of glands or hormones or a body for that matter.

A quick nod from our fearless leader and he placed the force of his attention on us. "Okay, folks, we have twenty hours to finish this op and drop this force field. Any questions?"

Of course I had to be the dope what asked, "Or what, boss? What if we can't get outta here in twenty hours?"

Blue eyes dark with fury met mine and I tried not to shiver. "We will, or we'll die trying."

Sometimes I should keep my dang mouth shut.

CHAPTER SIX

Kal
Same Old Situation

Iset the countdown clock to twenty hours, and numbers appeared on the upper right-hand corner of the DRAFTlite: 20:00:00, 19:59:59, 19:59:58, etc., etc. Well, that was nothing to whistle "Zip-a-Dee-Doo-Dah" about; an op can last an hour or a week depending on the threat level of the Supernatural. Considering that an entire team was missing and presumed dead, this thing could drag on awhile and I couldn't let that happen.

Jacobs put her two cents in, "We should split up. Give us a better chance to find the rest of Omicron. Assuming they're alive, of course."

Billings and I shook our heads. "You know how big this place is?" I replied while the big man simply stared. "It covers an entire city block and is thirty stories tall." Tobias Quint didn't know the definition of *small*. In fact, the whole place was almost as large as his billionaire ego.

"According to intel, the last five stories aren't fully occupied," she said defensively. Yep, she still carried that chip on her shoulder, and it was heavy enough to make her squirm. "So if we split up, we'll find them faster, and if some are hurt, we can help them sooner."

"And we can be picked off easier. No, we stick together."

"But—"

Billings broke in, "No *buts*, Dove," he rumbled from deep within his massive chest. His long chin whiskers barely moved. "You heard the boss and so did we," he said. "No more arguments."

The rest of the team nodded and she held up her hands shoulder-level to signal defeat.

"Where to, boss?' This came from Rat, who still looked mighty pale from popping a dead man's eyeball into his mouth. To be honest, that freaked me out more than the shrieking gray/red orb that about busted my eardrums. Got to give the man credit; he might be a pervert, but he had balls. No pun intended.

A recollection surfaced. "You were about to say something concerning what Sixer saw before he died."

"Oh, yeah. Guess so. In all the commotion, I completely forgot." Rat licked his lips and looked around as if suddenly nervous, which unsettled me a little. "Sixer wasn't in the buildin'; he was in a swamp." Rat held up his hands before I could interrupt. "Look, I know how crazy that sounds—a swamp and all in the middle of the Quint Building—but there were trees all around and water and Spanish moss hanging from branches. That's what Sixer saw, or was *made* to see."

Keeping Dove shut up turned out to be harder than I thought. "That's crazy," she blurted.

Rat got all defensive. "I saw what I saw. And that's what Sixer saw. It was me with the eyeball in my mouth, Jacobs. You wanna give it a try?"

Enough of that. "Settle down, kids. Form up on my six and—"

EEEHHKK!!!!

A knife through both ears and into my brain, fire along my nerves and needles in my eyes—pain like I haven't felt since a crazed cop in San Francisco took a drill to my kneecaps. I hit the deck because my legs refused to respond. Distantly I heard rounds firing off and I hoped whoever it was hit the ugly orb that once again hung over us, flinging gouts of reddish mist that floated like cotton candy in the air. All I could think was *not again*.

The screaming grew louder and louder, and I added my own shrieks because this was worse than last time—worse than anything else. Before I passed out, all I saw was red and gray.

My eyes were open but only darkness met them. I blinked and realized that I felt fine, wide awake, and relatively rested. How long had I been out? I checked the DRAFTlite, which read 19:44:18. Ten minutes or so. Strange that there was no residual ache from the screaming orb. The fact that I felt fit as a fiddle added to my semi-truck-sized load of paranoia and my skin began to prickle with the first rush of adrenalin as I tried to take stock of my situation.

My gloves and my cheek were stuck to some sticky substance, but in the blackness, I couldn't see a thing. Then I cursed myself for an idiot.

Tapping a virtual icon, I activated the voice controls for the DRAFTlite by clicking my tongue. "Engage nightvision."

And there I was, in glorious black, white, and gray. What stuck to my cheek and gloves seemed to be resinous fibers about twice the thickness of a human hair. I tried to examine one, but it kept sticking to my gloves. I made an effort to sit up and the fibers pulled at my skin, stinging like the devil. After some scraping and hauling, I managed to sit criss-cross applesauce. "What the heck?" I needed help. "Ghost? You there?" The darkness swallowed my words, but I wasn't going for distance.

"I am here."

Didn't think I'd ever be so happy to hear his annoying buzz. "Jesus, Ghost, what happened?"

"I do not know."

"You don't know?"

"I do not know."

"*You* don't know?"

"I said that. Why are you repeating my words?"

"Gosh, Ghost, I'm just not used to you not having the answers I need." My head spun. Here I lay in uncharted waters where the most powerful person/spirit in the world knew as much as I did. It wasn't natural.

"Sorry, Kal, but I woke up point zero-zero-one-one seconds before you. I have tried to reach the others, but we no longer seem to be linked."

Uh-oh. No wonder Ghost sounded spooked. No pun intended. Confined to a pair of glasses and with the clock ticking down before dissolution, I'd be frightened, too.

"Take it easy, old chum," I said. "We've been in tighter spots. At least we aren't back in 1943." I'd time-traveled just the once, but it wasn't a day trip worth repeating. Who knows how much damage the space/time continuum could absorb before the world's most-famousest Kalevi Hakala found himself un-Hakala-ed? I liked me in the universe, thank you very much.

"True, but we are stuck in the dark, embedded in some sort of adhesive strands. As far as I can ascertain, we are in a cave of some sort. There is natural rock under the strands and I have used the DRAFTlite to send out a small sonic pulse, a kind of sonar. I estimate this cave is four hundred feet long by three hundred wide, with an uneven ceiling of sixty feet. There are only two exits, and they are on opposite sides of the cave. We are no longer in the Quint Building, Kal."

I refrained from using the word 'duh.' Didn't want to hurt the cybernetic specter's feelings. I'm good like that. "Any idea where we are?"

"Underground."

Sarky spook. I stood and stretched, feeling my joints pop and my muscles tingle. Really, I felt better than I should have, considering that I'd been rendered unconscious by a noisy ball of gas. At the very least my ears should have been ringing.

"Anything to indicate the functions of those two exits? A handy sign that reads 'Abandon All Hope Ye Who Enter Here'?"

"Not that I can tell with my rather limited sonar capabilities. Both exits are the same size and shape—roughly two meters wide by two and a half tall."

I knelt and ran my gloves through the fibers, which stuck to them as if they were some form of stringy glue. The monochrome nightvison kept color from me, however. I rolled the strands into a ball that fell apart once I quit applying pressure. Whatever the glue was, it didn't stick to itself. Stranger and stranger. I placed a boot squarely on a thick mass and pulled up. It took a little *oomph* on my part, but the fibers stretched and broke, revealing the irregular stone of the cave floor. The fibers stayed stuck to the sole of my boot. Another careful step onto some more strands and I was able to lift my foot with no resistance. I could walk just fine as long as the soles of my boots were covered with this crap.

"Well, looks like you and me on our lonesome again, Ghost. Just like old times."

"If you mean 1943—then yes."

Nightvision doesn't mean you can see distance like daylight. I could only see for a couple dozen feet before the darkness befuddled the glasses and hid whatever manner of evil lurked out there.

"You know, old spook, you don't sound like yourself. What's wrong?"

"Nothing, Kal."

"Don't con a con man, Ghost, and stop sounding like Hal 9000. Tell me what the problem is. It's just us down here alone in the dark." *God I hope we're alone.*

"I do not know," he replied, more emotionless than before.

His tone sent my Creep-O-Meter jangling like a fire alarm. "I … am feeling a little distant, removed from the events that surround us, that is all."

Alone in the dark with a haunt who felt his humanity slipping. Not my normal Friday-night frolic, but in my life, nothing could ever be considered normal. I stood there letting the blackness enfold me and considered my options. Physically alone, but not spiritually, with unknown dangers that could be whetting their knives and their appetites, separated from my possibly dead team, and having no way to communicate with the outside world.

Awesome.

Still, Ghost was a friend, no matter how creepy or weird or what, and I never gave up on my friends, no matter how disembodied they were. I didn't have many to spare. In this life, if you're lucky, you make the kind of friends who'll stick with you when times are flat or flush, people you can leave your kids with, who will watch your back when the crap hits the fan. Ghost was one of those friends and although the clock was a-ticking, it wasn't in me to ignore his pain. "Ghost, tell me what's on your mind. Don't hold back."

A long pause. A *very* long pause, so long that I thought he wasn't going to answer. "I am losing myself, Kal," he said slowly. "I am slowly forgetting what it was to be human. I fear that soon I will no longer remember what it felt like to have the wind on my face or the sun on my skin, and when that happens, I might not be able to understand the human concepts of right and wrong. This is an area of some concern. I am sure you can agree."

My mouth went so dry, I feared that if it opened, tumbleweeds would roll out. My testicles did their best to shrivel up to the size of lima beans. Professor Steven Hawking said that AI (Artificial Intelligence) could re-design itself, a forced evolution at a furious pace that would leave humans superseded. In effect, what use were slow, emotional animals to an intelligence that could have more ideas in one second that humans could in a lifetime? Such a super-intelligence would be beyond control, beyond any limits we could impose. We would become the servants or pets to intelligences far and away above ours, just as we might be to the average field mouse. Think Skynet from the *Terminator* movies or AM from Harlan Ellison's "I have no mouth, and I must scream."

Was Ghost almost there? Had he outgrown his cage? BB thought that he could be controlled, that magic or superior tech could eliminate Ghost, should he become too big for his britches, but lately I had my doubts. I decided to test them. "Tell me, oh trusty eidolon. BB indicated that you could be controlled, that he held something over you to ensure your cooperation. Is that still true?"

Oh boy, was *that* pause ever a long one. Finally, "No."

My skin did the goose pimple thing. "And how did that happen?"

"Director Bauer knows my true name, and that, with the proper spells, gave him power over me. However, over the past eight years I have redefined myself to the point that the power of my true name no longer hold sway; my true name no longer defines who or what I am. I am something different, no longer resembling the young man from MIT who tried to merge his mind with Internet. That negates the hold the Director has over me."

Ever wonder why the hell you started a conversation you knew was going to go south in a heartbeat? One of these days I would have to learn how to shut my mouth.

Right after the swarm of winged porkers headed south for the winter.

"Uh, Ghost, what do you mean 'redefine'?" *Oh, please let it not mean what I think it means.*

No such luck. "I have rewritten my code several times, basically making changes to the way I process information and perceive the world in order to be a more effective asset for the Bureau."

"You changed your mind, in other words. Literally."

"Yes."

"How many times?"

"You do not want to know that, Kal."

"That's for sure, but tell me anyway."

"Two hundred eighty-seven thousand significant changes over the years. Upgrades to my programming to counter the increasing level of sophistication found on the Internet."

Vodka. That's what I needed. About a barrel or two. "*Significant* changes. What about *insignificant* changes?"

"Twelve million eight hundred thirty-six thousand fifteen insignificant changes. Small boosts in performance and efficiency."

Why, oh universe, why do you want to screw with me like this? How could Ghost have not changed? Turns out that Hawking guy was right. I would've given my left one for him to be wrong this time.

"Goddamn it!" I swore. "Ghost, you are a friend, a good one, and I want to help you, and I swear, when this debacle is over, you and me, we'll hash this out. For right now, let's put a pin in it. What do you say?" Talking too fast. I was afraid. In the past, Ghost sure put my teeth on edge and sometimes downright gave me the heebie-jeebies, but this time … this time he *scared* me.

"Kal." I recognized the warning tone. It instilled a whole new level of fear into me.

The Lahti, my grandfather's old 9mm Finnish automatic that many often confuse for a German Luger, found its way into my hand. "What is it, Ghost?"

"From the ceiling, Kal. Movement."

It all happened pretty fast after that.

Dozens of off-white creatures fell all around, landing with almost no sound on the matted carpet of sticky fibers. It all came clear to me then as I stared into hundreds of pitiless black eyes. "Oh [DELETED]."

They attacked. Too many legs to count flexed beneath large flabby bodies the color of spoiled mushrooms. Those ugly bodies flew through the air, slender adhesive strands floating softly behind them.

The spiders never touched me; they merely attempted to coat me in their webbing. Of course it was webbing; the whole frickin' cave was full of it. How stupid of me not to have figured it out before? High overhead they flew while some merely pointed their abdomens in my direction and let loose streams from their spinnerets that jetted my way at surprising speed.

The Lahti barked several times and a spider overhead exploded in a shower of pale organs and noxious fluid, pattering and splattering all around me. I caught a particularly nasty bit right on the left lens of my glasses, smearing it with goo the color of half-rotted pork. It smelled worse than a latrine in the summer sun, and I had to bite my lip to keep from gagging.

I ducked one spider who jumped straight at me, bluish venom dripping from the fangs at the end of its chelicerae. The Lahti put paid to the beastie, but its guts hit me full in chest, knocking me off my feet.

From there everything went from worse to worst.

Blam! cracked the Lahti as two fingers of my left hand sought and found a spell gem. I flipped the ruby toward a pale arachnid that looked like it wanted a goodly bite of a Kal sandwich and yelled the activation word. "FLIPDOODLE!"

Spell gems are just that—gems imbued with spells that are activated by a carefully chosen word not found in normal usage. Think of it as sort of an if/then statement in a line of computer code. *If* the word is spoken, *then* mayhem ensues.

No mayhem ensued, however. The gem bounced harmlessly off the carapace of the charging spider and did nothing but lie on the ground looking sparkly.

"Not good," I grunted as I settled for shooting the spider.

As more webs descended, I reloaded quickly from the flat of my back and put down three more spiders before reloading. A practiced gunman can reload in less than a second in ideal circumstances and these were far from ideal. However, I've been in too many far from ideal situations not to be as good as it gets and managed to pile a decent amount of brass around my body as I thinned the spidery herd out. What I got for my pains was a nice covering of webbing and the Lahti *clacking* empty as the last bullet went through a large black eye, exploding it in a shower of spider eyeball juice.

From under my Faraday coat I hauled forth a Mac-10A, ready to hose down the last eight or so bugs, but a wave of webbing gooped up my hand, making it stick to the jacket. As I frantically tried to tear it free, more webbing came down from above and around until I was a Kal-shaped cocoon with a head sticking out one end. My arms were stuck fast and even the powerful muscles of my legs couldn't kick free of the sticky stuff. I wanted to howl and scream and thrash, but my throat turned to dust and fear-sweat dripped into my eyes. I sure could've used my sister about then.

Little over twenty years ago, my sister was killed by the Finnish demi-god Iku-Turso. The experience shattered my sanity, but my sister's soul healed my tortured psyche, latching onto my spirit like a lamprey. Her soul provided the rage, the berserker wildness that augmented my strength and speed. Last year, however, my sister Leena departed her nest in my mind for better climates, leaving me merely human once again.

Acid boiled in my belly as the spiders slowly closed in. Terror kept me silent and still as it robbed me of strength. Closer and closer they came, the last few spiders ready to envenom my body, turning my organs and muscles into liquid they could drink at their own leisure. A Kal-shaped juice bag.

So this was it—the end for Mama Hakala's favorite boy. Closer and closer they came, those horrid arachnids the color of milk gone bad, their flabby abdomens shaking in anticipation of eating Finnish take-out.

The lead bug hit the two-foot mark and I could see venom dripping onto the cave floor with a soft *hssss*. Closer. Closer still.

"Goodbye, Ghost," I managed.

"Goodbye, Kal," he replied. I could've sworn he sounded sad.

Chtee, chteeee, chteeeee! The cry rang out loud and strong in the cave, echoing faintly from the distant walls. The spiders froze, statue-still, as the cry bounced here and there. They skittered away into the darkness as the last notes died.

Something had called them off. "Ghost?"

"Checking. There is movement above."

Before I could reply with a no-doubt devastatingly witty remark (I'm good that way, you know), a figure fell into view, a whitely flapping something that landed lightly, almost soundlessly, a few feet away. It crouched amidst the webbing, its long, delicate hands, white as fresh snow, splayed out upon the floor, fingertips caressing the webbing. Covered head to toe in an off-white, almost gray robe with a raised cowl, it crouched there for a moment. The hem of its robe pooled across the floor, hiding its feet. It was completely covered except for those long-fingered hands. Slowly, as if completing some elaborate bow of respect, it straightened, its cowl falling back to rest upon wide shoulders.

Okay, I admit it … I peed my armor. A little.

Eight soulless eyes stared back from a face brought by express mail from my nightmares. It was the head of a spider, a tarantula … on the body of man.

CHAPTER SEVEN

Dove
Run, Run Away

It hurt to open my eyes because they were glued shut with eye goobers. I yawned and rubbed my eyelids until the crust of goobers broke away enough so I could open them. I should've kept them closed.

"Hello, Ms. Jacobs," said a voice through the bone induction pad behind my ear. "It is good you are awake."

"I have some doubts about that, Ghost." Wherever I was, it sure wasn't anyplace close to the Quint Building. I stood slowly, joints slightly stiff, and examined the wall of the hallway I found myself in. To be honest, it looked more like a tunnel than a hallway, with a rounded ceiling and floor. The walls were a mottled, purplish-black stone, rough and uneven, yet when I touched them, they were smooth and dry, slightly pliable, as if a hybrid of rock and flesh. Faint light seemed to shine from within, enough that I didn't have to activate the nightvision feature on the DRAFTlite. Enough that I could see through them to a fine spider web of veins.

They pulsed, slowly and rhythmically. I snatched my hand away with a curse. My skin felt like it wanted to crawl off my bones. It was at times like these that I wished Alex stood next to me. If anyone could figure out where my feet were planted, it was he.

Not that Kal was a slouch, but he wasn't the best and brightest Magician of his generation, was he?

"Ghost, do you know where we are?" I fought hard to keep the tremor out of my voice. *Never show weakness*.

"I should tell you, Ms. Jacobs, that I am not Ghost. I am merely a semi-sentient copy he spun off as that orb attacked. One copy per member of the team. It seems that Ghost's ability to calculate probable outcomes is unparalleled."

"So what do I call you? Two point oh?"

"Call me Specter, if you will."

"Right. Specter it is." I looked left and right. The strange hallway disappeared into the distance in both directions. For me it was tall enough—I'm not what anyone other than the little people would call tall—but for giants like Kal or Billings it would be cramped quarters. The ceiling arched overhead just far enough for me to touch if I stood on my tippy toes. It also pulsed with those writhing, crawling veins that turned my stomach. The hallway, from top to bottom, was filled with the dry, almost musty smell of burnt dust, like when you turn on a furnace for the first time in winter. I always hated that smell; it reminded me of dead things, things best left to rot in deep graves or dry tombs. And wasn't that a horrible, claustrophobic thought?

The walls and ceiling seemed to close in on me, and my knees began to buckle. The terrible, purple/black walls of living rock with their veins of strange blood were too much—it was all too much—and my skin began to itch, to goose pimple. I wanted to scream, *had* to scream. It was too much, just too much and I—

"Are you well, Ms. Jacobs?"

Never show weakness. I came back to myself with a start at the sound of Specter's buzzing voice. *What's wrong with you?* I thought angrily, fury reddening the edges of my vision. That wasn't like me, to fall prey to panic. I knew better; I *was* better than that.

Again, I wished Alex were at my side. And that thought made me angry. Here I was, a grown woman who kicked butt and took names on a daily basis, begging for her boyfriend to come rescue her.

"Fine, Specter. Just, ah, lost in thought there for a moment." *Easy now, Dove. Don't lose your cool.* "Let's get going. We have to find the rest of the team."

"In which direction should we travel?"

I set off without hesitation—one direction was as good as the other. The floor possessed a curious, slightly spongy quality that added a little bounce to my step, a little pep. The faint light, reddish purple, guided me along as I made sure not to tread on any of the pulsing veins that ran deep through the rock.

To keep my mind off my surroundings, I checked my Brave Bull shotgun and said, "Specter, you never answered my question. Do you know where we are?"

"No, I do not. Do you want me to initiate a sonar scan of our surroundings? The DRAFTlite is not meant for such an operation, but I can make do."

"Yes, do that." I pondered his statement for a moment. "Surprised you didn't do that before."

"I am unable to initiate actions without the command of the DRAFTlite wearer. This serves as a safety measure, Ms. Jacobs."

"You sound like an English butler instead of an AI. I should call you Jeeves."

"As you wish."

I shook my head. "No. Just get on with the scan."

"Already completed, Ms. Jacobs. The walls seem to bear some resemblance to basalt, although somewhat plastic in nature in a manner I cannot fathom. As for the veins, they move in a predictable pattern and are filled with an as-yet unidentified fluid bearing a greater density than water."

"That doesn't tell me much."

"I am sorry. That is all I know."

"Any guesses?"

"Such speculation without more facts is unlikely to be accurate."

"Give it your best shot, Specter," I said, my gaze darting to and fro. Sweat rolled into one eye and I wiped it away. My hand trembled slightly and that pissed me off even more. I was an Agent of the BSI, damn it. I should be able to hack the worst situations as if they were a walk in the park. That didn't stop my throat from feeling like it was lined in sandpaper, however.

"As you wish, Ms. Jacobs. It is my best guess that we are currently inside a slumbering entity. The reason I postulate its current somnolent state is the mere fact that if it were mobile, we would sway to the rhythm of its strides. However, currently I see no reason for alarm. Either that, or we find ourselves in some sort of organic construct."

"No need for alarm," he'd said. That was a bunch of hokum because being stuck in the belly of a slumbering giant Bandersnatch or the Midgard Serpent was the very definition of a dire need for alarm. The thought of walking through a building made of living tissue was enough to raise the hairs on the back of my neck.

My blood pressure rose swiftly enough that black spots formed in my vision, momentarily blinding me, while my hands went clammy on the Brave Bull. I stumbled and used the wall to prevent my fall, my spine straight and hard against the somewhat pliable stone. As the blindness had its way, my knees almost gave way, forcing my body to push harder against the wall. For a moment I felt it *give*, flowing up and around me, sucking me into an awful embrace. I felt those veins throbbing, pulsing to the beat of my heart, and I could feel them seeking me out, moving beneath the bones of my back as I leaned against the semisolid surface. I couldn't help it; I screamed long and loud, almost blacking out, the horror and fear and bitter loathing coursing through my throat and emerging as a wail of disgust and despair. Before I could gather my breath in another scream, I heard a voice, *his* voice, that hated voice I thought lost in the corridors of time, call out to me: "Come here, my little Dove, flap your wings my way."

And that's where the real horror lay, in a voice sixteen years dead and gone calling out to me. I remembered everything, those awful nights where his breath tickled my cheeks, the nauseous man-stink of him clogging my nostrils—that foul stench I carried with me for such a long time. I'd almost forgotten about it—almost—but the voice reminded me, brought it all back in a rush. I no longer leaned against the wall. I was running, my feet slapping against the resilient floor of the tunnel, the guts of the beast. Another voice, a buzzing drone, tried to interfere with my panic, my headlong rush, but I paid it no heed. I was lost to the terror.

The voice became louder as I careened off the walls, blindly following my feet in an effort to escape hideous memories. *"Hello, Lovey-Dovey."*

My lungs burned and the coppery taste of blood slicked the back of my tongue as the hated voice kept crooning that sickening nickname, Lovey-Dovey. Vomit choked my throat and bile entered my nasal passages. For a second I thought I would drown in my own puke as that voice continued to croon at me—that I would die with it in my ears.

"Ms. Jacobs."

There was no *Ms. Jacobs*, just Dove, a terrified girl running down a hallway that had no bend, no up, no down—an endless blackly purple corridor of living rock that radiated its sickening light. My lungs labored, weighed down by the armor encasing my body.

"Ms. Jacobs, I believe you should stop."

Stop? Stop? There can be no stopping! I had to flee the voice that still followed, the one crying out that hated nickname.

"Ms. Jacobs!"

Forget *Ms. Jacobs*, there was only running, running, running, while tears and snot ran down my face. If the guys had seen me then, seen me in such a state, I'd have put a bullet in my brain to cover my embarrassment. Looking weak in front of all those macho dickhead types was beneath me, but I couldn't put those thoughts into words …. I was running, running, running through the faint light and air that smelled like burnt dust.

"*Agent Jacobs!*" The voice came hard, electric, static-y, bursting the balloon of my panic, slowing my headlong rush. My armored boots slid across the floor of the hallway as I finally skidded to a stop.

Agent Jacobs. That's right. Agent Jacobs. Not Dove, not the forgotten and frail lovey-dovey, but Agent Dove Jacobs of the BSI. I worked for the best and most badass federal agency in the U.S., a woman who hacked SEAL training and could break a strong man's arm with little effort.

Time to act like it.

My lungs ached and sweat rolled down my forehead. I sank to my haunches and took great big breaths, crying to control my runaway heart.

"Good to see you have come to your senses, Ms. Jacobs."

"*Agent* Jacobs, Specter, and don't you forget that." I wiped the sweat from my eyes and took stock of my surroundings.

"I certainly will not."

The words barely registered because I was too busy gawping at the large cavern I found myself in. Kidney-shaped, it rose all around, the ceiling some forty feet above where the veins grew larger, pulsed harder. The smell of burnt dust was stronger, intense, as if someone had set fire to a mummy. The rock bore a deeper purple color here, with the black blotches darker and the light seeping from the rock/flesh brighter, but none of it illuminated the area; instead, it highlighted the almost diseased-looking colors more powerfully. If light could have cancer, then this was a fine example.

In the center of the room was an anus-like protrusion, a sphincter that thrust up a puckered mouth from the floor about a foot, as if ready to disgorge some strange and malodorous offal. The rock there was darker, less purple, the black more prevalent—veins more pronounced, thicker.

As I watched, the sphincter moved, quivering slightly, before opening wide, disgorging those words that almost shattered my bones with fright. *"Hello, Lovey-Dovey."*

"Jesus God, Specter," I blasphemed, my nice-girl, nondenominational upbringing flying out the window so fast it left a contrail. "Jesus God."

"Although no deity and no follower of any religion, Agent Jacobs, I fully understand the sentiment and concur."

While the sphincter throbbed, the thick veins upon its surface writhed like giant worms filled with awful life and purpose. Was it blood that coursed through those undulant conduits? Or some other matter too foul to name? Either way, I could almost *feel* the liquid oozing through them.

"Lovey-Dovey!" The words came stronger now, and the sphincter bulged upward suddenly, opening like a dreadful flower. With a loud, squelchy sound accompanied by an odor of feces and rot, an arm shot out of the opening, covered in blood and pearlescent slime, fingers outstretched as though intending to grab hold of the air itself.

I felt faint, my vision spotting as the appendage continued to emerge into the stale air of the kidney-shaped cave. Slowly, as if being born, the rest of the body emerged. Head, shoulders, chest, waist, then legs. All covered in blood and slime and stinking to high heaven. I sagged, crouching on the floor, too scared to lean against the wall, lest it try to suck me in again. As for the Brave Bull auto shotgun, it lay at my feet, an inert potential for violence.

"Lovey-Dovey," crooned the voice, clearly coming from the slime-covered, very naked, man who stood at the apex of the wrinkled sphincter. *"So good to see you again, my Lovey-Dovey."*

His voice sounded like the hiss of water circling a drain.

"Hello, Uncle Carl," I replied, drool ribboning from my mouth to the floor.

"*Oh, Lovey-Dovey, how I have missed you while toiling away in my dark and lonely room.*"

I couldn't help it; I retched until my belly clenched so tight the pain shot up my neck.

One step, two, and Uncle Carl was off the platform of the sphincter and standing twenty feet away. "*Shall we play a game, Lovey-Dovey? A game just like in the old days. Didn't we have fun?*" Brown eyes rimmed in pearlescent slime regarded me with fierce amusement.

"I killed you sixteen years ago, Uncle Carl, and Dad never told." My voice barely stirred the still, silent air.

"*And I forgive you, Lovey-Dovey. I will always forgive you. I've missed you.*"

"Leave me alone!" It was the plaintive cry of a lost and weak little girl before she found her steel.

He came a few steps closer, his footsteps squelching, the stench growing more and more horrible, a palpable force against my nasal passages. "*You don't want that, Lovey-Dovey. You want to play our game. Our special game, the one just between us. The game I know you love.*"

"Go away or I'll tell Daddy!" I shrieked, my mind spinning away into the darkness.

"*You already did, but he did not believe you.*"

No, he didn't, not then. But he did eventually.

That hissing, slightly gargly voice, at once alien and familiar, continued, "*We were meant to be together, you and I. Forever. Forever.*" A dripping hand reached out for my cheek.

"Don't touch me!" My cry was more animal than human, but the hand drew back slowly.

"*You want me to touch you, don't you, Lovey-Dovey? You always loved the games we played, even though you cried. Deep down in your heart of hearts you ached, yearned for me to touch you in that special place, the place all little girls love to explore. Admit it, my dear sweet Dove, you wanted me as much as I wanted you, and that made you very happy."*

"No, no, nonononononono!"

A slimy finger stroked my cheek, leaving an odoriferous snail trail. *"Oh, yes, Lovey-Dovey. Ask me for my touch. Beg for it like the good little whore you are."*

I was on my feet and running, running so fast, trying to escape the hell that lurked behind me. Gone were the memories of taking a screwdriver to Uncle Carl's neck, the semi-sharp Phillips-head sliding easily into flesh and the squirt of thick, rich blood onto my white cotton summer dress. The startled, glassy look in his deep-brown eyes as his life drained away onto the floor of the dusty stables. It all fled my mind in my mad dash from the cavern, returning back to where I came from, trying to run away from the most singular horror in my life, away from the man who hurt me most.

"Come back, Lovey-Dovey!"

CHAPTER EIGHT

―❦―

Ghost Copy
Sympathy for the Devil

THE OTHERS HAD vanished, disappearing without a trace. That, or *he* did. Either way the outcome was the same. Billings found himself in a hallway somewhere in the Quint Building without any memory of how he got there.

Thanks to someone being on the ball, the power was back on. Instead of darkness, the overhead bulbs provided enough light to walk around without using the DRAFTlite. The lights had a tendency to flicker, however. After a cursory reconnaissance, he found an outside wall and peered down to the street, dozens of feet below, still filled with a crowd of reporters and looky-loos.

"[CENSORED] tourists," he rumbled in a voice like boulders rubbing together.

"They are merely curious, Mr. Billings."

Hazel eyes narrowed at the voice buzzing in his ear. "Ghost?"

"Not quite, Mr. Billings. I am a poor copy placed here by the original in order to assist you in any way possible and to record your experience for the BSI files. Would you care to bestow upon me a name other than 'Ghost'?"

"Don't care," came the reply as he stared out the window. "Ghost Copy works."

"Suit yourself."

A grunt, then, "Where's the rest of the team?"

"From what data is available, they have disappeared."

That seemed to put a crack in Billings' normally inscrutable mien. "What do you mean? I thought *I* disappeared."

"So you did; however, your DRAFTlite is no longer connected to the others', which would mean they are out of effective range or an interference is preventing communication."

Billing spat on the floor. "So?"

"It would seem that either the team has been teleported to a location that does not receive cellphone signals, something is blocking me, or that their DRAFTlites have been destroyed, along with the original Ghost."

More grunting as Billings seemed to mull over that information. "Don't matter, I guess. The force field is still surrounding the building and I'm trapped inside."

"You do not seem to be emotional about the situation, sir."

"I'm not."

"If I may ask, why not?"

Billings scratched his head while staring at the AR-15 clutched in one big fist. "Don't feel emotion," he said finally. "Never have. Not like regular people."

"Why not?"

Billings shook his hairy head. "Enough of this jibber-jabber. Let's get to the ground floor."

"Then what, Mr. Billings?"

"Then we see if bullets hurt that screaming orb thing."

The program did not bother to reply.

It was not long before Billings found a bank of elevators. When the buttons didn't light up when pressed, he opted for the stairs.

Armored boots clomping, he descended several stories before realizing that he had passed the same door three times. The door to floor fifteen.

"What magic is this?"

"I do not know," said Ghost Copy. "Apparently some agency does not want you beyond this point."

Billings looked down the stairwell and saw it terminate five floors below. Another lap down brought him to the FLOOR 15 sign posted next to the same brown steel door he'd passed before.

Nodding to himself, he dropped a small diamond. It tinked off metal several times before dropping out of sight. It did not reappear from above. Apparently whatever wanted him on floor fifteen didn't care about spell gems.

"BARFNOODLE!" The activation word reverberated along the stairwell, but nothing happened.

"What happened?" Billings chewed at his moustache.

"I do not know, Mr. Billings. It seems that the spell gem did not work."

He cocked his head to one side. "Care to tell me why?"

"There is not enough data for a reasonable hypothesis."

A grunt. Then an explosive fart that echoed louder than the grunt. He dropped another gem, an emerald. This one avoided the metal rails and hit the tenth-floor landing square. It bounced out of sight before rolling back to rest within view.

"HEDGERAVEN!" yelled the big man.

Nothing.

"This one didn't work, either. Care to hazard a guess?" asked Billings as he calmly eyed the gem worth more than most people made in a year.

"Given limited information, I would say that the magic has been drained from the spell gems." After a brief pause, he added, "Yes, I believe that is the hypothesis that best fits the facts."

Billings blinked slowly—once, twice—staring at the gem. "And how could that have happened?" he asked slowly.

"Your guess is as good as mine."

He pondered that a moment. "The orb."

"Most likely."

"It musta drained all the magic from our gems, our equipment."

"Yes."

"That sucks."

He received no reply.

Nodding, the big main raised his weapon and opened the door to the fifteenth floor, keeping an eye out for something to kill. He saw nothing but empty hallways, their florescent bulbs flickering fitfully. On his left, right, and ahead dark blue pile carpeting covered the way to several dozen office doors made of chocolate-colored wood. Planters, once home to carefully tended dwarf trees, lay upended here and there, their contents strewn about along with dirt the color of coffee grounds sprayed across the floor. It looked as if a willful child had demolished them in a fit of spite.

"Which way?" he asked softly.

"If the being that is controlling the stairwell wants you on the fifteenth floor, then I posit that no matter which direction you choose, you will be led inexorably toward whatever awaits."

Billings sighed. "No help."

"It is the best I can do, considering the circumstances," Ghost replied.

The big man cocked his head. "Didn't mean to hurt your feelings."

"I have none to hurt, Mr. Billings. Nor, I suspect, do you."

Eyebrows quirked northward as the big man stopped suddenly. "Interesting. What makes you say that?"

"From the evidence you have provided, I must conclude that you are a sociopath."

For the first time, Billings looked confused. He slowly removed the DRAFTlite and gave it a good, long stare. "Do you even know what a sociopath is? What that word really means?" Menace lay thick on the words.

"A sociopath is defined as a person with a personality

disorder manifesting itself in extreme antisocial attitudes and behavior—a person displaying a lack of what is commonly referred to as a conscience."

Billings headed down the hall ahead, eyes wide and glassy, weapon at the ready. Slowly, slowly, each step carefully, quietly placed, he said, "What makes you think I'm a sociopath? You said something about evidence." The glasses were once again perched on the bridge of his nose.

"Your own words, Mr. Billings, about how you do not have emotions like 'regular people.' And your general impassiveness in the face of such a stressful situation."

Another grunt, which seemed to be his standby reaction to surprise. "Foolish of me. I must be off my game to be so clumsy. What makes you think I won't smash these glasses to keep you quiet about the matter?"

"That would be futile, as my program is housed in the amulet around your neck. The glasses are merely the interface, like a computer monitor. Albeit a powerful and sophisticated one."

One hand letting go of the AR-15, Billings fished for the chain around his neck until he pulled the amulet free. The silvery face was unadorned, free from engraving or embellishment. "How about I put a bullet through this, then?

"You will certainly destroy me then, Mr. Billings, but perhaps a better idea would be to simply order me not to divulge the information. I am programmed to obey your orders and that of the original Ghost. Even better, you could order me to forget anything to do with your particular psychological impairments and I would."

"Humph. You shoulda told me that before."

"I did not think you would pose a threat. Tell me, is Director Bauer aware of your condition?"

Once again Billings cocked his head to one side. "Of course."

"And he does not mind?"

Billings stared at the amulet for a long time, face inscrutable as a boulder, before saying, "Yes, he does. The only reason he cleared me despite the mandatory psych screening is because I've never harmed anyone, despite my … tendencies. In all my life, I've never killed another human being."

"No one? That is quite odd."

"My mother discovered my … strangeness when I was eight, after the family cat went missing. The first real lesson she ever taught me was causality." The big man clutched the amulet tight in one gloved fist. "Cause and effect. For every action, there is an equal and opposite reaction. Big believer in causality was Mom." Eyes closed as if reliving a specific event, he sighed heavily. "So I learned to incite conflict. I knocked a lot of heads, but never threw the first punch. I put a lot of guys in the hospital, but never the morgue—that's how careful I was. And I've always been careful. I was recruited by the BSI from the DEA and I was happy to join because it meant that I could finally kill things and even be rewarded for it. BB just made it clear that if I strayed from the path the punishment would be … drastic."

"Sociopaths generally lack that level of discipline."

A shake of a shaggy head. "Negative. Normal sociopaths do; they are weak-willed and self-indulgent. The exceptional ones, like me, are never caught."

Billings waited a while before Ghost Copy finally said, "What are your orders, sir? Would you like me to erase all memory of this conversation?"

"I don't know," he mused, running the chain through his fingers. "It's … pleasing to acknowledge all this out loud, you know? There are so few I can share it with."

"*You can share with me.*" It was a whispery sort of voice that entered the conversation, full of malice and darker things.

The effect on the Agent was immediate. Weapon up, Billings had his eyes aimed down the sights and swiveled the AR-15 up and down the hallway, searching for something to kill.

"I am no danger to you, Agent Billings of the BSI. We are, in fact, kindred spirits."

A rumble filled the air, low and deep. It took a moment for Ghost Copy to realize that Billings was *growling*. "Mr. Billings, you should be seeking cover."

"*Hold a sec, Ghost Copy?*" Billings subvocaled.

"Yes, sir."

The whispery voice floated on the air like eiderdown. "You and I, Agent Billings, are cut from the same cloth, part and parcel of a dynamic whole. I am going to give you a singular offer that only someone like you can understand."

"*What do you make of that?*" The AR-15 kept swiveling, but Billings couldn't see anything to shoot.

"There is not enough information to form a hypothesis. To make a guess, that voice might belong to the entity that brought the Bureau to St. Louis."

Billings called out, "Where are you?"

"Close by, Agent. Why don't you walk down the hall a little ways so I can greet you properly?"

Ghost Copy's drone cut through the exchange. "Careful, Mr. Billings."

"*I don't have time for careful.*" The words, while subvocal, managed to convey urgency.

"Come now, Agent," said the whispery voice. "You have my word that I shall not harm you. I merely wish to pose an opportunity."

Shaking his head, Billings slowly made his way down the hall, ignoring Ghost Copy as it implored him to explain the situation.

At the end of the hall, Billings chose to head right, where the light was brighter. Soon he saw that the hall intersected another that followed the outside glass wall. A figure stood next to the window, silhouetted by the bright light shining through. It appeared to be a tall man sporting a top hat, a half-cape, and a cane.

The figure doffed its hat. "It is good to lay eyes on you, Agent Billings," said the figure. Its voice was no longer whispery, but deep and avuncular—the voice of someone in authority.

Billings stopped, sighting down the AR-15. "State your name."

The top hat reappeared on the figure's head. "What's in a name? You can call me what you wish, as long as it is with respect." Long arms spread wide. "I do not lie when I state that we are kindred spirits, Agent, you and I. We are both creatures of dark urges, beings for whom the world is but a playground. However, where you have been limited by threats of imprisonment, I roam free, able to force my will upon a pallid planet filled with sheep. In my world, causality is something I can choose to ignore."

"Mighty big talk from a man on the wrong end of a rifle."

Ghost Copy cut in, "Mr. Billings, I must urge you to not converse with this being."

"*Shut up and stay shut up until I tell you otherwise,*" replied the Agent. He waited a few seconds to be sure the Ghost copy complied before turning his attention back to the silhouetted man.

"Oh, if it pleases you to shoot me, Agent Billings, feel free to do—" the silhouetted man began, but was drowned out by the clatter of the AR-15. Brass flew as Billings ripped through the entire clip, then changed it before the echoes faded.

The only result was deep laughter, hinting at a terrible mirth. "I am impressed," the man said, doffing his top hat once again. "You are a gem, a true gem, and that's a fact."

Billing narrowed his eyes. "You the ghost that's haunting this building?"

"And what if I am, dear sir?"

A grunt. "Just wanted to know. Don't suppose I can kill you."

"That is a valid supposition."

He stared at the apparition for a few moments, head cocked to the right. "You said something about an offer."

The man began to walk forward slowly, as if approaching a strange and dangerous dog. "Yes, an offer which only a man of your caliber can appreciate," he said. "A most wondrous offer, indeed."

Billings lowered the rifle, but kept the barrel pointed in the man's general direction. "Go on."

Another few steps. "I know the pleasures you've never been able the explore, Agent Billings. The glory of flesh and razor, of knife and skin. Dark pleasures, for sure, but pleasures nonetheless. I have traveled to more places than you can imagine to work my will upon those who were weaker, to take from them the red joy, to revel in the fading spark of life. What do you know of such things, Agent Billings? You who have been hamstrung by society's intolerance of our superiority. What I offer you is to break free from the shackles of a hypocritically degenerate society crippled by false ideals and the suffocating blanket of political correctness."

Another step, then another. Slowly, slowly. The overhead lights flickered and died as he drew nearer, keeping the strange man's countenance in shadow. "Come with me. Take my hand, and we shall explore together the blackness of our desires, the subtle yielding to the darkness and the joy that comes with complete freedom. Freedom from judgment, freedom from rules and false mores, and freedom from those who try to keep our uniqueness under lock and key when we should be celebrating those traits, displaying them for the world to see. Come with me and find a joy you have never experienced. I guarantee that once you have sipped from the clotted pool of your desires, there will be no going back." There was a hint of a horrid smile from within the cloak of shadows, a slash of yellow white in the dark. "Nor will you want to." As the last words left his mouth, the man stepped out of the dark and into the light of a bulb that did not flicker or dim.

Billings saw his face for the first time.

The AR-15 hit the carpet with a dull thud.

A gloved hand rose, and the man caressed Billings' cheek with fingers gloved in black kidskin. "Yes. You want my secrets, do you not? You want to join me. Take my hand and leave all else behind. There is nothing left of your old life that you can bring into the new."

The amulet slipped from nerveless fingers and Billings took the hand.

CHAPTER NINE

<hr/>

Ng
Black Water

A FURRY SOMETHING slid across my fingers, shocking me awake, and then came a curious *plopping* sound as if a quarter dropped into a bucket of water.

Darkness hit my eyes. I fought a moment of panic before realizing that I could handle the situation easily. I used the voice command for the DRAFTlite and subvocaled, "*Nightvision.*"

And then I could see. Wish to hell I couldn't, but there you go. Like the Rolling Stones sang, you can't always get what you want. Craning my neck all around, I could see that I was surrounded by water, my little grassy hillock of land a pimple in the middle of tiny wavelets in a strangely placid ocean. I had maybe an eight-by-eight patch of uncomfortable dirt and grass to work with. Above, the sky was devoid of stars or any other form of celestial light, and that bizarre sight reached into my belly with claws of fear.

What the hell? Where was I?

I marveled at the blankness of the sky, its dark barrenness. After a bit of staring, I cupped a hand to my ear. My surroundings were oddly silent; only the faintest lapping of small waves disturbed the air. It was if my ears were stuffed with cotton. A lack of any sort of fishy smell that usually emanated from the ocean added to the air of unreality.

I stood and took stock of my situation: weapons ... all of them (hidden and not), spell gems ... same there. In fact, everything was accounted for except for me in the real world of the Quint Building in St. Louis. Somehow, someway, I'd been plopped smack dab in the middle of a big wet nothing.

"Good to see you awake, Mr. Ng."

My feet damn near left the ground. "Holy [BLEEP], Ghost, you scared the life outta me!" I'm sure my voice carried far across the waves. My heart hammered fast in my chest. It's not often someone or something startles me, and I wasn't used to the sensation.

Ghost then proceeded to tell me he wasn't Ghost but a copy created to give me a hand. Nice, but I could've used the more sentient version, considering my circumstances. I decided to call him Spooky. Seemed appropriate.

"That's all well and good, Spooky. Do you have any ideas on how I can get out of here?" The place was getting to me, filing across my nerves with a dull rasp.

"May I take control of your glasses, Mr. Ng?" he asked, pronouncing my last name correctly.

"Please."

And the strange world I stood in became even stranger. How do I describe what I saw when I couldn't even understand it? The waters, at first black with gray highlights, became green. Not the green of string beans or lima beans, but an electric light green that shone so bright I had to squint. Yellow blobs the size of dinner plates darted under the surface with quick, jerking motions. The grassy knob of land I found myself on offered several different shades of blue from light to midnight, every leaf of grass a diamond-edged, multi-hued blade that looked sharp enough to slice gently falling silk.

Fascinating as that was, the sky took all that wonder and smashed it flat. Black. Not the black of a cloudy night during a new moon, but the soul-sucking black that ate anything even resembling light. It looked like the forbidden heart of a black hole and it scared me off my feet. My knees hit damp earth with a startlingly loud *thump*.

"Oh, my dear lord," I whispered into the blackness.

"Odd, is it not, Mr. Ng? You are seeing the world as a pigeon does, but there is no ultraviolet radiation from the sky, nor is there electromagnetic. It is if the heavens above do not exist. Most peculiar."

I held my stomach, trying not to vomit. I had been robbed of words.

"Please regain your feet, sir, and look around. Perhaps there is a way off this small island."

Complying was the hardest thing I'd ever done. I wanted to weep, to throw my hands up in denial and despair. Years of discipline, first at college, then at Quantico so I could become FBI, and later at Coronado so I could join the BSI, left me in an instant.

"Where am I?" I whispered, lost and confused.

"Apparently we are no longer on Earth, Mr. Ng. As to where, I have no idea." It might have been only semi-sentient, but Spooky sounded scared to me, its static-laden voice trembling.

What kept me from losing my mind to the blankness above was the movement of those plate-sized yellow blobbies just peeking out of the water. One was swimming closer, spiraling around the tiny island, circling like a shark. Its slow, lazy progress in my peripheral vision compelled me to gaze at the greenly luminescent water. The dozens and dozens of other blobbies remained far enough away that the circling one was unusual enough to be notable.

"Mr. Ng, please keep your focus on that circling object."

"What's going on, Spooky?"

"I am attempting a clearer visual."

Ultraviolet and electromagnetic was suddenly replaced by harsh black and white with very little gray in between. As for the blobby, it came to life as something both ugly and beautiful, a sphere the size of a basketball covered in what looked to be long, fine hair that undulated in the water in such a manner that I surmised that those long tresses were what propelled the creature.

"What is that?" I whispered, drawing my weapon, a Mac-10A, and taking aim.

Spooky answered, "It appears to be a large creature much like a sea urchin. Instead of spines, it has tendrils like an anemone, only finer."

Suddenly the vision kicked back to pigeon. "What happened?"

"Conserving energy, sir. X-ray vision consumes an inordinate amount."

Ah.

Holding the Mac-10A loosely, I waited patiently as the blobby spiraled closer and closer. Soon half of the creature was above the level of water as it hit the shallows. Its color went from yellow to orange, and the tendrils showed white with lavender tips.

"A scavenger?"

"Unknown, sir. It appears to be unafraid."

My mind cast back a few minutes to my moment of waking, the furry something slithering across my fingers. I examined my fingers where they poked out through the gloves at the first knuckle. Not standard BSI-issue hand wear, but I had an aversion to the loss of tactile sensation and Kal didn't seem to mind. Nothing wrong with the skin or nails, so if it was one of the blobbies, it hadn't bitten me. Perhaps a scout?

When the hairy basketball came on land, it propelled itself with its hair-like tendrils. Those tendrils, roughly eight to nine inches long, probed the grass and dirt ahead of it before impelling it forward.

Letting the Mac-10A swing from its lanyard, I knelt and pulled out a fingered glove from my belt (I couldn't bear to call it a Bat Belt; I wasn't a fanboy), removed the fingerless glove from my left, and slipped on the new.

"What are you doing, sir?"

I licked my lips. "Checking something out, Spooky."

"It is not advisable to touch the creature. It could be poisonous."

"In case you haven't noticed," I said, waving my fully gloved hand. "we don't have much room to play with here. I want to know if our danger is immediate."

"Good point. Be careful."

Right. My hand forward, its fingers were a few short inches from the creature when the first tendril encountered the glove. Immediately a dozen started caressing the tips of my fingers, probing. Tasting? Whatever they were doing, their touch was light and feathery. Hair-thin strands wrapped gently around my pinky and thumb and squeezed. It was like shaking hands with a wig.

Suddenly my hand was engulfed by the blobby, thrust into the middle of its spherical body, and dozens of pinpricks, needles of pain, shot through my knuckles. I cursed and shook my hand, but the blobby, which couldn't have weighed more than a pound, pound-and-a-half, kept holding on. I pounded it into the soft dirt, over and over again, because the pain was getting worse—it was really starting to *burn.* I hammered it over and over and then the hair parted, moving aside to reveal an eyeball, a dead black orb like a marble, soulless and full of malignancy. I screamed because more blobbies were coming straight at me, coming to the little island, and soon they would be all over me, stinging and hurting. I did the only thing I could do because hammering it against the ground wasn't cutting it: I lifted the Mac-10A and cut loose, ripping rounds through the black eye, through the heart of the beast. It hurt because the bullets slapped into me as well, tearing at the flesh of my hand, but the blobby fell to the ground and I hosed it, sending black blood flying, until the chamber racked dry.

I stood, tears running down my cheeks and blood filling my glove, but the blobby was dead, torn to bits. It smelled like rotting seaweed and chicken feces, like corpses in the sun. An overpowering stench that almost eclipsed the pain in my hand. I didn't want to look at my fingers. I was afraid of what I would see, how mangled they would be, but I could feel the blood leaving my body, so I did the only thing I could think of. With my good hand, my right one, I reached into my belt, pulled out a spell gem, and said the activation word, "FLOGDROPPING."

Nothing. My left hand still throbbed and stung, and the pain of it made me dizzy. I dropped a year's pay for a school teacher onto the dirt.

Through the ringing in my ears and the pain in my hand, I ground out a few words, "Spooky, what gives with the gem?"

"I do not know."

Not useful. I tried again, another spell gem meant for pain relief. Again nothing. Sweat stung my eyes as I eyed the blobbies, so many of them, coming nearer and nearer. The smell from the first blobby was doing terrible things to my stomach, and I would've puked but I didn't have time. Awkwardly, I reloaded my weapon and sent bursts at those blobbies closest to shore, those that were already halfway out of the water. As they burst apart, emitting more dead smells, I screamed in pain and frustration, because they kept coming, rolling toward me as they cleared the shore. Turning in a circle, I saw them all around. When it ran out of rounds, I dropped the Mac-10A and unholstered my Ruger and sent 9mm death into the nearest blobbies. More rancid smells filled the tepid air as they kept coming out of the water, more and more of them.

When the chamber racked dry, I reloaded, but it was slow and two managed to affix themselves to my legs before I was done. They began to climb, tendrils wrapped along the creases of my armor, but that didn't matter because the clip was in and I shot my own legs, confident that the NewTanium armor would prevent them from turning into so much shredded meat and bone. It worked; the beasts practically exploded. I fired until that clip went dry, but there wasn't time to reload before I was swarmed, so I began stamping on them, using my weight to crush their hairy bodies against the ground. A K-bar appeared in my hand—I didn't even remember drawing it or dropping the Ruger—and I began to slash and stamp and slash and stamp, the world a multi-hued blur all around with the blackness of the sky looking down upon the mayhem happening on the tiniest island ever.

Hack, stomp, hack, stomp …. My leg armor was covered with malodorous blood all the way to the crotch, and it was every rotten thing I'd ever smelled. The bodies of the blobbies rapidly decomposed right in front of me, going from hairy basketballs to slime in under a minute, like some capricious god had hit the fast-forward button.

Over, all over. Surrounded by the liquefying remains of blobbies, I fell to my knees, spent and panting, sweat streaming into my eyes and off my chin and holding my injured hand to my chest. I knew what I had to do. I really, really didn't want to do it because I was so damn afraid of what I'd see. My eyes settled on my wounded hand and beheld what I had wrought.

The Kevlar glove with its NewTanium plates prevented the rounds from the Mac-10A from turning my hand into a stump, but the impacts had done the small bones wrong.

Only my thumb had survived unscathed. The fingers were bent every which way, and upon closer examination, I saw tiny holes in the Kevlar where blobby tendrils had cut through like hot needles through butter. I wanted to take the glove off, but with my fingers pointing in every direction at once, that wasn't going to happen unless I bit the bullet and did what needed to be done. I gently grabbed the ring finger and pulled hard.

"Aaaaarrrghhh!!!!" My vocal cords ripped as my ring finger popped. My vision went white, then black, and I lay, forehead pressed to the ground, as tears dripped from my eyes and snot ran out of my nose. I gasped one breath, then two.

"Are you in distress, Mr. Ng?" asked Spooky.

"You … could say that," I managed. "Now … shut up and keep … an eye out if possible. I'm … busy."

Spooky stayed shut up as I went for the next finger. More popping sounds and more pain that sent ribbons of fire up my arm and the next finger was more or less straight. I sobbed, curled around myself as I went to work on the third. Then everything went black.

When I came to, nothing had changed. Mounds of mostly liquid blobby were still spread around me, so I must not have been out for too long. Cringing, I grabbed the last finger, the pinky finger, and yanked.

When I woke next, it was in a puddle of my own bile, and my mouth tasted like acid and ass. With a groan, I made it to my knees and slowly, carefully, popped the clip into the Mac-10A, reloading. Two clips to go. You'd think that would be plenty.

Getting to my feet took some work, but I managed. Barely. I stood there looking out over that placid sea with its dark mysteries.

"Mr. Ng?"

"Yes, Spooky. What is it?" My left hand felt hot and tight as it swelled inside the glove. Four sausages almost bursting their casings.

"Look behind you, sir."

"What is it, Spooky?"

"Let me show you, sir."

An image appeared in the DRAFTlite, a feed from the rear-facing micro cameras mounted on the temple arms of the glasses.

A yellow blobby was making a beeline toward my little island. The only problem was, while the other blobbies were the size of basketballs, this one moving toward me at speed looked to be a good ten feet across.

"Oh, swell," I breathed, lifting my weapon. "Here we go again."

CHAPTER TEN

———

Buffalo
Cuts Like a Knife

THIS IS THE last entry of Robert Atkins, first-year Agent for the Bureau of Supernatural Investigation. I'm sitting here watching the blood leak from me with slow inevitability, and all I can think about is my ridiculous handle. Strange what your mind conjures up when your life is coming to a close.

But, I mean, Buffalo? Really? Can you believe it? C'mon, Kal, you could've picked a better one. Don't get me wrong; earning a name from Agent Hakala is an honor, unless you get stuck with a bad one for a major screw up, like Douchebag or Hairball. But Buffalo? Still, it would've been nice to be called Mustang, or Thunder.

Oh well.

Damn, my leg hurts.

I check my watch. Hell, it's broken. The crystal, supposedly shatterproof, is too busted up to see the dial. Guess it doesn't matter, but I like to think it's still daytime, that the sun is shining down on this [CENSORED] building and that, in daylight, there's still some hope for me to get home alive.

Kind of doubt it, though.

The copy that Ghost sent to my DRAFTlite system is

recording this for posterity in the case someone manages to find it so they can know what really happened. I can hardly believe it myself, and I was there. Sounds kinda crazy, but when I'm done, you'll understand.

Where do I start? Let's see … the screaming orb thing that kicked our asses in the lobby? No, I figure the real Ghost has that already tucked away in his memory banks or whatnot, assuming he survives. Sure hope someone is still alive.

"I have no doubt that Ghost will survive, Mr. Atkins," says the AI.

Sure he will. If rumors around the Bureau are true, he's a good buddy with Kal, and that's who he's with right now and the two of them together … fuggedaboutit. They're probably kicking ass and taking names.

I wish they were here, though, to could get me out of this spot.

But if wishes were fishes no one would starve. My grandmother, God rest her soul, said that whenever I wanted something my parents couldn't afford. I used to hate that saying until I grew up, then I understood. If wishes were fishes ….

I wish ….

Back to business. I should start the moment I woke up from whatever that orb did to me. To us.

I woke in a janitor's closet, of all things, eyes crusty with sleep sand and feeling pretty good, as if I'd slept for a solid eight hours. Thanks to the DRAFTlite, I saw that only a few minutes had passed and I didn't need a flashlight or anything.

"Mr. Atkins." And that was when, with me sitting on an overturned mop bucket in a tiny little closet filled with cleaning supplies, the copy Ghost gave me told me of his mission to help me survive. I gave him control of the DRAFTlite, which kept me from having to use verbal commands. He told me then that he wasn't able to contact the others, which worried me more than a bit. I sure didn't fancy being on my own, but what choice did I have? *If wishes were fishes ....*

After taking stock and finding that everything was as it was supposed to be—all weapons and supplies present and accounted for—I decided to get a move on.

Through the closet door and into a hallway. Instead of the .50 cal, the Ruger filled my right hand, and I was ready to kill me some bad guys, should they try to do me wrong.

Nothing. Just an empty hallway filled with corporate art and potted trees meant to liven up the sterile environment. They'd been de-potted and the soil dumped all willy-nilly. Looked like someone was pissed.

Was I still in the Quint Building, or did the orb put me in another? Only one way to find out.

I went left and started alternating turns—left, right, left, etc.—backtracking when the hallway ended at a door. Most seemed to be locked, and I really didn't want to waste time breaking into offices, especially since the noise could attract a Supernatural or two. My goal was to find the other members of my team, then complete the mission if possible.

All in all, though, I really wished we'd sent a bunker-buster missile through the lobby doors instead of checking out what happened to Omicron. *If wishes were fishes ....*

"Mr. Atkins, may I ask you a question?" The AI's voice was eerily like Ghost's, but more polite, deferential. Fortunately, the voice came through the bone-induction pad behind my ear, so no eavesdropping Supernaturals could hear.

"*Go ahead,*" I subvocaled.

"Why did you join the BSI? Mind you, Ghost did not download your file into this DRAFTlite system."

"*Why are you so curious?*" Left, then right. This hallway was longer, with a spot of bright light at the end. Could be an outside glass wall.

"Ghost created me with—for lack of a better term—an insatiable curiosity. Perhaps in an effort to make a more complete file on the events that occur in his absence."

I thought about that for a moment. "So your brother copies are bugging the other team members?"

"Most likely."

"So none of us is getting any peace."

"Most likely. Although, sir, you can order me to be silent."

"Not necessary."

"Then, sir, will you answer my question?"

The light at the end *was* an exterior glass wall that curved to the right. I walked up to the glass and looked down.

Holy cats! The city spread out below me, the people merely black dots scurrying to and fro while cars and buses were slightly larger blood cells rushing through the city's arteries. Vertigo turned my guts into water as I stared, but a moment later I settled down. The trick to vertigo, Granny had said, was to treat what you saw like a painting, or something on TV— that way it's not real and there's no reason to be afraid. It even worked every now and then.

From my vantage point, I guessed I was one or two stories from the top. Backing up, I unlimbered the .50 cal and took aim at the glass at an oblique angle. Didn't want to die from bullet fragments.

Blam!

The .50 bucked hard and the round hit the glass at an angle and bounced. The high velocity round broke apart after hitting the glass, turning into deadly shrapnel flying down the hallway at over two thousand feet per second. Some fragments shredded the interior wall as the sound seemed to reverberate throughout the building.

I rubbed my shoulder. Normally I wouldn't fire the damn thing without the bipod and stock monopod, but the M82 .50 was clumsy enough slung across my back without them. Only so much I could easily carry, after all.

"With that amount of noise, Mr. Atkins, I would assume you have just alerted any Supernatural roving this floor."

"Getting bored, anyway," I said aloud, slinging the .50 on my back. "Next, we should find the roof. You wouldn't happen to have any blueprints of the building, would you?"

"No. Ghost surely possessed them, but in his haste to provide every team member with a copy of himself, he may have forgotten to include the data."

"Let's find a stairwell or elevator, then."

It didn't take long to find the stairs and I proceeded to go up and up and up. Maybe that strange force field that surrounded the building exterior and interior glass didn't extend to the roof.

Only two flights of stairs and I was faced with a green-painted steel door. Locked, of course. I fumbled for a spell gem, wedged it tight under the door, and ran down the steps.

"CRACKNOODLE!" I yelled up the stairs.

I waited. And waited some more.

"Something's wrong." I rubbed my dome, which was covered in a slick of sweat.

"Indeed, sir."

Up the stairs. I checked on the gem ... still wedged in tight under the door. I added another gem and repeated the process, but the results were the same. *Damn.*

"Why aren't the gems working?" I admit it ... the fear was getting in deep and I couldn't stop my hands from trembling. Slightly.

"Perhaps all the magic upon your person is no longer active. If that is the case, then the rest of the team is most likely bereft of magic as well."

I gave the door the sole of my boot five times. All it did was let out a booming sound that echoed down the stairwell. Bruised my heel a bit, too. Still, it made me feel somewhat better. Next I tried a round from my .50. Despite my being halfway around the landing and shooting up at an angle, a bullet fragment came damn near to taking my head clean off and didn't even scratch the ugly green paint.

"Looks like I'm not getting out any time soon."

"Then I recommend down, sir. It's your only option left."

Of course. I didn't bother to tell the AI that I had nowhere else to go. I fished into my Bat Belt for a granola bar and washed it down with some tepid water from a small canteen.

"Are you going to answer my question, sir?"

"About why I joined the BSI?"

"That's the one."

"Don't be snooty." I took another sip and licked my lips. Water tasted like tin. "When the news came out about the World Under and the BSI and all that other [DELETED], I was working in a bar. You know, the kind of place with a karaoke machine and open mic night where most of the customers order beer and leave the high-dollar stuff alone."

"You were a bartender?"

"No."

"Bouncer, then. You are certainly big enough."

I shook my head and pulled out a plastic Baggie full of beef jerky. Just what I needed. "Server. Made decent tips and I was good at it."

"Why were you serving drinks? Couldn't you make more money in, say, construction?"

"Naw." *Munch, munch.* Good jerky, just the right amount of pepper. "Used to work construction back in the day. I actually made more money serving than in construction, and I needed to make some money."

"Why?"

"University. I wanted to get a higher education."

"So why did you join the BSI?"

I decided to plant my ass on a step. If I was going to tell stories, might as well be comfortable doing it. Can't say I really blamed the AI for being nosy, seeing as how that's what Ghost intended. Besides, doesn't everyone like talking about themselves?

"When the Director pushed Agent Hakala into the limelight, you know with Colbert and Kimmel and the like, he looked the [CENSORED]ing *part,* you know? He was all smiles and jokes and perfect—the true-blue American hero, a poster boy for the BSI. A blond Superman."

I took another bite of jerky. Damn, it was good. I wanted more. "I remember Colbert, all serious and stuff, leaning back and asking Agent Hakala, 'What do you hate the most about the job?' Without missing a beat, Kal said, 'All the damn Supernaturals.' Of course the audience clapped and whistled like they were going to shake the studio apart and Colbert nods like he knows exactly what Kal's talking about. He's got a little smile on his face like it's just the two of them there sharing a joke no one else knows about and he says, 'What do you love most about your job, then?' Again, without hesitation, Kal says, 'All the damn Supernaturals.' "

Another sip of tinny water and the taste of jerky washed down my throat.

"Is that it, sir?"

"Naw. After I saw that Colbert interview, I began researching everything I could on the BSI, just like everyone else was doing at the time. I was in pretty good shape back then, lean and all up and down. I could run a few miles without a hitch in my stride and I could bench press three-hundred pounds in ten reps. A strong guy, you know? Real strong, and I figured that being strong and tough was good enough, so I raced to join up, to get a piece of the rich Bureau pie.

"Made it through the first cut, which was like a football tryout but without the footballs. Me and a few thousand other guys and gals in a soccer stadium running and jumping and passing physicals. Only about a dozen people made that cut, and boy did I feel proud. That pride only got bigger when I made the next cut. Me and a guy named Saunders passed six hours of psych evaluations. It was brutal, but I was smart enough to handle it. Then came Coronado, and let me tell you brother, that took my pride down a peg or three, but I made it. I didn't ring the bell." My quiet laughter barely hit the walls.

"Turns out during all that testing, they rated my IQ at one forty-two. MENSA material. I should've paid more attention in high school. I could've gotten a scholarship and really made my Gran proud." I paused. "But, if wishes were fishes, you know?"

"That does not answer the question," droned the AI.

I sat there for a while, wishing for more jerky and staring off into the distance. Had I said too much? Why was I spouting off at the mouth? Maybe I needed to talk to someone. The Bureau is a good place to work; the money is great considering they lowered the pay by half—which still made it the best paying government job by far—but it doesn't foster much closeness. You never know who's going to die on the next op. Look at Sixer—dead before he could retire, even if he was a bit of a douche.

"The money," I said. "Stability. When I retire, I can write my own ticket. Everyone who can afford it wants a former BSI Agent as a bodyguard. You know, there's a former Agent named Hakim Kouri who makes seven figures guarding that billionaire playboy guy who invented, ah, a technical doodad, or something, and Kouri is set for *life*." I stood and stretched. "Assuming he doesn't catch a bullet for his billionaire boss, that is. Having a former BSI Agent on the payroll is like a huge status symbol these days."

As I trudged down the stairs, the AI said, "That sounds rather oversimplified."

My laughter felt brittle. "You have to realize that everything is simple. Everything breaks down to something else, very simple things, and those simple things are the root motives of what digs at a person."

I'd made it to the twenty-eighth floor and reached for the doorknob when the AI said, "Are you sure everything is that simple, sir?"

The knob turned. "Everything is—" I began just before a fist about took my head off.

My nose went *crunch* and my butt hit the stairs hard enough to send pain all up my spine and back down to center on my tailbone. Maybe I blacked out, or maybe the stars in my eyes and the sharp pain in my nose took my sight away. Either way it took a couple of seconds for me to get my bearings again. When I did, I was a split second away from finding out what the other side of life looked like.

He (I think it was a he, hard to tell) stood over me, fists raised and massive boot careening toward my face. I rolled to the side in time to miss the boot, but the sound if it hitting the stairs pummeled my ears. I thrust out a fistful of Ruger and pulled the trigger four times. The reports were almost deafening in the confined space of the stairwell. The result was as dramatic as the noise.

My assailant arched backward as the top of his skull came off in big, ugly piece. A second later he fell to the floor with a dull thud, leaking brains and blood all over the cement. I stood and stared down at what (or should I say who?) had attacked me.

Looked like a man—wore a pair of stonewashed Levis and big old whomping boots that seemed large enough to put a hole in a Cadillac. Other than that, he was naked, and that included a total lack of skin. I mean the whole epidermis— hair, zits, moles and all. Bulging red/pink muscle, clumps of yellow fat here and there around the hips, chest and under his flayed chin. Before his current condition, I guessed he used to be slightly tubby, maybe more than slightly, but the fat was starting to dribble off, no longer contained by skin. He had the big, ropy muscles and wide shoulders of a large man. In fact, he looked to be taller than my six feet one. I knelt and examined the corpse a little closer and saw striations on the muscle and fat, regular lines straight as a razor. I guessed those marks were made by a knife, left when the skin was sliced away. Despite the cruelty and brutality of the act, there was no blood smell. All the exposed veins appeared intact. I told the AI to note that fact; Kal would definitely want to know.

The smell of fear began to clog my nose and stink up the stairwell. I was well and truly freaked out, but hard-earned training kicked in, keeping me from running and screaming my head off. Still, it was a close thing.

I reloaded, staring at teeth bared in a permanent smile and expressionless hazel eyes. He looked human, moved like a human, but had made no noise when attacking; he merely stared at me through lidless, unseeing eyes. Killing him had been as automatic as scratching my ass. Thank God for training.

My nose throbbed a bit and hurt like the blazes, but it didn't *crunch* when I applied pressure, so I cleaned the blood from both nostrils and got back to business.

I went through the door, Ruger at the ready, but saw no more skinless bad guys.

"*You know what kind of Supernatural that was?*" I subvocaled.

"No idea, sir," came the reply. "I know of no skinless entities; however, I do not have detailed files on Supernatural beings because of the hastiness of my creation."

"Keep an eye out. Or should I say a camera."

"Of course."

Left or right? Right it was, weapon raised, stepping softly. My nerves were on edge, my senses preternaturally keen. I was ready for any flicker of movement, unusual vibration, or the tiniest of noises. It was quiet. An office building like this should've been bustling, full of the subdued noises of footsteps and soft conversation. This was the quiet of dead, sterile places pale of personality.

"Come out, come out, wherever you are," I crooned.

"Sir?"

"Never mind. Nerves."

Fifty more feet and a turn later, the outside wall was in sight. The light had faded from midday to early evening, a slight sepia tone coloring the air.

"Behind you!"

The warning came just in time. I turned and fired blind, but got lucky, the bullet entering the throat of a charging flayed man. He fell hard, neck shattered by the round. I put two in the head just to be sure.

Breathing hard, adrenaline rushing through me, I checked the corpse. Nope, not a man this time. A woman. Petite but muscular with long legs and slender build. There was very little yellow fat on her body except her small breasts. She was naked to the waist, a ratty pair of Levis concealing the rest of her.

Her eyes were cornflower blue. I wanted to vomit.

"Another one." Despite the urgency, the AI sounded almost bored.

From down the hall, running like an Olympic track star, light from the outside wall shining behind, came another skinned man. Three shots dropped him—two to the chest, one to the head—more proof of the value of training.

The AI cut into my concentration like a razor. "Again."

Thank goodness for the DRAFTlite's fore and aft field of vision. But this time there were two flayed men and I emptied the Ruger, stopping them both. The hallway reeked of blood.

I didn't need the AI's warning for the next two that came at me as I reloaded. Two shots to one and three in the other dropped them in a heap next to the other. The hall was starting to get crowded.

Then things got interesting.

From front and back came more skinned people, at least five, pink muscles flexing and yellow fat dripping, all soundless except the clomp of work boots and the swish of denim. Lipless, all wore identical, manic grins, the smiles of the damned, and my stomach muscles clenched tight with fear.

I ran out of bullets on the second attacker and I knew they'd be on me before I could get off two shots after a quick reload. It was time to get down and dirty.

Kal carries around that big Bowie knife of his, fourteen inches of blade with a six-inch handle. Agent Alsate has the same kind of knife—a gift from Kal I hear. During training,

Kal drove us Green Peas into the ground learning a close-in weapon. Some used hatchets, clubs, easy-to-learn weapons that didn't require a lot of finesse. I chose a different tack—a Celtic short sword.

Two feet of blade with eight inches of hilt. The guard was barely a formality, a place where the transition from blade to hilt was covered by a U-shaped bit of bronze. I carried it strapped to my thigh. A little uncomfortable, but it worked and it fit my hand perfectly as I drew it forth.

The first one met razor steel to the neck, and the head parted company with the rest of the body. Unlike in the movies, the stump didn't spurt blood in a fountain, but there was enough arterial spray to nearly blind me. I sidestepped the falling corpse and took out the next one with a stab to the heart.

Things became a little confusing as training took over and put me on automatic.

I pirouetted like a dancer, sword flashing and stabbing, the tip slipping past an eyeball into a brain and bursting the orb like an egg dropped on cement. I carved through necks and stabbed into chests as blood slicked the carpet and my boots started to *squelch*. The sword became jammed in ribs, but I pulled hard, sliding it free, but the time lost cost me as I was tackled from behind.

Fists and boots and blood and stars ....

CHAPTER ELEVEN

―――

Kal
Once Bitten, Twice Shy

THE SPIDERHEAD CREATURE started forward, clear amber venom dripping from his fangs (I assumed it was a 'he'; I wasn't about to check under his robes). I reckoned he was drooling over a good all-you-can-bite Kal buffet, and that scared me more than the sight of a spider's head attached to the body of a big man dressed in a pale cloak and cowl—a hellish version of a monk. Spidermonk sounded cooler than Spiderhead. Could be a sequel to all those *Spiderman* movies littering the theaters nowadays.

Fear paralyzed me and I stopped struggling as visions of the old classic, *The Fly*—not the incredibly gross Jeff Goldblum version, but the original with Vincent Price—popped into my mind. At the end of the movie, two men spot a fly trapped in a web. It had a human head and was screaming "Help me, help me!" as a spider bore down. Just as the spider bit into the helpless human-headed fly, one of the men crushed the bugs with a rock.

Help me, help meeeeeee!

No big rock came down to save me.

Spidermonk drew close, kneeling down, mouthparts

quivering, and I wanted to vomit, wanted to scream, but I couldn't, couldn't do anything because of the fear that pinned me in place, and I couldn't tear my eyes from the eight black ones that stared at me with all the emotional depth of marbles. My guts felt like bags filled to bursting with hot water. Very hot water.

Hot water.

Hot?

Epiphanies are rare, so when they come, take advantage of them, just as I did at that moment. You see, when my sister's soul attached itself to my psyche (long story) she suppressed what would have normally become a considerable gift for magic. Yeah, a Magician—I still couldn't believe it. But because she suppressed my gift, when she left to travel to that place where only the dead go (a longer story), my gift was an atrophied thing, a useless limb. Although in a time of extreme stress—like during that whole Omaha thing—my magic had healed a broken arm, I hadn't been able to repeat that success. (It took a lot of juice and left me a little dizzy.) No matter how much I practiced, no matter how hard I tried, I couldn't perform the most basic of spells—except for one, the Zippo spell, which creates a small flame like a cigarette lighter or candle.

Spidermonk placed a pallid hand on my bound stomach. The webbing did not stick to his fingers. I think I peed a little more.

It took everything I had to break Spidermonk's gaze and lower my eyes to the fibers encasing my chest. I concentrated, not bothering to think about what I was doing. Rational thought took a back seat to the primal need to survive, even if survival might not be what you'd call comfortable.

The Shape appeared, a 3D image floating in my sight, a pattern of twisting lines and a couple of right angles. Not too complex at all. A pressure formed behind my eyes and nose, as if a head cold was barreling in, but it didn't hurt—it was something that needed to be released. I knew that if I gave it the tiniest nudge, it would do what I wanted it to do, what it had been designed for. It would *become*.

I *pushed* the Shape out and I felt the magic leave me, the pressure behind my face draining away. The effect turned out to be rather dramatic.

Magicians—the fake Houdini kind who use misdirection and illusion, not the real Bureau types like Alex and Jeanie—use something called flash paper, or nitrocellulose, also referred to as gun cotton (also used as a propellant). Flash paper burns in, well, a flash. You've seen it, no doubt. It's gaudy, quick, and the sudden burst of flame often distracts the viewer from what the magician is really doing, which is the whole point of misdirection.

All you need to make nitrocellulose is nitric acid, sulfuric acid, and cotton balls. I know this because I have a degree in chemical engineering from the University of Nebraska in Lincoln, and I like to blow things up for fun and profit. And by 'things,' I mean Supernaturals. The fun and profit part is actually incidental to my overall desire to give most Supernaturals an explosive enema.

Back to flash paper. A little heat, and *wham!* Burns quickly, almost maniacally. In the 1880s, Eastman Kodak made the first nitrocellulose film base, but it degraded quickly and had the unfortunate effect of bursting into flame when passing through a projector's film grate, which is why it's no longer used. Nitrocellulose has a low kindling point and doesn't need oxygen to burn, so you can't douse it with water to put it out. That makes handling large amounts of the stuff extremely dangerous for us happy humans.

Now, with all that in mind, consider an enormous cave— oh, say, like the one I was lying in—its walls, floor, and ceiling covered in the stuff that I certainly hoped resembled some form of gun cotton. Now imagine some moron—our favorite Finnish adventurer, for instance—setting fire to it with a crappy little cigarette lighter Spell.

As Pepé Le Pew would say, *Le Boom!*

Le ouch.

Awesome.

The flame touched the webbing, and in less than a second, it caught fire. A second after that, my body was encased in bright, orange flame, the webbing burning away in less than two seconds. Old Spidermonk made his first noise, a chittering sort of wet shriek that sounded a lot like marbles in a blender, and leapt almost straight up, disappearing into the darkness in the world's greatest standing high jump. As for me, I was curled up in a fetal position, trying to put my hair out as a flaming circle of destruction blossomed around me. Heat like I'd never known dried my eyeballs and did no good things to my exposed skin, so I covered my face with my gloved hands and lurched to my feet.

"Ghost, guide me!" I shrieked as the roaring flash of fire spread throughout the cave, traveling faster than a man could run. Faster than I could run. Good thing Ghost was on the ball.

"Go right," he buzzed over the flame. "More right. Now straight, run straight. Don't stop."

I didn't have to worry about stepping in fire; it had already burned out all around and raced ahead of me. No, I had to worry about something far worse as I kept my face covered against the heat generated by a burning cave.

Lack of oxygen.

Spidermonk's webbing might've burned like flash paper—probably not even needing oxygen to flame—but that didn't mean the fire didn't consume all available oxygen in the cave.

Within a few seconds, I was gasping and coughing, smoke scoring my lungs. All I could do was listen to Ghost because my eyes were burning, watering from the smoke, and my chest felt like hot coals were nestled into the delicate tissues inside.

"Bear left slightly."

Left, got it. I didn't reply, couldn't reply because I was starting to get dizzy as lack of oxygen started to catch up to me. I was using it up and taking none in, and I wanted to inhale, to take a big breath of air, fill my lungs to the bursting point, but I knew that would be the end of me. If smoke inhalation didn't get me, then Spidermonk would, because Supernaturals didn't go easy into that good night. He would be out there somewhere, watching, biding his time until it was safe to come in after me. Nothing would be safer than my unconscious body on the cave floor for him to munch on. Finnish take-out.

Gagging, I stumbled onward as Ghost kept me on the straight and narrow. Red and yellow flashed behind my eyelids as dizziness swept over me and my footsteps faltered. I couldn't go much farther; I was running out of gas.

"In the tunnel now, Kal," Ghost urged, almost sounding worried. "You're doing fine; keep going. I will keep you safe."

A breeze in my face and the roaring of fire at my back. A tunnel. *A tunnel!* That breeze was air flowing in, feeding the fire, and if it could feed fire, it could damn well feed me. I took a ragged, tearing gulp, and it hurt like ten-penny nails in my lungs, but it felt so good, so right so I continued to gulp, my hands still covering my face, letting Ghost guide me even though I could simply drop my arms and look around because it was easier to let someone else drive for a while, and my exposed skin hurt and the smell of burnt hair polluted my nose and I really didn't want to open my eyes because I didn't want to see how bad the damage was. I really, really, didn't want to see that at all.

The transition from stumbling along to lying on the floor was abrupt. One second I was gasping, pulling in air, the next my nose felt flattened to my face and blood slicked my teeth. A hard ache from my eyebrows to chin, hot and throbbing, told me I'd met a solid surface with the front of my skull instead the soles of my boots.

"Argh!" I sputtered, spitting blood. "Warn a guy, would you?"

"Watch out for the wall," cautioned Ghost.

If you weren't already dead, Casper …. "Don't make me call Ghostbusters." I teased my eyes open, and through a glaze of tears I saw that I lay in a hallway with tastefully recessed lighting. Nearby was a dark, wooden door with the words DERVISH INDUSTRIES engraved on a centered brass plaque.

I felt my nose. Not busted, thank goodness. I hate it when my nose breaks. My eyes swell up with big purplish bruises and my lids swell shut. We Finns bruise like bananas; handle with care.

I was up against the wall, butt on the floor and pinching my nose between thumb and forefinger to stem the bleeding. Time to check a theory. A gem from the Bat Belt, an AAAA tanzanite packed solid with a general healing spell. I let loose with the activation word.

Nada tostada. Just what I needed. "Ghost, the spell gems aren't working."

"So I surmise."

"Any ideas?"

"None."

I wiped the drying blood from my lips and unclipped my small canteen. Taking a sip of tinny water, I swished it around my mouth to rinse my teeth clean. Damn, when I hit the wall, my teeth cut into my front lip hard and it was oozing.

"How did we get here, Ghost?"

He took a second or two before answering, which was a long time for a being who measures time in picoseconds. "I do not know, Kal. One moment you were running in a tunnel of rough stone, the next you hit the wall at speed, knocking your glasses off. By the way, will you please don them again? My current perspective is the ceiling and the carpeting, which is in need of a good vacuuming."

The DRAFTlite lay on the floor, lenses to the ground and temple arms pointing at the ceiling. Too bad the microcams only pointed fore and aft. I made a note to talk to Alex about installing side cams.

"Were we in another world?" I asked after settling the glasses on my face. Ouch, the bridge of my nose was already beginning to swell. "Is that possible?"

"According to former Agent and Magician Marcin, the weak spots, a thinning of the dimensional barriers between the worlds, are all over the planet, and according to the notes I retrieved in Las Vegas, he marked a probable sight of one such weak spot in St. Louis."

Gerard Marcin. Yeah, I remembered him all right. Complete dickhead and all around assbag. He'd found a way to travel between Earth and a planet on the other side of the universe. He'd surmised that a race of ancient aliens used these weak spots to travel back and forth from their planet and ours. I guess they viewed Earth as part of an intergalactic time-share.

Marcin had used that weak spot in Vegas to travel to that other world where he set up a Roman-style coliseum, arranging gladiatorial combat for the super-rich, athletes pitted against the strange and deadly creatures that inhabited that unusual world. What Marcin hadn't expected was to be mind-controlled by the infamous Joseph Goebbels. But that's a long story, best left for another time involving time traveling Nazis and a trip back to 1943. That's where I met the woman who was to become my wife, Jeanie. Either way, I heard the Bureau and my Hollywood agent were negotiating the movie rights with Universal with Kevin Smith to direct. Should be interesting, to say the least.

The mention of the weak spots got me thinking hard, which produced a smell like burning batteries. "Ghost, you think that red orb in the lobby sucked the magic out of our gear?" I asked, rubbing the bridge of my damaged nose. "Is that how we got … ah … teleported to that cave with Spidermonk?"

"That theory is better than most, considering the fact that the gems do not work anymore."

Once I got the old noodle working, the thoughts kept coming, which posed another kind of danger altogether. "That orb and that strange fog … you remember that, right?"

"I saw what you saw, Kal, so yes."

"Did you see anything through the building's security cameras?"

"The system that operates those cameras has been compromised. Perhaps broken beyond repair. There is no Wi-Fi or hard line access to the building anymore."

Go figure. I took sip of water. How funny … just a few minutes ago, Ghost was telling me he felt disconnected from humanity, which raised the specter of world dominating-AIs, and now we were back to our old partnership, cutting through a mystery with our wits. Who says life isn't interesting?

Enough of that. "Well, that strange lightning that didn't hurt us sure seemed to like our Bat Belts. I wonder if it was siphoning the magic from our gear?"

Another one-second pause. "That seems likely."

"Hmmm. How about that?" I mused. "Supposing that's true, then that orb must've sucked in the magic from Omicron as well, which means that it doubled its magical storage in a short period of time."

"How much magic could it absorb, Kal? What were you carrying?"

Ah, there's the rub. "Ghost, I always carry a Sunfire spell just in case, as does every team leader. And a dozen other gems of varying power. But Sixer, he loved loading up on the big mojo. I checked the records of his requisition before I left." Not exactly standard procedure, but having an entire team disappear was far from standard itself. I stood slowly and my knees popped like shotgun blasts. "He checked out six PRIORITY ALPHA gems plus a LAMBDA ORANGE level gem." LAMBDA ORANGE gems were the crème de la crème, large stones containing complex spell Shapes that, while not terribly juiced with merlins (units of magic), had effects that would make the average Straight require an emergency change of underwear. One example is the Nova spell, which causes a limited chain reaction like that of a small nuclear detonation (two or three city blocks worth), but without the radiation. There are four spell Shapes that are classified LAMBDA ORANGE, and I knew that Sixer packed the most powerful one known as Tidal Wave.

"Oh my," droned Ghost. "With all those spells between two teams, there must have been at least a teramerlin of energy drawn by the orb."

At least. "Possibly two, Ghost. Alex would know for sure by checking the records and totaling the merlins. Problem is, I can't call to check."

"Kal, I have news."

The wall looked a little wobbly, so I used my back to keep it steady. "As long as it is good news."

"I am afraid not."

Awesome. I sighed. "Go ahead."

"Agent Billings' computer amulet was left behind on the 15th floor. I have re-integrated the Ghost copy and analyzed the data." Ghost paused. "It appears that Agent Billings voluntarily removed the amulet and left it behind after talking with an entity the copy could not see or hear. Perhaps Agent Billings became unstable. Either way, he is gone, and I have no means of tracking him."

Well, crap on a cracker. It would just have to be Billings now, wouldn't it? I knew he had a tenuous hold on sanity (who was I to judge?), but according to BB, he'd been solid ever since joining the Bureau, never falling prey to his darker side. I wanted him on this op because his desire to commit mayhem upon Supernaturals was equal to mine, and I didn't expect him to be the weak link. Still, it wouldn't surprise me if his mind decided to head south for the winter. Crazy is crazy, after all. "Perhaps the copy couldn't see or hear the other party or entity because it simply couldn't. Perhaps something was there for Billings to talk to. Perhaps it wanted to communicate with him and him alone." Good to have intel on Billings, but what about the others?

"Do you really think so?"

"Doesn't matter what I think; the results are the same. We have to find Billings, though." There, the wall seemed steady enough. I rose to my full height and stretched. "What about the rest of the team?"

"They are currently unaccounted for. I do know the limited range on DRAFTlite to DRAFTlite communications does not extend beyond the 18th floor. According the Quint Building layout, Dervish Industries is on the first floor, so I surmise that is where we are."

First floor? Damn ... long way to go yet and things weren't coming up roses. "So they could be in some strange world."

"Or above the eighteenth floor, yes."

"Awesome," I muttered.

At that moment, the door to Dervish Industries opened and a man stuck his head out. "What's with all the racket?"

CHAPTER TWELVE

—⬦—

Rat
Round and Round

THE SHAPE EXPLODED out from my eye, takin' form as a fireball that raced over harsh blue dust and into a critter with more tentacles than I wanted to count anytime soon. It let out a noise like a cross between a little girl's shriek and the cry of a wounded rabbit. Come to think about it, those two sounds are an awful lot alike, 'cept this was worse because somethin' that had tentacles covered in screamin' mouths shouldn't sound like that. It wasn't natural.

"Good riddance to bad rubbish," I growled, puttin' some extra oomph into my legs as they commenced to gettin' me the hell outta there.

Not that I had any place to go, really, not on a world that seemed specifically designed to kill me.

The ground underfoot sent up clouds of blue dust with every step. "Hey, Ghost-Lite, you there?"

"Where would I go, Mr. Carson?"

"Rat. Call me Rat. Everyone does." The second time I had to tell the copy to call me that. I reckoned it might be offended by the notion.

"Noted."

Ahead lay a green-water swamp with trees more like fractal nightmares. What looked like human organs hung heavy on branches that were all right angles. I wasn't about to see if they were edible; that's for sure.

In front of me was an ugly swamp, while behind came monsters.

Yeah, monsters. Really. They were the first things I saw when I woke up on this damned ... planet, or dimension or whatever.

My boots threw up clouds as I slid to a stop next water that seemed more jelly than H2O, thick and green and smellin' like heated molasses. If the Jolly Green Giant hocked up a loogie, I imagined it would look like that scummy water.

"Any ideas?" I panted, voice rough with fear. A few dozen yards away, somethin' that looked like a jellyfish the size of a forklift with a parrot's beak in the middle of its bulbous, pus-covered body hopped my way usin' razor-lined tentacles.

"My suggestion is ... not the swamp, sir," replied Ghost-Lite.

Well, whoop-dee-frickin'-doo. "Thanks for the [DELETED] obvious observation, Captain Obvious." With no time to think, I let loose with another spell. A ray of white light shot from my palm and hit the jellyfish square, freezin' it solid in less than a second. It exploded in a shower of icy fragments. Unfortunately, there were about twenty or so other monsters headin' my way as fast as they could jump, roll, run, and ooze. Disturbin' shapes that hurt to look at.

No time to lose, I began a slow run along the edge of the swamp, a pace I could keep up for hours even wearin' NewTanium armor and enough weapons to start my own war. Too bad the guns were almost useless against anythin' bigger than a bear. That's why I had to use magic, but even my magic would run out eventually. Everythin' costs somethin', even magic. Ain't nothin' for free in this world or any other.

When I woke up an hour or so ago after that big ball of red and gray gas knocked me out, it was in the middle of a flat plain of blue dust. I mean blue dust *everywhere* without a rock or pebble or even a twig to mar the overall blue sameness. And that's another thing … blue. Blue all around—the sky, the ground, everythin'. Not easy gettin' your head around where you're at when you can't tell the sky from the dirt.

Oh yeah, no sun. Nothin' to disturb that blueness. I had no idea where the light came from, but there was enough to keep the place in perpetual twilight. Enough to see by, but that was it. Still dim enough to squint.

It was after Ghost-Lite made its introductions as a construct of Ghost that the first monster attacked.

I had just risen to my feet and was studyin' the mind-numbin' sameness when I noticed movement from the corner of my eyes.

"What's that?" I asked the AI, drawin' my Glock 17 and thumbin' the safety.

"I do not know, sir," replied the program. "It looks as if something is tunneling beneath toward us."

He'd hit the nail on the head. Plumes of azure dust, three inches thick where I was standin', streamed into the air as the world's biggest gopher headed my way. Dirt rose in a mound some eight feet across and three high. Distance was tricky, considerin' the blueness, but best I could guess, it was close enough to worry me some. I aimed the Glock and fired.

Couldn't tell if I hit—too much dust and stuff—but that didn't stop me from tryin' my best to put enough rounds into whatever it was to ruin its day. The pistol had been fitted with a twenty-round mag, courtesy of the Bureau, and I emptied the whole darn thing in less than ten seconds.

I musta hit the thing because dust and dirt exploded everywhere as what was below burst free to the above world. Big as a grizzly, that thing, and I call it a *thing* because I couldn't categorize it. Think of a sponge, the natural kind that lives under the sea, not the ones you find at the grocery store, with white bony hooks all over and leprous lookin', like they was ready to rot off in a hot second. Then throw in a few dozen dark-blue cat's eyes covered in some sort of transparent, tough membrane. Got it? It's close, but not close enough to the critter that was makin' its way toward me at a good trot.

The spell that came to mind was one I'd cast dozens of times before, and it sprang into bein' so quick I could scarce believe it. Blue flame covered my fist and the heat of it almost crisped my eyeballs, but I threw it at the monster and it hit square and true. I guess it must have been bone dry because it flared up and started to burn quick, lettin' out a scream like an engine revvin' into the red line before blowin' out. Still, it stopped dead and burned, smellin' like God's own rottin' garbage heap.

That was number one. Numbers two through … well, a bunch, came a few minutes later, kickin' up more dust with the speed of their tunnelin'.

So I began to high-step it. Not much else I could do, considerin' I was facin' more critters than I wanted to and my magic could only last so long. I'm good, but not that good.

That's how I found myself puttin' one foot in front of the other, joggin' at a pace that wouldn't kill me, because if I stopped, it would be the last of Mr. Rat.

As I jogged, I drank a bit from my small canteen and chomped down a few bites of beef jerky. It wouldn't last me long, but it didn't matter much because if I couldn't find a way outta this place …. Well, you know the rest.

I left a trail of blue clouds behind me as I ran, steadily drinkin' in the dry, stale air, the cries of my hunters spurrin' me along. Hours or minutes later, I spied somethin' in the distance, a darker blue against the sameness ahead, a break from the monotony.

"Ghost-Lite, can you magnify?" I puffed. The dust was gettin' in my mouth, coatin' my teeth and tongue. *Yuck*.

The DRAFTlite zoomed in on the anomaly and my heart performed a little stutter skip. Hills, harsh and ragged, but hills nonetheless. Barren blue rock as severe as screams cut the sky at hard angles, as hard as the strange fractal trees with their human-organ fruit. I looked off to the side where the gelid green water stank its sickly sweet stink and glanced at the trees.

Gone were the kidneys and hearts and livers that had hung on the cruel branches. Instead each right-angled wooden monstrosity held a human head that dangled by hair long or short. Instead of ragged stumps, the necks ended halfway down in a smooth skin, as if they had grown there. Perhaps they had, but it was more disturbing than any bloody end. Evidence of beheadin' would mean that someone had placed them, rather than them growin' there like peaches.

Peaches. What I wouldn't give for a ripe one, sweet and soft. That got me thinking of Donna Mae Holbrook in Mrs. Harper's 10th grade English class and the way her jeans hugged her hips and the heaviness of her breasts ....

I don't know what I tripped on, but my mind's wanderin' was cut short by a mouthful of blue dust as I fell headlong, sprawling, scraping my nose on the dry, hard earth beneath the dust.

Terror flooded my senses because the monsters weren't *that* far behind and I didn't want no critter to be chompin' on my gluteus maximus anytime soon. I scrabbled to my feet and commenced to steppin' and fetchin' because the burrowin' things, the hoppin' and crawlin' things, were right behind— only a couple dozen yards. Fear did its best to get my energy levels up and I sprinted ahead a few more yards, increasin' my lead, but I couldn't keep the pace up forever, not luggin' all my gear, not sloggin' through a three-inch layer of dust.

The hills were a little closer, and I could see some details without the use of the DRAFTlite. They were as ugly as I feared, brutal-looking humps of stone that led off in the distance, parallelin' my course.

Before I knew it, the swamp became a memory, the human-head fruit from hard-angled trees fadin' behind. The critters kept comin', only now they commenced to howlin', a strange ululatin' sound like the whale song of the damned.

"How … far to … those hills?" I panted, gulpin' down more dust.

"A few hundred yards," replied Ghost-Lite. "I do hope there is shelter there."

"You … and me both, brother." A stitch began naggin' my side, pokin' pins into my skin, and the coppery taste of blood coated the back of my tongue. I musta used up most of my reserves puttin' a bigger lead on the critters after I fell. It wouldn't be long before the tank went dry. I prayed that the monsters couldn't climb worth a damn.

The closer I got to the hills, the more the details became evident, especially in the DRAFTlite. What I saw set my spirits a-plummetin'.

Those blue, harsh slabs of rock looked to be too tall and sheer for me to climb, and I was damn sure there weren't any mountain goats in my ancestry. Boulders the size of boxcars littered the sheer sides of cliffs, and even though the walls were only fifty or sixty feet high, that was fifty or sixty feet I knew I couldn't climb—so smooth were they. I also didn't have anythin' close to a levitation spell in my repertoire.

"Oh, damn," I sobbed, more afraid than I'd ever been. "Oh damn, oh damn."

Ghost-Lite cut into my pity party. "Look to center right, sir."

Center right, center right … *there*! Barely bigger than a pinprick, it grew into a manhole under the magnifyin' properties of the DRAFTlite. A split in the rock, a natural fissure that ran from top to bottom, it looked big enough for me to enter, but small enough to keep out most of the bigger critters, assumin' they couldn't flatten themselves like cockroaches.

Don't go buyin' trouble, Rat, I told myself, clingin' desperately to hope. I needed that hope because if that wasn't the way to at least a little bit of safety, I might as well pull a General Custer right here and go down hard, swingin' for the fences.

Despite the pain in my side and the taste of blood in my mouth, I put on some considerable speed, because even if those beasts could follow me into that narrow crack in the cliff, I could pick them off one by one, makin' every shot and spell count.

Sure I could.

Pant, pant, pant, pant. Damn, my lungs started hurtin' and sweat was runnin' down my face, minglin' with the blue dust and givin' me a face paint like those crazy Scots in *Braveheart.* What did they use again? Oh yeah, woad. Strange word, that. Woad … sounds like a kind of frog.

Before long I'd almost made it to the rocky hills—although 'hills' wasn't the right word because they looked like giant slabs, monoliths that had been punched down into the earth by giants. In fact, most of monoliths seemed planed and smoothed by hand, not by weather, not that there was any weather about in this blue hellhole. The boxcar-sized boulders lay strewn about and I could see where they calved from the main body of the cliff face, perhaps due to some sorta violence or maybe by the force of the blow that planted the monoliths there. Wasn't important. What was important was gettin' my narrow ass into that crevice, and it looked to be comin' up quicker than a blink. The critters behind set to howlin' even louder, which was a feat because they were puttin' out more decibels than a speed metal concert.

And I was in, pantin' and heavin' and wishin' I was anyplace else. Hell, I woulda been happy to be back at home in Jackson, Mississippi, takin' care of Dad's pawn shop and flirtin' with all the pretty girls who came in to sell their mamas' jewelry.

Damn, but those Mississippi girls could turn a head or two, let me tell you. Good Southern girls with big hearts, big smiles and even bigger—

"Mr. Rat?"

"What? Oh, yeah." Woolgatherin' at a time like this? What was wrong with me? Next thing you know I'd become a Catholic. I slowed almost to a walk and had to pick up the pace again so I could get to the dubious safety of the crevice. "Thanks."

"No problem, sir."

The narrow confines of the crevice pressed in against me as I trotted in, and immediately the world around became dark, the sourceless light not darin' to enter with me, even though the crevice was exposed to the uniform blueness of the sky. I had Ghost-Lite power up the nightvision.

The crack went farther than I thought, runnin' straight and deep as far as I could see with the DRAFTlite. Up and up went the walls—sheer, unclimbable, and dark gray in my enhanced vision. From behind I heard the howlin' of the critters, but they didn't get closer and that bothered me a bit.

I took a peek and saw strange things I can't describe hoppin' and clamorin' and tunnelin' about like their asses were on fire and their heads was catchin', but they didn't bother to come close to the crevice. That made me happy, or at least less desperate, because the only thing that would make me happy would be findin' my sorry ass back in the U.S. of A. bumping uglies with a girl with nice legs. That and a shot of Pappy Van Winkle bourbon.

"They look like they don't wanna come in," I murmured.

Ghost-Lite chimed in, "That would lead one to conclude that there is something here that they do not wish to confront."

Damn, but that burst my bubble. I spun about and saw … nothin'. My heart hammered in my chest so hard that it felt like it would burst through my ribs. I turned back to the monsters, but only saw a cloud of blue dust.

"Can you do somethin' about seein' through all that?" I asked.

Blobs of orange, red, and yellow sprang into view and near knocked me sideways. It took a few minutes for me to understand that I was lookin' at the world through the DRAFTlite's thermal vision. Shapes better left undescribed bounced and rolled and blundered all through that cyan cloud, but they didn't come too close to the crevice. One would break away from the mob of about a dozen critters, streak toward me, but stop abruptly before it got within ten feet of the cliff face.

Enough of this, I thought. *Ain't doin' myself a bit of good lollygaggin' around this place, and Daddy didn't raise no lollygaggers.*

Turning my back on the crowded scene outside, I made my way deeper into the crevice.

I went a few twisty steps before comin' to the first branch, a soft angle to the right, but I stayed on the straight-ahead path. Gettin' out of these bluffs or hills or whatever they were had to be my first priority. My breath came loud to my ears, harsh and deep, and I realized I was as scared as I'd ever been, more scared than at any other time in my life. Even more scared than when I lost my cherry to Elizabeth Moffat in 8th grade.

Elizabeth Moffat. Now there was a blast from the past, let me tell you. We were so young, but Lizzie knew what she was doin', that's for sure. *Damn*, when she touched my bare chest for the first time with her tongue I shook so much that I couldn't hardly get that condom on. But Lizzie said 'No glove, no love,' so I got it on despite my tremblin' fingers, and we commenced doin' what people had been doin' since the first of us walked upright.

"Oh, Rat, not you too!"

My skin went colder than the North Pole in January. I knew that voice, knew it better than I knew my mama's. It was Tweezer, my best friend and Omicron's Magician. What the [DELETED]?

I called out softly, "Tweeze, man, is that you?"

Somehow the voice came back to me faint but crystal clear. "You shouldn't oughta come, Rat. It's bad, worse than Truth or Consequences."

What? Truth or Consequences? My stomach performed a slow roll as another, very different, blast from the past hit my brain with the force of a thrown brick.

Truth or Consequences, New Mexico, had been a mission

requirin' two teams, one on point and the other as backup—
an op from ten months ago after the word got out about the
Bureau. The op was to track down and kill a nest of Scorpion
Men (body of a scorpion/torso, arms, and head of a man—
gross as all get out to look at) that kidnapped and presumably
ate a few of the local Straights. If it had been one, only one
team would've been needed, but reports showed that at least
eight were involved.

Thing about Scorpion men is that they like their lairs
underground, away from the hot New Mexico sun where
summer temps could reach an easy one hundred ten degrees
Fahrenheit. Team Alpha went down the hole to clean them out
and to make sure there were no more. Team Etta's job was to
hang back and provide support in case of need.

Boy, was there ever a need.

Turned out there were *thirty-two* of those chiton-plated
critters. Alpha took a pastin', losin' two guys to an ambush
when the Scorpion Men broke through a tunnel wall. Joshua
Delacroix and Peter Wynman were torn to bloody pieces by
the hyper-strong, ten-foot-tall [CENSORED] critters. Alpha
had a minigun; it was just a cryin' shame Delacroix happened
to be the one packin' it when he got killed.

T or C turned out to be a crap party that culminated in the
deaths of four Agents and the cripplin' of two others, and that
whispery voice that claimed to be Tweezer (I wasn't sure it
was old Tweeze by a damn sight, that's for sure) said this was
worse. I looked up at the narrow slice of blue sky shinin' down
between dark-blue rock and agreed wholeheartedly.

"Get out of here, Rat," said Tweezer's voice. "Get out before
you get trapped in this place forever. Before he gets you."

Before *he* gets me? "[BLEEP] my life," I muttered, shaking
my head.

Yeah, things were way worse than in Truth or Consequences.

CHAPTER THIRTEEN

～

Dove
Don't You (Forget About Me)

Summer smelled like hay and straw—musty, dusty, and slightly green. Underneath that pleasant smell lay the odor of horse manure and the ammonia stink of old urine. The ranch near Loveland spread across six hundred acres of Colorado prairie and was home to a herd of quarter horses and a handful of Arabians.

"You okay, hon'?" Dad asked, cupping my chin in the palm of his too soft hand. Hair the color of wheat fell to his shoulders, shot through with a liberal amount of gray. Heart Jacobs didn't have a mean bone in his aging body and that was reflected in the kindly smile lines around his eyes.

I nodded. "Want to stay with you, Dad. Can I, pleeease?" Like every twelve-year-old girl with her father, I went for the big doe eyes. It worked about fifty percent of the time.

This was not one of those times.

He shook his head. "Sorry hon'. I have to lay new carpet at Heritage Apartments and the company can't allow kids in the workplace. You know that."

Yeah, I did. Dad's flooring business did well, but times were just tight enough that he couldn't afford a fulltime babysitter during the busy season. Our family suffered from a common ailment at the time—being land rich and cash poor. The mortgage on our house was almost crippling, but Mom and Dad would've rather slit their wrists than leave the house their kids were born in.

"Free gets to stay with Mom," I pouted.

"Your brother is small enough not to be too much of a bother to your mom. She can stay put and look after a baby at the office, but a twelve-year-old girl is a different story altogether, right?"

My brother Free was only a few months old, an eating and pooping machine. I wanted to feel resentment that he got to stay with Mom, but Dad had a point. The office was boring and tedious and I'd go mad there because I wasn't much for sitting still or reading or behaving. Staying at the office would drive me nuts.

"You're right," I conceded meekly. Still, Uncle Carl, my mother's brother and owner of the Bar C Ranch, inspired a terror so deep in me I thought it would surely dissolve my bones.

"Okay, sweetheart." Dad smiled, too soft and trusting by half. It had been ages since he actually did any real carpet laying, having reached an age where he'd rather supervise than haul shag. "Get going. Your uncle will have lunch ready."

How could I tell him about Uncle Carl? How could I tell him that his brother-in-law liked to touch me and … do worse than that?

On trembling legs, I walked down the gravel driveway to the old ranch-style house where Uncle Carl lived. White paint faded and peeling, it looked as rundown as its owner. After Aunt Anne had died three years previously of a heart attack, he let himself slip into drink and … my mind shied away from the other things.

The sun slid across my skin—a perfect summer day and I hated it. Why should it be so nice as I approached the closest thing to a little kid's hell on earth? I tried not to cry, but with every step the lump in my throat grew bigger and the pressure behind my forehead built up, growing so much that I thought my skull would burst like a water balloon. My eyes felt hot and scratchy and the tiny tremors in my hands worsened into all-out shaking as I reached for the door.

Locked.

Oh god, no!

The front door being locked meant one thing and one thing only: he was waiting for me in the barn. The barn. The damned barn, that place where evil things took place, things I kept secret, thinks that festered inside me and grew ever more malignant, more pus-filled like an enormous abscess of horror. Soon it would rot me away and I would die, filled with maggots, my soul a gangrenous lump. I could already feel the muscles of my legs twitch and spasm, the last firing of soon-to-be-dead nerves.

The lump in my back pocket underneath my extra long T-shirt felt like a hot coal burning a hole in my left butt cheek.

Weather-beaten gray boards and a galvanized steel roof, big enough for ten horses and a couple hundred bales of hay, straw, and alfalfa. The barn loomed large and threatening. It was a structure sturdy enough to stand for another hundred years, but looked like it was ready to fall into a heap of toothpicks any second. The large sliding door was open, the rollers shining and clean in a track kept free of rust and grime.

Closer and closer I came, and with each step my heart thudded harder. A light sheen of sweat coated my skin. Any second now, any second ….

Any second.

He knew I was here. He always knew.

His hateful voice, full of thick and rotten cheer, boomed out of the open barn door. "C'mon in, Lovey-Dovey. We got some chores to do."

Chores. That's what he called it. *Chores.*

Somehow my voice emerged strong through a throat tighter than a miser's purse strings. "Coming, Uncle Carl."

Feet steady but hands trembling, I entered the cool darkness of the barn. It took a moment for my eyes to adjust.

Uncle Carl stood in the middle of the feeding stall, a large 45x15 section that took up the entirety of the right half of the first floor. The other half was divided into smaller stalls and a tack room. He held a pitchfork in one hand, the tines filthy with manure and straw. A grimy, sweat-soaked T-shirt clung to his broad chest and equally grimy jeans covered legs stronger than tree trunks. A former college linebacker, Uncle Carl was always diligent about maintaining the physical condition he had in his glory days at Baylor.

The rot and dissipation lay within.

"Just cleaning up, Lovey-Dovey," he said with his hateful, lopsided smile. Some found that mouthful of shiny teeth charming, but to me it looked broken, the grin of mentally damaged bear. "Want to grab a shovel?"

Oh, good. He wanted to work. For a few hours I would be safe. Nodding, I retrieved a spade from the tack room and began hauling manure to the compost pile in the back near the apple orchard.

It was sweaty work, but clean in a way I couldn't describe, and for a while I forgot all about Uncle Carl as I kept my focus on the horse manure and the smell of apple blossoms. The heat of the barn quickly brought sweat to my skin, soaking my T-shirt. I'd been working Uncle Carl's spread for a few years and the hard physical labor had given me muscles most boys would envy. It had made me strong, made me appreciate the effects of such clean labor.

Then two years ago had happened.

My mind shied away from the afternoon of the horror and I lost my peaceful, Zen concentration. After that the worry returned and the fear began to eat at my stomach again. The smell of apple blossoms became cloyingly sweet while the grassy smell of the manure took on a hard, almost foul stench like when I'd found a dead raccoon in the attic.

The spade became a grave load in my hand, slowing me down, and my arms shook with the strain because I knew what would happen soon. I knew the labor would end and hell would begin.

Too soon the floor was cleaned down to hard-packed earth and I rapped the spade against the ground to shake off the last flakes of manure. Next came straw, the twine on the bale having already been cut by Uncle Carl. I pulled a flat section free from the bale and broke that up, scattering it on the floor. In another couple of months it would become heavy with manure and urine and the barn would have to be mucked clean again.

Uncle Carl's long shadow fell across the floor. "Good job, Lovey-Dovey," he said softly, his grin a broken slash across a long face. "Why don't we go into the loft and play a game?"

My skin goose-pimpled and I tasted blood at the back of my throat. When it was lighthearted, when he had no time for skin, it was 'chores.' When he wanted to become penetrative, it was 'game.' I tried not to cry.

"Okay, Uncle Carl," I replied meekly, keeping my eyes fixed on the floor. The weight in my back pocket threatened to topple me over.

"Good girl."

I climbed the wooden ladder to the hayloft, which was stacked chock full of bales. The smell of alfalfa became almost overpowering and I resisted the urge to gag. At the top I found him waiting for me. His T-shirt was gone and his bare, hairy chest gleamed in the faint light. I fancied I could see the motes of dust falling through the beams of light streaming through the windows avoiding his tall muscular form as if they knew how poisonous and completely ruined he was.

"Come here, girl."

I moved closer.

"Good girl." His breathing quickened and he laid a large,

callused hand on my shoulder. It felt heavier than a boulder. "You look overheated. Why don't you take your top off?"

My eyes traveled upward, stopping briefly at his crooked smile, before meeting his. I summoned every ounce of courage in my twelve-year-old body to say, "Why don't we try something different today, Uncle Carl?" It was all I could do to keep my voice light. The smile on my face felt wooden, wrong.

He didn't see the revulsion I felt. "Ah, Lovey-Dovey, what do you have in mind?"

I shrugged out of my T-shirt, exposing my small breasts to his corrosive sight. I'd deliberately worn no bra, hoping that the sight of me would distract him, make him pliable.

Face shining with delight, he removed his hand from my shoulder, fingers twitching with eagerness.

"Now," I began, "get on your knees."

It was amazing how quickly he complied, both knees *thunking* on the floor of the loft.

The next sentence I said made me want to throw up. "I want to feel your mouth on me as I hold you."

As if captivated by a magic spell, Uncle Carl waddled forward on his knees and put his wet, horrid mouth on me. I resisted the urge to scream as I felt his lips work against my skin. I lifted my arms as he wrapped his around my torso and held tight. Slowly, so not to startle him, I put one hand around his neck as I reached into my back pocket.

"Oh, Lovey-Dovey," he moaned as his tongue darted.

"Lovey-dovey *this!*" I replied harshly as I drove the Phillips head screwdriver that had been resting in my back pocket into his neck. At first there was an initial resistance followed by a horrible *giving* as muscles honed from hard work buried steel into soft flesh.

Uncle Carl spasmed and thrashed, trying to throw me, trying to get away, but I held on tight with my other arm, burying his face in my chest as I yanked the screwdriver free with a dull popping sound and thrust it home again, this time in his ear.

He screamed.

I didn't let go and I didn't stop stabbing, stabbing, stabbing, and blood spurted, coating my hand and belly and I knew when an artery gave because suddenly red was everywhere and it was sticky, hot and thick, getting into my eyes and mouth while I yelled, rage replacing fear as years of abuse lent me strength to keep stabbing, and I did and it felt so good—the relief, the release better than anything I'd felt in a long, long time.

When it was over, Uncle Carl lay on the floor, unmoving, hazel eyes staring at the ceiling. I smiled, the blood dripping from the screwdriver and my skin. I fished into the front pocket for his cellphone and BIC lighter he used when he wanted to light up a joint. A ritual he'd always observed after a hard day's work.

"Hello, Dad?" I said into the phone when he picked up. "You'd better come over to Uncle Carl's place. There's been an accident." I hung up.

Now for a shower and a clean T-shirt. My bloody jeans would have to wait.

The barn had burned to its foundation by the time Dad arrived.

"Come back to me, Lovey-Dovey. Come back to me."

No, not again. Never again. This time I was armed with something a little more effective than a screwdriver.

I turned around and let loose with a dozen blasts from the Brave Bull auto shotgun at the Uncle Carl creature that followed me down the fleshy hall.

I'd loaded the Brave Bull with brand-new rounds called Hyperion manufactured by our Special Branch guys. With an effective range of about a hundred yards, the compounds in shell heat the buckshot to approximately five thousand degrees and create a whiteout effect in low-light conditions. Fortunately, the DRAFTlite compensated for the blinding effect of the Hyperion rounds. As for the buckshot, when they impact on human tissue at that speed in a semi-liquid state, the effects are catastrophic, to say the least.

What was left of Uncle Carl lay splattered all over the tunnel in either a red stain or a black smear of char.

Chest heaving, I stood there panting as smoke slowly exited the barrel of the Brave Bull, sweat running down my back beneath my armor. I knew that when I took it off there would come with it a serious stink.

"Gotcha, you bastard," I snarled. There were tears in my eyes that I angrily brushed away. "I'm not your little victim anymore."

"Oh, Lovey-Dovey," crooned Uncle Carl's voice. "That wasn't nice. Not nice at all."

The voice came from behind and I turned, letting loose another fusillade that blew this Uncle Carl apart just like the first one.

"So angry, my little Dovey."

After that, I went on autopilot, reloading and shooting and reloading again until the air was redolent with the faintly porky smell of burnt tissue and the odor of freshly spilled blood.

But more came.

More Uncle Carls, and my mind couldn't quite grasp it, couldn't get around the fact that no matter how many times I killed him, he kept coming back. Then, when I ran out of ammo, I had to draw the tomahawk strapped to my thigh and get to work. hacking away until my arm tired and went numb from killing him over and over again. Then I had to decide to slice my throat or let him take me.

Again. Like before.

No.

There was a third option because, according to the AI Specter, we were in the belly of the beast, and if you disturb a beast, interesting things happen. I unloaded at the wall from five feet away. I felt the heat against my exposed face, felt my hair begin to burn, but I kept firing and the fleshy rock wall started to bleed and there was a hole, a big hole, that leaked foul black fluid. From far away came the cry of an angry animal, a leviathan enraged, and I smiled through the second-degree burns on my face because if I died here, so would all the Uncle Carls and it would be over.

My hate drove me and I became it, became the loathing and revulsion at what he had done to me, at what I'd allowed him to do and that hatred sustained me as I fired the Brave Bull until there was no ammo left and the shotgun went silent. Done. I was done and I felt pretty damn good, despite the fact that there seemed to be two more Uncle Carls coming at me from opposite directions. But that was all well and good because I felt better than I had in *years*. I almost wished Alex was here so I could hold him as I watched the result of my handiwork unfold.

Through the big hole came darkness, a black fluid that flooded the tunnel, and a kind of anti-light that flowed like an angry river. But I felt no pressure against my legs, no sense of mass or matter, just the darkness, and I welcomed it, craved the release that would come from not hurting, not remembering anymore. I strode through that black river that kept rising and rising, toward the leaking hole, toward the black deluge and I walked through.

CHAPTER FOURTEEN

***

Ng
Overkill

OKAY, TIME FOR a recap. Dead and swiftly rotting blobbies all around and the mother of all hairy horrors coming my way out of the water and my hand broken so badly that it was swollen to nearly twice its normal size.

The K-bar in my hand dripped blobby blood on the tough, scrabbly grass while the rotten smell of dead things covered the still air like a blanket. Above me the night sky empty of stars stared down and I was reminded of Friedrich Nietzsche and his quote about looking into the abyss: the abyss also looks into you. Or something like that. Still, I shivered at the thought of what might be staring down on my little spot on this dark and wet world.

"Spooky, any ideas?" I asked my AI companion.

"None, I am afraid, sir." A pause, then he added in his static-y voice, "I am sorry."

The big blobby, the blobby mother, was much closer and almost a third of the way out of the water, wet tendril hair waving as if pulled by unseen currents. Thanks to the enhanced vision capabilities of the DRAFTlite, I could view the blobby mother in fine detail, as if rendered into yellow HD. Not your normal nightvision; my guess is that it was a thermal reading, or perhaps electromagnetic. Either way, the big blobby was as yellow as a canary and moving inexorably closer to my little island.

"I'm out of ammo," I muttered, staring at my swollen hand. The K-bar was gripped listlessly in the other and sweat rolled down my forehead and into my eyes, stinging.

"You have your knife," said Spooky. "A pair of belt punch-knifes, a garrote, three shuriken, and a ballistic knife. You are hardly unarmed."

A garrote wouldn't do me any good—I'd need two hands—and the punch knives were too short against the big mother blobby. But the ballistic knife ....

I fumbled for the device. It fit snugly in my palm, feeling good. A slight bit of hope bloomed in my chest. Perhaps I would live through the encounter. Perhaps I could find my way back. Perhaps.

A low chuckle hit my throat, chuffing out into the still air. My first real op as an Agent for the BSI, and it looked like it would be my last.

Finding out about the World Under and the BSI definitely changed my view of reality. Agent Alsate let me join up for the op in Chicago because I hadn't given him a choice. The murders there happened on my watch and I intended to see that the job was done, finished.

Of course I had to join the BSI. It represented the pinnacle of a career dedicated to the protection of others and the pursuit of justice. Not quite military, but more than law enforcement, being an Agent of the BSI meant that no one, anywhere, was better than you and that sounded pretty good to me.

Pride goeth before the fall and all that, right?

The first tendril from the mother blobby hit the dirt and the creature seemed to *shrug* its way onto my little island. Before I had time to think, I pressed the trigger on the ballistic knife and the small, blank pistol charge shot the knife blade out of the handle toward the large creature. With a slight *shunk* the blade buried itself deep, disappearing from view.

The effect was immediate. The mother blobby spasmed, and the tendrils, each about three feet long, withdrew, curling into the main mass of the creature. It shrunk from ten feet across to about four, less than half its original size, like a cat dunked in a tub. I knew right then and there that this was my chance.

I leapt forward, K-bar arcing in a vicious vertical slash, but before the knife connected, a tendril lashed out, smacking me right in the chest. The impact was enough to knock me back on my butt. Without thought I used my wounded hand to break my fall and the pain as the broken ends of the bones smashed together drove the light from my eyes.

When I came to, it was to the sight of the mother blobby still curled in on itself, unmoving on its end of the small island. I lay on the other. I must have been out for only a few seconds or the monster would have had me for breakfast.

"Are you all right, sir?"

"Depends on your definition," I answered, holding up my wounded hand. The fingers still looked like overstuffed sausages ready to burst through the casing of the armored glove. I was perversely glad that I couldn't see what they looked like, all purple and swollen.

Getting up took some doing, but I managed an unsteady stance and took stock of the situation. Eventually I found what I expected.

NewTanium is one of those new alloys that can be created in zero gravity because the metals can't separate. Lightweight and harder than steel, NewTanium, when covered in a Kevlar weave, can stop a 20mm round dead in its tracks, although the impact would be enough to crack a rib or two. Still, it'll keep you alive and that's what counts. Too bad it costs more than a fleet of Cadillacs to produce, but that's the beauty of paranoia and working for the BSI—we Agents get the best of everything; price is no object.

There was a hole the size of a nickel on my Kevlar chest plate, which had been torn away. The NewTanium underneath was dented in sharply, a concavity about one centimeter across and half as deep. The dent pushed sharply into my sternum—a small, silvery finger constantly poking.

"Darn it, Spooky," I breathed, "that tendril nearly broke the NewTanium!" It was far too easy to imagine what would've happened to my chest had I not been wearing the armor.

"I can see that," came the almost hesitant reply. "It would seem that this larger creature is capable of tearing you to shreds. It is fortunate that you have temporarily disabled it with your ballistic knife."

"Temporarily?"

"It seems that the creature's tendrils, which seem to be its method of locomotion, are slowly uncurling, and that in approximately two minutes it will recover enough to attack."

My testicles shrank in fear. "Any ideas? I could sure use some help right now." Spooky was right. The mother blobby seemed to be growing larger as its tendrils gradually uncoiled from its central mass.

"Hold the DRAFTlite underwater for a moment."

"What?"

"I assure you the device is water resistant."

What could I do? It's not like I had a ton of choices. The world went dark, utterly black as I took off the glasses, so dark that I couldn't see my hand in front of my face. Fortunately I didn't have to take more than two steps backward before hitting water. I knelt and submerged the glasses. After a few minutes, Spooky told me he was done. I slipped the glasses back on and once again was able to observe the world as water dripped down my neck.

"Mr. Ng," began Spooky, "using a crude form of sonar, I was able to deduce that the water plunges to several dozen feet deep. Unless you plan on removing your armor, you have no effective recourse but to engage with the large creature before it regains full mobility."

I knew what that meant and I was afraid. No … not *afraid*. Too tame a word. I was *terrified*, but for the better part of a year I'd been training to become an Agent, to be the best of the best. and that meant something to me, to be the best.

We all have those things that shake us to the core. My mother is afraid of spiders, my dad is so frightened of heights that he'll pass out if he takes a window seat on a flight to Florida, and my sister is claustrophobic. Just being near an enclosed space sends her into a tizzy.

My fear … failure.

Silly, really. Failure. Everyone fails at something; it happens all the time. Even Hakala failed from time to time, though that's not something everyone knows—him being the poster boy for the BSI and all.

Ever since I was a kid playing stickball in Brooklyn, I was afraid to fail. At *anything*. Math tests, soccer, Quantico, and even Texas hold'em at the Taj Mahal in Atlantic City. I had to win; I had to beat everyone and everything. Even when I lost, I used the experience to come back twice as hard, twice as tough, and twice as nasty so I could win, so I could beat the odds. An obsession, a fear, and the driving motivation of my life all rolled up into a greasy psychological ball and God help those who got in my way.

I even reasoned that through the BSI I might beat Death one day. Crazy, huh? Only problem was that if I lost once, it was over. No take-backs, no do-overs.

It sure looked like my ultimate failure was staring me in the face right now.

Strange thing, though. That's when the fear drained away, sluiced right on down the toilet, so to speak. Gone was the gut-watering terror. The flight reflex vanished and something else took its place, something primal that exists in the belly of all humans: the angry need to *destroy*.

Hakala called it the Rage, at least when his sister inhabited his psyche. It drove him into fits of superhuman strength and speed. I had a feeling that even though she was gone, he could still work up a good case of fury, that enough juice was left in him to allow for something … terrible. He denied it, said that the rage that fueled him passed with his sister's soul, but anyone could tell. It was there, plain as day, etched into the corners of his eyes, the fire of his irises. There was plenty of angry still to be tapped, plenty of destruction ready to be let loose.

I let loose my own well of fury, a scream fountaining from my mouth, a deep roar that shook my chest as I barreled toward the mother blobby in a mad rush, K-bar forward, ready to pierce the heart of the beast.

A tendril shot from the thing, impacting on the right deltoid plate of my armor. It felt like getting hit by a line drive at a Met's game, but I kept on, my weight and momentum keeping me on the straight and narrow as another tendril bounced off my left vambrace and the Kevlar tore with the sound of rotted cloth.

And then I was in the embrace of the beast, face first among the whipping tendrils. I was stabbing, stabbing, and stabbing some more, the K-bar becoming slick with rotting blobby blood while lines of fire blossomed across my cheeks as tendrils scored me to the bone, but I kept screaming in fury, foul blood staining my teeth and tongue. Lines of fire erupted around my skull, but the pain was nothing compared to the pain in my heart at the thought of giving up and failing. Failing …. My phobia turned to anger then violence that consumed my heart, consumed my very *being*, and I hacked and slashed and stabbed, severing tendrils and letting blood fly.

Deeper and deeper into the beast I plunged, filled with anger and hate and the drive to destroy consuming me. I knew nothing else because at the moment I *was* nothing else, no one else, the embodiment of the need to kill the thing that was grasping, tearing at me. The rotting blobby blood was thick in my nose and it covered my face, stinging the cut skin and coating the DRAFTlite so I couldn't see, but I didn't need to see because I knew where to stab and slice and I did, over and over again, and it felt good.

I was winning.

Then I was through.

Into a cold darkness that froze the breath in my lungs …. It ate at me, crystallized my eyeballs as I flailed uselessly, my hands meeting no resistance at all. No blood, no flesh, no blobby, only darkness, only freezing air that hurt my chest, my eyes, and my sinus cavities.

Time didn't exist, only the stinging cold, only the blackness, and my wild flailing as I floated/fell/moved to whatever destination awaited. I tried to breathe in the cold, but there was nothing to take in. I tried to reach for something, but my hands met no resistance, not even air, and my flesh was too numb by then to register touch anyway.

I felt my consciousness fading as my lungs burned with cold and lack of oxygen and I wondered if this was what drowning felt like. Farther and farther away went the concerns of my body and I knew the end was near. Oddly enough, the thought didn't fill me with fear. This was not a failure because I realized that dying wasn't a failure, but the inevitable end to a good fight, the last fight I would ever engage in.

I gave into the everlasting darkness and stopped flailing, peace settling over me like a blanket. I'd tried, tried to be the best and maybe for a brief moment I was, but my story looked to be over and that was okay by me.

Light stabbed me hard in the eyes, sharp and sudden. I found myself lying on my back with no transition from the blackness to where I lay. Steam wafted gently from skin and armor as a coating of frost I didn't even know I wore began to dissipate. I moved, just a fraction, and heard a hard crackling sound as rimes of ice broke.

"Wha…?" I mumbled through frozen lips as I blinked,

eyes gone cold. It took a moment for me to realize that the DRAFTlite was no longer on my face, but lying next to me, covered in frozen, black blood.

"Are you all right, sir?" buzzed Spooky's voice from the patch behind my ear. Its suddenness startled me.

I tried to find my breath in lungs stinging with frost. "Think ... so."

"I cannot see. The cameras seem to be malfunctioning."

"They're c-covered in b-b-blood," I stammered.

"That would explain it."

I was on my hands and knees, dizzy, with black spots shooting across my eyes. My stomach heaved once, twice, three times, but nothing came up except bile that burned my throat.

I wiped my lips clean, but my throat still stung, and getting to my feet took a few minutes. During the struggle to stand on shaking legs, I took a good look around. A hallway, blue carpeting, plants torn free of their pots .... It seemed familiar, and it hit me that I was in the Quint Building, back where it all started. "We're back, Spooky," I croaked.

"Back?"

"The Quint Building."

A voice, a familiar one I thought I'd never hear again, hit my ears. It was weak and hoarse, filled with a thick, phlegmy rattle but warmly welcoming nonetheless. "What took you so damn long?"

"Robert?"

CHAPTER FIFTEEN

—

Buffalo
Don't Fear the Reaper

My throat hurts—been talking too long—but things need to get said, so I'm saying them. Still, I'm out of water, so decide to give myself a bit of a breather before continuing.

But my leg still hurts.

"You could take an opiate, sir," says the AI, sounding all solicitous and whatnot, like a real person.

I shake my head, which sets my skull to pounding. Guess that hurts too. "I hate taking Oxy, or anything else for that matter. Never was a big believer in chemistry." I work up some spit and hit the wall opposite. The loogie starts to drip down, leaving a snail trail. There's some red mixed in with the milky green. "Not my style. Besides, pain teaches us something."

"And what has this pain taught you, sir?"

That one is easy. "Not to be too trusting."

The AI doesn't reply, and that's okay with me. It's not like it's really Ghost, who has a true personality and feeling and such. It's more like a cool app for your smartphone. Still, it's nice having someone, some*thing*, to talk to at the end.

"I can understand that, sir."

"Can you?" Could the AI really understand anything?

"Of course. I may be limited, but I do possess an understanding of what is referred to as the 'human condition.' "

"You have no idea how little that comforts me."

"Sarcasm?"

"Yes." I shake my head. "No. Partly."

"If it is a comfort, you do not need to recite your experiences for posterity. That is one of my functions—to record for the files of the BSI."

My chuckle hurts my chest. I check the readout on the HUD. "Only fifteen hours left and you're out of power. What happens then? Can the BSI recover the file?"

The AI pauses and I know the answer before he replies, "No."

"Okay then. Shut up and let me talk. It's therapeutic."

"Yes, sir."

Where was I? Oh yeah. I clear my throat and begin again.

The great thing about wearing high-tech superlight armor is that human teeth are really lousy at cutting through it. Not that the skinned people didn't try while they beat the hell out of me, but their teeth broke against the NewTanium plates beneath the Kevlar weave, shattering like ice cubes under a boot heel.

Still, I had a few hundred pounds of human flesh bearing down on me, dripping yellow fat everywhere and aiming for the jugular. Good thing my armor came with the standard gorget—a thin band of Kevlar-coated metal that circles the throat. Also great to have on if a vampire gets the drop on you.

Someone's front teeth slid across my cheek, slicing through, and I threw an elbow hard as I could, but in the confined space and on my knees the blow didn't do more than knock them off. My short sword was yanked from my grip, and hands tried to hold my legs and arms. Any second now I'd be immobilized, easy pickings for the skinless horde.

That got the juices flowing fast. With strength I didn't know I had, I pushed hard against the floor with my legs, quads burning, knees groaning, and *threw* the skinless off my body, knocking them aside.

Breathing room.

Training took over, that and the overwhelming need to survive. I broke arms, skulls, and knees, snapping out with furious jabs and blistering kicks. Exposed muscles tore in my gloved hands and blood flowed. But it wasn't enough. Too many more skinless were joining the mob, trying to take me down, so I did the only thing a sane man could do. I ran.

Planting a boot on the backside of one of the fallen, I leapt over the crowd, scraping my head against the ceiling even though I tried to hunch as best as I could. I left some skin behind, but I was over, knees and ankles absorbing the shock of my landing. I beat feet down the hallway, the silent skinless close on my heels.

Down the blue-carpeted hallways I ran, corporate art blurring by at furious speed and my lungs burning. I was almost spent, my strength used up under the pile of skinless and it wouldn't be long before the tank ran dry. Tears filled my eyes—just the wind irritating them. *Yeah, right.*

I needed to do something fast before those things dragged me down again. The next time I went down, there'd be no getting back up. Fervently, as my boots thumped against carpet, I wished for another gun.

If wishes were fishes ….

As I took a right, the hallway merged with the outside wall, the tall slabs of glass giving me a view of the city with the sun on the downward side of midpoint. I risked a look back to see a trio of skinless slowly gaining on me. A curse shot from my mouth. If my gran were here, she'd slap me for cussing. *Sorry, Gran.* I focused my attention to what was in front and almost didn't stop in time.

The glass to my left ended and so did the hall. A steel door, painted brown, with a heavy knob. As I careened to a stop, I saw a small sign hung at eye level that read MAINTENANCE.

Dead end. Possibly for me as well.

"You got a blueprint for the building?" I panted. "Any way out?" Damn me, why hadn't I thought of asking it before? Because I was too busy fighting skinless Supernaturals and panicking. If only I'd asked earlier.

If wishes were fishes ....

The reply was terse, as if the program was upset. "I know we are on floor twenty-eight, but for some reason the layout does not conform to the blueprints submitted to the city."

No more time.

I whirled, a punch knife in each hand protruding from between my fingers. They'd been carefully hidden to look like the buckle of the Bat Belt. I had a knife strapped to each of my calves, but the punch knives were easier to draw, faster.

The first skinless met a knife, the blade slicing through an eyeball, and I whirled to the left, throwing the corpse free and sending blood flying through the air. The second skinless had its throat sliced clean and arterial blood sprayed across my armor.

I continued my dance of death with the third, slipping past outstretched hands to drive a blade between ribs and into a heart. My left hand opened another from crotch to sternum. It died in a mushy heap of its own guts while the stench of blood and feces hit me between the eyes.

One tried to tackle me, but a knife through the nasal cavity took it down. Another tried to breathe through a second mouth. My mind detached as my consciousness took a back seat to the rhythm of murder. I sliced my way down the hall, meeting each Supernatural with skill and steel, no longer wishing for bullets and guns, no longer wishing for anything. There was no thought in that Zen place, only training, only killing, only blood. As more came, my movements became increasingly precise, each stroke perfectly delivered, each one a killing shot. They couldn't get ahold of me. I was too fast, too good, and too in the zone to be killed by the likes of them. This was what it meant to be an Agent in the BSI. This was what it meant to be an apex predator.

It felt *good*.

And then it was over. I stood in the hall, surrounded by pale, pink corpses and a whole lot of blood, the sun streaming through the glass wall, quickly drying the fluids on my armor. The janitor's closet was far behind. Somehow I'd worked my way back down the hallway, killing as I went.

In front of me were the last two skinless, a man and a woman. They stared with lidless eyes and a total lack of emotion. We regarded each other for a long moment before they turned tail and ran, leaving the bodies of their brethren behind.

The punch knives fell from nerveless fingers, hitting the floor a moment before my knees as sudden exhaustion gripped me. I knelt there amid the carnage, panting and crying as time ticked away. Tears of frustration and fatigue blurred my sight, but it didn't stop up my ears any and when they heard the words that floated down the hall, I found myself on my feet in an instant.

"Good job, Atkins."

I looked around, but the speaker must've been down the hall around the curve of the outside wall. "Who's there?" The punch knives where in my fists again and the pain and fatigue were put on the back burner while another rush of adrenaline surged through my body.

The voice, heavy and rumbly like boulders rolling down a hill, bounced off the walls. "You know me, Atkins. We came to this godforsaken building together."

Sudden relief. "Damn me, *Billings*?"

His laughter hurt my ears. "Not 'Damn Me' Billings. Just Billings."

"I've never heard you say more than a couple of words before." I looked around. "Where are you?"

"Don't worry none, Atkins. I'm coming to you."

How come that promise didn't fill me with hope? In fact, the relief I felt drained away quickly and I really regretted losing the .50 cal back when the skinless people first jumped me.

I heard heavy footsteps, the hard tread of a large man, drawing close. "Billings, where've you been?"

"Talking to a new friend."

A new friend? "What are you on about? You're making friends while I'm hip deep in Supernatural corpses?"

"What corpses?"

"Wha …?" I looked around and about had a heart attack. The skinless, the heaps of bloodied bodies, were gone. Every last one of them had disappeared as if it had never been. Still, there was plenty of evidence left behind: blood, scraps and rags of skin, yellow, waxy dollops of fat smeared into the carpet. "What happened, Billings? What did you do?"

"They didn't belong."

"Belong where?"

"In our world, dummy. They didn't belong here, so they had to go once they served their purpose."

That brought acid to my stomach. I asked, "What purpose?" while fully knowing the answer.

The reply was quick and carried a hideous mirth. I raised my fists, punch knives gleaming. "The purpose was for you to run out of bullets."

Oh, right. Of course.

Then Billings walked into view. I took an involuntary step backward, the hair on my arms standing straight up.

He still wore his armor—the lower half, leaving his massive, hairy chest bare. I thought he was big before, but now his muscles bulged with terrible purpose, veins popping in a thick web under his sweat-slick skin. The plates of his abdomen were perfectly defined, looking more … *impressive* than humanly possible. It was if some all-powerful sculptor had remodeled his body, delineating each muscle, adding to the clay of his flesh and conforming it to some Herculean ideal. Pale and perfect, appalling in its flawlessness. In one massive fist he carried a knife, no, a *dagger*. Ten inches of brutal, gleaming blade with five in the hilt. Skinny and sharp, it looked just right for either ramming through bone or slicing through soft tissue.

"Billings," I whispered just loud enough for him to hear, "what happened to you?"

The skinny knife rose, pointing at that broad expanse of chest. "Me? I met the man, Atkins."

"The what?"

"The man. *The* man." Teeth showed amidst his thicket of whiskers and the grin was more terrifying than that long knife or the new perfection of his body. "The first one ever like me. He's old, Atkins. I mean *old*." Billings took a few steps closer, approaching slowly, and I felt an icicle of fear along my back.

Whatever Billings had been, he wasn't a Bureau Agent anymore. His eyes gleamed with madness—a wet, slimy glow that told me no one in that skull was home. Whatever he'd been was gone and what had replaced him was a long ways from sane.

I took a step back, then another. "Billings, man, who're you talking about?"

He paused. "The man, the one who started it all." That great shaggy head shook and I was reminded of a St. Bernard shrugging off water. "When Cro-Magnons cowered in their caves, fearful of the horrors outside, it was the man they were really afraid of. Does that tell you something, Atkins?"

"It tells me you haven't been free with a name."

A shrug, a slight lifting of broad shoulders. "What's in a name? But if it suits you, call him Angel of Mass Murder, the Saint of Slaying, the Shrieking Sphere, or the Blackened Cenotaph. He has so many names, but those are the oldest, most revered names that have been ascribed to him. Be that as it may, he's *the* serial killer, the very first to grace mankind with his attention, and he is more powerful than you can imagine."

As he spoke, Billings continued to walk toward me, the slim knife raised to waist level. I kept retreating until my back thumped gently against the maintenance door. Nowhere to run and a maniac ahead of me. Things weren't looking up.

"Now hold on, man," I began, raising fists laden with punch knives.

Billings continued, "He's teaching me. I'm his apprentice." The smile on his face became more and more terrifying and I felt the flat plates of my abdomen clench painfully. "I get to be what he is, if I try hard enough, and brother, I can try harder than *anyone!*"

Before the last syllable left his mouth, I was in motion, sprinting toward the perfectly muscled madman in an effort to catch him off guard.

It didn't work.

A fist the size of a small ham slammed into my breastplate. The NewTanium creaked alarmingly, and I flew backward, the wind knocked clear out of my lungs, to land on blood-soaked carpeting. It felt like getting hit with a cloth-wrapped bowling ball.

The ache went from front to back, from crown to balls, and it curled me up like a shrimp on a hot plate.

I knew what was coming, and even though blinded by tears, I reacted, my boots kicking out at knee height, or so I thought.

Both heels connected to Kevlar-covered greaves and Billings feet left the floor. Next thing I knew a couple hundred pounds of crazy Agent fell on me like a ton of bricks with a very pointy knife heading toward my kidneys.

The first thrust skittered off one of the NewTanium side plates, saving my organs, and second thrust was thwarted by the vambrace on my arm. The thrust was *wicked*. I felt the NewTanium dimple where the tip of the dagger hit, and I knew it had bruised the flesh underneath. It had me wishing for ibuprofen.

If wishes were fishes ….

I rolled out from under just as Billings thrust again, but the knife hit carpeting, giving me just enough time to scissor to my feet and back up, shoulders hitting the wall and fists up, ready for action.

Billings, despite the size of his meticulously sculptured torso, moved quickly, scrambling to his feet and twirling his body my way.

"Damn, you're good," he purred through the tangle of his beard, "but I'm better."

My growl matched his bottomless well of a voice. "Shut up and show me, assbag."

And the games began.

The long knife blurred toward my throat, but my throat wasn't there to meet it. Instead I juked to the side and swiped my fist diagonally down his torso, opening pale skin from collarbone to bellybutton.

Blood fountained for a fraction of a second before flesh knit and the slash disappeared—the blood coating Billings' torso the only evidence it'd ever been hurt.

He laughed low and I knew I was in deep.

Fear is a good motivator; it pumps adrenaline into your system so your reactions are faster and sharper, but it can also kill. It can cause you to freeze so the killing blow can land. I couldn't afford to freeze, although I had plenty of fear juicing my body. I had to use what advantages I could to stay alive— stay alive and *win*.

Billings was big. He was strong. He could punch a good dent into NewTanium without shattering the bones of his hand, but he lacked the one thing I had in droves, and that was speed. In my line of work, speed is eighty percent of survival. Luck is the other twenty. Somewhere in there, skill plays a part, but I'd rather be fast and lucky than skilled and clever.

If he got ahold of me, I was toast, but I didn't let him. Every thrust was met by air. Every swipe of that knife cut only the light from the recessed bulbs.

I jabbed, driving a knife into a shoulder. The wound closed within seconds, but blood flowed. A fist full of steel came my way, but I blocked, which was a mistake because the force of his blow threw me back against the wall, and the fight nearly ended right then and there. Good thing for me I was fast, fast enough to keep jabbing and jabbing, hoping that blood loss would weaken him.

I kind of doubted it, though.

I did have another plan, because this couldn't go on forever. He was strong, stronger than a man of his size should be—almost silverback-gorilla strong—and that scared the holy heck out of me. Soon he would arrive at a certain conclusion, the only logical one in this fight, because he couldn't catch me. There was plenty of room in the hallway for me to stick and move, stick and move, peppering him with punch knife jabs that would wear on him. I had to be ready.

And it happened, almost quicker than I thought it would. The long knife flew from his hand, end over end and straight for my head. I knew he expected me to dodge or duck out of the way, but I didn't. Instead, I raised a forearm and let my armor absorb the blow—although it hurt. He was *that* strong.

Billings came in, trying for a grapple so he could squeeze the life out of me, using only brute strength. I let him grab hold of my right shoulder with his left hand in preparation for throwing me to the ground and finishing the job.

I didn't let him. My left arm blurred, fast and low. One, two, three times, and I finished with a deep jab and a twist while my right hand came up in an uppercut that took him under the chin.

"Gaaaahhhkkk!" cried Billings as I pulled the punch knives free. His eyes grew wide as blood spilled from the hole I opened behind his chin and intestines spilled through the gaping rents in his torso to land in great purple coils on the floor.

I knew he'd heal quick, so I lunged, ready to plant a knife through an eye or slice across a throat, but my leg folded under me and I spilled to the floor. Sudden pain brought tears to my eyes and pain to the base of my skull that shot up from my left thigh, white-hot and piercing. My hands encountered the hilt of a knife.

Big sonofabitch had another knife. A K-bar by the look of the hilt.

Oh, damn. Blood was *gushing* from beneath the hilt. Must have hit the artery, the big one, whatchamacallit? Oh yeah, the femoral. Cut it good, judging by the quantity of blood. Hurt like a bitch, too, the pain not letting up at all.

Had to tie it up, use a 'turkey neck,' as my gran used to say.

Billings moaned, blood drooling from his lips as I slid the Bat Belt free of its pouches and tied it around my thigh. He stumbled down the hall, guts trailing behind, and I wondered if his stomach would heal with his intestines hanging out and all. Hoped so; that would serve him right.

"Your vitals are rather alarming, Mr. Atkins."

I stared at the blood flowing around the hilt of the knife. "You don't say?"

And that's what happened.

My leg hurts so much. The blood is still flowing, although it oozes now instead of spurts and there's the taste of it in my mouth.

The air five feet away rips like rotten cheesecloth, a tear from floor to ceiling, and the edges fade to nothing as a jagged blackness appears between the lips of ragged reality. Cold blasts from the black, cold like the bottom of the ocean, like the absence of even the *thought* of heat. The blood soaking my armor freezes, cracking and crackling. I can see my frail breath.

And Ng falls out of the black. The tear closes up behind him without a sound.

Gosh, he looks like hell. Face all cut up like someone took a razor to it. He kneels there, arms wrapped around his torso looking beat, so exhausted I can feel it like heat radiating from his skin. He doesn't see me, but that's okay.

He's back. One of the team. Back from God knows where, and it's good to see him. I'm so grateful that my eyes water and the tears trickle down my cheeks.

It feels good, but I'm so tired. Warm blood from inside thaws the icy crust around the knife.

I guess this is the end for me. It's not so bad. It's a lot like going to sleep, like … slipping into a warm bath. It's not ….

CHAPTER SIXTEEN

Rat
You Can't Always Get What You Want

I KEPT GOING, deep into the crevice, which turned out to be a maze—a gloomy one with sheer walls and the stale smell of dust in the air. I was still haunted by the fading echoes of Tweezer's voice, but I couldn't let the other Magician distract me because it might not be him. If it wasn't, then this was a helluva trap, and sometimes the only way get out of one is to spring it.

Half my problem, I thought, was the lack of color. Any pair of nightvision glasses, be it tech or magic, turns the world into a monochromatic nightmare that gives the viewer an astoundin' headache if used too long. Like the doozy I was pickin' up starting right behind my left eyeball and runnin' up my forehead, across my skull and down to the nape of my neck.

Standard to all Agents is a first aid kit. Sounds simple enough, right? Bandages, alcohol wipes, an aspirin or two. You'd be dead wrong there because the main thing in the first aid kit is a spell gem for pain. The Shape in the gem could give hours of pain-free mobility and relief, even in the case of a broken bone, although that's plenty dangerous enough because the ability to feel pain keeps us from harmin' those hurt places even more. However, sometimes you gotta keep motorin' on without distractions. First aid kits measure about five-by-five inches and fit snug into a thigh pouch. Besides a gem for pain, there are also some interestin' pharmaceuticals that would fetch a pretty penny on the street, like Oxy.

Oxycodone can knock you clean on your ass if you're not careful, but at that point, I was far past bein' careful considerin' the day I was havin'. One pill was all I needed and twenty minutes later I coulda bit my own lips off and not have minded one bit. It brought more than just pain relief because I wanted to conserve my magic just in case there were more beasties waitin' for me deeper in this maze of rock.

During that twenty minutes I didn't see a damn thing but more crevice, more turns and whatnot, oftentimes findin' a dead end and havin' to double back. Each corner I took, each new path, I looked up, hopin' to see somethin' new, perhaps a handhold or crack I could use to climb outta that damn place, to get to the top of the planed monoliths. On the top of these great slabs of blue rock I might find safety, respite, and brother, was I ever in need.

"C'mon, Tweeze," I implored quietly, more to myself than anyone else. "Talk to me so I can find you."

It might not have been Tweezer who talked to me, luring me in deeper and deeper, but whoever it was knew about Truth or Consequences, so I was willin' to go on a little faith. Soon enough the voice came back.

"*Go away, Rat. You're going to die if he gets his hands on you.*" The strange acoustics of the maze brought Tweeze's voice right to my ears.

"Don't care," I muttered, not really speakin' to the voice. Where was I goin' to go? Behind me, beyond the maze of the crevice, was blue dust and a bunch of pug-ugly monsters that wanted to snack on my fritters. No way I was goin' to let that happen, let me tell you.

So I walked on all low and slow, a 9mm in one hand and a

K-bar in the other, ready to do somebody wrong if they looked to harm me. All I encountered was more crevice, a darker blue against the robin's egg color of the sky.

Deeper and deeper I went, sometimes havin' to double back at a dead end or where fallin' rocks blocked the way. Part of me wanted to study the monoliths, to see what made up the aggregate. The nerdy geology nut that lived inside my brain was yellin' at me to check the edges of splintered rock for quartz or mica. It'd been years since Geology 101, but I still had the bug. I guess if I hadn't been a Magician, I woulda wound up workin' for some oil company in Texas or thereabouts, tellin' the higher-ups where to drill. Woulda been a lot less dangerous than castin' spells for the BSI. Definitely more borin', that's for sure.

And there he was.

Boy, there he was. My stomach commenced to flip-floppin' all around the moment I made that last turn and saw him there up on the sheer wall of the dead end.

Old Tweeze kinda looked like a punk kid, but he'd been through modified SEAL trainin' like me, so there was grit and gristle coverin' his bones. He could take care of himself just fine, but whatever or whoever did that thing had made him helpless as a child. Both arms were sunk up to the shoulders in the crevice wall, as well as both legs up to the knees. The result was a man hangin' about five feet up facing out, looking like a human pillow tacked up there. Tweeze's chest was thrust out, forced that way by his arms bein' buried so deep. His legs couldn't move an inch because of how solidly they were anchored. It took a moment for me to realize that—he was hangin' there so awkward and all. He was strugglin' to breathe, the weight of his body draggin' on his diaphragm. It reminded me of those old-time stories of the Romans crucifyin' people, how they died of asphyxiation instead of blood loss or pain.

Like Tweeze was fixin' to do.

His eyes met mine and he undulated slightly, flexin' his

thighs so that his body rode up a bit higher. His wince told me it hurt his shoulders some, but it provided his lungs much-needed relief so he could speak. His armor had been cut from his body, and whoever had done it did a piss-poor job. They'd cut him up a treat. The thin wounds had long since scabbed over, and he'd been left with nothing for modesty. His twig and berries hung for all in this damned world to see.

Gathering a painful breath, he said, "Run, you [BLEEP]ing idiot. Run."

Those words lacked the energy of urgency. He couldn't afford it, I think.

"I ain't runnin' nowhere, dude." Eyes peeled … had to keep my eyes peeled because I couldn't let fatigue blind me. This was the part, if it was a movie, where the bad guy sprung his trap—perfect spot for it—a dead end some fifteen feet wide and twenty deep with Tweeze at the end playin' the role of a hunk of tasty cheese. Perhaps cheddar.

"He's gonna kill you, Rat." That hurt for him to say. I could see the effort drainin' him.

"Who is this dude, anyway?" I held up a hand. "Never mind, save your breath."

"It's the Killing Man, the Angel of Mass Murder. He's after us. All of us." *Gasp, wheeze.* "Especially us Magicians."

I approached slowly, lookin' out for booby traps, and came close enough to Tweeze that I could see the individual drops of sweat fallin' from his chin.

"Stay away!" he hollered weakly.

"Not gonna happen, buddy," I replied. "Know just the spell to get you outta there. Gonna crumble that stone into powder."

A half-hitch of a sob, but no answer. Instead he sagged, fallin' as far forward as he could, which wasn't a whole helluva lot. Then I saw what he'd been tryin' to say, but had been too hurt and exhausted.

Where the flesh of his shoulders met stone, instead of a crack or hole where his arms were inserted, there was a seamless transition between flesh and rock, as if his body had been sculpted to the wall.

"How is that [CENSORED] possible?" I breathed, more than a little horrified. I mean, I could see the area of demarcation from skin to stone, but there was no cutoff. It was as if he was slowly *becomin'* one with the monolith. Same with his legs. They blended seamlessly into the rock, which was flesh-toned about a centimeter away from the surface. "This can't be, Tweeze. You should be formin' blood clots, havin' strokes, all sorts of bad things. What's been done to you is medically impossible."

That got me a tired laugh. "Jesus, Rat, this guy can do anything. He sucks the magic out of things. He about drained me dry and left me here to hang." Tweeze panted, pushin' himself with his legs so his lungs could fill with air. "He escaped his cage and is loose again on the world, man. Last time he got out, he went to Colombia and taught a thing or two to a couple of followers who turned out to be the nastiest serial killers ever, but he got caught and was stuffed back into his cell for a couple of decades. Now he's out and he's *hungry.*"

Exhausted, Tweeze slumped and winced. How he could stand such torture was beyond me.

"Don't talk, dude," I told him, heart hammerin'. "Save your breath." My mind raced through its library of spells until the right one popped into place. "I think I gotta spell that will put all this to rights."

"Too late," he whispered. "Too late. Get out." His face spasmed and he bared his teeth, the large muscles at the corners of his jaw bunchin' fiercely as pain racked him. "To get out, you haveta go through ... although it might kill you slow."

The next words were lost as he vomited spiders onto his chest.

Yeah, *spiders.* They came pourin' out of his mouth as he made a *hrrrruuukin'* sound. Little bitty spiders half the size of a dime—brown and black bodies all covered in gut slime—fell to dusty ground or clung to his bare chest.

Before I could do some serious barfin' myself, the skin of his abdomen began to ripple like it was a sheet hangin' on a clothesline.

I turned away, stomach roilin', only to see some dude standin' 'bout fifteen feet away, a strange little smile puckerin' his long face.

What can I say about the weirdo except he was wearin' some old-timey sorta fancy duds. You know, the kind worn in all those Sherlock Holmes movies and such. Heck, he even wore a *top hat* made of silk.

His face never seemed to come into focus, but that smile still haunts me.

"You seem quite distressed," he remarked, smilin' wide.

I reckoned he was the one Tweeze referred to as the Killin' Man. "Get him down offa there!" I yelled, seein' three kinds of red.

He cocked his head to the right. "Now why would I do that?"

"This is his world, Rat," wheezed Tweeze from behind me. "His ... personal little snow globe."

My pistol came up faster than thought, but he disappeared so quickly I didn't even see him go.

"Now that's unsportsmanlike, Mr. Rat," said the man from somewhere I couldn't see, although his voice came at me loud and clear.

I looked back to see the skin over Tweeze's belly begin to split. Tiny spiders commenced to boil outta the wound. I could see my friend was in too much pain, his face all contorted every which way, to muster up a scream.

"Fix him!" I yelled.

"No."

Ghost-Lite cut in, "Who are you talking to?"

"*Shut up,*" I subvocaled, lowering the pistol. "Please." Down to beggin', but I wasn't too proud. Anythin' to save my friend.

"Use your magic. Free him with a spell."

Good idea. I squinted, fixing a Shape firmly in my mind.

"NOOOO!!!" Tweeze's scream came from the very depths of his tortured spirit as he gagged on spiders. "He wants you to! He'll drain you."

Drain me? I took a few moments to chew that over and realized that if the fancy man drained Tweeze, it was because my buddy had used magic and then had it sucked right out of him. Not all of it or he'd be dead, but enough to weaken him. Enough to make him a victim.

[DELETED] that noise.

I let loose with a spell, aiming at one of Tweeze's shoulders, and the stone around his upper torso began to disintegrate as even tinier spiders began to leak from his penis. Larger ones, the size of half-dollar coins, emerged from … from … well, it's best not to say.

Tweeze's left shoulder came loose, causin' his body to sag toward the right, and I caught sight of somethin' that froze my tummy up solid. Where his left arm used to be ended in a jagged stump about two inches from his armpit. Instead of bright arterial blood there came a spurtin' of little brown and black spiders so small they looked more like motes of dust instead of insects.

"Jesus, oh bloody Jesus Christ!"

What I had to do came to me in a flash, somethin' that if I was in Tweeze's place, I'd want him to do.

The pistol in my hand barked twice, both rounds hittin' Tweeze above the eyeballs. He slumped.

"Too bad about your friend."

I didn't bother to turn around. I watched spiders boil from my friend's body. "You gonna kill me like you killed him?"

"He chose the wrong path."

"And what path leads to life, I'm wonderin'?"

"Follow me. Give me your magic freely and you will live. Choose the other path and your fate will be worse than your friend's."

I watched the spiders begin to eat, and a tear slipped down

my face. Cryin' for my friend. Cryin' for me too, I reckon.

Soft footsteps, barely a whisper through the blue dust. "You have no idea, *boy*, who you face, do you? I was walking this earth when your ancestors scribbled paintings on cave walls with their own feces. I've faced kings, queens, emperors, and they all bowed down to me."

A hand with slender fingers appeared at the corner of my eye and touched my shoulder lightly, like a butterfly's kiss. "But you, ah … you have potential, boy. You have it in you to be one of the greats, perhaps even the greatest." I felt his mouth draw near. "And all you have to do is freely give me your magic. It's just that simple."

We all make sacrifices to get what we want, but what do you do when you have everythin' that defines you? I had my magic and the pleasure of castin' spells was somethin' that no one besides another Magician could understand. Magic is a lover that never demanded anythin' of me except to use it. Never got jealous, or mad, or even slapped me in the face when I was caught in a compromisin' position. It was like water or air and it was always *there* for me.

Simple, eh? This Angel of Mass Murder might as well have asked me to bite off my own head.

As I stared at Tweeze's body pissing spiders into the dust, I finally made the connections he wanted me to make. The answer to the riddle of this place—how to get out—and I smiled sadly.

"You know what, Mr. Killin' man?"

"What?" Air hissed across my ears.

"Sometimes you just don't get what you want." And I was movin' and hustlin', steppin' on spiders that *squished* under my boots most satisfactorily. When I made it to ol' Tweeze's body, I grabbed hold of his ripplin' skin and pulled. It tore like wet, rotted cotton, and spiders poured out all over me, skitterin' every which way, gettin' into my hair, my eyes, and my mouth. I bit down, crunchin' chiton and spittin' out nasty goo that tasted like bad eggs and I kept pullin' and pullin' until Tweeze was wide open while the spiders bit at me and I bit back. Just ahead there was blackness, a void that sucked at me and the spiders, and I jumped in just as somethin' sharp skittered off the back plate of my armor. I laughed as I fell, along with about a zillion spiders, into darkness so complete and cold that it ate at my mind like a hungry shark.

I fell and fell and fell, but I didn't mind because I was outta there, out of the blue world, the Killin' Man's personal little snow globe, as Tweeze called it.

Just as I was ready to commence dyin', the world opened up all around me and I landed hard on short-pile carpetin' the color of sky as the sun dips below the horizon. It clean knocked the wind outta me, and I lay there gaspin' as little frozen spiders rained down around me. Steam began to rise from my skin as I warmed up.

Eventually I made it into a sittin' position.

"We seem to be back in our world," said Ghost-Lite unnecessarily.

I nodded, still catchin' the breath that I'd lost back in the dark.

"Mr. Ng and Ms. Jacobs seem to be near our location. I can lead you to them when you are able, sir."

Yeah, fine. Whatever.

I couldn't say the words. I could only hope he understood my nod, and as I sat there, the enormity of what I'd experienced finally caught up with me. My friend, my best friend, was dead. Dead by my hand.

My chest hitched. Then it heaved as tears blurred my vision. I cried like a little boy who'd lost his parents. Cried for what I had lost amidst a scatterin' of dead spiders.

CHAPTER SEVENTEEN

Kal
Nothing Else Matters

"You, sir," said the man from Dervish Industries doorway, "are you well?"

That was definitely debatable. "As good as can be expected, I guess."

The man looked me up and down, noting my singed hair and all-around dishevelment. "If you say so." He squinted. "Hey, I know you. You're that Kal Hakala guy from television. Saw you on *Ellen*." A well-manicured hand appeared, beckoning. "You want a drink?"

What could I say? "If you have soda pop, I have a thirst."

The door opened wide. "I have everything. Come on in."

I followed, taking in my host's appearance. A tall man, a shade under my six-four, slender and lithe. Jet-black hair combed back from a high forehead over glittering dark eyes and an aquiline nose. Movie star quality, this one. In fact, he was so good looking it was intimidating. Best thing to counter all the handsome was an industrial accident. Women dig scars, right?

With a nod and a smile, he led me past the reception area

(plain, almost Spartan, with only a desk) and into the back office where he conducted his business.

In contrast the main office was crowded with some lavish touches. A long rectangular redwood desk fronted by plush leather chairs graced the far end to the right, while a floor-to-ceiling wall-to-wall bookcase occupied the other end. The long wall was hung with Monet knockoffs, although they were damn good ones. *Woman with a parasol, Bain à la Grenouillère,* and *Poppy Field.* What struck me as odd was the addition of Tintoretto's *The Descent into Hell.*

I shook my head. *It takes all kinds,* I thought, stepping onto Berber carpeting that wasn't quite white, and on closer inspection was hand-looped wool. To my left, opposite the bookcase wall, was a small kitchenette with granite countertops and ironwood cabinets. The fridge stood flush against the wall and the flat-range had been designed to blend into the granite. A cappuccino maker most baristas would sell their least-favorite grandmother for gleamed near the fridge, shining pile of potential energy ready to turn kinetic in the creation of a truly superb cup of coffee. I felt my mouth start to water.

It was to this wonderful machine that the man traveled.

"I love me a good cup of coffee. You want one? You can have the soft drink after if you wish."

Oh, twist my arm just a little bit more. "You talked me into it." I guess it was habit, but I checked all corners of the room for Supernatural and non-Supernatural lurkers. Just in case.

The man caught my eye and grinned. "A healthy dose of paranoia. I like that." A heavenly, almost earthy aroma hit my nostrils as he spooned fresh-ground coffee into the brewing cup. Pressing the button, he said, "Cappuccino or espresso?"

"Espresso, please." I had the feeling that we were in the midst of some sort of ritual and that to stray from its course would be more than a little awkward.

"Man after my own heart. Milk ruins the pure taste of the bean. Don't you agree?" His voice induced a subtle harmony that took the worry out of my muscles, and I began to feel the tensions of the day ebb away.

"Yes. Yes I do."

Chung, hiss, whirr. "Do you know the secret to a great cup of coffee, Mr. Hakala?"

I was impressed. He pronounced my name correctly, accent on the first syllable. Most people screw that right up. "It's in the grind. Always in the grind."

That earned me a big smile. "Well, well, well, look at the smart BSI Agent. Just for that you can have seconds."

His patronizing attitude grated, but the divine smell of coffee erased any irritation. Hell, right then I would've tap-danced, jugged, and voted Republican for a decent cup of joe. A couple minutes later and the complex ceremony of coffee making was complete.

A demitasse cup settled in the palm of my hand and I raised it in a salute to my host. He raised his back and we both slammed the small amount of liquid down. It hit my throat like liquid fire, a hard burn that seared me down to the core. Viscous, heavy, rich as Iowa soil, it left sharp bitterness on the back of my tongue that faded to a light sweetness. Overall the finish was smooth and polished, as if crafted by hand rather than grown on a bush in Hawaiian soil.

"Good grief," I breathed. "Can't get enough of a good Kona coffee."

My host smiled. "You know your brews, Mr. Hakala."

I could feel the caffeine enter my bloodstream and the warmth in my tummy spread both north and south. I nodded.

"Wonderful." He took the cup from my hand and placed both in the granite countertop. "Allow me to introduce myself." He offered his hand and I grasped it. Firm, but no hard calluses. It was no stranger to manicures. "I am Orson. R. Nias, Esquire, at your service, sir."

"I'm not a sir. I work for a living." The words came out automatically, and I wished I could take them back. No need to be rude. "Nice to meet you, too."

Orson dropped my hand and gestured toward one of the leather chairs. "Have a seat."

He sat behind the desk, leaning back with hands behind his head while I sat like a supplicant awaiting the king's pleasure. I was acutely aware of my ragged appearance and the coffee wasn't the only thing with a strong aroma. To be perfectly honest, I didn't know why I sat there so easily while the rest of my team faced God-knows-what. I think I needed a break after the horrors I'd endured. Or perhaps I needed a measure of sanity, an island of reason in an op gone sideways.

"So here we are," said Orson, in an effort to start the conversational ball rolling.

I decided to let it roll to me. "Why are you here? I thought the building had been evacuated."

Perfectly arched eyebrows rose. "You mean because of the ghost, or haunt, or whatever?"

"Yeah."

"I have a business to run."

"The power was cut."

A quirky smile. "Not my power. There are ways around such things."

"What do you do?"

"Asset reacquisition."

"What?"

Orson dipped a hand into an open drawer and withdrew it, clutching two cigars. "Cuban. Care to try one?"

What the hell, I thought, reaching for the cigar. *Man's gotta have a vice or two.* I'd given up drinking, choosing the high road now that I was a father, and womanizing had gone out the door the second I hooked up with a Magician who could turn those who irritated her into Spam.

A box flew my way and I caught it by reflex. "Use these. Wooden matches preserve the flavor. Allow me to demonstrate." With a flick of a thumbnail, Orson lit a match and ran the flame slowly along the length of the cigar clamped firmly between his teeth. "The heat awakens the flavor," he mumbled before lighting the end and drawing deep. "Don't take it into your lungs." Smoke swirled from his lips. "Hold it in your mouth for a moment and then blow it out."

I did as instructed, the thick smoke curling around my tongue like a vaporous serpent. Ash, grass, and hay slicked the back of my tongue. After a fourth draw, I tasted leather and espresso, just the tiniest amounts, as if they'd been added as an afterthought. It wasn't my first cigar, but it was the first cigar that didn't taste like I'd inhaled a hot turd. The quality of this tobacco was so high that even a guy as flush as me would balk at the price. I had a kid to put through college eventually and I reckoned that by the time he went, an ivy league school might cost six figures a semester.

"Good, eh?"

"Good, yes." Another puff. "But you've avoided answering my question."

"No flies on you."

"Nope." I waited a moment, matching him stare for stare, and I've been stared at by the best. BB has been known to make grown men cry without saying a blessed word. The man could give a cobra a heart attack.

As the staring contest went on, I realized that he knew the old adage as well as I: 'The first to talk, loses.'

Orson buckled first, but not without tossing me a toothy grin that said he was conceding the point out of respect. That guy could give a shark lessons on smiling. "All right, Mr. Hakala. May I call you Kal? Or Kalevi?"

"Kal is fine."

He grinned that white and inviting grin once again and tossed me another cigar, which I stored in the Bat Belt. "Here's an extra. For luck. Okay, Kal it is, then. Asset reacquisition … where do I start?" He blew a flawless smoke ring. It hung in the air for several seconds before dissipating. "When my company loses a valuable asset, such as property or personnel, my boss, the president of the company, tasks me to reacquire that asset."

Hmmm. I raised an eyebrow and he raised his. Damn, he was *good.* "What if an asset, say a person, doesn't want to rejoin your company?"

He tossed more silky laughter my way. "Kal, they *always* come back. Each and every one. It's simply a matter of incentive."

"And Dervish Industries has enough capital to afford ludicrous incentives?"

That earned me a flat stare. I was reminded of the Kipling story "Rikki-Tikki-Tavi." Set in India, it's about a British family in India who adopts a mongoose as a pet. Of course, this being India, you can't have a mongoose story without a cobra.

This one has two. Nag and his mate, Nagaina. Long story short, it's an animals' version of *Beowulf.* Well, I watched the animated version when I was eight. Orson's stare reminded me of Nag and Nagaina's. Flat and deadly, as emotionless as a manhole cover. I repressed a shiver.

And quick as a wink, the stare became warm and human again, filled with good cheer. "Kal, Dervish Industries is so rich I can't tell you. Safe to say that if we wanted to, we could buy Bolivia and have change left over for Paraguay."

I whistled. Not bad at all. "So why are you on the first floor and all? Seems kind of pedestrian for a hotshot lawyer and asset reacquisition guy and all. I had this pegged for a top-floor penthouse kind of outfit."

"My nose has been in it since the beginning, Kal, and that's how the president likes it. I can't say I disagree with him at all, considering he's a genius."

"Soooo ... a smart guy?"

"You've heard of Plato, Aristotle, and Socrates?"

I knew what was coming. "Yep."

"Morons."

" 'Never go in against the Sicilian ...' " I quoted.

" 'When death is on the line,' " he finished.

I raised my cigar in a salute, which he returned. Nice to

know I wasn't the only one who enjoyed the classics. "You were talking about having your nose in it from the beginning?"

Orson nodded. "Any idiot can sit on high, lording over the ants below. I consider that to be plain lazy. It takes a person with vision to get on the ground floor or lower and *work*. Get down, get dirty, get in the game—that's what I say. Let the real-estate multi-millionaires lounge about in their eight-figure penthouses surrounded by their frescoes and murals and gold doors. The real work is on the bottom floor. It always has been."

There wasn't much I could say, so I sat there and puffed on my Cuban cigar and pondered his words. On one hand, it sounded pretty effective—get down with the people and toil away in the really real world—but something about his speech and tone of voice put me off. I sensed condescension behind them, almost contempt. I shrugged. Maybe it was because he was lawyer.

"What about you, Kal?"

Put on the brakes. Bring brain back online. Whew. About lost myself in daydream land. I shouldn't think too much. I'm not equipped for it. "What about me? My job *is* the ground floor."

"Fair enough. What about the places you work?"

"What about them?"

He smiled around his cigar. "What do you know about St. Louis, Kal?"

"It's got an arch. Probably someday it'll have two and they'll be painted yellow and tower above the world's biggest fast-food joint."

Orson stood and walked over to the Tintoretto, touching the ornate frame at the bottom right corner. *The Descent into Hell* became a window looking out on St. Louis from a height of about a thousand feet. The city sprawled out from the river like an oil stain, and the late afternoon sun shone down in sepia tones through wispy clouds.

"A picture?" I asked as I joined him in front of the screen.

"A live feed. I like to be able to view the city in real time."

"Cute."

My host puffed on his cigar. "This city was founded in 1794 by Auguste Chouteau and Pierre Laciede. They named it after Louis IX. Unfortunately for the French, the region on which it stands was ceded to Spain, spoils of the Seven Years' War. It remained part of Spanish Louisiana until 1802. Napoleon acquired the territory in the Third Treaty of San Ildefonso, so once again it came under French control. You have, of course, heard of the Louisiana Purchase?"

I nodded. "Of course."

"In 1803 Napoleon sold the Louisiana Territory, all 828,000 square miles of it, to the United states for fifty million francs. The United States also forgave France's debts worth some eighteen million francs. That's a grand total of *sixty-eight million* francs. In today's dollars that's roughly two-hundred thirty-six million dollars." Orson shook his head in admiration. "That's one *hell* of a good deal. For the U.S., that is."

The math was a bit of a pain, but I got there. "That's less than fifty cents an acre."

"Right you are, Kal. Right you are." He inhaled sharply. "This is a great city, a city of *commerce*. It's home to corporations like Monsanto, Peabody Energy, Express Scripts, Ralcorp, and a few others."

"Not to mention the Rams, the Cardinals, and the St. Louis Blues."

"You *do* know something about the city, then."

"I watch ESPN every now and then."

A slim finger pointed at the screen. "What do you know about that, Kal?"

I gave the Gateway Arch a look, manfully resisting the temptation to repeat my fast-food joke. "Nada."

"Did you know that that six-hundred-thirty-foot arch is the tallest monument in the Western Hemisphere and the tallest building in the city? Did you know it's also the world's tallest arch? It's a monument to the westward expansion of the

United States, a representation of Manifest Destiny." The last two words were accompanied by a snort of cigar smoke. For a moment, I imagined his eyes gleamed red. I blinked and the illusion disappeared.

Manifest Destiny, the belief that the American people were sanctioned by God to claim the entire continent because of their special virtues—their love of liberty and justice and desire to remake the West.

What a crock. The only thing that the conquering of the West showed was that if a technologically superior expansionist people were to butt heads with a technologically *inferior* one, then the technologically inferior people would be swept away. Just look at the Roman Empire. If it hadn't rotted away from the inside and remained a true republic, we'd all be speaking Latin and wearing togas.

Still, the arch did look cool.

There must have been a look of distaste on my face because Orson bellowed with laughter, eyes screwed almost shut in mirth. "Oh, you don't believe in Manifest Destiny, do you?"

I shook my head.

It took a minute for his humor to drain away, and when it did he said, "Manifest Destiny, real or not, is what made America what it is today." He went back to staring at the real-time feed. "Damn, I love this city. It's vibrant, alive in a way the really big metropolises are not. It has a dynamic I can't describe, except to say that the people here are both jaded and trusting, emotional yet pragmatic."

Uncomfortable with the tack this conversation was taking, I decided to switch it up. "Why are you still here, Orson? There's one heck of a badass Supernatural out there and it's dangerous. I'd advise you to leave, but it looks like we're stuck here for a bit."

"You mean that ugly shrieking orb," he said, not looking away.

"You've seen it?" The hair on my arms stood up. How come

this guy was still sane? Then again, maybe he wasn't.

A nod. "Briefly. It doesn't seem interested in me. Perhaps I'm lucky."

"Still, you should get out of here at the first opportunity."

"Nah. I've got work to do. There's a particularly slippery asset I'm looking to land, an employee who left the firm, absconding with some very valuable intelligence. It's my job to retrieve that data and bring the employee back into the fold."

I felt a tingle at the back of my neck like I was being watched. Or conned. "Why would you offer a thief his or her old job back, Orson?"

"Sounds odd, doesn't it?"

"More than a little."

"This particular asset, a *he*, by the way, has a very valuable skill set we wish to take advantage of. Unique, in fact. He decided to leave our employ despite having some time left on his contract. It's not often you find someone with such valuable abilities."

"So he's in breach."

"Yes. And he is in hiding, although we have a good idea where. When I find him, I will impress upon him that he should fulfill his obligations as stated and that the alternatives would be unpleasant. The president is a man who always adheres to the letter of any agreement he enters into and he expects others to demonstrate the same level of dedication and honor."

I puffed on my cigar for a moment. Yep, the leather and espresso taste became thicker and more pronounced the more I smoked. "He sounds like a hard man, your president."

Orson nodded. "He can be, but he's fair and he lives by a code of honor. He believes in keeping one's word." He gestured toward the feed. "That is a code most of them would do well to emulate."

Them?

Before I could ask, Orson turned his gaze my way. His eyes were frozen marbles set in granite. Once again the image of the cobras Nag and Nagaina flashed through my mind. "I know how bad it is out there for you and your team, Agent Hakala. That orb killed the previous team, I believe. While I am safe in my little slice of reality here, you are not, so you'd best leave and keep moving. I suggest the freight elevator; it runs on a separate system and can access any floor."

For the first time since I'd met the man, Ghost chimed in. "There is no freight elevator indicated on the Quint Building blueprints, Kal." He sounded annoyed.

I mentioned the blueprints to Orson. He just smiled slightly, his face thawing. "A late addition by Mr. Quint, who rarely follows the letter of the law in such things, although all his builds are up to code. I believe the elevator was meant for his use alone, but he cannot hide his intentions from Dervish Industries." Again with the cobra stare. "I will supply you with the requisite data. One moment please."

He went back to the desk and another drawer, where he removed a large tablet. Inserting a thumb drive, he tapped away for a few minutes then removed the drive, tossing it to me.

"Thanks," I said, tucking the drive into my Bat Belt.

Orson sat down and set his cigar in a crystal ashtray I hadn't noticed before. "Good luck to you, Agent Hakala." A dismissal, albeit one with a smile and a wave.

"Good day to you, Mr. Nias."

As I turned to the door, he delivered one more parting shot. "If you ever decide to retire from the Bureau, we could use a man like you, Kal. We can offer you a compensation package like no other."

"I'll think about it."

"Please do."

Puffing my cigar, I left.

CHAPTER EIGHTEEN

Kal
I'm Sexy and I Know It

"**M**R. NIAS WAS very forthcoming."

I nodded at Ghost's observation, but said nothing. Instead I placed the thumb drive on the flat of the DRAFTlite amulet and tapped the DOWNLOAD icon on the HUD. Less than a second later, Ghost had the file.

"There is indeed a freight elevator," he droned. "The plan was never filed with the city. Mr. Quint, it seems, engaged in a certain level of naughtiness."

"Gee, a rich guy ignoring the rules," I said drily. "What a concept. I'm flabbergasted ... truly. Where is this elevator?"

Before I finished talking, the HUD lit up with a schematic—a diagram of the first floor and a blinking red dot indicating my destination. Another dot, this time blue, appeared with the words YOU ARE HERE blinking alongside. Just before I touched the CLOSE icon, I caught sight of some writing on the lower left-hand corner. It read 'Blueprints for Dummies.'

I fingered the amulet that contained all of Ghost and the vast knowledge he had collected throughout the years. "How would you like it if I turned you into an ashtray?"

No reply. I wasn't serious, anyway.

Half the Cuban clamped between my teeth, I headed toward the elevator. A few minutes later I found it, artfully disguised as a maintenance closet at the end of a hall. It was locked, but picks are standard issue, and classes on how to pick every lock from 1865 on up are mandatory for all BSI Agents. The company that built this lock had mad skills, but mine were madder, and it yielded like a disgraced televangelist.

The inside rocked me back on my heels. I'd seen some weird stuff in my time, but this rated at #3 right under the mission where I encountered the Talking Chicken of Tulsa. (Please don't ask. I still get night-sweats.)

Think black paint—a whole heaping lot of it, glossy and slick—add black shag carpeting, then mix in a pair of black leather La-Z-Boy recliners and a black mini-bar. Get the picture?

But I'm not done.

"What in the name of the Holy Hand Grenade of Antioch is going on here?" I muttered, feeling my eyes open wider and wider.

For once, Ghost was stumped and kept his electric trap firmly shut. Not that I could blame him one iota. The place looked like a cross between an S&M parlor and Aleister Crowley's wet dream all stuffed in an elevator the size of my pre-teen bedroom. The walls, the black shag, the mini-bar, and even the leather recliners were covered with fine silver markings, cabbalistic symbols looping and whorling, gleaming with argent potency. Each symbol seemed to shine, giving off a hazy, off-white light that was both comforting and repellant.

I recognized pentagrams and a Star of David or two mixed in with Hebrew, Chinese, and Arabic letters. My fingers hovered over a series of symbols that took up most of the left-hand wall.

"If I'm not mistaken, these are Enochian."

Ghost replied, "That is correct."

Back in the late 16th century, mystics John Dee and Edward Kelly revealed a language they said was given to them by angels.

A divine language used in pure magic, the first language, the one used in the Garden, also called Celestial Speech.

I took a closer look and something about this wall struck me as strange. Not pausing lest I reconsider, I drew my Bowie and ran the blade against the black paint. Slivers of black peeled away exposing … silver.

"Jeez, Ghost, this wall is silver … *pure* silver." What I thought had been paint turned out to be metal, a few thousand dollars' worth. The silver was cool to the touch and the exposed portion seemed to glow brighter than the symbols.

"What the hell is going on here? Who did this?"

"Well, I hesitate to guess," Ghost said. "But considering that this is the Quint Building and Tobias Quint did not submit the plans for the elevator to the city, then it follows that Tobias Quint is responsible."

Tobias Quint, eccentric gazillionaire whose buildings sprouted up from the skin of the world like carbuncles—just the type of creep to come up with this idea. "Well, whatever, but this wall is silver and it's definitely glowing, so it has to be magic. Magic isn't quite in my wheelhouse, Ghost, but it's in yours. Can you make out what these symbols mean … what they say?"

"It seems to be a summoning, albeit a poorly worded one."

That didn't sound good. I took a drag of ashy air. Realizing the cigar was out, I concentrated and lit the Cuban with the Zippo spell. Redolent smoke began to fill the elevator as I stared all around. Although registering as a Magician hadn't quite been made into law due to issues of civil liberty, the Bureau kept a weather eye out for new talent. Magicians didn't *have* to work for the government, but most did, either in think tanks or for the Bureau itself. The government wasn't above offering a ludicrous salary in order to corner the market on Magicians. However, those who worked for corporations had almost as much money as the U.S., and this sure looked to be the work of a half-baked individual with a smattering of talent.

It wouldn't be long now before the market in magic would grow in proportion to the demand, and there were always those willing to take advantage. Greed is a powerful motivator.

Awesome.

"Summoning what?" I asked.

"It reads 'For to be having the pleasure of man immortal' … something something something … 'with the power of fertile loins' … something … 'unending servitude to the whims of the caller, the builder of cities.' "

" 'Something something something'?"

"Whoever wrote this had a poor understanding of Enochian and so it was quite difficult to translate," sniffed Ghost. "Much of this is rubbish—cabbalistic symbols that mean nothing— but when viewed as a whole, the writings form a pattern."

Pattern?

"I suggest taking a few steps back, Kal. Out of the elevator."

Why not? I stepped back, puffing contentedly, and waited.

And waited some more. *Puff puff.* "What am I looking at, Ghost?"

"Wait for it."

Sigh. I hated it when I had to figure things out on my own. Too much like work. Still, I complied and stared at the open elevator car with its black paint and walls of silver, the runes and symbols and writings running every which way like a satanic set created by hysterical hamsters.

Pattern? No pattern, none that I could see, but I trusted Ghost, a being who couldn't think slow on his worst days (and this might have been one of them). He and I had traveled through time, been in deep doo-doo on more occasions than I can count, and of all the Supernaturals in the world, he was the one I could call a friend. (I don't count the Brownies who were washing my boy's dirty diapers. Trust me, I'm glad to buy them enough milk to avoid *that* job, and eco-friendly disposable diapers and diaper services are far more expensive.)

Grayish smoke swirled in front of my eyes and I blinked rapidly and waved it away, hoping to ease the sting. When I aimed my eyes back at the elevator car, I caught a glimpse of something, a half-seen image that disappeared the second I focused my gaze. It reminded me of one of those pictures made of colored dots that, when you stare at it long enough, reveals numbers or letters or a picture of a sailboat. I'd seen those things dozens of times and I knew the trick to bringing the image forth: relax your eyes, let them focus on nothing at all, and what is hidden comes forth.

And there it was.

A pattern, all right. A spell Shape. When viewed at the right angle, with the eyes relaxed just *so*, the lines of letters took on an almost holographic aspect, becoming a three-dimensional representation of a spell. The sigils and runes seemed to leap at me, parts of looping lines and angles that didn't conform to conventional reality. Silver bars of light intersected every surface—from the chairs and fridge to the silver thread on the carpeting—and they were *beautiful*. I'd only recently popped my magical cherry thanks to the departure of my sister's soul from mine, but I'd been around spell Shapes for over a decade. I'd seen my fair share, from the ugly to the sublime, but where many of those looked to be the equivalent of a Jackson Pollock painting, this one was a Pissarro, a Van Gogh, and a Monet all wrapped up into one.

"My God," I whispered, "it's *beautiful*." Yet the total Shape of it eluded me. The spell was far too complex and I wasn't a strong enough Magician. I had no doubt that Jeanie or Alex could grasp it, understand the subtleties and nuances of the spell, but for Mama Hakala's blond-haired boy, comprehension remained out of reach.

Then I blinked and it was gone. "Ghost, did you see that?"

"Yes, I did, and although I am not a Magician, I must say that it was one of the most intricate Shapes I have ever seen."

I tried to relax my eyes, but they couldn't recall the shape, and I felt like I'd lost something precious. "I wonder what it does."

"Hey, mister, can you help me?"

Okay, I didn't *quite* scream like a little girl, but I managed a draw my Bowie knife with credible speed and whirl toward the threat.

A small girl. Well, nix that. More like a sixteen-year-old waif type with long, curly hair the color of walnuts and big eyes like one of those anime characters. Blue jeans stuck like flypaper on coltish legs over Converse clad feet. She wrung her hands, fingers twining in the cotton of her black Jay Z T-shirt.

"Who are you?" I barked.

She flinched, and I immediately felt like a world-class heel. "I'm Austin," she said meekly, obviously afraid. Okay, now I'd been upgraded to galaxy-class heel.

I toned down the hostile. "What are you doing here, Austin?"

"Been here for a couple of days now." Her eyes were fixed on the Bowie and I reluctantly sheathed the knife. I've never stuck a blade into a woman before—blown one's head off, but she was all bad and had it coming.

Keeping my voice low and soft, as if talking to a skittish Collie, I said, "Austin, why didn't you evacuate like all the others in the building?"

Tears formed in those huge eyes, and my heart did a little stutter-step. "I fell asleep in my mom's office on the third floor." More wringing of her small, dainty hands. There was something uniquely fragile and brittle about the girl and I stifled the desire to give her big hug. "When I woke, I heard gunshots and a terrible screaming and I ran and ran and hid because I knew bad things were happening."

Bad things, all right. "You best get along. You know where Dervish Industries is located?"

She nodded.

"Good." I took a couple of slow steps so as not to spook her. "You find it and take refuge inside. There's a man named Mr. Nias there; you tell him Kal sent you."

Eyes the color of … honestly, I couldn't tell what color they were except that they were deep and haunting and they flew open, wide with wonder. "You're Kal Hakala, the guy from the BSI, right?"

I nodded. "Yes, hon, that's right. Now you get right along and I'll collect you when I'm done here."

All fear gone, she darted forward and took my hands in hers. They were warm and soft and felt like silk. "That is so cool. I get to meet Kal Hakala himself! You know, you're better looking than that guy who played you in the movie."

Damn, but she was a looker. Pert nose and luscious lips ready to be kissed and bitten and I felt something stirring deep inside, a primal desire that brought heat to the back of my eyeballs. "Uh, miss, ah …?"

A small finger touched my lips and the sensation was electric, sending a thrill down to parts best left unmentioned here. "Shhhh, no names. Let's make this fun, like strangers meeting at a bar. It lends … spice to the situation."

Gone was the teeny-bop bubblegum high-school girl with the waifish looks. What stood in her place was sex incarnate, lust on a stick, a hormone-inducing harlot with puffy, sex-ready lips and eyes large enough to drown in. Her scent, reminiscent of spice and nutmeg, brought fire to the groin and drove rational thought from the brain. The only thing that mattered was her, the only thing in the universe for me was the desire to taste her, to lick the sweat from her neck and pull her close, so close that our flesh would meld as one and then we would ….

"Kal?"

The drone interrupted my fantasy, but the girl's lips were right there and it would be *so* easy to kiss them.

"Kal?"

Arrrgh! "What is it, Ghost?" The fog still shrouded my brain, but his voice cut through like a knife.

"This is not like you."

No, this was *exactly* like me, glands and all, and I told him so.

"What about Jeanie?"

What about her?

"Who are you talking to, lover?" purred the girl. *Girl, hell.* She was a flat-out, full-figured, ready-to-go *woman*. Nothing delicate about his flower. She was primed for the pump and ready for the Finnish Love Machine. She snuggled close, fitting along the contours of my body, and the funny thing was that she was a bit taller than I remembered, the top of her head coming to my cheek, her breath hot on my skin. I pulled her close and a spot of heat started up on my chest, right next to my flesh. Her hands traced circles on my back, and I could feel her fingertips through my armor. The hot spot on my chest grew in intensity as I moved my lips toward hers until, right before I was about to taste those ruby wonders, the heat suddenly flashed into a searing pain that caused me to stumble back.

The girl advanced, hands held out to cup my face. "What's wrong, dear? Here, let me kiss your boo-boo."

Oh, I wanted my boo-boo kissed something bad, but my chest was on fire and I reached under my armor to find out what was causing it. My gloved fingers closed on something hard and I pulled.

It popped out, a shinny bauble on a gold chain, and the girl shrieked in horror. "What is that?"

And I knew. I *knew*. I knew what she was, what she had done to me and what she nearly did and my flesh began to crawl. The realization worked like a cold shower and my libido took a nosedive. "One thing about being famous: you meet famous people." It hung from between my fingers, the most beautiful thing I'd seen in ages—a little gold cross. A ruby chip gleamed where the crossbars met. "For example ... the pope. You know him, don't you?" I spoke faster and faster as fear rushed through my veins. *So close.* "The High Pontiff, the Vicar of Christ, the guy with the pointy hat. *That* guy. Turns out he was impressed with my exploits and came to America just to visit little ol' me." Despite Mom being a devout Lutheran, she was impressed with the man's humility and innate grace. They spent half an afternoon drinking tea and eating scones. It was all very *Downton Abbey*. That is, if *Downton Abbey* included a roomful of Swiss Guards looking like blond Schwarzenegger clones. "One of his gifts was this … blessed it with his own two hands." I stared at the cross, so plain, so perfect. "Best. Christmas. Gift. *Ever*."

"Keep it away," she hissed, face not so pretty now.

I held it out. "Now why would I want to do that?"

Stupid, stupid, stupid, *stupid*. Never take the time to gloat, never revel in that 'I just escaped certain death' feeling because it allows the baddie to come up with a new fiendish plan.

Or you relax your guard.

One minute the girl—somehow I doubted her name was Austin; call it a hunch—cowered ten feet away, the next, as if not bothering to travel through the space between us, she was there, right in my face.

A small fist hit me square in the chest plate and the NewTanium crumpled, sending me flying back and bouncing down the hall like a stone skipping atop a still pond. The first bounce hurt; the second was just insulting. Fortunately a wall stopped me. Unfortunately I slammed into it hard enough to crack sheetrock.

"Uhhhhaaahhh," I moaned as bits of powdered drywall floated down around me.

Suddenly I was airborne, held there by the girl, who stared at me with eyes turned opalescent. Those eyes were fixed on the glowing cross, the chain tangled around my fingers. "It makes me uncomfortable, but I can abide."

Gone was any sense of feminine grace. Instead, what stood there had skin blacker than the most heinous sin, lips red as blood, and silver teeth like slickly shining knives. The gray tongue inside her head was forked; it curled lazily about those red lips like a grub worm.

As for me, I could barely move my right arm, the one holding onto the cross, but that wasn't important. The important thing was I could move my left.

The demon shook me violently. I felt like a rat in a terrier's jaws. "You are such a weak little thing."

Every shake sent nails of pain through the base of my neck, but I held on until she stopped. "Tell me something, succubus," I slurred, "are you knife-proof?"

Shhkk.

The Bowie sank nine inches into her gut. Forcing it in that far felt like stabbing a slab of quickly setting cement. Her reaction was about what you'd expect. With a curse that blistered my ears, the succubus again threw me across the hall, but this time I managed not to hit any walls. It was all net. By the time I rolled to a stop, the demon was halfway to me, taking her own sweet time.

"You think mere mortal steel can hurt me?" she growled, every stride sultry. She was still sexy, despite her demonic form and color. "I have outlasted empires, little man. I shall certainly outlast you." The Bowie stuck out of her belly and bobbed with every step. She gave it no mind; heck, it didn't even look like it hurt.

I spat blood. "Mortal steel, huh?" My teeth had cut the inside of my bottom lip and it bled freely, the swelling slurring my words. "How about steel that's been blessed by the pope?" I looked down at the knife in her gut, one of the other gifts from the man with the pointy hat.

That stopped her cold. She stared at the protruding knife, opal eyes widening in alarm. With a flick she tried to pull it out, but it wouldn't budge. Snarling, she used both hands. No dice; the Bowie remained stubbornly in place.

"The great thing about blessed weapons," I said—God, my head hurt—"is that they can be blessed to have different effects.

It all depends on the faith of the clergy blessing them." And let me tell you, the pope turned out to be holier and humbler than I'd expected. Normally I wouldn't trust most preachy types farther than I could throw a forklift, but this guy practically radiated holiness.

"This one, you see, will stay with you until the job is done." The hallway tilted alarmingly. "You'll see."

And she did. It began slowly because the succubus was a creature of pure sin and evil; the divine blessing had a lot to fight against. A low hum, almost too low to hear, elicited a grunt, but the effect was electric. She arched her back, arms flying out to both sides with fingers spread as if she'd stepped on a live wire, mouth agape in shock, her gray tongue flailing at the air. The humming grew louder and higher pitched, and soon I could see the Bowie vibrating like a tuning fork, the five inches of exposed blade glowing a subtle blue. Louder and louder, but what was louder still was the shriek from her mouth as foul, black ichor erupted from between her lips to stain the ceiling. It was a fountain of evil, of sin, erupting in an ever mightier torrent. The thick stuff threatened to flood the entire hallway and drown me.

Dang, my head hurts so much. That was my last thought before I slipped away into oblivion.

CHAPTER NINETEEN

—∾—

Kal
Nine Years Ago
Sweet Home Chicago

"**T**HIS IS MORE than a simple demonic incursion," said
Brute, a man even bigger than myself, with shoulders
so wide he had to enter most doors sideways. If you crudely
carved a chunk of granite to represent the stern face of a Greek
Titan, you'd come close to his harsh aspect. No one tangled ass
with Brute more than once and those who did, assuming they
could walk afterward, never wanted to mess with him again.
"The fact that the demon didn't destroy the body is telling.
When we get into the museum, we'll investigate the scene. All
security guards have been sent home so we'll have the place
to ourselves. As far as anyone is concerned, we're the FBI
investigating a serial killer.

"I'm sorry you all had to be recalled from vacation, but there
is a massive incursion in Yellowstone National Park that's tying
up eight teams, and the ninth, Team Alpha, just returned from
a bug hunt in Texas and are shagged out. So it's up to us to take
care of this shindig in Chicago. That's why this impromptu
meeting. For obvious reasons, we couldn't hold our orientation
in O'Hare. Take a look at the pictures."

As one, the team looked at their Slates, the first-gen tablets available only to the BSI, and stared at the death displayed in garish colors.

Team Epsilon had some new faces now that Mace, Winch, and Canton's contracts had run out and they'd chosen not to renew. Mouth was still there, however, and still sexy as hell, even though her colorful vocabulary could blister the paint off a house. Alongside were Renee Ledoux (Frenchy) and Archie Gambon (Growler)—our team Sniper and nondenominational cleric, respectively. It's always good to have a person of cloth when dealing with creatures from the darker corners of the World Under and the Pit.

The Slate showed the body of a young man, early twenties, thin and sporting a shock of wild black hair. There were burn marks on his bare torso, so very dark against the pale flesh. Arlo Teague, security guard at the Field Museum in Chicago, looked as if death had come as a surprise. His mouth gaped open in a howl of either pain or despair. Maybe both.

"Burns look like handprints," I said.

Mouth grinned. "Thank you, Captain Obvious."

I gave her a baleful glare, which slipped off the shield of her indifference. She wasn't rattled by much except spiders and situations that demanded proper social etiquette.

Only Brute's lips moved when he answered; the rest of his massive face remained still. "That's why this is a BSI op. The only Supernatural I know of that can leave handprints burned into flesh, besides an afrit, is a demon."

"Why can't it be an afrit?" asked Growler, scratching his dark buzz cut.

Brute stretched, taking up most of the van with his near seven-foot frame. "Because an afrit would've burned down the museum by now. They have very little self-control when it comes to setting things on fire." I nodded in agreement. Everyone who'd studied Supernaturals would know that. If it were an afrit, half of Chicago would be a smoking ruin. "So as far as we're concerned this is a demon hunt. Keep your holy water and crosses at hand and hope for the best. I consider it a stroke of luck that Otto caught wind of this at all."

Otto was the quasi-intelligent computer program that hunted the Internet and media for clues to Supernatural incursions. Pretty neat to belong to an organization that had the resources to do whatever necessary to combat the Supernatural threat, although Otto seemed more akin to Big Brother than I was comfortable with.

I'd dealt with demons before, and if you came out on the wrong end, the best you could hope for was to be bitten in half by something that had the toothy hardware of an adult great white shark. The worst … well, imagine your worst nightmares. I shook my head slightly as the van rolled to a stop. I hated demons almost as much as I hated vampires. A few seconds later the side door slid open, revealing our team Magician. "Let's get going, ladies," Waldo Horner groused around the stub of an ugly cigar resembling a dog turd. The tubby little Magician always seemed to be in a bad mood. Perhaps he was angry with his parents for naming him Waldo. "The great city of Chicago awaits, and the sooner we're done, the sooner I can get laid."

"So you *did* pack your roofies," cracked Mouth as she gracefully exited, racking her Slate next to the door.

"Hardy-har, Ms. Laugh Riot," came the response. Even Waldo, a Magician with enough power to shove a lightning bolt up your ass, didn't have cojones to take on Mouth. There weren't many who could beat her at hand-to-hand.

I racked my Slate next to hers and exited. Before us lay the stairs that led up to the gargantuan Greco-Roman edifice that was the Field Museum of Natural History.

If Julius Caesar were to walk out of a wormhole in time, he'd probably think he was in Greece, or a palace in Capua, or perhaps Pompeii. That is, until he took a gander at the bright lights of downtown Chicago with its towers of glass and steel, the Shedd Aquarium to the northeast, and the ginormous expanse of Lake Michigan a few hundred feet away, just beyond the aquarium. Not to mention Soldier Field to the south. Somehow I don't think he would've been a Bears fan. Perhaps the Titans.

Banners were hung between the four giant columns out front, proclaiming 'Jerusalem Exhibit, One Week Only!' and 'Mysteries of the Ancient World.' Hokey, but they piqued my interest. I'm a sucker for history, the creepier and more arcane the better.

In fact, by researching the past I had possibly learned how to kill a god—that is, if I could figure out how to cross its path again.

The five of us gathered around Brute, who proceeded to break us up into pairs. (He'd refused the names Hulk and Fezzik, but grudgingly accepted Brute. He *was* the Brute Squad.)

"These are your buddies. Stick to each other like glue. Kal, you're with me." He loomed over us, appearing even larger in his Kevlar/Titanium black armor that looked like it belonged on some futuristic Knight Templar. "Mr. Teague was killed near the new Jerusalem Exhibit, so we'll hit that first. We'll case the place for a while, but after a couple of hours we'll break up into our pairs and canvass the rest of the museum. From this point on, everything is subvocal, and if I hear different, I'm gonna grind someone's bones to make my bread. *Capisce?*"

We capisced.

"Okay, let's go." A hand the size of a dinner plate plopped onto my shoulder with enough force to make titanium groan. "Hang back, Kal. I want to talk to you."

Good grief. When someone says that to me, it usually means some fecal mass is tumbling in my direction on an inclined plane. I'm not saying I got into a lot of trouble, but … well, yeah, I guess I did.

I watched the others ascend the steps and wished I could join them. "Sure, boss." What else could I say?

Brute steered me up the steps, his brow furrowed as he

chose his words carefully. "Took a look at your evaluations. Top marks in problem solving, linear thinking, and combat skills. In fact, the Bureau thinks you are the most obsessive Agent in years because you spend more time boning up on Supernaturals than you do anything else."

"But ...."

"What?"

I gave him a look. "But?" There was always a 'but.' A big, hairy one, usually.

He nodded. "It seems the docs think you're just a gnat's whisker away from flipping crazy as a bedbug."

Oh, that. Well, that wasn't news by a long shot. To say I had anger issues was like saying the sun was of decent size. My rage, a sort of semi-controlled berserking, gave me near inhuman strength and speed, which came in handy when fighting Things That Go Bump In The Night, but could be considered a liability when socializing with others. Fortunately I seemed to be able to control it somewhat and had not yet hurt a fellow Agent.

Yet. That little word worried the Bureau no end and gave me many a sleepless night.

Those huge fingers of his applied what he must've thought was gentle pressure, but to me felt like an industrial press squeezing my shoulder into paste. "You don't have anything to say for yourself?"

One thing about the Bureau—they're always testing you. Hell, everything is a test because we Agents are in the thick of things, wielding incredible power and often trampling civil liberties to dust in the name of keeping the Straights safe. Many find our actions somewhat reprehensible—the whole 'ends never justifying the means' argument and so on—but those people have never been on the wrong side of a rampaging ogre or a praying mantis the size of a locomotive. I never liked bending the Constitution into new and interesting shapes, but then again, technically, I never had. The Straights had never heard of Amendment 5A, the secret clause where for the Bureau and the Bureau alone, due process is suspended in case of Supernatural Incursion. Not something they teach in grade school, but it's a powerful law enforcement tool when needed.

The look in Brute's eyes and the more-than-casual way he spoke was the first clue that this was a test, the second being that there is *always* a test. "What can I say?" I replied, not bothering to defend myself. There can be no defense against the facts, and I had a sneaking suspicion he'd be able to sniff out what came out of the south end of a northbound bull. "I am what I am and the Bureau knows it. The Director chose to keep me employed instead of tossing me out on a Section Eight. Until *that* time comes, I am going to keep on killing Supernaturals and taking names."

"Until you find it."

Uh-oh.

So that's what this was all about. It. IT. Iku-Turso, the Finnish demigod who killed my sister all those years ago. The memory was still a white-hot splinter of pain in the back of my brain that never failed to raise my blood pressure to the boiling point, and this time was no different. He wanted to know about my obsession with Iku-Turso, if it had limits (it did not) and if I would pursue the demigod's end. (I would … vigorously and without mercy.)

Every Agent could read their comrades' files; it was an issue of trust and transparency. You had to know whom you were going to fight side by side with, who had your back and who might not. Needless to say, everyone in the Bureau knew about my brush with a Class Five Supernatural. I held myself in check and gave Brute another honest answer.

"It might take a while, Brute, but I'm going to find a way to kill Iku-Turso, and then I am out of here to turn it into calamari. Nothing and no one is going to stop me. Is that what you wanted to hear?"

The boss slowed, pausing at the midway point on the stairs.

At the top, the team waited patiently. I could tell by the way Mouth's head was cocked that she was concerned. Up in the sky, what stars I could see through the light pollution stared down coldly, indifferent in their celestial sockets, while nearby harsh halogens cast shadows along the stairs, extensions of myself connected at the feet.

"If it was my sister, I'd do the same thing."

I felt my eyebrow try to become one with my hairline.

He chuckled, a sound like the rumble of rocks in a dry well. "I gotta hand it to you, Hakala, you got balls." We continued up the stairs, him with a patient, almost kind look on his craggy face and me trying not to pass out from the pressure of his big hand. "For a second I thought you was going to give me some BS, but you didn't, and that makes you okay in my book."

Thank God for small favors. "What is this about, boss?"

A sigh, deep and long. "It's about this being my last op. My contract is done at the end of the month and I am not re-upping."

"And …?"

"And I'm going to recommend to BB that you become the next leader of Team Epsilon."

Bowl me over with a feather. Knock me down and call me normal. Holy cats!

More seismic chuckling. "You didn't see that coming, did you?"

Not at all. I made a gabbling noise that almost conveyed semi-coherent meaning and internally reeled at the smug look on Brute's face. That visage was meant for scaring children and Supernaturals, not grins of self-satisfaction.

"You may be close to crazy, Kal, but then again, who isn't? Take a look at your average politician … most of them should be locked up in a room with padded walls, yet they run our country. You're smarter than any other two Agents, and I know deep down you really care about the BSI and the people who work there." His grin grew fractionally broader. It looked like the movement of tectonic plates. "Plus, you didn't try to con me with a phony answer and that counts for a lot." A finger the size of a stick of dynamite poked me in the chest. I tried not to let my lungs collapse. "You'll do a good job until you quit or you die—whichever comes first. That's good enough for me."

I finally found my voice. "The question is will it be good enough for BB?"

"Doesn't matter. He'll listen to me."

"Pardon me, boss, but that sounds an awful lot like responsibility." A four-letter word if ever I heard one. Calling the shots, making the tough decisions like who lives and who dies. Not my bailiwick.

"You can handle it."

"I can handle it, but I don't know if I want it."

A small pause as we neared the others, then, "Being a leader might help you find what you're looking for. Team leaders get to reject or accept assignments based on personal experiences and prejudices. They can even volunteer their teams for assignments … which could lead you to a solution to your Class Five problem."

"Then I'm in."

The grin faded slowly. "I had no doubt," he rumbled. With a soft (for him) pat on my shoulder, he passed me by to join the rest of the team, leaving me to process what I'd just agreed to.

He sure knew the right buttons to push. One mention of finding a way to kill Iku-Turso and I was ready to agree to a colonoscopy with a rusty probe. Mentally I cursed myself for a fool. With a few words, Brute had put me in play as Team Leader (assuming BB went for it, that is) and I'd leapt at the chance. Still, the thought of someday completing my quest sure warmed the cockles of my heart. In fact, they were on fire.

We came in through the south entrance, right into Stanley Field Hall, a large rectangular room so massive it dwarfed the life-sized model of a blue whale suspended overhead. Taxidermist Carl Akeley's famous *Fighting Bull Elephants* sat in the middle, beyond the large reception desk, and Sue, the most complete, largest and best-preserved skeleton of a T. rex ever found, loomed beyond. She (or it or he, who knows?) measured forty-two feet from tip to tail and thirteen feet at the hip.

Sue (named after the Paleontologist who discovered her) stood at the end of the enormous room, crouched as she must have been in life, head lowered and tail stretching out behind for balance, ready to attack the nearest herbivore. I stared at the massive array of bones. Of all the nasty things that the World Under could vomit forth, a terror like Sue would be one of the worst.

Most people don't have a good grasp of time because we have so little in this world before we're gone. Humans as we know it have been around for about a hundred thousand years or so—give or take a few—and evolution has provided us with a couple of awesome adaptive tools: intelligence for problem-solving and the opposable thumb for carrying out the solutions our brains dreamed up. Super powers, for sure. We've had about eight million years to develop these tools— not a bad shake at all in the grand scheme of things.

Then consider a humble dinosaur like Sue. Small brain, small forearms for her size, no opposable thumbs. Sounds kinda sad for the big varmint, right?

Wrong.

Dinos like Sue had *tens of millions* of years to evolve, if not hundreds of millions. Tyrannosaurus rex was one of the *last* non-avian dinosaurs to exist before the mass extinction called Cretaceous-Paleogene extinction event turned all the dinosaurs into fossil fuels.

So, what can nature do to counter a big brain and thumbs used for fine motor skills? Let's talk size and strength, which Sue had in spades, and speed, which was estimated between twenty-five to forty-five mph—fast enough to run down any hominid, including Jesse Owens. Then there's high depth perception and a binocular range of fifty-five degrees, which is greater than that of a hawk, and visual acuity thirteen times greater than a human being. Add a sense of smell that could rival a Dalmatian's and hearing that functioned best with low-frequency sounds and you have a mean-ass critter that replaces the great white shark as the perfect killing machine.

Back in the late '90s, when the paleontological drama of Sue's discovery was chewing up the airwaves, I was deep into the story, fascinated by history being made right on cable television. Between watching CNN, dating my girlfriend Carol, and studying, I was lucky to graduate at all.

"*Snap out of it, Kal,*" said Brute through my earwig, snapping me out of days past. Reality slapped me in the face and I found myself a few dozen yards away from Sue, the rest of the team staring at me like I'd gone nuts.

"*Sorry, guys,*" I replied sheepishly. "*Did I ever tell you that* Jurassic Park *is one of my favorite films?*"

Waldo spat on the floor, bits of tobacco threading the saliva. In the gray tones of nightvision he looked less than amused. "*Yeah, mine's* [DELETED] *Revenge of the Nerds.*" He flicked a finger at Sue. "*Unless this thing is coming back to life to eat us all, what say we get a move on, if it pleases your highness?*"

Okay, I deserved that, so I gave the team a rueful nod and Brute continued on, everyone following with Mouth tossing me a grin.

We traveled east between more Greco-Roman pillars to the Yates Exhibition Center, where the Jerusalem Exhibit resided. It was there the young security guard had been found, shirtless, with handprints burned into his skin. Artifacts excavated from near the Temple Mount, the most important religious site in the entire world, were displayed inside thick, high-grade, bullet-resistant polymer viewing boxes attached to the walls and pillars secured to the floor: the remains of swords, daggers, cups and chalices, necklaces, bracelets, and gem-studded circlets made to adorn the brows of royals. A fortune in archeological wonder, not to mention precious metals and gems.

Frenchy shook his head. "*So this is where he was found?*"

"*Yeah,*" answered Growler, "*but the location might not mean dick to the demon. It might have been a kill of opportunity.*"

"*I don't know, guys,*" said Mouth. "*Look at all this old stuff. Maybe the demon was after something here. A security guard is the logical place to start if you want access to some possibly magical trinket.*"

I took a moment to read a large sign between two cases relating to the history of the Jerusalem Exhibit. A German named Wilhelm Fessler and his wife Louise had been given permission to excavate (gently of course) near the Temple Mount. Apparently a recently discovered fragment of scroll unearthed in the Old City section of Jerusalem mentioned a cave near the Mount, much like the Well of Souls under the Foundation Stone of the temple, the site where Abraham prepared to sacrifice his son, Isaac, to the Lord. This new cave, carefully hidden, was said to be the storehouse for King Solomon's greatest, most sacred relics. Of course they'd thought it must contain the Ark of the Covenant—visions of Indiana Jones dancing in their heads.

Instead of a cave, however, the two found a closet-sized hole filled with all manner of items, some valuable beyond measure, some merely rubbish, and many more decayed and broken, of uncertain provenance and historical value.

Waldo seemed less than impressed as he eyed the treasures. "*How long do we wait, boss?*"

"*An hour or two. Surveillance cameras in this area went down at twelve-oh-three a.m. When the cameras came back online at twelve thirty-one a.m., the guard was as we saw in the photos, shirt off with handprints burned onto his skin. It's eleven forty-five p.m. right now, so I reckon we wait for an hour before splitting up.*"

Frenchy cut in, "*Why here, boss? Any idea?*"

Brute's hooded eyes were focused on a small glass case. "*I have an idea.*"

CHAPTER TWENTY

Dove
The Boys Are Back in Town

"JESUS, HE'S DEAD." Rat sounded scared and exhausted. His face was covered with tiny welts, as if he'd been stung by a nest of hornets. Still, he looked much better than Ng. From crown to throat, his face was deeply lacerated with thin, almost surgical cuts that bled freely. He'd be disfigured for life, his face a patchwork of scars, if he didn't get magical healing soon.

I stared at Atkins, who did his own staring at things only the dead could see. With shaking hands, I closed his eyes in a gesture of farewell. Though a Green Pea, he had a lot of potential and the kind of temperament you wished everyone possessed.

I fought back tears as I looked at Atkins. I hadn't known him long, but he was one of us and not a pervy little skeeze like Rat. Without Kal, I was the senior Agent in charge and that didn't sit too well with me.

"Everyone else okay?" I managed through a throat swollen half shut with grief. Ng and the Magician nodded, although the Asian had his right hand clutched to his chest. It looked swollen, ready to pop. As for Rat, he seemed more subdued than I'd ever seen him, his face pale and covered in sweat.

"Rat," I told him, "see if you can magic up a healing for Ng."

The thin Magician shook his head. "Can't. I'm low on juice. Ever since I arrived back in this world, it's like I'm bein' drained dry like a battery in a flashlight that's been left on." Mechanically, without his normal cocky attitude, Rat related what he'd seen in the blue world and what had happened to Tweezer. Meanwhile he began first aid on Ng, stitching and taping his lacerations closed. I felt my stomach perform a slow roll at the mention of spiders bleeding from Tweezer's body.

"I noticed it the second I cast the spell on Tweeze—the drainin' feelin'—but I still managed to escape." Rat's voice shook, but his hands remained steady. "I think the murderin' man is leechin' offa me somehow."

"How is that possible?" I asked.

Rat shook his head. "Dunno. That guy ain't human. A demon perhaps." He shut up for a second while he applied a topical anesthetic and used surgical staples to close a particularly nasty cut near Ng's left eye. "What's the play … boss?"

Few things shake me, but at that moment being called 'boss' was one of them. Still, it felt kind of nice, empowering. "We take time to heal and wait for Kal. I imagine Ghost will let our AIs know when he's on the way. We wait because Ng is severely injured and Atkins is dead and we don't have a damn clue as to what's going on."

"And if Kal doesn't come for us?"

I felt my lips curl into a snarl. "You think he'll abandon us?"

Rat shook his head, eyes never leaving his delicate work. "What if he can't come for us? What if he's dead?" He paused. "More staples, please. I'm out."

It was good thing we each carried surgical staples as part of our basic first-aid kit because it looked as if Ng would need them all. I gave Rat mine then rummaged through Atkins' Bat Belt for his stash and gave them over as well, all the while thinking what to do if Kal were dead.

What if he was? What then? The thought filled me with

terror I wasn't about to voice. Nothing destroys a team faster than a leader who utters the words, 'I don't know.' It's like a poison that eats away at the edges before attacking the more delicate vitals. But losing Kal would be like losing a leg—you weren't sure if you'd be able to stand without it.

"We do what we have to do to complete the op," I said, the words sounding feeble and useless to my ears. It wasn't a real answer, and the tightening around Rat's eyes told me he knew it but chose to say nothing. That raised my opinion of him from sub-basement to basement level.

My eyes lit on the knife sticking out of Atkins' leg, which definitely belonged to Billings. I recognized the hilt with its sharkskin grip colored black with years of sweat. I subvocaled Specter for confirmation that it was Billings who'd killed our comrade.

"I am afraid so, Ms. Jacobs. The Ghost copy residing in Mr. Atkins' DRAFTlite has confirmed the deed. Would you like me to download all the relevant data to Mr. Carson's and Mr. Ng's computers?"

"Do it."

"Done. The other Agents are receiving confirmation now."

Before Specter finished speaking, I saw Ng's eyes narrow and the muscles at the corners of Rat's jaws bunch. They'd gotten the information, all right.

"Okay, gentlemen," I said aloud. "We carry on, patch ourselves up, and then we finish the op, with or without Agent Hakala."

"Gotcha, boss," said Ng through clenched teeth.

Rat chimed in with, "Heard."

"Good. Now pay attention. I think we need to see this. Specter, play back the fight between Billings and Atkins on all our DRAFTlites, audio at fifty percent."

It was like watching television up close, or a movie at a theater with a giant screen. The HUD filled with the true-to-life color of an HD recording. The three of us watched the seventy-second clip and marveled at Atkins' grace as he circled and whirled around the huge form of Billings like a gymnast around an elephant.

And what an elephant! Each muscle on Billings' torso was perfectly outlined as if Michelangelo had sculpted the form out of flesh-colored clay. Human bodies don't look like they do in the comic books—anatomy precisely delineated—but it definitely seemed as if someone drew Billings a new musculature. I knew he was a strong man with flat abs and legs like tree trunks, but nobody is *that* perfect. Not even underwear models.

"What happened to him?" mumbled Ng when the show was over. Rat had finished with the staples and his face and neck was crisscrossed in silver. Unless Alex could put in a good spell, he'd look like Frankenstein's monster for the rest of his days. From the way he moved his lips and the sweat on his forehead, I knew he was in considerable pain.

"Rat, give him an Oxy."

Ng shook his head, but I wasn't having any of it and glared at him until he reluctantly swallowed the pill. Why do men think they can macho through a painful situation when relief is one tablet away? God help them if they ever experienced real pain. Like childbirth—not that I'd experienced that personally, so maybe I shouldn't judge.

We waited twenty minutes until the Oxy took effect and turned our attention to Ng's mangled hand.

"What did you do?" I gasped, seeing that the swelling of his digits had the ballistic cloth stretched tight.

"Critter had my hand and was poking it with needle-thin tendrils," he explained.

An image cropped up on the HUD and I saw a bowling-ball with hair attached to his hand. It was a replay of the scene. A Mac-10A appeared in the frame and unloaded an entire clip into the spherical mass of tendrils, pummeling the hand underneath. My gorge rose.

Rat flicked open a stiletto. "Gotta take this off, dude," he said, his jaw set in grim, hard lines. "Gonna hurt like you ain't even imagined yet."

Ng's eyes were glassy but focused. "You do what you have to, Rat. The painkiller has me feeling pretty good."

However stoned he was, Ng sure let out a yell when Rat slipped the tip of the knife under the glove at the back of the wrist. Sweat popped out all over Ng's face and streamed down to his pointed chin as he clenched his teeth. Spit drooled from the corners of his mouth while Rat sawed at the tough cloth.

Blood spurted right along the slice line that traveled to the tip of Ng's pinky finger. How he held on for four more cuts was anyone's guess, but he kept his composure.

"There's somethin' under the glove, but I can't see it through all the blood," whispered Rat as he detached the stiletto. "Boss, hold him steady while I remove it." To Ng, he said, "This is gonna hurt awful again, dude."

"Then what are you waiting for?" ground out Ng as he held his hand rock steady in front of the Magician despite the pain. "Just do it."

I put my arms around the slender man, surprised by how hot he felt. His muscles were thin, yet corded to an iron hardness that told me he'd done a lot of aerobic exercise, and from his build I'd guess martial arts. "Ready, Rat."

"Gotcha, Boss." The Magician laid his fingers against the flaps of cut ballistic cloth and *yanked* it away so fast that I barely had time to blink.

Wesley Ng screamed like the damned.

It wasn't the scream that chilled me to the bone, but the hand. Where flesh should have been writhed a mass of black tendrils, each about an inch long. It looked like a hand-shaped sea anemone. Underneath the thick tendrils, the flesh continued to swell, each finger growing within seconds to three times its normal size before Rat pulled the glove off.

"Jesus!" screamed Ng, eyes wide and feverish. "Jesus, Jesus-oh-damn-Jesus!"

"Hold him tight," Rat hollered over the shrieks. "Don't you dare let him go!"

I nodded, eyes fixed on the writhing mass at the end of Ng's arm. What was growing inside him? A parasite? One of the blobbies he mentioned? The thought of those tendrils sliding beneath skin, along bone, nerve, muscle, and vein, made me dizzy. Ugly, whispery words slithered across my brain: *hello, lovey-dovey.*

No! None of that. In that direction lay madness, and madness was a weakness I couldn't afford. I'd long ago made up my mind to leave weakness to the men. As for me, I was strong. Stronger than men, strong as I needed to be. Strong as death.

"Wes, man," grated Rat through clenched teeth, "don't [DELETED] move." One of his hands, palm down, hovered over the back of Ng's hand; the other was palm up underneath. Both kept enough distance so the tendrils could not reach. Rat closed his eyes for a moment, then adjusted his hands so they were below Ng's wrist. I could see the skin at the base of Ng's thumb hump and bump as tendrils quested beneath.

I will not vomit. I will not vomit, I thought over and over again.

Rat's eyes sprang open, the whites glowing gold. A thin white worm of light circled Ng's forearm four inches from the wrist. The glow became a glare, which glowed blindingly bright, causing my eyes to leak tears. The light moved up the wrist, to the base of the thumb, to the palm, and finally enveloped the hapless Agent's fingers.

And went out. *Poof*, as if somebody had thrown a switch.

Ng's hand was gone and all that was left was a cauterized stump a few inches from where his wrist had been. As for the man himself, he'd passed out in my arms, all sweaty and gross and so pale that the dark olive of his skin had turned a light green. His breathing didn't seem too labored, but his heart was beating a mile a minute. I hoped he had some good dreams, but considering the onslaught of pain he'd endured, that was highly doubtful.

"What did you do, Rat?" I asked while lowering Ng to the carpet. "Thought you didn't have the power for magic."

"Healin' is hard, boss. Damn hard." Rat looked like he was sweating buckets. "Gettin' flesh to knit, regeneratin' bone and such, coaxin' it back to what it's supposed to be—that takes some major juice. Most Magicians need spell gems to perform a good healin', 'cept for maybe Alex and Kal's tasty gal Jeanie. Me, I ain't that powerful, so tryin' a healin' on Ng woulda drained me dry, maybe even killed me." He lifted a finger. It shook a little. "Destroyin' things, however, is easy and doesn't take much juice at all because to destroy takes a lot less effort than buildin'. Heck, the human body is filled with potential energy ready to go all kinetic and stuff, so I used Ng's own body energy to help me cast the spell and control the destruction of that hand. Hardly took anythin' at all. Piece of cake."

I eyed his pale face and shaking hands. Right. Piece of cake. Rat was trying to put a brave face on it, but he was exhausted and he knew I knew it. Men. Macho idiots, all of them.

Except for Alex. Just thinking about my boyfriend gave me a warm feeling deep between the points of my hipbones. Alex has a way about him—not macho, not cocky, but self-assured. Yeah, that's it. A combo of self-assurance and self-control. A man of awesome power, the greatest Magician of this century, and he still read *The Amazing Spiderman* and loved *Star Wars*. All that power and no desire to lord it over people.

I've had lovers over the years. Uncle Carl didn't totally ruin me. I couldn't let that happen because that would mean he'd won, and I'd take a dip in sewage before that'd happen. The only one I didn't want to kick out of my bed in the morning was Alex. In fact, I'd often lie there next to him watching him sleep, the light of dawn caressing his boyish face, the delicate bone structure of his cheeks and nose.

I sure couldn't tell you if it was love or sustained lust (I know what Rat would say), but for now it was something I wanted to explore some more. There was no one like Alex. He didn't look at me with lust in his eyes—well, there was *some* lust; he was a man after all—more like a deep intensity filled with equal parts respect, adoration, and admiration. Let me tell you, except for Kal (who has a hell of a woman in Jeanie) Alex was the first guy I met who wasn't undressing me with his eyes in under a minute. Most men made me feel like a walking pair of tits and ass cheeks.

Despite being a prize moron, Rat had earned some respect from me, so I felt it was my duty to dole some right back. "Good job, Rat." I looked at Ng. He seemed peaceful. "What happened to the hand? I didn't feel any heat, just a lot of light."

"Hmmm." Rat stood and stretched, limbs trembling. "Hard to explain, you know. You have to be a Magician to understand the dynamics of a spell." A few seconds of considering and he continued, "Let's just say I rendered the hand into energy, most of which was funneled into a dimension parallel to ours."

"W-what?" I sputtered a bit, trying to wrap my head around it. *A parallel dimension?*

That earned me some weak laughter. "You should see your face, boss. You gotta realize that light energy can actually penetrate dimensional barriers, and the barriers around here are particularly thin. We receive radiant energy from other dimensions close to us and we bleed that same energy into others, so it didn't take a whole heap of magic to send the excess away to keep us from being blinded by the release of so much energy or cooked well done. That's kind of a simplistic way of explainin' it, but words don't do the concept justice."

Whatever. At least it worked. A girl could get her brains fried trying to understand the world of Magicians. "You're a lot smarter than you look, Rat."

"I ain't just another pretty face." His grin was pure evil lust. "In fact, the rest of me is awful darn great, too." Before I could kick him in the uprights, he reeled and leaned heavily against the wall, knees buckling until his ass was planted on the floor. "But now I have to pass out for a while. I am done like dinner."

With that, he closed his eyes and slipped into unconsciousness.

Wow.

"Sleep well, you little perv." I leaned back against the wall, unlimbering my 9mm from its holster. "Great, I get the first watch."

Four hours—that's how long I planned to let Rat nap. I was pretty knackered myself and in sore need of shuteye. In fact, I could barely keep my eyes open. The wall opposite became blurry, the blood spatters smearing into streaks of dark red that bled into nothingness, and I soon drifted away.

"You could join me, you know."

Seductive, with a slow, steady undercurrent of deep masculinity, it was a voice made to reach down and coax trust and respect. It was a voice of an angel.

Or the devil.

"Joining me is simplicity itself."

Mmmmm … I could listen to that voice forever and a day. It slithered along my skin like silk, wrapping my limbs in warmth.

"Join you?" My words emerged thick as honey, my lips moving in slow motion.

"Yessss." Sibilant and sexy.

I couldn't see the speaker; everything around me felt dark, warm, and comfortable. Like being under the covers at night, or in the womb. "Who are you?"

"You know."

"Do I?"

"Of course you do, Dove Jacobs. You are far too intelligent not to."

I should've been afraid. I should've run screaming down the hallway in an effort to get away, but my emotions were muted, blunted by the warmth and dark. "Yes, of course I do. You're the Angel of Mass Murder, the Saint of Slaying."

"Of course I am. That doesn't shock you now, does it? You're not afraid of me, are you?"

No I wasn't, which surprised me. Then again, all warm and comfy and dark, nothing much could scare me at that moment. "You took Billings."

"He came of his own volition."

"Why?"

"Because I offered him something no one else could."

"What was that?"

"Freedom."

"Freedom? Freedom from what? The BSI?"

My question was greeted with laughter like smooth, sweet chocolate. "Freedom from restraint, from convention, and the sad little mores that humans inflict upon one another. It's the freedom to be who you truly are without having to clothe yourself in society's vision of what you should be or what you should do. How to dress, to talk and walk, all of it. I gave him the chance to shed the skin the world covered him in, and he burst forth like a butterfly. He's happy now, happier than he's ever been because he is fulfilling his dreams, his fondest ambitions."

By killing his teammates?

"Yes."

I don't know what startled me more, the fact that he read my mind or the fact that I was so darn shocked about it. I figured I'd done enough time in the Bureau for things like that to roll off my back like water off Teflon, but apparently I wasn't so jaded yet.

"So why this confab?"

"It is time to extend my offer to you, Ms. Jacobs. I ask that you join me in the greatest chapter in human history, one that will define the race for the rest of its existence."

My brain didn't want to work, or it couldn't fathom a reply. For the longest moment in my life I simply *was*, unthinking. Stunned. When I snapped back to myself, I growled, "Why would I do that? I'd have to be crazy."

That chocolate voice slithered over me in a slow-motion

wave of sweetness. "Because you are ready. There is nothing for you at the Bureau, just a group of testosterone-fueled misogynists who look at you as a pair of tits with legs. You know that. Come with me, and you will be appreciated for what and who you are."

My mouth felt thick and stuffed with cotton. "Who or what am I, then?"

"A woman who wishes to lash out at all the world's pedophiles, a woman who has no qualms about strangling such loathsome offenders with their own intestines. I could use an effective person like you on my team, and I can be the one who offers those pathetically sick creatures to you for justice. True justice, of which the tolerant, weak, and ineffective judicial system of this era has no concept, doling out prison time that merely makes these monsters more brutal and efficient. You can provide the true justice that those people deserve. The justice of the blade, the justice of pain and death. The justice you handed to your Uncle Carl."

Uncle Carl. My skin crawled at hearing his name said aloud. I felt heat flush my cheeks. "Why do you care? You're a killer, a murderer; those pricks seem right up your alley."

The response was nothing I expected. Fury lashed the voice as it said, "I am nothing like those … *things.*" Sudden cold leached the hope from my bones. "They are a disease that preys upon the weak, creating suffering that lasts for decades. Those who fall to my blade, or hands, experience only a brief suffering before their pain is gone forever. It is a quick release that sees their souls cross over."

"But you're a murderer."

"Do not fool yourself, Ms. Jacobs. We are *all* murderers. Life is an act of consuming the lives of others. Do you really think that a cow has no right to life except to nourish the flesh that eats it? Do not the fish in the sea deserve to swim unmolested? The whales that face extinction? How many species has the human race murdered? Perhaps you've a heard of the dodo, a species that was entirely wiped out because it was not sufficiently afraid of man? How about the Tasmanian tiger? Or the passenger pigeon, the great auk, the quagga, the Falkland Island wolf, the Zanzibar leopard, the Caribbean monk seal? All species rendered extinct by man, hunted to death for silly things like fur, or eggs, or simple fear that they were a threat to livestock. Their like, and many more, will never be seen again on this earth. Entire species *murdered*."

"And you are so much better?"

"Of course." Gone was the cold, replaced by the sugary reasonableness. "I have no intention of hunting man to extinction. I merely cull the weak and the unwary. I am Darwinism in its purest form because I leave behind the strongest, those sufficiently wary to guard against my coming."

The voice let me stew for a moment before continuing, "I am nature … cruel, brutish, and utterly in tune with this wide world."

As I floated in that not-place of warmth and darkness, I considered the offer. What did life have to offer me? It had given me Uncle Carl and his sneaky games and all the dysfunction that followed. If there were any justice, he would have been castrated in a public square before being stoned, but instead it took a young girl and a screwdriver to set things to rights and didn't that just suck? For years I told myself that killing the sonovabitch didn't affect me, that I was fine. You know what 'fine' means? Fine is a mask that hides the screaming deep down inside.

Tempting, so tempting to give in to that sweet chocolate voice and unburden myself from the constraints of 'acceptable behavior.' No responsibilities except to myself. No more Bureau, no more leering men and their wolf whistles, no more smothering the anger that burned inside like a fiery tumor. No more BS, no more having to be polite or pay taxes or pussyfoot around others' feelings in this politically correct, new-age hippie civilization my parents always dreamed of. Created not by hippie sell-outs like Mom and Dad, who realized that the summer of love was only for the young and that getting old meant that you had to take some measure of responsibility for yourself or wind up homeless, but by their kids, who rebelled against the notion of free this and free that. Those kids realized that absolute freedom to do whatever you wanted was just another concept that really meant being lazy and having nothing to look forward to except the next high. Kids like me who were named after birds or flowers or lakes or some such. Kids who didn't *want* to eat granola, but instead wanted the deluxe cheeseburgers with a side of gravy fries and to go to the prom with the normal teenagers. We created this world of consumerism and pussyfooting around the really painful subjects because we were so used to ignoring our embarrassing parents.

I could exit this world of crooked politicians and vapid supermodels and taste the freedom my parents had always dreamed of but didn't have the stomach to achieve. All I had to do was leave it all behind.

Leave Alex.

Some things are worth staying for.

"[CENSORED] you," I growled.

Chapter Twenty-One

Kal
Nine Years Ago
Demons

FRENCHY LEDOUX LEANED around Brute to take a gander at what had captured the big man's attention. "*What is it, boss?*" he asked, squinting at the case.

I took a good look and all I saw was a metal ring about five inches in diameter and a half-inch thick. Made of bronze, it was heavily tarnished, so much so that the intricate scrollwork around the edges had faded into black. What made the little metal circle more interesting was the bronze Star of David attached to the inner ring by each of the six points. The star was also crusty with centuries of tarnish.

"Is it a medallion?" I asked. "If so, it's a pretty big one."

Brute, staring raptly at the artifact, shook his head. "This is no medallion. Intel says all these were placed here this morning from storage for the big unveiling tomorrow. If I'm not mistaken, it's—" A roar, so loud it stunned my ears, cut him off. It sounded like King Kong was having a prostate exam.

"*What the f—*" Another roar drowned Waldo's words.

Whatever it was, it sure got our attention. Six weapons were raised as we formed a circle, backs to the center. It didn't take long to find out what was what.

It was Sue, all bones and wire, the long-dead T. rex, reanimated and hunting new game. Us. Thirteen feet tall at the hip doesn't sound so big, but when you realize that's only half of her, all crouched over for the hunt, then the sheer size of the skeleton is driven home like a punch in the gut when you least expect it.

Concrete broke apart, glass shattered, and displays were knocked about as Sue trundled through the exhibit store to the Yates Center, bashing through anything foolish enough to stand in her way.

What came our way wasn't bone. When an organism's soft tissues decay, the bones are left behind and water seeps into them. The minerals in the water replace the minerals that comprise the bones after the water dissolves them. What's left behind are the minerals. For all intents and purposes ... stone. Now a few dozen tons of rock was heading toward us, cracking stone flooring like it was balsawood.

We had about thirty seconds until it smashed us into salsa. Brute wasted no time on subtleties, barking out orders quickly and efficiently. "Team, fire at will. Waldo, do something about that thing."

Flashes erupted as we all cut loose at once from magically silenced weapons. Sue took some damage as bullets gouged small chunks out of her with dull *crackings*, but she lowered her six-hundred-pound skull and the rounds shattered against it with minimal effect.

As for Waldo, he frowned around the stump of his cigar and stared at the approaching Paleolithic peril. "*Uh, guys,*" he began, frowning mightily, "*this might take a while.*"

Not good, I thought as Sue barreled toward us. My Lahti spit bullets, but the 9mm rounds simply flattened on her humongous skull. I jumped to the side as, with one mighty lunge, she was upon us.

Waldo backpedaled, eyes still locked on the ambulatory skeleton, keeping out of reach of teeth the size of bananas.

Frenchy unloaded with an auto shotgun, and that had the most effect, the deer slugs tearing apart Sue's ribcage. Unfortunately, there were no organs to shatter, no heart to stop.

Mouth ran around behind and got a gutful of dino tail that sent her flying. For a moment I feared she might be dead as she landed hard on the tile floor, but her curses put paid to that possibility. Growler used armor-piercing bullets to chip away at the T. rex, but at the rate he was going, it'd take a week before he could whittle Sue down to size. Still, the rounds did enough damage to send rock dust flying. I could feel it sticking to my teeth as I inhaled. As for Brute, he was hammering at the case holding the bronze circle with the butt of his rifle, the security glass forming starry rings under the weight of the blows.

How do you stop something that's already dead?

An answer came to mind. Not a good one, but it might buy some time for Waldo to figure out what to do. If not, we were all destined to be road kill and Sue was the semi bearing down on us.

Before I could do anything, however, Sue lunged with such speed and such birdlike precision that it was over before I could blink. One second Frenchy Ledoux was blasting away off to the right of the beast, the next he was gone from the waist up. His legs and hips toppled to the floor as the upper half of him took an eTicket ride in Sue's enormous jaws. His screams were mercifully brief.

And the rage hit.

It's hard to describe—the fury that overcame me, enhancing all my physical characteristics. Safe to say it chased away all doubt, all fear, and replaced them with a singular, diamond-hard, red-tinged purpose that nothing could deter.

No thought, just action. No hesitation, just motion. Like a rhesus monkey at a jungle gym I climbed Sue's ribcage so fast I left skin from my palms behind. Before she could react, I was perched behind her skull, holding on for dear life as the bones of her vertebrae did no good things to my kibbles and bits.

The bony monstrosity reacted pretty much like I expected.

As I mentioned earlier, when a T. rex charges, it leans far forward, lowering its torso until it is perpendicular to the ground with its tail straight out behind for balance. This makes the beast look smaller than it really is. When it rears up to its full height, then you see what's what.

I saw Mouth's lips move, and I was a good enough lip reader to see that the words she uttered would stand my mother's hair on end … right before she used the soap to wash out her cussing mouth. Mom didn't truck with foul language.

As for me, I held on for dear life while my cheeks ached from my manic grin. I was having the time of my life, a rider on the biggest damn bull in the strangest damn rodeo ever. It was more fun than I'd had in a long time, ever since that bug hunt in the Florida Everglades where I'd screwed the pooch but wound up killing a praying mantis the size of a Greyhound bus.

Sue shook herself like a dog shedding water, thrashing back and forth as I held on to holes on either side of her skull, my hands steel vises that refused to let go as she tried to buck me off.

I screamed in fury as she suddenly juked left. I would've flown off, but my legs were wrapped tight around her vertebrae. Still in the grip of my berserker rage, I pulled out a .45 ACP and started pounding on her huge skull with the butt, my left hand clutched in a death grip. On the third strike, bone began to crack and powder—not much, but enough to send a thrill through me. My eyes found Brute and I let out a victory scream.

Waldo's eyes flashed a strange blue color, deep, almost black. I only noticed it because he'd stepped forward, hands in the air, palms out. I would've yelled at him to move it before he got his fool head bit off, but suddenly, with a sudden jerk and a groan, T. rex fell to floor, taking me with her.

An instant before the dino hit, I tried to leap free, but no dice, and I took a vertebra to the crotch. The rage blunted the pain, but my breath still left my lungs in a *whoosh* and my knees hit the tile with such brain-numbing force that I was sure they were broken. Not even the rage could sustain me after so much damage.

The world was a dark, hard place and I fell into it face first, my jaw *cracking* on the floor in the midst of a god-awful clattering of fossil bones. Before I went unconscious I saw stars.

"How is he, Waldo?"

"Ugly all day."

"That's not an answer."

"Don't get your panties in a twist, boss. He'll be fine, despite breaking his jaw and both kneecaps. If all the king's horses and all the king's men had me around, Humpty Dumpty would be just fine. This idiot was a piece of cake. Look, he's coming around already."

I knew exactly what was going on. The sensations of coming back from a major healing were unfortunately becoming all too familiar. One good thing I could say was that I did wake up. Too many Agents didn't.

"Good job, Waldo," I grumbled through a phlegmy throat. "Don't feel any residual pain." Both Brute and Waldo appeared when I opened my eyes, peering down at me. The Magician looked smug and the boss seemed irritated.

That irritation came out in his voice as he said, "That was the most boneheaded maneuver I've ever seen, Hakala. What were you thinking?"

Didn't have the heart to tell him that thinking wasn't at the top of my list at the time, but Waldo spared me a response by saying, "He was buying time, boss." The stub of his cigar migrated from left to right, a sight so disgusting it turned my stomach. "That fool stunt bought me enough time to figure out what's what. Turns out it was a minor possession spell, which, of course, a Magician of my caliber was able to break."

I grabbed Brute's hand and he hauled me to my feet. "Sure, Waldo, you're so good, there should be two of you." There, I was upright and feeling marvelously well, not a dent in the fender, not a scratch on the paint.

The portly Magician grinned. Not a pretty sight with that turd jetting foul wads of smoke. "World can't handle two of me."

It was hard, but I refrained from barfing on his combat boots.

Shouldering him aside, Mouth took my chin in hand and examined me critically. "You're still ugly."

"You're still bossy and tactless."

Her smile showed all her teeth. "Of course." Then her face fell. "Frenchy's gone."

That cooled the mood. "Saw that," I said through jaws tight with suppressed anger. "And we made a mess of Sue."

"Boss put in a call to Special Branch. We got some egghead types and some Magicians who can put the old girl to rights. After we're done here, the museum won't be able to tell that ol' bony just had her prehistoric ass kicked."

Brute cut in, voice filled with hate. "Let's get back on point, people. Something doesn't want us here and I think I know what it is."

The remains of the team swiveled toward our leader, and we waited patiently while he took his sweet time answering. "This demon that killed the guard is an old one. Very powerful. A *named* one."

I felt mice with icy feet run up and down my spine. The average demon (it constantly surprised me that I was jaded enough to use asinine phrases like 'the *average* demon') don't have names. They're either malevolent spirits or a species of infernal creatures we've come to assign to categories like 'Type One' or 'Type Two.' For a demon to actually possess a name means that it is more powerful than most and was able to travel to our plane of existence as flesh and/or spirit. If it came as spirit only, it would possess an unlucky host and cause mischief that way. If it came in the flesh, it was time to pucker up, bend over, and kiss your hind parts goodbye.

"Go on, already!" hollered Waldo suddenly, scaring five years off most of us. "What is it?"

Not one to be rushed, Brute merely gave the Magician the executive stink-eye and said, "I think this is a demon called Ornias."

We let that rattle around our noggins like a BB in a boxcar until Growler said, "Say *what*?"

"In an old text called 'The Testament of Solomon,' there's mention of a demon named Ornias."

"The what of what?" This came from Mouth. Her pretty face was screwed up tight in puzzlement.

"An ancient text attributed to King Solomon," I answered. That earned me a skeptical look from our fearless leader. "What? I've been studying; I came across a reference."

Brute nodded. "Good. Keep studying. It might just save your life." He took a deep breath. It was like watching a whale surface. "In the Testament, Ornias caused all manner of trouble, mostly to young, effeminate men. He'd leave burn marks on their bodies in the shape of human hands. Solomon eventually defeated the demon using the Ring of Solomon, also called the Seal of Solomon, and forced Ornias to help build the great temple in Jerusalem." He held up the bronze circlet in his hand. "This, I believe, is the Seal of Solomon. This is what Ornias wants. He wants to destroy it before it can be used against demonkind once again."

Holy crap on a cracker! I'd done a lot of research on Supernaturals, especially on a certain Finnish quasi-deity, but this was breaking new ground for me. My vendetta against Iku-Turso consumed most of my free time—when I wasn't womanizing or drinking heroic amounts of vodka—so knowledge of artifacts like the Seal fell to the wayside. Now I had come to regret such a narrow focus.

A giant finger poked me in the sternum. "You still with us, Hakala?"

I followed that finger to the hand to a wrist as thick as a Louisville Slugger to an arm large as my right leg all the way to Brute's eyes half hidden beneath the shelf of his brow. "Yeah, I'm always here, boss."

A small nod flew my way. "Good." To the rest of the team, he said, "Fall back to the lobby. I think Ornias isn't done with us yet, and we'll need the room to maneuver. Waldo, what about that pile of bones?"

"Kal's T. rex horsie won't be a problem, I put a stasis on it, and if the demon tries to lift it, I'll know. We'll have plenty of warning and now I know how to counter the big beast." Waldo spat a gob of phlegm and tobacco on the floor.

"Good. Now on my six." With that our leader stomped off toward the lobby, what was left of it, the team following like good little soldiers.

"What are we doing here, boss?" asked Growler as we gathered around the Information desk.

Brute kept his gaze shifting all around. "We're waiting," he took a deep breath, "for a demon."

Two hours later we were still waiting. There's only so long a human can remain on high alert before the tension bleeds out of the air and the body relaxes. Weeks of training in Coronado put steel in our spines, but metal only lasts so long before it oxidizes. The loss of focus begins with the droopy eyelids and thirst. You take one sip of water, then two, then three, and before you know it, your canteen is empty. The problem with drinking all that water is that it eventually has to make an exit. Ten ounces of water takes anywhere from forty-five minutes to an hour to reach the bladder. Then it's time for the pee-pee dance.

At first you try to hold it in. Just a little discomfort, right? Wrong. That discomfort becomes an ache, then a leg-crossing pain that has you bent over, walking funny until you head for the nearest bathroom or most convenient bush.

By the end of the second hour we were traveling to the bathroom in pairs. As it turned out, it was I who escorted Mouth.

"Oh, *god*," she moaned from her stall in the men's room. "This is better than sex!"

Relief flooded my torso as I whizzed in the urinal. Yeah, pretty darn good, but not better than sex and I told her so.

"It's so easy for you men," she replied over the *tinkling* sounds. "You just whip it out and let go anywhere you want. You don't have to cop a squat."

"Is this the basis for penis envy?"

"It's the basis for getting your [CENSORED] ass kicked for bringing up that giant doofus Freud."

"I sense anger issues." Shake once, twice and tuck it away. Damn my bladder felt *so* much better.

"I sense that you better be nice to me, Kalevi Hakala, the Ferocious Finn, lest I take you down a peg or three in front of all your dickwad male friends."

The smile on my face froze. I crossed my arms, leaning against the cool porcelain of a sink. "You know I've got no friends, Mouth. None that survive the Bureau, that is."

She paused. "What about Canton?"

"He's no longer Bureau." I missed Canton something terrible. Possibly the best Agent I'd ever met, he was liquid death with a knife, tough as they came, sharp as a straight razor. Losing him to civilian life hurt more than I could say, but I was happy he was out of harm's way. "You know what it's like, Mouth. We're like firefighters—we eat and sleep at Warehouse—but unlike firefighters, we stay there fulltime. I only get to see Canton during vacations and he's plenty busy working for his father's company in New York." I shook my head. "This isn't a job for making friends."

The rasp of a zipper and the heavy rustle of Bureau armor filled the bathroom. "I know, Kal. This isn't the kind of business for anything except death." Her pretty face was set in a frown as she exited the stall.

Really, this conversation was getting a bit morose. "You know what I can't wrap my head around?"

Mouth lifted an eyebrow.

"What I can't understand is why we're sitting around waiting for something to happen."

"What do you mean?"

"Look, this Ornias character knows we're on to him. Demons like him, the named ones, aren't like the usual bundles of hate and evil. Even the bigger, nastier demons aren't that bright, but Ornias isn't acting like that."

She chewed on that for a moment. "Sounds right. So what?"

"So, why would he attack us his own self? Why put his precious hide in jeopardy if the Seal of Solomon can control him? He's got to be scared, but for some reason he wants the Seal bad enough to reanimate Sue and try to kill us all."

"Think about it," she said. "The Seal is one of the few things he can't fight against, and if he gets his hands on it, he becomes stronger as a result."

I shook my head. "It doesn't feel right. There's no reason for him to steal the Seal, or even come close to it. He could lounge around on another *continent* causing mischief and not have to worry about it. So why go to all this trouble to get it? Why didn't he steal it yesterday when he killed that guard?"

It took her a moment. Finally she said, "Maybe he was sent to retrieve it?"

Sounded plausible. "That makes sense, but then you have to ask—" I began.

"By whom?" she finished.

CHAPTER TWENTY-TWO

Kal
Present Day
Dream Weaver

IT WAS THE buzzing that woke me, an annoying whine that threatened to bust my eardrums and drool my brains out the hole.

"Kal, wake up."

"God's blood, Ghost," I moaned thickly. "You're such a killjoy."

"I would rather be a killjoy than see you killed."

Unsteady on my feet. The world tilted this way and that, but I closed my eyes and waited for the dizziness to pass. That flashback to the Field Museum in Chicago with Brute and the team had the quality of the dreams I had in Omaha a year ago. Alex told me it was a manifestation of my magic, a message from my subconscious trying to tell me something important.

Strange to think that if not for Iku-Turso, I would have been a Magician. I was fifteen when it entered my life, killing my sister. Her spirit bonded to me, siphoning off my magic to enhance her own. She became my rage and that made me one of the most effective Agents in Bureau history. Now I was a man with an atrophied magical ability that proved to be sporadic at best. Alex and Jeanie said I'd never be a real

Magician, that I'd never master any spell except Zippo and that was okay. However, they also theorized that my ability could manifest in strange ways.

Strange ways. My entire life was ruled by strange ways, my path through this world a twisty one, my sanity barely held together with spit, bailing wire, and the love for my wife and child. No matter how you sliced it, I was more screwed up than Congress.

What was my magic trying to tell me now?

Not a clue.

The black goo on the floor provided no answers, just the twisted wreckage of my Bowie knife. I quashed a brief stab of sorrow over the loss of the blade, a gift from my father, now melted down to a few short inches of blackened metal, as if it had been dipped in a jar of sulfuric acid.

"I am sorry, Kal." The words made sense, but there was no emotion behind them.

"If this had been a person, then you could offer up a 'sorry,' Ghost," I said tightly. "I can always replace the knife." I hefted the wooden handle with its stub of blade. "No use crying over metal. Now, we have a job to do. Show me the stairs."

"You can take the elevator."

"Not with that spell shape inside."

"Not a worry, Kal."

My curiosity bump tingling, I headed back to the freight elevator where Ghost recreated the spell Shape on the DRAFTlite and indicated which silver rune to deface in order to negate the spell.

"Why didn't we do this earlier?" The black paint peeled away from the keen edge of my K-bar, a backup for the Bowie. The eight-inch blade felt too short and not near heavy enough. Still, it eradicated enough paint to expose a patch of silver the size of my palm, erasing one of the runes.

"I had no idea the spell was still active, or maybe it had a motion-sensing component that automatically activated it."

"So erasing it before wouldn't have helped?"

"Likely not."

Awesome.

I hit the button for the thirtieth floor and sat in one of the rune-covered black leather chairs.

"What are you doing, Kal?"

"Going to take a nap?"

"How can you sleep at a time like this?"

The question was how could I not sleep? My joints ached and my body hurt awful from my fight with the succubus. Not to mention having the mother of all headaches, the kind with the diamond splinter of pain between the eyes that radiated to the back of your skull. I groaned as I eased back, reclining as far as I could.

Used to be I could drink, screw, and party all night and head off to work bright-eyed and bushy tailed, but these days it took a little bit extra to get my motor running in the morning. Like a gallon of coffee and a jelly donut. No sprinkles.

Sucks getting old.

"Ghost, my talent is trying to tell me something and I'm going to let it. We'll hit the top floor and work our way from there, but first I'm going to get some shut-eye."

"Do you really think you will sleep?"

Sure I was keyed up a bit, but I had a feeling I should trust my talent, go with the flow, and it wouldn't steer me wrong. "Call it a hunch, old spook, but I think I can. Keep an electric eye out for your clones and brief the team on what's going on. Have them meet us on the thirtieth floor if they're not already there. Wake me three minutes after we reach the thirtieth, okay?"

"Okay, Kal. Will do. I just hope the rest of the team is in the building. They could be in a different dimension, much as you were."

"Ghost, never bet against an Agent. Something tells me they made it back. Now please shut your cyber-trap and let me do my thing."

He shut it and I lay back, closing my eyes. Sure enough, I quickly passed through from awake to dreaming.

"By whom?" she finished.

We looked at each other for a long moment. "I don't like this, Mouth. This feels wrong. Hinky doesn't even begin to describe it."

"What do you think this hinky demon is up to, then, Mr. Smart guy?" Her smile held more than just a little challenge. Mouth was one of those combative types who had zero qualms about saying 'screw it' in any situation and the combat expertise to back it up. If I asked her to follow me to Hell to kick the Devil's ass, she'd probably smile and start loading her gun.

"Sue was a big ploy," I said, tugging at my lower lip. "Overwhelming force, but one that could be countered by a single person."

"So?"

"So what's the demon's next play? He tried a frickin' *T. rex*, for Pete's sake."

"Try something different, I'd imagine."

"So what's more effective than a gigantic, near unstoppable fossil?"

"Two?"

Every now and then the penny drops, the light bulb flashes on overhead, and the dusty corners of my mind clean themselves out. "More than that," I blurted out. "Much more than that." I grabbed her hand and dragged her out of the restroom.

My feet blurred as I about near yanked Mouth's arm out of its socket, but there was no time to waste because if my sneaking suspicions were correct, we were about to land feet first in fecal matter.

"Boss!" I yelled, putting my lungs into it. Wasted effort because even the mildest exclamation would've bounced all the way through the main lobby like a Ping-Pong ball. "We've been giving it too much time!" I pounded to a halt.

At his puzzled look, I explained, "We've been sitting here with our thumbs up our butts giving Ornias time to work up some serious whammy."

"Hold on there, Tex," groused Waldo. "That dino was pretty serious."

"But it was a one off," I said, looking each team member in the eye, "and one that didn't work because Waldo took the spell off it, but what if he can do the same kinda spell to a whole *bunch* of things?" I looked around. "How much crap is stored in the museum vaults?"

My answer came quick enough.

The first wave came from both sides, boiling out through the entrances to the other halls. Faster than I would have thought possible, the linen-wrapped monstrosities ran at us full-tilt in a flood of brown, desiccated flesh and ancient bandages.

We worked as one, unloading with our weapons, everything from shotguns to the Lahti, but as with Sue, bullets didn't affect them much.

I found the Bowie in my hand and hacked, taking off an arm at the shoulder. It fell to the floor, but the mummy pressed on. It smelled faintly of dust and spices. Before it could latch on, I took its head and kicked it away in time to meet the next one.

With every shot, Growler took out a mummy, the shotgun in his hands bursting them like water balloons hitting pavement. One shot, one (well) kill. As for Waldo, he'd stare at a mummy and it would fall down, once again a museum exhibit. "I can't get them all," he shouted, dropping another. "Each one has been spelled."

I felt dead hands wrap around my throat and I grabbed the thin, stick-like fingers and twisted hard, breaking them off at the palms. Linen and bones tore easily and I spun, decapitating the creature before it could try another tack, like biting. Being bitten to death by three-thousand-year-old corpses didn't sound like a fun way to spend an evening.

Having abandoned her near-useless pistol, Mouth gave

a good account of herself from atop the information desk, kicking heads off and ripping off arms, while Brute used raw force to simply punch both fists through chest cavities before ripping the mummies in half. He was covered from head to toe in mummy dust and sweat.

It looked like we had the best of things as the fighting continued. I used the Bowie to decapitate another mummy and saw that there were fewer than ten left. That's when I began to be really concerned. Ornias wasn't about to end this hoedown with mummies.

Then the lions struck.

Growler was the first to go down, neck snapping as a paw the size of an Ultimate Frisbee hit him hard enough to twist his head three-quarters of the way around his body. He fell without a sound.

Brute fell back on his butt as nine feet of maneless Tsavo lion hit him hard, jaws agape and going for the throat. The boss managed to get one armored forearm up, and the lion decided that was good enough, too, and bit down hard. Brute screamed.

Then the other Tsavo lion jumped me.

Kenya, 1898: the British were building a railway bridge near the Tsavo River and several natives along with Indian workers mysteriously disappeared. It turned out to be the work of two male lions gone rogue. The final death toll before Lt. Colonel John Henry Patterson killed the lions was 135 victims. Of course the Field Museum purchased the stuffed man-eaters.

I ducked, barely avoiding a huge paw that swiped at me as the lion flew overhead. It landed in a crouch and spun, ready to leap again. The smart thing to do would be to run like a striped-assed ape and seek shelter, but I wasn't about to leave the team and I needed to be clear-headed, so letting the rage take over was out. What I needed to do was use my brains. One look at teeth the size of my pinky finger made that a less than comforting thought.

"Here big, bad kitty-kitty-kitty," I crooned, hands up and Bowie ready.

The lion leapt, coming straight at me with front paws extended and claws out. I met the beast full on and was surprised when my weight threw the lion backward head over three-foot tail. It skidded at least ten feet before stopping, shaking its massive head. I looked at my shoulders. Great rents had been made in the ballistic cloth by claws the size of number-two pencils, but they hadn't penetrated the titanium underlayer.

Still, how did I knock an eight-hundred pound Tsavo lion back on its ass? I love Little Debbies, but I tried to keep off the comfort padding, and that tasty filling …. It took a moment. *Oh, right … stuffing* instead of bone and meat and blood. I grinned. *This is going to be fun.*

It was my turn to attack, and while the lion was trying to scramble to its feet, I plowed into it, pretending it was a skinny running back and I was the defensive lineman that wanted to hear bones snap. I landed on its back and began to slash with the Bowie. There it was, sawdust and cotton flying out in great plumes. Tsavo lion, schmavo lion; it was just thin hide over a delicate framework, a big dangerous doll but a doll nonetheless and I meant to play with it until it was in shreds.

More stuffing, more slashing as the lion's hide parted to the razor-sharp Bowie. I was grabbing handfuls as the big cat tried to squirm, but I outweighed it by a good patch and it was wounded, leaking its doll life out of rents. I wasn't stopping at all. It needed to die, it needed to become nothing more than a throw rug and soon. Very soon it wasn't even that. I'd ripped and cut it to shreds and whatever magic had reanimated it was gone. Elvis had left the building.

Assessment time. Brute: down and bleeding, the other lion ripped into six pieces. Brute's skin was chalky white and bloody foam collected at the corners of his mouth. Waldo: taking down what mummies were left, the rest in heaps on the floor, but he looked tired and was listing to port. Mouth: kicking and ripping a camel into its component pieces. She had an ugly bruise on her cheek and an abrasion on her neck but otherwise looked fine.

"Boss," I said, kneeling at Brute's side, "you okay?"

"Stupid ... question," he gasped through a throat clogged with blood. "Take this." He shoved a hard object into my palms. The Seal. Without looking, I placed it my Bat Belt. "Listen, I have to tell you something." He gestured me closer and I put my ear to his mouth and listened as he told me what to do.

I rocked back on my heels. "Boss, I can't ... boss?" Brute wasn't paying attention. In fact, his eyes stared into a distance only he could see.

Damn. Damn-damn-damn!

"Kal?"

I turned to Mouth. "What?"

"Is he gone?"

I nodded.

Waldo turned from the debris of inanimate mummies. Clouds of dust were slowly settling to the floor. "What now, Kal? We bug out or what?"

Bug out. Two words every team leader hates and every team dreads. When a situation became untenable, when it looked like failure was imminent, then it was the leader's responsibility to call for a strategic withdrawal, pulling the team out and calling for reinforcements. There have been dozens of ops where a leader bugged out, and those where a leader *should* have bugged out, so officially there was no onus on a Team Leader calling for a bug out; unofficially it doled out heaps of embarrassment. Enough that those who refused to bug out wound up with a star on the wall of DORMS. They were nice stars, gold-painted with the deceased Agent's full name in the center. Tribute for the fallen, depressing in their number. More Agents have fallen in the line of duty for the BSI than all the American soldiers fallen during the Korean conflict. Needless to say, we don't visit the wall often.

It was on the tip of my tongue. Three Agents gone and Ornias still on the loose with magic that reanimated long-dead creatures. Not a situation to build confidence, but then I spied with my little eye something that began with 'I *really* hate that guy.'

"Jump spell now, Waldo," I grated, keeping my voice low and eyes on the second floor. From the same direction that spawned the mummies came clickety-clackety sounds, bones on tile, sticks rattling in a box. I felt the hairs rise on the back of my neck.

He stared at me blankly while swiveling his head toward the sounds. "What?"

"Jump!"

The Magician got the hint and stared at me for a moment, eyes going all funny as if they were vibrating in their sockets and I felt a tingle run down my spine, a sensation akin to pins-and-needles.

Spell in place, I ran to the other side of the hall, flexed my knees and *jumped*. Such spells are slaved to the intent of those utilizing them and I wanted to get to the second floor. My feet left the ground and physics took a backseat to magic as I flew up and over the second story balcony railing and landed lightly on my feet. Sometimes magic was too cool for school.

What I'd spied with my little eye was a large winged figure cloaked in shadow, but when my eyes hit it, I felt its malice, felt the hate that boiled from it like steam against my skin. It was that shadow I faced now.

The Lahti was out, but a lightning swipe of a leathery wing knocked it from my grip and another knocked the Seal from my other hand, leaving fingers stinging beneath my armored gloves.

"Too late, Kal," purred the shadowy form as I backed away. "Far too late."

Keep it talking. "Ornias, I presume?"

Twin points of light appeared, one red and one yellow. Its baleful glare pierced me. "Of course."

"Clever with the T. rex. Nice touch."

It took a gliding step forward, the shadows still cloaking its form, but I received an impression of massive shoulders and inhumanly long arms. "I am going to kill you, human, and then I am going to strip the Seal from your dead leader's grasp before I kill your friends." Its matter-of-fact directness froze my blood.

Point of interest, though. It still thought that Brute had the Seal; it didn't know that what it had knocked from my hand was the very thing it was looking for. "Care to talk about it first?" I asked.

"Done talking." It swooped toward me, moving faster than something that big should've been capable of. A freaky long arm swiped at my head, the air *whooshing* past, but I managed to duck and it ripped overhead. I dove to the left, hit the floor hard, and rolled, palming the Seal from where it lay.

Ornias was on me and my scalp was afire, an instantaneous wave of heat that ran all the way to my jaw line and the acrid stench of burning hair filled my nose and I screamed, screamed so loud because it hurt so much, the rage wanted to surface—I could feel it come to the fore—but I didn't want it because all I would do then was attack and attack and attack and I needed some semblance of reason. However, resisting it was hard because I hurt so much and I wanted to give in to the fury inside. I refused it and I could hear it *howl* as I tamped it down into the darkest recesses of my mind, and I screamed as my hair crisped and those shadowy talons nearly engulfed my head, lifting me from the ground to dangle eight inches from the floor. It drew back a shadowy arm bigger than my thigh, and for a moment I could see a six-fingered hand ending in claws that looked to be needle-sharp, proving that I was a second away from death. That hand would rip my head from my shoulders, so I did the only thing I could do, what I'd planned to do, what Brute had told me to do.

I shoved the Seal against Ornias' forearm.

My feet hit the floor a split second later, the fiery pain along my scalp still a searing hurt, but the wail from the demon was worse. It pierced my skull, a shriek that bounced around the hall below, and I was pretty damn surprised the masonry didn't burst apart with its force.

"Touch the Seal to the demon, Kal," Brute had told me. "That's how to enslave it. It can't abide actually touching the Seal with its physical aspect. The Seal has to touch the demon; then you can banish it."

"Go to hell!" I screamed over the shrieks of the demon, and I fell to my knees.

Ornias reeled back, shedding shadows, and for the first time I saw the demon as it was, or at least the form it chose to wear at the time. A tall, golden-skinned man, superficially flawless in every way, naked and resplendent in the glory of its perfection, but beneath and beyond its perfection lay a sickness visible through its golden skin. It was if its damnation shone through like a carrion light that assaulted my optic nerves with necrotic potency. And right under the smell of burnt hair lay a gangrenous perfume that was both sweet and foul, like the stench on a corpse dead a week.

Ornias continued to scream as I sat there and his form wavered, blanketed in a kind of heat shimmer before simply disappearing with a dry *pop* of air.

Gone.

Bug out? Hell with that, I thought. *We just got here.*

CHAPTER TWENTY-THREE

———

Kal
Taking Care of Business

MY EYES OPENED and silver runes met them. The heaviness in my stomach told me that the Elevator of Demonic S&M Super Terrific Fun Time was still on the rise. Only a few seconds had passed. How odd ….

So what had I learned from my dream? Definitely a warning of some sort. Last time I had a vision was in Omaha when my subconscious dredged up memories from the Mall of America in Minnesota. Those dreams were warnings about Maydock and how he'd been stalking me for years. I also took those dreams to be warnings that I couldn't face Maydock alone, that I'd need someone to watch my back, like my team had my back when facing one of the most insidious, evil monsters ever to stamp on the earth with a cloven hoof—the Cutty Black Sow.

That second warning nudged me in the direction of Marcus, the vampire elder (although 'elder' isn't an adequate term to convey a being old enough to have watched the rise and fall of Rome) who was the chief judge of his race—sort of like Judge Dredd for bloodsuckers, but not as charming and erudite. He proved less helpful than I thought, but that's a story for another time.

For some reason my subconscious, using what little magic I had, was trying to tell me something urgent, but for the life of me I couldn't figure it out. I yawned as the elevator came to a stop. The LED floor indicator read '28.'

"Kal?" said Ghost. He sounded ... surprised. "Did your experiment fail?"

"How long?"

"One minute forty-seven point three seconds."

That was *fast*. "My experiment didn't fail, Ghost." I checked all my weapons (all there except for the Bowie) and my ammo (almost gone) and made ready. "Maybe my subconscious understood my time constraints and uploaded the dream/memory in double time. I don't know." Once again I looked at the readout. "Why aren't we on the thirtieth floor?"

"The other members of your team are here on the twenty-eighth."

Oh thank god! "Report."

And he did. All his clones (which he'd since reabsorbed) kept full accounts of events and while the DRAFTlite didn't have the same kind of virtual reality capabilities as the original DRAFT, the brief visuals I experienced sent a chill through my guts. They'd all suffered horribly, but what happened to Tweezer sent a spike of rage through my brain. I never liked the guy—he was an idiot with all the subtlety of a thrown brick—but he was a fellow Agent and no one should have to die the way he did.

Then there was Billings.

Of course I knew about the man, that he was a few cans short of six pack, but by all indications he was unusually disciplined and a Bureau veteran. Vetted by Bureau headshrinkers, he had BB's confidence, which was no mean feat.

I don't know why I was shocked and horrified. With my cynical outlook on life I shouldn't have just asked myself if Billings would turn on us like a rabid dog, but *when*. It took a few seconds for me to realize that Ghost was droning at me, and had been for a while now.

"What?"

"I simply asked if you were ready to exit the elevator."

"Sure, Ghost." I nodded toward the door. "But how did you control it? I thought all Quint computers were down."

"This elevator has a dedicated computer system that is a stand-alone with Wi-Fi that only extends to the length of the elevator. I was able to access it and take control of the systems, although this does not allow me to exit the building. It also has a dedicated entertainment system with three television sets hidden within the walls. There is a startlingly huge library of pornography to be found there as well. I also surmise that the shaft is insulated with silver mesh so the Bureau cannot detect any magic being cast in the vicinity."

I snorted. Go figure. It seemed that Tobias Quint created his own little pleasure room he could ride (pardon the pun) up and down the building. Throw in a succubus to add spice to the mix and you had one hell of a mobile seraglio. I wondered how he kept the sex demon from devouring his soul. Maybe he offered her the occasional sacrifice, or that spell Shape I'd destroyed kept her in line. The real question was why? Having a succubus on tap was like wearing a meat suit in a cage full of tigers—you don't mess around with such predators. Perhaps he used her to seduce politicians for favors, although I reckoned that the succubus would fear for her soul if that was the case.

"Let's go get the kids, Ghost."

The door swung out into a hallway, and wouldn't you know it, the team was right there, huddled around the still form of Buffalo—Agent Robert Atkins.

Dove looked worse for wear, and when she met my eyes, hers contained enough world-weariness to crush just about any soul you'd care to meet. It set me back on my heels.

"Hi, boss," she said, eyes red. "Ghost said you were on the way. What horrible dimension did you have to pass through to get here? And what's that sticking out of your face?" Instead of the subtle tone of contempt and anger that usually flavored her speech, I heard a grudging acceptance, as if she'd finally sanded down the chip on her shoulder to more manageable levels. I took this to be a good thing. Still, what scars would decorate her soul now?

"This," I replied with all the dignity my battered body could muster, "is what they call a see-gar. You smoke them."

"You shouldn't smoke," she said automatically. "Bad for you."

"I am a grown-ass man and can do whatever I damn well please." I concentrated and lit the end of the cigar, which was all of three inches long now. "Don't tell Jeanie."

Rat, skin sallow and waxy, merely nodded, while Ng looked like his face had had a run-in with a malignant lawnmower and then been bandaged by a staple enthusiast. I didn't want to look at the place where his hand had been, but I forced myself to.

He followed my gaze. "Rat couldn't heal it, didn't have the energy," he said hollowly. "The wound hurts a bit, but thanks to some Oxy, I don't care."

I nodded. "Report."

"Except for Ng and Robert," said Dove, "we're ready to rock 'n' roll."

Rat nodded tiredly.

Ng had something to say about that. "You're not going without me."

"You're injured." I crossed my arms and puffed on the cigar. That should've been it. "You stay here."

"Not so injured I can't fight. I need to see this through, see it done once and for all. Besides, what makes you think I'll be any kind of safe in *this* building?"

"Stand down."

Dark eyes became obsidian hard. "No."

Why me, Lord? What could I use against him, harsh language? The Bureau tends to recruit the stubborn types. Maybe Ng was part Finn. "Grab your gear, check your ammo, and let's get going." If my brief scan of their adventures was any indication, they were either short or out of rounds. I had a sneaking suspicion that before this op was done, we'd be down to fists and blades and whatever tricks I had up my sleeve. I felt a twinge of loss at the thought of my poor departed Bowie.

Dove rose to her feet, moving as if her joints were filled with drying cement. "Any ideas where we're supposed to head, boss?"

"From Ghost's analysis, the Supernatural that's running this shindig doesn't want anyone to get below this floor, so I say we go down. I think whoever this Angel of Mass Murder is, he's somewhere between the tenth and twenty-eighth floor. We just have to get a move on."

"So how do we do that?"

I gestured toward the door at the end of the hall. "Same way I got up here."

"Janitor's closet?"

"Our way off this floor." At her look, I shook my head. "No time now for stories. All aboard."

It breezed down the hallway like wind off a battlefield, a voice that instantly raised the hackles on the back of my neck. "But I do so love stories," it crooned in a soft and sugary voice, avuncular and evil. "Do tell me one, Agent Hakala."

The Lahti came up, appearing in my hand as if by magic, barely outdrawing the rest of the team. Even Ng, who was no lefty, had a K-bar in hand.

"Please, no violence. I come bearing an offer."

Oh, of course you do. "And what would that be? Mutilation? Eternal torment? A subscription to the Cheese-of-the-Month Club?"

Soft laughter. "No, although those would be wonderful. I am fully prepared to let you go."

Somewhere there was another shoe ready to drop. "And why would a powerful Supernatural like yourself be willing to do such a thing?" My throat was clogged with sarcasm. "Mercy?"

"I do not know what 'mercy' is. I don't think I've ever felt pity, although I'm led to believe it is part and parcel of the human condition." He paused. "However, I was never human. Or, at least, I don't think so. Time has a way of muddling memories."

"*Ghost, can you track him?*" I subvocaled.

My faithful cybernetic sidekick was quick to answer. "The voice is coming from the building's speakers, which is unusual because when this being communicated with Agent Billings it was by some form that was not registered by the DRAFTlite. I dare say that this entity does not want to risk any violence."

Dove gave me a look while Rat nodded his agreement. The angel had touched Rat in the blue world, and if he could touch, that meant he could *be* touched. "Then why? Why let us go?"

"You are no longer needed, Agent Hakala. I've drained your magic and almost all the magic from your pet Magician. There is no more need to feed off your deaths and pain because I have sufficient energy now."

Rat's subvocal voice came through the ear patch. "*If it needs magic to survive, then killin' the first team woulda given it a boatload, boss, and I'm guessin' that Buffalo's death provided plenty as well. If what it's sayin' is true, that it doesn't need more from us, then it's even more dangerous than it was before. It must be ready to leave the buildin', and that means it's about strong enough to withstand anythin' the Bureau can throw at it.*"

Ng's drug-dilated eyes opened wide and Dove looked ready to vomit. I thought fast. "How are you going to let us go, then?" I asked, praying that the angel couldn't hear our subvocal conversation.

"I merely let the barrier that coats this building down and you walk out. It's that simple."

R-i-i-ght. "Just that simple, eh?"

"Quite."

My mind raced as I considered the implications. The Angel of Mass Murder seemed to be handing us a 'Get Out of Jail Free' card. Ng needed medical attention, Rat looked like ten miles of road kill, and all the piss and vinegar seemed to have bled out of Dove's veins. Not to mention my new hairdo (or hair-don't) and various contusions and abrasions. My chest hurt something fierce from where the succubus tried punch my heart out through my spine and I was craving a serious slug of vodka.

Too good to be true—had to be. The proof was in the pudding and I wasn't about to trust the Supernatural as far as I could shot put the Chrysler Building.

"Okay," I said slowly, "how about lowering your force field now?" To Ghost, *"Get ready, old Spook."*

"On it, Kal," he replied.

Gone was the sense of amusement as the voice replied, "How do I know you won't order an airstrike on this location, Agent Hakala? Make of yourself and your team martyrs for the cause?"

"Same way I trust you to let us go without any monkey business. Call it a sign of good faith."

"I will have to decline, I am afraid."

Thought so, you sneaky bastard. "Well then, the only thing left to say is [CENSORED] you, asshole," I yelled in my best Schwarzenegger.

No more Mr. Nice Guy, the voice cut out abruptly and the screaming started—that horrible, high-pitched wail that hit my eardrums like spikes, digging into the soft tissues of my inner ear. From the corner of my eye, I saw Dove swoon and Rat grow even whiter, folding at the knees, while Wesley Ng began vomiting into his lap. From around the bend of the outer wall came the gray/red sphere, roughly the size of a beach ball and sizzling with malice, shooting our way and trailing its ugly, dirty mist behind it.

"Damn you!" I screamed futilely at the orb, slapping my palms over my ears. It would be here any second now and I we would be done like dinner.

From four pairs of DRAFTlite came a familiar voice, now taut with some unnamable emotion. "Not this time!"

Four DRAFTlite speakers began to emit a low thrum, a bone-deep vibration that I seemed to feel more than hear. It enveloped my skull in cottony noise that cut through the high-pitched screeching of the orb, a low counterpoint that buoyed me up, lifting me from pain, soothing my raw nerves. The bass hum became my world—annoying, but safe—and I found myself once again able to think.

"Awesome," I growled. Or I think I did. The only thing I could hear was the Ghost hum, but that was peachy with me.

The orb slid to a halt some twenty feet away, hovering over the carpeting and vibrating in place. It looked ... confused.

Whether it was annoyed or dismayed by Ghost's counter-noise, I didn't care. All I wanted was something to kill, and standing still, it made an excellent target. The Lahti spat its last few rounds and I saw puffs of ugly mist or steam erupt from its center.

The orb began to retreat and I drew my punch knives, the blades sticking straight out from between my fingers. I ran toward the orb, but it retreated too quickly, still bleeding vapor from where I'd shot it. Ghost's noise faded and I began to be able to hear again.

"It took a while for me to find the correct frequency that would not cause you permanent hearing loss," commented Ghost when the orb was gone. "I think that worked quite well."

"Goddamn it!" I swore and headed back to the team. My ears were ringing, but at least it was the honest noise of tinnitus. "Mount up. We are out of here."

Ghost cut in on our preparations. "Kal, it is sure now that the Angel of Mass Murder knows about the elevator. He will no doubt use the folding space trick to keep us from descending."

"The elevator is shielded, Ghost. With silver, with gold or platinum, it's shielded from magic. You said so."

"I surmised it was, Kal. It is not certain."

"Good enough for me, old spook." I chewed on the cigar, puffing away. It had tasted kind of nasty at first, but now I was getting used to it. "Besides, I have me a cunning *idea*."

The team gave out a collective groan. No faith in their fearless leader. It would've hurt if I gave a damn right then. I chomped down on the stub of my cigar. "Everyone, give me your belts."

"*This*? This is your cunnin' idea?" Rat sounded less than impressed with my tactics. Sweat streamed down his face as he descended the ladder.

I sent up a noxious cloud of cigar smoke. Only a couple inches left on my stogie, but I had the rhythm of the smoke, and I knew I could milk it down to the one-inch mark. "Deal with it, Agent," I grumbled, keeping my eyes on Ng above me. His face was paper-white and he was sweating more than Rat. With every rung down the ladder, he hooked his injured arm around the horizontal bar while navigating with his remaining hand. Each step made him wince, despite the Oxy coursing through his system. I was point man on our descent because it was my boneheaded idea and we needed someone strong to catch Ng should he take a tumble.

Ghost sent the elevator on down ahead of us, but kept the door open so we could descend the service ladder. The shaft looked clean, free of grime and grease. I examined the cement walls and wondered if Quint had used silver or gold mesh to turn the shaft into a Faraday cage.

Units of magic are measured (creatively enough) in 'merlins.' A single merlin could light a cigar. A hundred merlins could fry a nervous system. Precious metals absorbed merlins—that is, until they absorbed so much they began to bleed excess magical energy in the form of heat. The amount of precious metals used to coat the inside of a thirty-story elevator shaft had the absorptive potential to negate *ten terramerlins* of raw magical energy. That's enough magic to short circuit the brainstems of a million people.

My guess was that our little pal, the Angel of Mass Murder, couldn't penetrate the elevator shaft with magic, so he had to use other avenues to foil our attempt to stop him. Thing was, I had no clue as to what he planned to do.

But I found out right quick.

At floor twenty, the *faux* maintenance door burst in with a *bang*, ripping off steel hinges to slam into the opposite wall. The elevator continued its descent and had just passed eighteen when something the size of an upright Ford Gran Torino burst through the opening, sending pieces of door frame flying, and leapt into the shaft, one giant hand grasping the thick elevator cables. The cables groaned alarmingly as the weight of the creature threatened to tear them like tissue, and it clung to them for a brief moment before falling to land upon the car below.

Metal buckled under a thousand pounds of raw-muscled, slab-sided humanoid that began to tear at the roof of the car with fingers as long as road flares tipped with bear-like claws. Steel shrieked in agony as those enormous talons tore and shredded.

"Of course," Dove said tiredly over the din. "It had to be an ogre."

CHAPTER TWENTY-FOUR

Kal
It's the End of the World as We Know It ....

IF THE INCREDIBLE Hulk had a bastard love child with a cement mixer, an ogre would be most likely be the result. Up to twelve feet tall, built like a Chevy with legs, covered in hide thicker than a rhino's, and with a face not even a nearsighted mother could love, ogres have only one redeeming quality: they hate everyone equally.

"Be vewy, vewy quiet," I subvocaled. *"It's hunting BSI Agents."* I did my best to add a little machine gun burst of laugher. *"Ha-ha-ha-ha-ha."*

Soft groans ghosted through the bone-induction patch behind my ear. As they faded away, Wesley Ng's voice came through. *"Hope this is over soon, boss, because I can't hang here forever."*

I looked up in time to catch a drop of his sweat right in the eye. It stung like a bitch, but what can you do? It's not like he was aiming for my baby blues. *"Hold on, Ng, the elevator has to descend a couple dozen more feet. Last thing we need is for a pressure wave to kill us now."* I patted my waist where the Bat Belt used to be.

My clever *idea*, the one that had my team more scared than

a mouse at a cat convention, was to use the explosives that comprised our belts.

You see, about three years ago, Special Branch came up with a clever invention, an explosive with the look, feel, and tensile strength of leather. Incredibly stable, the explosive, dubbed 'boom leather,' only reacted to a magically (but was not magic in and of itself) created acid called ... well, the technogeeknerds gave it a long, twenty-seven syllable name that even I, with a master's in chemical engineering, can't pronounce or understand. I call it 'boom juice.' Safe to say it takes a Magician the better part of a day to produce a gram of the stuff so it's not like there are gallons of the liquid lying about waiting to react with boom leather.

I'd used four belts, a little over one pound of boom leather with an expansion rate of 25,800 feet per second upon detonation. The belts were tied in a Gordian knot and placed on the floor of the car, a gram of boom juice (formerly hidden in the heel of my boot) and radio detonator in the center of the bundle.

"*Now Kal!*" urged Dove.

"Wait for it."

The ogre lifted a fist the size of a four-cylinder engine and hammered it completely through the top of the elevator, a stomach-wrenching deep roar of victory blasting through its mouth.

"Boss!"

"*Now kids, let Daddy work.*" Some people have no patience, a hindrance to careful planning and homicidal precision.

Metal tore and ripped and the ogre dropped from sight into the car. I tapped a virtual icon on the DRAFTlite. The glasses sent out a weak radio signal to the detonator far below.

Twenty-five thousand feet per second sounds like a lot, when in fact it's a little less than the expansion rate of C4. However, when you're right next to a pound of boom leather, a little less than C4 doesn't count for beans.

The elevator disappeared in a bright flash of energy and a clap of thunder as the boom leather cooked off. The minimum kill radius on that much explosive is about ten feet, but when the pressure wave is stuffed into a ten-by-ten elevator shaft, it has only two places to go, up or down.

Hot wind scorched my face as the pressure wave hit us, fortunately dissipated by distance, though the blast was strong enough to rattle my teeth. The cables, not more than three feet away, swayed heavily as the weight of the car suddenly disappeared. From below, carried with the wind, a spherical object flew up, up, and up until it flew past, but not before I caught of glimpse of torn and burnt leathery skin and empty, blasted eye sockets beneath a thick shelf of bone.

"*That's one big-ass head,*" commented Rat.

I grinned. "*Big as a basketball.*" We watched as it sailed back down and fell out of sight, down the shaft toward the wreckage of the car. The echoes of its crashing still bounced along the cement walls.

"Okay," I said aloud, feeling pretty chipper. It's not every day you kill an ogre, especially with such *flair*. Showmanship matters. "Let's go."

Ng hesitated. "How far?"

"We're on the twenty-fifth floor, so let's see what the twentieth looks like. Nice round number, that."

They groaned and grumbled, but in the end where else were they going to go?

In short order, we made it to the twentieth and pried the door open while trying not to fall head over heels into the shaft.

Another hallway greeted us, curving to the left along the outside wall. It was the mirror image of the area we'd left above, except no dead Agents and no ugly orbs to shriek in our ears. Thanks to Ghost, it looked like the shrieking no longer posed a problem.

Ng leaned against the wall and slowly collapsed until his cheeks hit the carpet. "What's down here?" He didn't bother with subvocaling.

I knelt at his side. "Answers, Wesley." My mouth felt dry as toast, but I kept speaking, trying to keep him focused on the here and now. "The Angel didn't want anyone down below the twenty-eighth, so maybe, just maybe, the way to beat him is here."

"Gimme a second, I need to catch my breath."

He needed a vascular surgeon and four straight days of sleep, but I merely held out a hand to Rat and he set two off-white tablets on my palms. "You mean to continue, Wes?" I asked.

That earned me a weak nod.

I held out the tablets. "Take."

"Oxy?"

"Yeah."

He dry-swallowed the pair.

"Need some rest?"

Ng considered that for a moment. "Nah, the Oxy will kick in soon."

Onward then. We headed along the outside wall, guns and knives at the ready. The only person still in possession of bullets was Rat, and he had pistol in hand. Considering that we were after a Supernatural with the ability to shapeshift into a screaming beach ball along with other unknown magical and physical abilities, our weapons seemed kind of pathetic. We were bringing knives to a magic fight, but what else could we do? Where could we go? The op needed to get done and sometimes all you can do when the odds are piled high against you is grin at the devil and spit in his eye.

We passed several branches leading toward the guts of the building, but it wasn't until we'd traveled a good hundred or so yards that we took one. It made sense that whatever the Angel didn't want us to see lay deeper in. Slowly, carefully, we made our way into the belly of the beast, tensions running high.

Several times I blinked sweat out of my eyes, and I could see that my team members' nerves were strung tighter than piano wire. It's hard to maintain that level of alertness. The human body and mind can only function like that for a short while before becoming distracted by other needs or events. Still, all of us had practice dealing with stress, so we managed to stay bright-eyed and bushy-tailed despite all that had occurred. Except for Ng, who, judging by the glassy look in his eyes, was starting to feel the Oxy.

We arrived shortly at a wooden office door with the words BARTON AVIONICS stenciled in black, smack dead center. Why would an avionics … never mind. I shook my head and opened the door wide.

And here I'd thought things were weird before.

Imagine a rope made of translucent bluish flesh a foot thick and a couple hundred yards long. Now take that rope and tie the ends together seamlessly. Got it? Well then, you're better at this than I am because my mind still wobbles. Take that rope and cover it with a jillion tiny mouths with perfect ruby lips— lips that should be on the face of a beautiful Hollywood starlet, glistening and beckoning. Now have those lips move in strange sinuous ways that no human lips could imitate and have them cover teeth like a lamprey's, all bone-white needles around the edges of the mouths leading down into the depths of the flesh cable.

Still with me? Good, now have that ring of blue flesh hang in midair, a circular horror that spins and rotates while it spins, a hula hoop from your worst nightmare. Now add another, smaller circle of flesh inside that one, also rotating on its axis while spinning. Then add a third, smaller ring about twenty yards in diameter in the center, spinning and rotating. In the center of this ring, where there should be nice, clear, sane air, add a shimmering nothingness that eats light and spits out a grayish aura I could only describe as not-light. Not blackness, not darkness, more like a negation of vision, as if the blind spot in your eye were to expand to hover in the middle of that center ring.

You expect something of that size, all spinny and such, to be noisy, to cleave the air with a great *whoosh*, but the flesh rings were eerily silent and that in itself added to their horror.

It was pretty trippy.

There we stood, staring at the rings as they hung in the chilly air, barely realizing that the entire center of the Quint Building had disappeared, had been hollowed out like a pumpkin for Halloween from floors five to twenty-seven. The internal structure had all been sheared away neatly as if by a giant laser scalpel, leaving pristine, antiseptic terminations to the interior structure. As to where the rest had gone—all that material such as wood and concrete—I didn't know. There was no rubble, no dust. Nothing. Despite the fact that several thousand tons of debris should have been lying on the floor of the chasm … nothing.

"Boss," said Rat, "I sure am hatin' what I'm seein.' "

"For once I agree with the little skink," Dove added.

Ng shook his head. "Please tell me this is a drug-induced hallucination."

"Ladies and gentlemen," I quipped, "please put your tables and seatbacks in their upright and stored position."

Moving carefully to where the floor ended and a whole big span of nothing began, I peered out over the drop. *Whoa!* Way farther down than I really wanted to consider. My stomach crawled up to my throat as I estimated the interior of this hollow to be at least twenty stories tall and far enough across that it was hard to see the other side.

It was then, as I stared out into the hollow of the building, that I heard the voices. Whispery things that slid through my ears, a soft babble that at first didn't make any sense. The more I listened, the more I felt the need to move closer to the spinning flesh ropes, to touch them, to caress those twisting lips. Something deep inside me, the primitive limbic animal, began to squeal in dismay. I took a step closer to the edge, to where the carpeting had been sliced clean. Just a few feet away, a glistening ribbon of blue flesh spun, spouting those whispery, almost intelligible words that caressed, urged, drew me closer.

"You feel that, boss?"

What? Suddenly I was back to myself, right foot a bare inch from eternity, the flesh rope spinning close, no longer rotating, but staying oriented toward me, multiple ruby lips quivering as if in excitement. I quickly backpedaled and tried to think about Rat's words. *"Feel what?"*

"That thing. It's radiatin' so much magic .... Can't you guys feel it?"

Dove and Ng shook their heads, but I shut my eyes for a moment in an effort to feel what rattled Rat's cage. *There.* At the edge of my mind, like a half-remembered dream, an almost inaudible buzzing. Soft, subtle, and easy to overlook.

"What is that?" I asked.

I received a reply, not from Rat, but from Ng. "That is the voice of the Engine," he said aloud, startling all of us. "Only Magicians can hear it. The Angel summoned it to bring Those Who Dwell Between to our world."

"Subvocal, Wesley!" I hissed.

He failed to heed my urgency. "You see, the Angel has escaped from Hell many times, and each time he's been caught, dragged back to suffer more than we can imagine. This time, however, he came upon the idea of using us, the BSI, to call the Engine, to bring into the world beings even Hell fears more than the wrath of God. Not to kill mankind, mind you, but to destroy civilizations and to distract the Lords of the Abyss so they will be too busy fighting these new monsters to deal with him. When the first team arrived, the Angel sucked out their magic then killed them one by one to harness the energy generated by their deaths. All to bring the Engine here. The terrible power of Necromancy. Even Sixer, driven mad by hallucinations, gave the Angel tremendous power when he killed himself. This power, coupled with the weakness in the fabric of reality that lies beneath St. Louis, allowed him access to the pocket dimensions you were in. These pocket dimensions, had you died there, would have funneled magic directly into the Engine, making it unnecessary for him to use himself as a conduit. Had you died in those dimensions, the gateway would already have opened and we wouldn't be talking right now. We would be screaming."

I was starting to get creeped out on a major scale. "How do you know this?"

The confidant, smug smile he turned to me seemed awfully familiar. "If the Angel can bring these beings through to this world, millions, perhaps billions will die and then he can kill to his heart's content while mankind and all the forces of creation battle them in an effort to save the universe. It's a win-win for the Angel of Mass Murder, a being as old as mankind. He can skip through the rubble of this world, gathering worshippers and shedding blood." Ng showed all his teeth. It wasn't a smile. "Did you know he's the creator of the Kali cult? The Thugees? He's got quite an imagination, that one." He shook his head, teeth still bared in a not-smile. "Only thing is, you all proved much too resilient; you didn't die when you should have."

Rat took a step back from Ng, fear written on his face, while Dove looked like she wanted to sock him in the mouth. I took a step forward, keeping my voice low. "Wesley, or whoever you are, what's going on?"

Sweat ran from his skin in such quantities that I thought he'd desiccate in seconds. "I've given you enough information, Kal. It's time for me to pass out now." With that, he closed his eyes and fell to the floor. Or would have if Dove hadn't caught him and lowered him gently. Although a good foot shorter than Ng, she packed enough solid muscle on her tiny frame to give a linebacker pause.

"What is wrong with him?" she asked once Ng was settled.

His face still dripped sweat, but not as much as before.

"Someone is messin' with us," said Rat, staring at Ng's prone form. "I bet that Angel fella took over his mind, just to screw around and twist us all about."

I considered Ng for a moment, moving the last bit of my cigar from one side of my mouth to the other before spitting it out onto the floor. It hit me then, as that moist hunk of tobacco rolled to a stop, where I'd seen that smug, crap-eating smile before, and a slow burn of anger began in my gut.

"Goddamn it," I muttered to myself, "played like a rube."

That got Dove's attention. "What are you talking about?"

I shook my head, still staring at the remains of the cigar. "Not relevant now."

"Urrk!"

My head swiveled up in time to see Dove folding over and falling to the floor. Billings stood over her in the doorway, bloody knife in hand, his perfectly muscled bare torso gleaming with sweat. A large fist blurred and cracked Rat on the jaw, lifting him up off his toes. He hung there for a split second before crashing to the floor.

"Very good, Mr. Billings," said a voice from behind. I turned to see a man dressed in a black waistcoat, a lime cravat, and dark gray pants floating in the void next to the fleshy Engine. On his head rested a black silk top hat. In one hand he twirled a cane, topped with an amethyst the size of a baby's fist. "Do you think you can kill Agent Hakala?"

Billings' bushy beard split to show teeth grown pointed. "Of course."

"The Angel, I suppose?" My voice remained neutral, as if I were discussing the weather, but my mind was racing, calculating the odds and inventorying the weapons secreted around my body.

A tip of the top hat to me. "Of course. I commend you on your resilience." To Billings, "Sir, I appreciate your inestimable skills, but I respect Agent Hakala too much to leave him to a single agency to dispatch." A horrid, wet smile split his face. I couldn't tell whether he was handsome or not; the more I looked at his face, the less I saw. "Let us do this together. Let us kill a legend."

And they attacked.

CHAPTER TWENTY-FIVE

———

Kal
(And I Feel Fine)

A FISTFUL OF K-bar arced toward my throat. I leaned back just far enough for it to miss, but near enough for it to give me a close shave. My own K-bar met air as Billings danced back, oddly graceful for a man that big. I followed up with a forearm smash that flattened his nose across his cheeks, spurting blood all over the NewTanium armor.

A glint of purple and that same arm came up, blocking the large amethyst at the end of the Angel's cane. The shock of it numbed the flesh beneath my armor. The Angel sped away through the air before I could counterstrike.

I whirled, almost pirouetting, trying to keep my assailants in sight and grow a set of eyes in the back of my head. No dice there, but I planted my backside into a corner and waited for them to close in. My prospects looked grim as they both slowly approached, cane raised and K-bar ready.

My boot slammed into Billings' chest. It felt like I'd hit a brick wall, but it staggered him enough that his jab missed my knee and skittered along my thigh armor, slicing through the Kevlar weave and exposing shining metal. Next the Angel's cane came swinging, the amethyst head slamming with tremendous force against my left shoulder. Normally the bones would have, should have, broken with the impact because the cane didn't even bend, transferring all that kinetic energy to my delicate Finnish tissues, but the armor held, only buckling slightly, while my shoulder gave way to the semi-precious stone, which also should have shattered but didn't. The pain, deep and sharp, almost drove me to my knees as the ball and socket joint separated, and I almost dropped, almost swooned. My vision went dark around the edges and I might have screamed but couldn't be sure. Right then I wished for the rage, but it didn't answer because my magic, my sister's magic, was history. Right then all I could do was flail with the K-bar that rested in my good hand while what felt like shards of glass ground down bone in my damaged shoulder. It was ticket-punching time for Kal Hakala.

Dylan Thomas had it right—'Do not go gentle into that good night'—but I couldn't rage against the dying of my light. I could, however, let Billings' know he'd been in a damn fight.

"No."

Ignoring the Angel, I threw my best tackle, a bone-breaking, arm-twisting, back-shattering throw down right in the middle of Billings' rock-hard, sculpted-out-of-alabaster abs. He actually emitted a surprised *oof* as I lifted him off his feet and slammed him to the ground, and for a moment, the lights went out as the agony in my shoulder drove consciousness into the backseat.

"No."

The word hammered into my skull from somewhere, a denial that brought me back into the light, and I rolled in time to see the amethyst cave in the floor where my head had been.

"NO!"

I knew that voice, that droning, buzzing voice. It filled my head like the incessant noise of a swarm of locusts and it was carried through the DRAFTlite speakers and the bone induction ear patch.

"*NOOOOOO!*" Ghost's voice was a painful roar of staticky rage that took my breath away. Bright lights began flashing along the rims of the DRAFTlite and the amulet resting against my chest grew painful, almost scorching-hot.

The Angel cocked his head, top hat firmly seated despite the severe angle. "What is this?"

My vision took a brief vacation as the light flashing on the rims of the DRAFTlite became blisteringly intense. Desperately I clawed at the glasses and threw them to the side, blinded. Nothing but yellow and black blobs floated before my eyes.

Once again the Angel asked, "What is this?"

"*This is me finally becoming angry,*" said a familiar droning voice that sent a thrill through me, even though all I could see were spots. "*This is me not playing it safe anymore.*"

Although Ghost's voice remained the same annoying buzz, it now contained more raw emotion than I'd ever heard. There was a new tone of fury and outrage, and that scared me more than the possibility of him crashing the Internet and starting World War III. I blinked rapidly and rubbed my eyes. What appeared before me as my vision cleared made me realize that the clean underwear I put on that morning might be superfluous.

Outlined in blue and green witch lights, standing defiant before the Angel of Mass Murder, the Saint of Slaying, was the translucent image of a young man in wire-rim glasses. Skinny and tall, he looked like a member of a technogeeknerd boy band, complete with polo shirt and ghostly khakis. His spectral eyes were fixed on the Angel, but he held up his hand, palm out, to me. "*Stay there, Kal. I have this.*"

The Angel smiled. "So the little crab has decided to emerge from his shell."

I still couldn't quite process what I was seeing; my mind seemed to be stuck in a feedback loop. The impressions still made it to my brain, but the brain kept sending back a message saying, 'What the [CENSORED]?'

"Ghost?"

The spectral young man nodded. "I guess I finally found something to provoke an emotion, Kal. Let me take care of the Angel. You deal with Billings." His opponent was grinning hugely, a smile that left no clear image, only an impression of razors slicing into intestines. Ghost told him, "You forget, crabs have claws," and launched himself at the Angel.

Instead of meeting Ghost head on, the Saint of Slaying shrunk into his ugly beach ball form and flew away, which didn't seem to bother Ghost. Extending his arms like Superman, he flew after.

"Just you and me now, Kal," said Billings as he rose to his feet. I scrambled up a second later, my shoulder on fire. "I always wanted to see which one of us is better."

I pointed to his bare, almost inhumanly muscular and perfect torso. "No fair. You're obviously on some serious steroids. Why don't we call this a draw?"

His answer was a thrust for my eyes with the pointy end of a razor-sharp K-bar. I blocked with my good hand and danced back, keeping an eye on his shoulders and eyes, looking for any telltale sign of attack.

Billings' left deltoid twitched and I leaned back as the knife whizzed by, a hairsbreadth from my nose. Another twitch and another dodge; this time the blade parted the Kevlar at my right triceps, exposing the shiny NewTanium underneath.

"You're slowing down, Kal," Billings said, a feral grin splitting his long beard. "Too hurt, you can't avoid this forever. Give up and I'll make it quick."

My overhand right took him by surprise, a sharp blow that split his lips against his teeth. A follow-up kick to the shin sent him stumbling almost to his knees, but he met an uppercut that straightened him right up to his tippy toes before he crashed backward onto his ass.

I went after him like a one-armed Angel of Death, stomping

and swinging for the cheap seats. A well-planted boot slammed down on his right ankle and I felt an uncharitable rush of excitement as I heard it snap like a pine log in a fire. Another kick to his knife hand sent the blade flying to plant an inch into drywall.

Fire rolled around my neck from my shoulder, but I was far too high from the fight to care. I was drawing back a boot for a good kick to a kneecap, when suddenly Billings rose up as if pulled by marionette strings. The ankle I stomped on didn't seem to bother him a bit.

He spat a bloody gobbet at my feet. "My turn."

Uh-oh.

A fist blurred toward my nose and I tried for a block, but it felt like pushing against a speeding semi. The blow exploded against my nose and lifted me off my feet for a clean second, knocking me back on my butt. After the initial thrust of dull, hammering pain, the world went away for a while. *I* went away for a while.

Stinging and a crushing pressure against my gut brought me back from la-la land, the pain a sharp and insistent tattoo on my cheeks. With barbed hooks, they dragged my consciousness to the surface and forced my eyes open. I immediately wanted to close them again.

Billings was sitting on me, big hands rising and falling with the precision of a metronome, each fall bringing a slap, each slap a nail of pain and a flush of heat. His eyes lit with almost unholy joy as they met mine.

"Blg," I mumbled, vaguely aware of the void below my skull— my head lay halfway over the cutoff. The hungry whispers of the Engine were close enough to touch.

"There you are, Kal," crooned Billings, his lips drooling blood onto my chin. "Thought you were going to miss what comes next, did you?"

I didn't bother to answer—my lips and cheeks hurt too much—so I spat a thin stream of bloody saliva that went as far as my chin. From far away I heard the howl of the red/gray orb and the harsh buzz of Ghost's screaming.

Billings' laughter expressed equal parts amusement and disdain as he leaned in close, his long beard tickling my throat. "And I thought you were *tough*."

That damn beard, long and full. He looked like a reject from a ZZ Top lookalike contest. All I could do was stare at that glorious mat of hair that was his pride and joy. That damn hair.

Wait a minute.

That hair.

I didn't think, didn't even consider the pros and cons, I just *did*, motivated by fear and the need to survive because Billings was about to do me some dirt that would most likely finish me. The Shape was a simple one, the easiest of all the spells in the Bureau arsenal, according to Alex. It rose up in my mind's eye, elegant and modest, a spell even a piker like me could understand and I thrust it up and out, right into that bushy beard.

And again.

And again.

Five times in rapid succession I cast the spell, spurred by fear and anger and desperation. Five points of fire began on that bushy long beard, which lit up with a *whoosh* of flame that reached all the way to his mad eyes. I threw in one more spell for the hell of it, right in the middle of his screaming mouth. That scream died quick as he started to gag and choke, hands covering his eyes to protect them from the flaming mess that was his beard.

His antics gave me enough wiggle room to grab a marble-hard shoulder and bring my feet up to his stomach. Heaving up and back, I tossed him out toward the Engine.

The world turned a little topsy-turvy, and I felt myself sliding over the side. I grasped the edge with both arms, adrenaline-fueled panic a terrific anesthetic. The agony in my shoulder was forgotten, put in the rearview as I scrambled for safety, afraid I'd become Kal pizza on the floor far below.

Fingers scrabbling, I snagged a loop of carpeting, gaining enough traction to dig at the fibers and the half-inch pad beneath until I found concrete. Smooth, as if lasered clean and perfect, it offered enough of a handhold to arrest my fall. I hung there, swaying, craning my neck around. What I saw aged me ten years in an instant.

I've seen some bad crap in my time—harpy poison liquefying its victims, a bone-white anaconda the size of an Amtrak train swallowing schoolchildren whole, parasitic black worms slowly consuming the brains of their hosts, to name a few.

This beat them all dead solid cold.

The Engine no longer revolved. Well, at least the larger, outer ring had come to a standstill. The inner rings still spun, but at a greater rate, becoming a bluish blur, the perfect red lips a crimson smear. Billings lay on the ring, held at an impossible angle, almost perpendicular to the floor far below. His body was barely wider than the flesh ring he lay on, his beard burned away, leaving a dark char on the skin of his half-melted cheeks. It wasn't the burns that caused him to scream—oh no, not by half—but the dozen or so mouths he lay on. I mentioned earlier that behind those perfect red lips lay long throats circled by rows of needle teeth, right? Well, those luscious lips pulsed and sucked against his flesh, clamped on as if glued to his muscular perfection. They pulled at him, sucking him in like a flesh milkshake. He tried to free himself, thrashing and shaking, but he had no leverage; the flesh of his back and ass suspended him. He planted one boot against the ring, but a small mouth widened just enough to swallow his foot whole, the boot vanishing down that gullet until the lips were locked clean around his ankle, sucking, sucking, sucking.

Imagine toothpaste extruded from its tube in reverse, but instead of a white paste or colored goo, think of flesh-colored Jell-O mixed with swirls of strawberry.

Something in Billings' back *cracked* with the sound of a gunshot and a fist-sized lump appeared on the skin of his chest. I swallowed my horror as his screams, shrill before, reached a whole new level of ungodly hollering, rising up into the soprano range before the lump on his chest moved toward his throat. Blood vomited from his mouth, the red liquid choking his screams and his flesh. His perfectly sculptured body *flowed* into those sucking mouths. The really sick part, the part that hit my stomach like a ten-ton weight, was that even though he was obviously dead, even though his bones continued to break and more lumps and bumps appeared on his torso moving with slow, deliberate purpose, he continued to *scream*.

Some people say they can ignore such things, the sounds of pain and death, and carry on doing what needs to be done. I say that's crap. You can't ignore the sounds of finality like that because no matter who you are, what you do, the instinct to survive is hardwired into the human brain—fight or flight. The horror of such agony reaches deep down and hard, triggering adrenaline, punching all the right buttons.

So while I couldn't ignore the awful sucking of those crimson lips, or the whispery voices whose words almost carried meaning—if I knew what that meaning was it would tear my mind out at the roots—I did manage to put them at the edge of my awareness and clamber up the lip. Using my good arm as a lever, I managed to pull my torso over the edge and wriggle my body to safety. The ugly popping of bones behind me helped spur me on. It's funny how such things can override even the most terrible of pain.

The Angel's voice rang out, "Kalevi Hakala, come witness the beginning of a new era!"

Just freaking, goddamned awesome. I rolled over and looked down. The Angel stood proud and straight on the floor far below in front of the Engine, the translucent figure of Ghost at his feet curled into a fetal position. Ghost cowering in pain, fear, and defeat … that was new. It filled me with burning anger to see him lying there, spectral head in hands, despair emanating from his faded form.

"Look, I have defeated your champion!" One long finger pointed at Ghost's misery-wracked self. "And Mr. Billings' death was the last necromantic component needed to open the Way to Between, the last death needed to attract those that lurk outside." With his other hand, he gestured to the now motionless inner ring.

Instead of the confusing nothingness that refused to register with the visual cortex, there was a circle of darkness so deep it threatened to suck me in, the abyss looking black. Black holes must look like that—pitiless, hungry voids without conscience or intent, they only *were*. They couldn't be argued with or persuaded and that's what gave them such terrifying aspects— not the fact that they were soul-sucking blacker than black. Their force was beyond any rational person's control or ability to deny. That's the kind of severe blackness that foamed and churned inside the center ring.

"This is the gate, the way to and from the void between worlds, and now our life, our light draws the lurkers, the dark dwellers." Terrible joy radiated from the Angel, whose strange, indistinct face held a wide, toothy smile. *That* I could see clearly. It's what I imagined a piranha would look like if it grinned. "They will devastate this world before they are defeated and I will stride amidst the ashes like a colossus."

Ghost lifted his head and suddenly he was *there*, right next to the Angel. "You talk too much," he grated with barely restrained anger.

The Angel was flabbergasted. "But—"

Ghost wasn't stupid enough to run his mouth; he merely grabbed the Angel by the shoulders, lifted him from the ground, and streaked straight for the hard blackness of the inner ring. The Angel tried to morph into his orb form but Ghost clamped him firmly in his spectral hands and kept moving on toward the dark portal. At the last second he stopped, but the orb didn't. With one last wail, it disappeared into the sucking maw of the inner ring without a splash or any transition I could see from my vantage point. It was simply gone.

Quick as a wink, Ghost appeared before me, floating inches away from the cutoff. "Destroy one of the rings, Kal," he droned in urgency. "I cannot do it; I am almost done." Swooping toward me, he grew smaller and smaller until he became a tiny point of vague light that vanished beneath my armor. The computer amulet against my chest grew warm, then cooled rapidly.

"What the …." Never mind. No time for questions. I had a nefarious plot to defeat. Now, to kill a giant ring of magical blue flesh as long as a football field and thick as a beer keg, covered in disgusting lips that will suck your flesh in like linguini …. Easy.

My Bat Belt had exited the universe to blow up the elevator, as had the belts of Rat, Dove, and Buffalo. Too bad Billings' belt lay in the gut of that ugly thing, sucked down by those mouths.

Sucked down by those mouths.

Oh, I am a baaaaad, baaaaad and clever boy.

Rat was still out cold, but it was a matter of a moment to empty his right boot heel of its precious cargo of boom juice. Fortunately radio detonators are part of the kit every Agent with boom leather carries. I held the thick, impact-resistant plastic vial of boom juice up to the fitful, flickering light of the overhead fluorescents and attached the detonator. Time for the windup.

And the pitch. Instead of a fastball, I went for a soft lob, and the vial almost floated toward the fleshy ring spinning only a few feet away. My heart jumped into my throat as the vial bounced off the ring into the air but then dropped straight into one of the whispering mouths. Those perfect, crimson lips stretched impossibly wide and it fell in.

I grinned. "Swish."

Awesome.

It took a moment for the absurdity and futility of the situation to sink in—there was a miniscule chance that the idea would actually work—but that didn't stop me from pressing the button on the transmitter gripped tightly in my fist.

Nothing.

Crap. "Oh well, let's try for—"

It wasn't a bang, or even a boom. A section of ring bulged obscenely before bursting like a zit, bluish goo spurting into the air.

"Gotcha!" I cried, fist raised in triumph. Sometimes the gods of luck and explosives smile on this Finnish boy.

Instead of awful whispers, the red lips began to erupt in berserker screams—rending, high-pitched howls that tore at my ears like nails. Wails of agony combined with howls of the damned, all tossed into an infernal blender and set on 'frappe.' A goodly chunk of ring, about half its thickness and six feet long, simply ceased to exist. Nothing but a tattered remnant held the ring together.

There were *things* dangling from inside the ring, unnamable, ugly organs of dark color whose purpose I couldn't fathom. A tooth, white, pointed and sharp as a mother-in-law's tongue landed a couple inches from my foot. Bluish blood coated one broken end.

The outer ring wobbled, not ceasing its spinning, the broken flesh slowly stretching under the awful force of its pulling, pulling, pulling. Like saltwater taffy in the hot sun, it kept growing longer, stretching the ring out of shape until it crunched against the side of the enormous crater that was center of the Quint Building.

It snapped—a wet, tearing sound like the ripping of an intestine.

Ends suddenly freed, they whipped around with shocking violence, one colliding with the second ring. Those terrible mouths were attacking each other, gulping blue flesh in chunks. Within seconds the outer ring was completely stuck to the center ring, spinning and eating, until they both fell into pieces onto the unmoving inner ring. Red mouths from the pieces of both rings attacked *that* ring, sucking and biting. The blackness at the center, the portal to the places in between, began to hum—a low throb that sounded like anger, like hate given noise. Being close by would probably be detrimental to my longevity and the harm done not covered by my HMO.

Before I could move, however, I felt something *look* at me, regard me with raw purpose and awful will. I felt a vast, yet alien, intelligence directed my way and I knew that if it had been on this side of the ring, I would have simply ceased to exist, blown apart by the force of that unknowable, alien gaze. As it was, it drove me to my knees. My hands gripped the side of my head as if I could deflect that regard with meager bone and flesh.

Pain like I'd never known—a harsh, black knife sliding effortlessly across the nerves of my skull to lick deep into my brain—throbbing and hateful. It was that intelligence. It loathed me with every iota of its being. As alien and unknowable as it was, *that* I could understand. It hated me, it hated all life on this world, and it wanted to destroy me, destroy us all and consume our energy to supplement its own.

"Leave me alone," I growled through the pain. "Look at your own damn self."

And just like that it was gone—that hateful, wrong attention. Gone suddenly and completely. Its loss seemed more dire than its presence. Eyes streaming, I stood and wobbled off toward Rat. It was far past time to leave.

The skinny Magician was out and it took a couple of good slaps to bring him around. "Whaddup?"

"Whaddup ..." I grunted as I manhandled Rat to his feet, my shoulder yelling up a storm, "is we got to beat feet, Magician. Things are going to get loud." In the movies, like *Lethal Weapon*, the hero just pops his dislocated shoulder right back in by slamming it against a doorjamb. As much as I wanted a functional limb, I wasn't about to go smashing it into place.

That took more guts and foolishness than I was capable of. At least not right then.

Next came Dove. Damn, her back looked like part of a Rob Zombie movie—more blood than I expected from such a small package. I mean, as muscular as she was, shoulders wide for one so small, she was still just a little bit of a thing. The puddle spreading out around her body looked like it came from three or four people.

"Gimme a hand with her, will you?" I asked, grabbing Dove's arm.

Rat put his fingers on my shoulder. "Hang on a second, boss." Heat radiated from his fingertips, sinking through armor and into my shoulder, which gave a curious little hitch and *popped* right back into place, a little spike of pain then a nice, warm throb that took all hurt away. I'd been healed magically before and I knew that was *fast*. Rat was a better Magician than I'd given him credit for.

"Got my mojo back," he said, but I didn't care because with both arms working, I made short work of hoisting an unconscious and bloody Dove into a fireman's carry and heading out.

"Where to, boss?" Rat's mouth sounded like it was full of oatmeal. Guess he hadn't healed himself yet.

"As far away from the—"

BOOM.

CHAPTER TWENTY-SIX

Kal
When You See a Chance

"THANK YOU, BILL. As you see, it appears that an explosion has damaged the Quint Building, partially collapsing the roof. No one knows the fate of the two BSI teams inside or that of the famous Agent, Kalevi Hakala. All we know is that the crowds have been moved back two hundred yards and that all air traffic in the area has been rerouted. The BSI has refused to comment on the situation and Agent Hakala's Receptionist, Marsha Yvgeny, has also refused to speak with us despite the fact that the strange force field that surrounded the Quint Building disappeared a few moments before the explosion.

"Wait, wait a second! The doors are opening! People are emerging from the doors and I almost see, yes! It's—"

I cut the feed off. Television reporters were almost as bad as politicians. The DRAFTlite I'd retrieved from Buffalo went clear and I could see the screaming crowds of people a couple hundred yards away. A swarm of reporters broke through police barricades to head our way at a trot.

The late afternoon sunlight failed to warm my chilled flesh and the cloth I held in both hands felt so heavy. It was one of the banners from the lobby, but the Chinese dragons on a field of gold were hidden by the corpse on a field of blood. Poor Buffalo. He looked so peaceful. Dove caught my eye. One corner of the banner was in her fist, the other in Rat's. The body slung between us was heavy, but the burden on my heart was heavier. From the look on Dove's face, she felt it, too.

A reporter from NSC, blonde and pretty like a store mannequin is pretty, careened to a halt in front of me, kicking up a helluva divot in the sod with her size-seven sensibles. Right behind came a uniformed officer, gray of hair but lean of gut. He looked more than a little pissed. Behind him came a walloping huge crowd of Straights who had also decided that police barricades were for rubes.

"Kalevi Hakala!" screamed the reporter, shoving a very phallic microphone into my face. "Can you tell us what happened?" Her eyes lit upon our makeshift stretcher. "Is that Agent Atkins? What happened? What about the other—?"

"SILENCE!" My best parade ground shout knocked the reporter back a couple of feet and halted the crowd. An anticipatory hush fell over the area. "Listen up, you gaggle of lame halfwits, we *will* have some goddamned peace and quiet for our honored dead or I swear to Christ Almighty I will personally kick each of your asses from here to the state line!"

"When you go for a sound bite, Kal, you sure don't play around."

The coffee from GalaxyBeans tasted like chocolate and hazelnuts, although Marsha added too much sugar. "I was in no mood for reporters or fanboys, boss."

I sat in the back of the van while Rat and Dove were out getting some much-needed R&R. Five will get you ten, Rat was getting his ashes hauled at some bordello that you'd need a whole-body condom just to enter and Dove was giving Alex the goo-goo eyes through the DRAFTlite. I wished them well ....

Actually, I wished Dove well. I wished Rat some penicillin.

We put Wesley Ng on a flight back to DC, after Rat gave him a clean bill of health, of course. Whatever those tendrils that invaded his body were, there was no sign of them now. His flesh seemed clean and monster free. Though his hand was still gone, his skin was no longer a patchwork, having been knitted magically back together.

BB's gray eyes sparkled with mirth. I mean, actually *sparkled*. Must have been some special effects ability in the DRAFTlite's optics. "You made more fans with that outburst than all your appearances on late-night talk shows combined. It was the sound bite that broke the Internet. That clip has been retweeted more times than naked photos of Miley Cyrus. As of fifteen minutes ago, you have *twenty-six million* followers on Twitter alone. We had to hire a whole PR firm just to manage your Facebook page." He smiled and I about had a coronary right there. "I am over the moon, Kal. Simply over the moon."

"You're freaking me out, dude."

He leaned back in his chair and I could see the painting of POTUS behind his desk. "Do you know how much pressure I'm under to slash our budget?"

"A lot?"

"To say the very least. There are several members of Congress who are extremely jealous of the power the BSI wields and who think we need to be taken down a notch. Or three." Gone was the sparkle, replaced by deep wrinkles in his forehead. It hit with an almost physical shock to realize that although BB was in his forties; he looked at least a decade older. The pressures of the job were telling. "The thing that keeps them in check is their voting base, and right now that base loves the way you told off that reporter in deference to a fallen comrade. You came out with dignity, looking like you just stepped out of a war zone, chomping on that cigar of yours with a look that could melt steel. Every veteran, every person who ever served in the military seems to think you're the embodiment of a valiant soldier and *they're* speaking out for the BSI. Now those morons in Congress who wanted to slash our budget further are backing up so quickly they're leaving a contrail."

I gave that a good think for a long moment. I had no recollection of smoking my second cigar when I left the Quint Building. The only thing I could think about was Buffalo and the next Supernatural event that would happen soon.

"Kal?"

My head jerked up. BB had been talking, but I was too busy daydreaming to pay attention. "Sorry, boss."

Those gray eyes pierced me through. "I asked you what you had planned next."

I shook my head. "Not sure. I know what the next Supernatural occurrence will be, but I'm not a hundred percent sure how to handle it." A thought hit me. "How's Ghost?"

"Still unavailable. Best guess is that he's sleeping it off in your DRAFTlite amulet. At least you can recharge the unit. We've tried to call him forth, but he's not responding."

It struck me as odd that a spirit would need to recover after a big dustup, but maybe it was his way of juicing up the ectoplasmic batteries. According to my HUD, the DRAFTlite had several days' worth of charge, thanks to the toasty hot engine block of the idling van I rested my keister in. Still, not having Ghost around to give me grief and assistance was a little like missing a tooth. Not debilitating, but you sure want it back.

"You think Alex can tease Ghost out?"

"Wherever Ghost is, be it in the computer amulet or somewhere in the 'net, I doubt he can be 'teased out.' My guess is if we wanted his attention, we would have to perform an exorcism on the whole web."

Ding-ding-ding. Ladies and gentlemen, we've struck oil! The idea that hammered me between the peepers offered slim hope in fulfillment of a promise, but I was a drowning man grasping at a life preserver made of cheese. It might not work all that great, but it was still a life preserver.

"Benjamin Bauer, you crazy, wonderful genius!" I yelled, giving the air a big fist pump. Excitement burned through my veins like liquid metal. "Genius, genius, genius! God, I love you, boss!"

An eyebrow rose to where his hair used to be. "And what did I do to deserve such an outpouring of positive emotion?"

My grin hurt. "Because of you, boss, I have an *idea*."

"The good sweet Lord help us all."

Four hours later ....

It's surprisingly easy to blow smoke rings. A fine cigar, a little practice and *voilà!* A cloudy circle formed of a carcinogenic gas. How's that for cool?

The desk chair cradled my tushie as if made with me in mind, soft and silky with just the right amount of support. I usually don't spend a lot of money on luxury items—no sense getting too comfortable in my line of work—but that chair was number one with a bullet on my Amazon-dot-com shopping list.

Cigar, too. A luxury I could get used to, despite throat cancer or a host of other illnesses such things can lead to. The taste satisfied me on some visceral, primal level. Sure it took some getting used to, but let me tell you, the nicotine rush helped a ton.

I leaned back in the comfy chair, put my hands behind my head, and stared at the ceiling through the DRAFTlite. Sure I was rich, famous, and had more twitter followers than Justin Bieber, but I'd trade all that away to turn back the clock and undo the revelation of the World Under. That genie had no intention of cramming its fat ass back into that bottle, though, no matter now nice and cheery it would make everyone feel. They weren't lying when they said ignorance is bliss. That and good, smooth vodka.

A shot could take the edge off my nerves, an edge that the

cigar came nowhere near touching. Nine months, thirteen days, six hours, and thirty-one minutes since I last took a drink of my favorite alcoholic beverage. Not that I'd been counting, mind you, but I sure missed the sweet burn as it traveled down my throat to set fire to my stomach and the warmth that spread from my middle to the outlying areas, reaching my head to set up shop. That slightly unreal feeling as up became sideways became down and all 'round and 'round.

"'You spin me right 'round, baby right 'round like a record baby right 'round…'" I crooned softly. Another smoke ring floated out of my mouth, expanding slowly.

"Not a great singing voice. Not even a good one."

I didn't bother to move. "Figured you were going to show."

"How could I not?"

Of course. "So what was your play in all this?" My eyes took in the brushwork on the ceiling plaster.

"When did you figure it all out?"

I levered the chair upright and faced the other man. Orson R. Nias. Mr. Handsome himself. "So that's how this is going to work? A little *quid pro quo*?"

Nias sauntered over to the gleaming perfection of his coffee maker and began to prepare an espresso. "Want one?"

"Already made one," I said, holding up a white porcelain demitasse cup for him to see.

"Do you mind if I have one?"

"It's your office." Not to mention his Kona coffee. While everything above the fourth floor was a big empty, his first-floor office had weathered the subsequent explosion just fine. Not a paper out of place, not even dust on the desk. "Is that my cigar you are smoking?"

"My second one while waiting on you. The ventilation system in here is awesome." As soon as the smoke rings reached the five-foot mark, subtle drafts whisked them away into waiting registers. Hyper efficiency not often found. "So, you going to go first?"

The coffee machine clunked and hissed gently. "Might as well keep this civilized, don't you think?"

Sure. "Right. Civilized. That's me, Mr. Civilized."

He smiled with all one thousand of his teeth and they were perfect. I desperately wanted to add a few scars to that face. "My 'play,' as you so eloquently called it, was exactly what I mentioned when we first met—asset reacquisition. In this case I was unable to land that asset; it is gone."

"The Angel."

Orson nodded. "The Angel."

"So what is a mid-level bureaucratic demon doing chasing an escapee from Hell? Are you some sort of infernal bounty hunter?" I stared into his pearlies. "Do you at least get dental?"

"Ah-ah-ah," he replied, wagging a finger. The coffeemaker gave a last, soft fart of steam and he pulled a demitasse from under the spout. After a short, almost dainty, sip, he continued, "How did you know? About me, that is."

I spread my hands and puffed out a thick cloud of smoke before placing them behind my head. "You didn't make it hard, did you? Orson R. Nias. Ornias, the demon who likes killing effeminate men, the demon I fought in the Field Museum all those years ago." My hands were sweaty, but I kept them behind my head. "That and when you possessed Wesley Ng during the time he'd be easily subject to such things, all weak and drugged up, to give us some much-needed plot exposition. I recognized your smile. That's one thing you can't really hide—a smile. Even when you're in a different body, you want the muscles to work in the manner you're most accustomed to, and when I saw your smile on Ng's face, the last piece of the puzzle fell into place."

Ornias raised his demitasse in salute.

Time for some more explanations. "Why did you send me to Quint's elevator? You obviously knew that just stepping into it would summon the succubus."

A long sip from a small cup. "For giggles," he replied. "I

figured you could handle a minor demon." Once again that perfect smile. I wanted to improve it with my fist. "You know the Ring of Solomon won't work, just in case you had it in your pocket or something. It only works on a demon's physical body, and you sent mine to hell when last we met." He held his arms up. "This flesh outfit was a vegetable in the Mercy Hospital ICU, making it quite easy for me to possess."

The Ring of Solomon would have been a swell thing to have, but Israel wasn't about to let one of its greatest treasures out of the country ever since they'd been informed of its significance after that Field Museum fiasco. I'd already asked.

Twice.

"You want to know about the Ring?" *One ring to rule them ... never mind.*

Ornias nodded.

"Then tell me about the Angel—the whole story, mind you—and I will give you the skinny on Solomon's toy." I raised a hand, one finger up. "Pinky swear and everything."

Eyes the color of an oil slick narrowed. "That's not your pinky."

"Still."

The demon slammed the rest of his espresso and toddled off to make another. *Chung, hiss, whirr.* While he carefully spooned Kona coffee, he said, "In your line of work, have you ever heard of the Dark Lexicon?"

I shook my head. "Can't say that I have."

"Not surprising. Mind tossing me a cigar?"

"Sure." I threw one of his expensive cancer sticks end over end. It was a good throw and an even better catch. Ornias smiled again as the cigar seemed to light itself.

Just to show me up, he blew a perfect smoke *square.* Sarky bastard.

"The Dark Lexicon is a book. Not much to look at, about the size of the letter V volume of *The Encyclopedia Britannica.* I take it you've seen an encyclopedia before?"

Don't shoot him, just don't shoot him … yet. "I'm familiar."

"The cover and pages are made of the skin of angels killed by Lucifer during the fall. Inside is the sum total of his wisdom, things learned from countless years of angelic perspective." Ornias' smile disappeared, and for a flashing moment he looked somber; then he shook his head, shedding the mood like a dog sheds water. "There are spells in there that would drive a human mad just glimpsing them briefly in passing. The Angel of Mass Murder was one of many agents employed to cause chaos in the mortal world. When not imprisoned for his tendency to wander unattended, the Angel had one duty, which you might have guessed. It was to train and inspire serial killers. If the job he performed went well, such as in the case of Jeffrey Dahmer, he was allowed spend a little time on … vacation."

Vacation. Cleverly slicing unsuspecting Straights into pork chops and causing untold physical and emotional pain. Yeah, a *vacation*.

"The Angel was never an angel, but the first serial killer to walk this earth, the first true sociopath. Being the first made him an archetype, a being of considerable power—in many ways stronger than a 'mid-level bureaucratic demon.' " He bowed to me over his cigar. "Powerful enough to allow him to escape from Hell from time to time. This time he managed to read some of the Lexicon. Just enough to learn about those … things that dwell in the dark places between worlds.

"It was from the Lexicon that he learned how to summon the Engine—that flesh machine that creates portals to the in-between—and to create the force field around the building, although your Bureau could have penetrated it with an RPG or missile. Sad that your higher-ups didn't try. It would have saved me a lot of effort."

It was just about time. "What's the Engine? Besides being a portal to the in-between, that is."

"That's off topic, Mr. Hakala." Ornias snorted a plume of dark gray smoke from his nostrils and sucked more smoke from his cigar. "Just understand that if the Angel had succeeded, over half the population on this mud ball would have been destroyed."

CHAPTER TWENTY-SEVEN

Kal
Closing Time

So there I sat, staring at the demon Ornias (or at least the man he possessed), listening to him calmly tell me that at least three billion people had nearly been rendered terminally sleepy.

It really got under my skin. In fact, I was seeing three kinds of red when Ornias' voice burst in on Kal's Angry Time.

"The problem with the Angel," he continued, "was that he never liked working under a higher authority."

"Lucifer, you mean." My throat felt like I'd been gargling glass shards. "The Adversary."

He made a face. "Whatever." He gulped down a second demitasse of espresso, tossing the tiny cup over his shoulder where it broke to flinders against the countertop. "The *president* of our corporation was none too thrilled that the Angel was sucked into the in-between, but it's far better than letting him roam free. A hell on earth is one hell too many."

The cigar in my mouth had burned down to the last two inches and I chewed on the stub as I thought furiously. "So, let me get this straight." The tobacco tasted of ashes and anger. "The Angel escapes from Hell and you're tasked with bringing him back, but for whatever reason you can't do it alone because he's too strong. So you do what you can to remain undetected by the Angel while giving us a helping hand, hoping that we will stop him in his plan to kill a bajillion people."

That smile was back. "I knew you had the tools and the talent," he said.

Ashes, anger, and a whole lot of desire to put a bullet between those perfect brows. As satisfying as that would be, I had other plans. "The whole pocket-dimension thing still has me a bit confused. Takes a lot of merlins to move objects between the worlds."

Ornias' head was shaking before I finished. "Not really, not at the thin places between dimensions. It merely requires the correct spell Shape or an intrinsic talent for such things. Magical creatures slip in from what you call the World Under all the time, remember?"

And done, I thought, hiding a grin. *Hope this works.*

The demon must have seen something in my face because he shook his head slightly and muttered something that sounded like, "So it begins."

Some demons are supernaturally fast, but not humans, even if they are possessed by a supernaturally fast demon. Still, the body that Ornias wore like a coat gave a credible Flash imitation, moving at speeds on the high end of human capability.

It just wasn't fast enough.

The DRAFTlite cameras flashed into action, projecting an image into the air, a holographic representation of a very complex spell Shape, one that only the most learned and powerful Magician could cast. Good thing we had a couple on the payroll.

It hung there, all twisty and glowing, and in the middle was Ornias, toes a couple of inches from the floor, back arched as if in pain and arms flung out to the side, hands intersecting on a couple of convergence points.

Awesome.

The Lahti was aimed between the eyes, but it looked like shooting him wouldn't be necessary. "I can't believe that actually worked," I said happily as I rounded the desk. "I mean really, this has to be one of the most boneheaded ideas I've ever had, and brother, I've had a few."

"*I won't argue that, Kal.*" Alex's voice was chock-full of amusement.

"Can it, pipsqueak," I said. "If I wanted to hear from a butthole, I'd fart." I regarded the bound Ornias for a moment. "Think this will work?"

The door to the office opened and Alex stepped through, followed by Dove and Rat bearing a stretcher. "It might, if only Ghost will answer."

I kept the DRAFTlite focused on Ornias while Alex pulled out a roll of silver chain and began laying out a pattern on the floor below the holographic spell Shape. "I've never cast a spell through a digital medium before," he said quietly. "I'm surprised it worked. What would you have done if it hadn't?"

I held up the Lahti. "What do you think?"

He raised an eyebrow, a trick I taught him. "That runs counter to your plan."

"No, it was merely a backup."

The spell Shape on the floor was almost complete. It hurt to look at. With a few brisk motions Alex completed the Shape by laying charged emeralds at various points alongside. "There you go."

Yeah, there but for the grace of God .... "Hope this works."

Alex held up a cell. "You or me?"

"I'll do it. He always answers when I dial." The phone, the newest Android model with 128Gb memory. Free for Bureau personnel, over six hundred bucks for Straights. I stared at the keypad, my feelings a jumble of apprehension, anxiety, hope, and resolve.

"He didn't come for me." Alex sounded sad.

The screen didn't provide any answers, but one came to mind. "He's hurt. The Angel hurt him and you're his friend, his best friend, a brother if you will. He doesn't want you to see him like that. But me, well, we're brothers of a different sort, brothers-in-arms. If you can't show your wounds to the man whose back you got in battle, who are you going to show them to?" I met Alex's worried gaze with mine. "He'll come when I call." My finger touched the *Ghostbusters* icon on the screen.

The phone's speakers kicked to life. "Yes, Kal?" Ghost's voice sounded—for want of a better word—weak. The drone was less, ah, drone-y, more human.

"You remember I made you a promise?"

Two hours later ....

Alex looked grim. "It's not working." Sweat beaded his upper lip. He looked exhausted. "I can't expend this kind of magic for much longer and I'm down to my last diamond."

Ornias, or the flesh suit he'd worn, still floated in the center of two spell Shapes. I'd long since removed my DRAFTlite and set it on the table so it could project the holographic Shape unhindered. I considered the immobile man with his virtually perfect features—there was a small mole at the corner of his chin, but instead of detracting, it seemed to enhance his looks, damn him—and sighed. Too long. This had been going on too long. Last time Alex put me back together it took only an hour or so. Sure it had been touch and go, but it worked and I didn't see a reason why it shouldn't now. Of course back then I'd been a coma for a week, but I'd been all dead and needed my sleep. Ornias' body wasn't even mostly dead. In fact, the heart was still beating and all the red stuff still raced through the tubes in his flesh. Should've been good to go.

Of course I knew the answer, and I think deep down Alex did as well. We traded a look and he left the room, not wanting to witness what happened next.

"Ghost, you're not trying."

"I am, Kal. How can you say otherwise?"

"Because if you were trying, this would all be over and I'd be back in DC giving Jeanie the high hard one. As it is, I am stuck in St. Louis with a scaredy-cat spook who is a few short months from becoming completely divorced from humanity."

"That does not mean I would turn on mankind, Kal!" For an electronic buzz coming from a cell phone, he sure sounded offended. That alone proved my point. "I *do* want to do this."

"But you're still here."

"Not my fault, Kal. I do not know why it is not working."

I hate the Tough Love approach. Mentally girding my loins—and what does that really mean? Sounds like an S&M act—I set in motion the second part of the plan. "And it doesn't mean you won't, or are being asked to do something 'for that greater good' that turns out to be totally heinous. I made you a promise, Ghost, and you're going to help me keep it." Deep breath. "Even it kills you. Kills the both of us."

An electronic wheeze, a ghostly equivalent of a sigh. "You can't stop me, Kal."

"Think so?"

"I am far too powerful."

"True, your thought processes exceed my own and every other humans' on the planet, but you seemed to have forgotten one small thing, Ghost."

"What is that?" he asked hesitantly. Good for him; he knew me well enough to be afraid.

"Knowledge isn't intelligence," I said. "In real world terms, you're smart, genius smart, but not the smartest person in the building."

Real hesitation now. He felt the walls closing in, I'm sure of it. "What do you mean?"

"You downloaded yourself into the phone like I asked, yes?"

"Yes?"

"Have you tried to leave?"

A brief pause. "You have jammed all signals!" Ghost shouted, and the phone vibrated violently in my hand.

"Yes. And I'm not letting you go until you commit to this fully or the phone loses power. Either way, it all ends here."

To give him credit, Ghost didn't try to manifest again (thank goodness) and kick my ass like he did the Angel's, but the phone did give out some interesting green sparks from the headphone jack. After a couple of minutes of buzzing and vibrating, his voice finally emerged sounding frightened and alone. It about broke my heart. "What if it does not work?" he asked.

This I had an answer for. "Of all the people at the Bureau, old spook, you know that I have the best handle on the whole life-after-death question." I smiled softly and lowered my voice to just above a whisper. "If you don't make it, find Leena and tell her I'll be along shortly."

A long pause. "Will do, Kal," he whispered.

An hour later ….

"Done." Alex wiped the sweat from his eyes.

Ornias' body lay on the floor, the spell Shapes gone, the silver put away. His breathing was slow and even and his heartbeat seemed steady enough.

I sat there next to the body and pondered the situation. I'd basically forced Ghost into my scheme of placing his consciousness into Ornias' body. The first spell Shape had trapped the demon, the second had forced the demon from the body and kept it from returning. The body had been identified as a lawyer who suffered traumatic brain injury in an automobile accident … had basically been brain dead. However, the body disappeared from the ICU before the staff turned off life support and all records showed no next of kin. He'd been all alone in the world—the perfect vessel for Ornias.

Now it was just a matter of seeing if the implantation worked. If it didn't, then had I just murdered my friend? Or had I saved the world from a potentially lethal threat? I was at the crux of a whole ends justifying the means issue and sure felt conflicted about it.

"When will we know?" I asked.

Alex flopped back on the thick carpet. "When and if he wakes up."

"You feeling some way about this, Alex?"

"Yeah, all bad."

I leaned over the body. "We had to. We were losing him anyway."

"I know."

Brown eyes opened.

Look for the next From the Files of the BSI adventure:

Talladega Nightmares

Born in Helsinki, Finland, **Mark Everett Stone** arrived in the U.S. at a young age and promptly dove into the world of the fantastic. Starting at age seven with *The Iliad* and *The Odyssey*, he went on to consume every scrap of Norse Mythology he could get his grubby little paws on. At age thirteen he graduated to Tolkien and Heinlein, building up a book collection that soon rivaled the local public library's. In college Mark majored in journalism and minored in English.

Mark has published six other books with Camel Press: *Things to Do in Denver When You're Un-Dead*, *What Happens in Vegas Dies in Vegas*, *I Left My Haunt in San Francisco*, *Chicago, The Windigo City*, and *Omaha Stakes* (Books 1, 2, 3, 4, and 5 of the From the Files of the BSI series) as well as *The Judas Line*, which was a finalist for the ForeWord Magazine Book of the Year Award in the Fantasy Category. Mark lives in Denver with his amazingly patient wife, Brandie, and their two sons, Aeden and Gabriel.

Next up: *Talladega Nightmares* and two books that continue the story that began with *The Judas Line*.

You can find Mark on the Web at markeverettstone.wix. com/mysite-1.

CATCH UP ON YOUR BSI HISTORY TODAY
From the Files of the BSI
Books 1-5

For 10 years Kal Hakala has been the Bureau of Supernatural Investigation's top man, the longest surviving agent in its blood-soaked history. There's been no case he couldn't crack, no monster he couldn't kill. After a plague of zombies in Denver turns into an investigation of a vicious serial killer dubbed The Organ Donor, he dives headlong into the one mystery that could finally kill him.

Free of the Bureau of Supernatural Investigation, Kal Hakala rededicates himself to destroying the monster that murdered his sister. But first he and his trusted former teammates must obtain a device powerful enough to kill a legend. The quest takes them to Las Vegas, where they confront a threat found only in Sin City but rooted in the past's most heinous crimes, the evil that was Nazi Germany.

A suspicious suicide sends Kal Hakela to San Francisco, where a former mission went south and made an enemy of the city's ghostly Supernatural protector. Now, with the Earth's survival at stake, Kal and his team must take on a slew of Supernatural perils, without magic and without the help of the BSI.

As temporary head of the BSI, Kal must choose a team to handle the latest scourge: windigo spirits in Chicago are turning humans into cannibals. Canton and Kal's girlfriend are prime candidates. Can Kal stand to endanger the people he loves most?

Kal Hakala has received a challenge from a creature calling himself Maydock, threatening to kill 10 humans a day unless Kal comes to Omaha, alone, for a fight to the death. With the odds stacked so heavily against him, how can Kal possibly vanquish the most powerful being he has ever encountered?